NEW YORK TIMES BESTSELLING AUTHOR

SHARON SALA

A Field of Poppies

Copyright 2012 by Sharon Sala
ALL RIGHTS RESERVED
ISBN: 9 781469 937175

This novel is a work of fiction. Names, characters, places, and incidents are either the product of the author's imagination, or, if real, used fictitiously. No part of this book may be reproduced or transmitted in any form or by any electronic or mechanical means, including photocopying, recording, or by any information storage and retrieval system, without the express written permission of the author of publisher, except where permitted by law.

Cover and book design by

THE KILLION GROUP

www.thekilliongroupinc.com

DEDICATION

It is commonly accepted that we do not choose our family – only our friends. But like every accepted adage, there is always an exception to the rule, and that is where the secrets come in. Families are notorious for keeping secrets that can destroy an innocent life, and that is where choice becomes the solution. We either take control of our destiny and go forward, or remain passive and let life pass us by. What the victim does not always understand is that, by choosing to do nothing, a choice has been made to let the secret stand.

I dedicate this book to all the people caught between a rock and a hard place, who chose to become warriors in their own defense rather than victims – who chose to laugh in the face of destiny and create their own paths.

To warriors everywhere.

You know who you are.

CHAPTER ONE

Poppy Sadler hated rain and it had been raining for hours – the kind of windless downpour that shrinks a person's environment into a worm-hole view of the world and sends a spirit into emotional demise. Without guttering on the old clapboard house that was her home, she couldn't even see the street. A wet gray curtain had been drawn between her and the rest of humanity.

But, if Poppy was honest, she would have to admit it wasn't the rain sapping her twenty year old soul. It was cancer. The cancer eating away at her mother's body was also destroying her family.

Ever since Helen Sadler's diagnosis, nothing had been the same. Her daddy, Jessup Sadler, moved with an invisible burden that had made an old man out of him before his time.

Her brother Johnny was a trucker. BC, before the cancer, he had always come home at least once a month, sometimes more. Yet the day he heard about his mother's diagnosis, within a week he had a new job for a different company that demanded a move to Atlanta, and then he used distance as an excuse not to visit. She guessed he didn't want to be around to watch their mama die.

That was fine. She still had Daddy. He wasn't perfect and had his own way of grieving, but he loved her and was good to her, and that had to count for something.

Only last night Daddy hadn't come home.

Poppy didn't want to think that he'd fallen off the wagon again, but past history was a hard fact to ignore. Because they shared the family car, she'd already been forced to call her boss at the restaurant to tell him she'd be late coming in. If it hadn't been for the rain keeping away most of their usual customers, he would have been pissed.

She kept glancing at the clock and trying not to panic. If Daddy didn't get home soon, she would have to take a cab to work, which would be six dollars she didn't have to waste.

When her phone began to ring, she cringed. If it was her boss again, she was screwed. She saw Caller ID and the floor began to tilt. It took her a moment to realize there was nothing wrong with the floor, just with her, and grabbed onto the back of the sofa to keep from falling. This couldn't be good news.

She closed her eyes before she answered, as if being sightless would make the hearing of it easier to bear.

"Hello."

"This is Doctor Mackay from Saint Anne's Hospital, may I speak to Jessup Sadler?"

"Doctor Mackay, this is Poppy. Daddy's not here. Can I take a message?"

She heard him hesitate. He'd been her mother's doctor for the past seven months and knew the family well. She could almost hear what he was thinking.

"I'm sorry, Poppy. This isn't good news. Your mother passed away a short while ago. You should take comfort in the fact that she wasn't in pain. One moment she was breathing and then she wasn't. I'm very sorry for your loss."

She couldn't breathe and talk at the same time without screaming, so she nodded, and then realized that was stupid. He couldn't hear her nod.

"Poppy?"

She pinched the bridge of her nose so hard her eyes watered so she could focus on that pain instead of the one in her chest.

"Yes, I'm here."

"Are you okay? Where is your father?"

She could, at least, address the last question. "I don't know where he is. He didn't come home last night."

"I'm so sorry. Is there someone else you can call?"

What good would it do to tell him her brother Johnny had abdicated the family? At any rate, he was too far away to be of help. There were a thousand questions in her head, but the only one that came out was something out of her control.

"What happens to Mama?"

"We'll call the funeral home. They'll contact you later today. Again, I'm very sorry for your loss."

It was the dial tone in Poppy's ear that broke her focus. Her legs gave way as she sank to the floor, but before she had time to come completely undone, she heard shuffling footsteps on the porch, as if someone was cleaning their shoes on the mat, and then finally the knock she'd been waiting for!

Daddy!

She scrambled to her feet, wiping tears as she ran.

"Daddy! Daddy! Where on earth have-"

It wasn't Jessup Sadler.

Two men in full-length raincoats were at the door dripping water all over the threshold. They flashed badges.

Cops?

One stepped forward.

"Are you Poppy Sadler?"

Something told her this was more bad news and wondered what would happen if she denied it, but they were waiting for an answer, and the cop who'd asked looked kind.

"Yes."

"Miss Sadler, I'm Detective Amblin. This is my partner, Detective Duroy. We're sorry to inform you that your father is dead. Someone reported a body in the Little Man River early this morning. It was your father, Jessup Sadler, and we have a positive ID."

Poppy blinked.

"This isn't happening," she muttered, and then closed the door in their faces and began to walk away. "I must be dreaming. That's it, I'm still asleep and when I wake up none of this will be real."

She thought she heard a series of sharp knocks and then someone calling her name. She frowned. That sounded loud and real. She looked back just as the door swung inward.

It was the same cop. Maybe this wasn't a dream.

"Sorry miss, but we needed to make sure you're okay."

She folded her arms across her chest in a subconscious need to shield herself. "Are you real?"

The cops shared a look then he nodded. "Yes, ma'am, we're real."

Shock spread through her body, leaving her with nothing but a whisper to voice her disbelief.

"Then you were telling me the truth? Daddy's dead, too?"

The cops shared another look and walked inside without an invitation.

Kenny Duroy was an underweight, middle-aged cop with little to no patience who ate his weight in sugar on a weekly basis. When he heard the word "too" his suspicions rose. His voice was challenging as he crossed the room to where she stood.

"Who else is dead? Is there someone in here that-"

She started to shake. "Mama died this morning. The hospital just called."

Duroy's inner alarm system immediately subsided. That wasn't what he'd expected her to say.

Mike Amblin wondered if he looked as stunned as he felt. Damn, but he hated this part of his job, and Kenny had already stepped up as the bad cop. It was time for him to come in as the good one.

"Your mother just died? Was it here in Saint Anne's?"

Poppy stifled a moan. She was shaking so hard she could barely speak.

"Yes, from cancer." And then it hit her. If Daddy was dead, how did he die? "What happened to Daddy? Did he get drunk and drown?"

"No ma'am. He was murdered."

The word was like a fist to her gut.

Mike watched her chin come up and for the first time he saw fire in her eyes.

"Murdered? Are you sure he didn't just slip and fall into the-"

Duroy interrupted. "One gunshot in a body can be an accident or a suicide. Three gunshots is a murder. Do you know who-"

Whatever it was they wanted to know would have to wait. Right now she needed to faint.

Amblin saw her eyes roll back in her head.

"Catch her, Kenny!"

Duroy leaped forward but not fast enough to stop Poppy's descent. She slid to the floor without making a sound, as if all the bones in her body had turned to dust.

"Damn it. Way to break the news," Mike said, as he dropped to his knees beside her. "Find the kitchen. Bring me a wet cloth."

A little surprised by the panic he felt, Duroy sprinted for the next room while Mike felt for a pulse. It was there, beating steadily.

He felt bad for what had happened. They'd had no way of knowing about Sadler's wife and couldn't imagine what this young woman must be feeling. He eyed the dark circles under her eyes and the thin contours of her face and wondered if she got enough to eat. She was pretty, in a tall, lean way and with more long, black hair than seemed fair for one woman to have. He smoothed a lock of it away from her forehead and then looked up as his partner came back with a cloth still dripping water.

"It's clean," Duroy said. "The whole place is clean."

Mike frowned. "Just because someone's poor doesn't mean they're dirty. Now shut up before she wakes up and hears you saying something else stupid."

Kenny's face turned pink. "Sorry. I wasn't thinking."

Mike pressed the wet cloth on Poppy's forehead, then on her cheeks, then beneath her chin. When she began to come to, he rocked back on his heels.

"Miss Sadler...Miss Sadler, can you hear me?"

Poppy's eyelids were fluttering. When Mike heard her moan, he hoped she wasn't the kind for hysterics.

Her eyes opened.

Their gazes locked.

A thousand thoughts went through his head, but all he managed to say was, "you fainted."

"Obviously," Poppy mumbled, and began to get herself up off the floor.

Mike helped her stand, steadying her until he was sure she wasn't going to buckle, then handed over the wet cloth.

"This is yours. We…uh, we got it from the kitchen."

She clutched it absently against her belly, unaware it was soaking into her blouse. The room was spinning. She could hear someone screaming, but it took a few moments for her to realize the sound was just inside her head.

"Daddy's car. Have you found Daddy's car? It's a 1999 Ford. The left rear fender is black, but the rest of the car is blue."

They looked startled. It was an odd question, considering everything that had happened.

"No ma'am, we haven't, but when we do, it will have to be taken into evidence."

She shoved a hand through her hair, unaware it was trembling, and then looked down at the front of her shirt.

"How will I get back and forth to work? I have to bury Mama... and now Daddy, too." She choked on a sob then took a breath, struggling to maintain some composure. "Just look at me. I'm all wet. I'll have to change before I go to work."

She was rambling. Mike had never seen anyone blink in slow-motion. Obviously she was in shock.

"Considering everything that's just happened, don't you think you should call in sick today?"

Panic spread across her face.

"I can't. The boss would fire me and I need the job. Will you give me a ride to The Depot? It's on-"

Mike realized she was going whether they took her or not. "I know where it is and yeah, sure, we'll give you a ride. On the way we can talk. There are a few more questions I need to ask you."

"Whatever," Poppy mumbled. "I'll be right back."

She made it out of the room, stumbling and swaying with every other step.

Duroy gave Mike a dubious look. "Do you suppose she's gonna be okay going to work and all?"

Mike was mad but he didn't really know why.

"Hell no, she's not going to be okay. She may never be okay, again. But she wants a ride to work, it's raining like crazy, her mother just died, and we just pulled her father's body out of the Little Man, so I'm gonna give her a ride, and then we're going to go find that fucking car."

Kenny's eyes widened. He'd never seen his partner get this worked up about anything or anyone. Ever.

When Poppy came back, her hair was pulled away from her face, she was wearing a different blouse and a hooded raincoat over her clothes. She got her purse, checked to make sure she had her house keys, and then turned on a porch light. But it was the composure on her face that seemed out of place.

"It might be dark by the time I get home," she said, then tucked her purse beneath her arm. "I'm ready to go."

"Yes, ma'am," Mike said. "After you."

They exited the house. Poppy paused long enough to lock the door, then made a run toward the car while the rain pelted her body and washed what was left of the tears off her face.

"In front!" Mike said, and quickly opened the door.

Poppy ducked inside as Duroy jumped in the back seat. Mike circled the car and then got in behind the wheel.

"Terrible weather," he said as he waited for her to buckle up.

"It fits the day," Poppy said, and then stared blindly out the window as Mike backed into the street.

Poppy eyed the houses as they drove out of Coal Town, and wondered how long it would take for the news to spread. Everyone here knew everyone else. She'd thought everyone liked her Daddy. Obviously someone hadn't liked him as much as she'd believed.

When they began to cross the bridge over the Little Man, she closed her eyes. She couldn't bear to think about his body tossing about in the downpour, waiting to be found.

Mike felt her anxiety. She was most likely thinking about her father's body being pulled out of the river below, but they had to cross the bridge to get to her job.

All of a sudden a stooped figure jumped off the footpath and into their lane of traffic. Duroy braced himself against the back seat as Mike slammed on the brakes.

"What the hell?" Duroy said.

"It's Prophet Jones," Mike said, as the car slid to a halt.

Poppy recognized the old homeless man who roamed the streets of Caulfield. She'd heard stories that he'd once been a preacher, but didn't know if that was true. She'd never seen him this close before.

"What's happening?" she asked.

"Sit tight," Mike muttered, and jumped out in the rain, quickly grabbing the old man standing in front of the car. "Damn it, Prophet! You nearly got yourself killed! What are you doing out in this weather?"

The old man's eyes were red-rimmed and swollen and it was hard to tell how many layers of clothing he had on, but it was completely sodden and molded to his skeletal body. He twisted out of Mike's grasp and began to shout.

"The devil! The devil is afoot!"

Mike stifled a curse. Prophet was a menace to himself.

"Yeah, well the devil isn't here now," Mike said. "Come get in the car with us and we'll take you some place dry."

He reached for Prophet's arm, but not in time. Before he knew it the old man had bolted in the opposite direction in a scuttling, crab-like motion. Mike thought he was going to have to chase him down to get him off of the highway when Prophet suddenly jumped back on the footpath and kept going.

"Crazy old bastard," Mike muttered, and got back in the car. Despite the raincoat, he was now soaked to the skin.

"What the hell was that about?" Duroy asked.

Mike wiped his face and put the car back in gear.

"Just Prophet being Prophet. He wanted to tell me the devil was afoot."

Poppy shivered. From her viewpoint, there was more than a note of truth to the statement.

Mike waited until they'd crossed the river before he returned to the subject of Poppy's father.

"Miss Sadler, I'm sorry to keep pressuring you, but it's important that we find out as much as we can early on. Do you understand?"

She nodded.

"You asked if he'd gotten drunk and drowned. Was drinking a problem for your father?"

"It had been years ago, but not lately. However the stress of Mama's health was weighing heavy on him. I just assumed that's what must have happened. I shouldn't have."

"Was your father having problems with anyone?"

They braked for a red light. Poppy eyed a pink dress on a department store mannequin and wondered how much it cost. She'd have to buy something to bury Mama in and pink had been her favorite color.

"Miss Sadler?"

She realized he was still talking and made herself focus. "Sorry, uh, not that I knew of."

"He wasn't angry with the boss after he got fired?"

Poppy reeled as if she'd just been slapped. Her eyes darkened. "Daddy got fired? When? I didn't know. He never said."

"I'm sorry. I assumed you knew. We were told it happened about a week ago."

Poppy mind was racing. "Oh my God! That means he lost the medical insurance, too. He would have been crazy worried about that and he never said a word. Mama's hospital care... all those doctor bills." Her face twisted with sudden rage. "Exactly what was it he did that got him fired, or did Mr. High and Mighty Caulfield decide Mama's care was costing him too much money and they just kicked us to the curb?"

Mike felt bad that he was making it worse, but they had to know all they could to figure out who had wanted Jessup dead bad enough to pump three bullets into his body.

"I don't know, Miss Sadler. We have a man checking into it."

She shoved her hands through her hair again, but the anger had steadied them.

"It doesn't matter. Nothing's going to bring him back. Nothing's going to bring either one of them back."

She suddenly threw back her head and laughed. The sound gave Amblin chills, as did the raw anger in her words.

"There should be a law in the universe that if you are born into hell, you get a free pass to heaven when you die. It would make the current facts of my life somewhat easier to bear."

Mike glanced up in the rearview mirror at his partner's face, and then stared straight through the windshield. The despair in her voice was palpable.

"We're very sorry."

"Yes, well… thank you. In the meantime when you find Daddy's car, if you find it and do whatever it is you need to do, I would appreciate it if you'd let me know when I can have it back. I have nothing else to drive and no money to buy another one."

"Do you have any idea where he was going when he left your house last night?"

She looked at him as if he'd lost his mind. "The same place he went every night after he got home from the mine and cleaned up... to Saint Anne's to sit with Mama."

Justin Caulfield stood at the windows of his office overlooking the Little Man River, but it was without focus. He'd heard all about the body they'd found this morning, but it had gone in one ear and out the other. He had a much bigger problem, and for once, it was something the Caulfield fortune couldn't fix.

His great-great-great grandfather Wilson Caulfield had immigrated to North America from England in the mid-eighteen hundreds, investing all he had into mining and lumber and made a fortune his heirs continued to grow. It had given Justin an opulent life and an edge he'd taken for granted.

Caulfield Industries kept the city of Caulfield alive and prosperous, except for the people who worked the mines. They were the have-nots who lived on the south side of Little Man, leaving the north side to the well-to-do.

The northern residents called the settlement across the river Coal Town, and the south, being less concerned with names and more concerned about putting enough food on the tables to feed their families bore the name with silent indignity.

But Justin's concern at the moment was personal and involved his only child - his fourteen year old daughter, Callie, who was on the verge of dying.

Before Callie's diagnosis two weeks ago, they'd spent months in the corporate jet going from state to state – hospital to hospital, and he'd spent hundreds of thousands of dollars on specialists trying to find out what was wrong with her.

Her symptoms began with her feeling slightly listless and fatigued, to constant nausea, shortness of breath, and lately, coughing up blood. By the time they finally had a diagnosis, Justin considered it closer to a death sentence than he might be able to handle.

According to the team of doctors who made the diagnosis, she had an auto-immune disease called Goodpasture's Syndrome. The cause was not fully understood, but researchers had theories ranging from an inherited factor, to exposure to deadly chemicals, and even the possibility of something viral.

The symptoms were many and varied, while often mistaken for the flu, but the bottom line was bleeding in her lungs and the danger of renal failure.

The treatments ranged from oral immunosuppressive drugs to the use of a process called plasmapheresis, which basically involved cleaning her blood of the lethal antibodies by separating the red and white cells from her plasma, then putting them back into a plasma substitute and returning the clean stuff to her body. The process seemed like a scene out of a bad Frankenstein movie, but he wouldn't argue if they could just make it work.

A couple of weeks ago he'd called his mother, Amelia for help and she'd come from her opulent retirement home in Florida back to Caulfield without hesitation to help in anyway possible.

Last night Justin had spent his time in Callie's room cursing God. Her struggles to breathe were brutal to witness. And if that wasn't enough, as the doctors had warned, her kidneys were failing. If she survived the treatment, she would most likely need a kidney transplant, but only if they managed to stop the bleeding in her lungs before she bled out and died. He was sick at heart and as mad at God as he'd ever been.

Today he felt like an old man. Callie was the future of Caulfield Industries, and if Callie died, there would be no one left to take his place, because his ability to father children was over, as well.

When Callie was seven, he got an infection. Before they could stop it, he lost the function of one kidney and rendered him sterile. Should Callie get to the point of needing a kidney transplant, he would not be able to donate, and should she not survive, the Caulfield dynasty ended with him.

His fingers curled into fists as he pounded the windowsill. A vein rose in his neck, pulsing vividly from the sudden rage that engulfed him.

"Damn you, God. You want to hurt someone? Hurt me. Don't take it out on an innocent child."

In the middle of his rage, there was a knock at the door. He turned away from the window, pulling himself together with the mastery born of years of practice as his secretary entered.

"I'm sorry to interrupt, Mr. Caulfield, but there is a detective from the police department who would like to speak with you."

"Show him in."

Justin was all cordiality and smiles as he seated the man across from his desk then settled back into his own chair. "Detective Harmon, right? I remember you from the policemen's ball."

Harmon, a three-year veteran of the force was pleased that Caulfield knew him.

"Yes sir."

"How can I help you?" Justin asked.

"I'm sure you know by now that we pulled a body out of the river this morning."

"Yes, I heard that as I came into work. Very tragic. This rain is a deluge, so I assumed it was a drowning."

"No sir. It was not. We've got a murder on our hands."

Justin eyes registered surprise. "Murder! Really?"

"Yes sir, three bullets in the body."

"I am sorry to hear this. So what is it you need from me? Is the family in crisis? Are they going to need someone to pay for the burial?"

"That's real generous of you, Mr. Caulfield, but it's not why I came. The deceased has been identified as one of your former employees. A man named Jessup Sadler."

Justin frowned. "I'm sorry, Detective, but the name isn't familiar to me. I employ thousands of people across the state. Surely you understand."

"Yes, sir, I do. But we were told the man had been working

for you at Caulfield #14 for more almost thirty years. He was up for retirement in a couple of months, but was fired last week. He lost his pension and his health insurance, which would have been a terrible blow to the family since his wife is in the hospital dying of cancer. We thought, considering the drama of the circumstances, you might have remembered why he was fired, or who he might have had a grudge against."

"Ah, I see where you're going. Okay, just a moment."

Justin picked up his cell phone and scrolled through the contacts until he came to the name Tom Bonaventure, who was the foreman of Caulfield #14, then gave Harmon the info.

"I'm sorry I'm not familiar with the personnel problems, but I really don't involve myself in the day-to-day issues of the mines. I will let Bonaventure know you're coming and that he's to cooperate fully with your investigation."

"Thank you, Mr. Caulfield. We appreciate your assistance," Harmon said, and stood up.

"Happy to help," Justin said, as he walked him to the door. "As for the victim's wife, that's an unfortunate situation. I don't know the details of his dismissal but I'm not comfortable about the timing of when he was let go. I'll make sure his wife's medical bills are paid and his family is cared for. Under the circumstances, it seems only fair that they still get his pension, as well."

"That's real generous of you," Harmon said.

"Not a problem. I'll have my legal department take care of it," he said. "Have a good day, Detective," and then closed the door and returned to the desk to put in a call to Bonaventure. It rang twice before the call was picked up.

"Caulfield #14, Bonaventure speaking."

"Tom, this is Justin Caulfield. Thought I'd give you a heads up. The local police will be paying you a visit shortly."

Bonaventure was nursing a hangover and trying to hide the fact. Hearing the cops were on the way didn't help his misery.

"What's going on?"

"We had a man on payroll named Jessup Sadler?"

Bonaventure frowned. "Yes. Why?"

"They pulled his body out of the Little Man this morning. He'd been murdered."

"Oh, man. That's awful. I liked Jessup. He's the one I fired last week for coming to work drunk."

Justin frowned at the news. He turned toward the windows and looked down just as the detective bolted from the building and made a run through the downpour for his car.

"While it's company policy to fire a man who's drunk on the job and I know it's well within your authority to make that judgment, you should have taken his time on the job into consideration and simply asked him to turn in his retirement papers a couple of months early. He gave thirty years of his life to the company. Firing him like that will give the company a bad name, like we're cheating him out of what he'd rightfully earned."

Bonaventure felt his testicles drawing so far up his ass he wasn't sure if he'd ever be the same, and was immediately thankful Caulfield couldn't smell *his* breath.

"Yes sir. I understand. If there's another incident, I'll check with you first."

"Thank you. Carry on," he said, and disconnected.

The problem that had arisen had just been neatly solved. Delegation of duties was one of Justin's best traits.

CHAPTER TWO

The chatter on the police radio was disconcerting. It made Poppy wonder what the code was for finding dead bodies then wondered how these men lived and worked at a job where everything was a matter of life and death.

Because of Jessup Sadler's chosen lifestyle, she'd grown up with the possibility of cave-ins at the mine. She'd always known that death could be imminent. But it had never seemed real until this morning, and never had she imagined her daddy would become a murder victim. She hoped God was happy about the lesson she was supposed to learn because right now she was pissed.

The farther she rode, the more her shock dissipated, leaving nothing behind but pure rage. They'd had months to mentally prepare for her mother's passing, but this had taken her completely by surprise. She didn't know who she was madder at – the person who'd murdered her daddy, or God for letting it happen. As they stopped for a red light, she realized they were almost at the restaurant.

"If you take the next right into that alley it will take me to the back door of the restaurant. Vic doesn't like the help coming in the front door and parading through the dining area. He's already going to be mad at me for being late, so there's no need adding to the issue."

Mike frowned. "Vic Payton who used to wait tables here is your boss?"

"Yes, since just before Easter."

"How do you go from waiter to boss in five short months?"

“You get engaged to the owner’s daughter,” Poppy said. “Turn here.”

Mike glanced at her profile. Except for a complete lack of color in her face, it would have been impossible to tell her world had been decimated.

He took the turn into the alley then stopped at the back door to the restaurant. The downpour was incessant. He was hesitant to let her leave, and yet had no real reason to stop her. The weather sucked, but it wasn’t weather that was breaking her heart.

“Here’s my card, Miss Sadler. If you need anything, anything at all, feel free to call.”

Poppy dropped it in her purse. “Thank you for the ride.”

She jumped out, slamming the door behind her, and within two steps was inside.

Duroy got out and into the seat she’d just vacated. He couldn’t remember being this cold and wet.

“So, what do you think?” he asked.

Mike was watching the windshield wipers uselessly swiping at the downpour. “I think life just kicked her in the teeth.”

“Yeah, she got a rough deal for sure,” Duroy said. “Where to next?”

“Saint Anne’s. We need to see if Sadler’s car is there and if there’s security footage showing him coming and going. Maybe we’ll get lucky and see him leaving with someone.”

“Luck is good,” Duroy said.

“It’s a place to start,” Mike said, gave the back door to the restaurant one last glance.

He kept telling himself Poppy Sadler was a big girl from a tough side of town and not some delicate little socialite, but he still felt guilty as he drove away.

Vic Payton liked his fiancé, Michelle, well enough, definitely coveted her family’s social standing, and loved the power that came with his new position. He’d always had a thing for Poppy Sadler, but she’d never given him the time of day – or anyone else at the restaurant, for that matter. She was friendly and polite and did her job, but she came across as cold as ice. She didn't party. She didn't hang out with the other women on the job. She just worked her shifts and went back across that bridge to Coal Town like it was heaven on earth and he didn't get it.

Vic had been born in Coal Town and spent most of his twenty-seven years trying to get out. When the opportunity presented itself, he took it *and* the boss's daughter with open arms. Now he had to make good to keep Michelle happy and prove he was worth the promotion he'd been given, which meant reading Poppy the riot act if she ever showed up.

Everyone on the morning shift knew Poppy had called in this morning. They all assumed it was because of the weather and that she just wanted to sleep in. It had set a sour tone for the rest of the crew. They were going to be watching him to see how he handled it if she ever came in. And he was ready. He'd do what he had to. Just because she was pretty didn't mean she got a free pass. Not on his watch.

When she finally appeared on the floor he excused himself from a customer and strode toward her.

Poppy caught up with Jewel, the other waitress on her shift, at the coffee urns. The fifty-something woman was the no-nonsense type and prided herself on never missing a day of work. She gave Poppy a cool glance and then kept pouring fresh water into the coffee urn.

"I see you decided to show up," she said.

Without elaborating, Poppy picked up an order pad and slipped it in her pocket.

"Finally caught a ride in. Sonny said you'd been covering my tables. I owe you one."

"Whatever," Jewel said. "I'll finish out the tables being served to get my tips and then they're all yours."

Poppy was oblivious to the chill in the woman's voice. It was all she could do just to focus.

Then Vic tapped the counter behind her.

"Poppy! In the kitchen."

Too numb to be concerned, she followed him through the swinging doors.

He'd barely cleared the dining area before he turned and unloaded, right in front of Sonny the chef and his assistants.

"I don't tolerate tardiness and you know it. I assume you have a good excuse for showing up two and a half hours late for work?"

Poppy had one – two actually – but she didn't feel like sharing. If she said it aloud, it would make it final and she had yet to get to that state of mind.

"I'm sorry. It won't happen again."

Vic glared. "That's all you've got? I'm sorry?"

She lifted her chin, and as she did their gazes locked. She saw anger and pride in Vic's face and understood why he was behaving like a tyrant, but she wasn't in the mood to kiss ass.

He took her silence for defiance, but the longer he stared the more certain he became that something was wrong. She was unusually pale and her fingers were shaking. Because the behavior was so unlike her, it disarmed him.

"Just get back to work and see that it doesn't happen again," he muttered.

She went back into the dining room before he could change his mind, and slipped into the routine without a single word of explanation, leaving the rest of the crew to think what they liked.

It wasn't until a couple of her regulars came in for their mid-morning coffee that the fragile hold on her sanity began to unravel. They sat at their usual table and then waved her over.

"Poppy! Did you save us any jelly doughnuts?"

"Hey Bug. Hey Charlie. Where's your ark? I thought you two would know better than to get out in a flood."

The old men laughed. "Twenty-two years of coal dust went and fogged up our brains. All we do now is follow our bellies. What about them doughnuts and coffee?"

She tried a smile. It felt strange on her face but hoped they wouldn't notice.

"I saved you some. Be right back."

She returned quickly with the doughnuts and coffee then moved on to her other tables to top off their cups. It wasn't until she walked past her last table that she realized word was beginning to spread about her father's murder.

"...heard it on the news right before I drove down here. They pulled a dead body out of the Little Man. Said they he was all shot up. Scary shit, hunh? I guess he pissed off the wrong person and that's what he got."

"Really? Did they say who it was?"

"No. They were still notifying next of kin. Imagine getting that wake up call."

Then the woman looked up, saw Poppy and pointed toward her coffee cup. "Hey, honey, I'd like a little more."

Poppy managed to pour the coffee without making a mess and quickly headed for the counter, pretending to switch coffee pots and wipe up a spill to get herself together.

Jewel saw Poppy stagger as she reached for the cleaning rag then noticed her hands were trembling.

"What's the matter with you? Are you sick? If you are, you shouldn't have come in and spread your damn germs around."

Poppy flinched as if she'd been slapped, then turned on Jewel, spitting words in short, staccato bursts.

"Thank you for your concern but you can't catch what's wrong with me."

Jewel took a quick step back, thinking Poppy was going to hit her. Not once in the four years they'd worked together had she ever seen her act like this.

And once again, it was anger that pulled Poppy back from the edge. She picked up an order and walked away, blanking her mind on everything but the job. All she had to do was get to the end of the day and then she could scream.

But not now.

Not here.

Not in front of people who didn't have her back.

Vic kept watching Poppy from across the room, convinced something was wrong. He was considering sending her home when his cell phone rang. When he saw it was his fiancé, Michelle, he mentally shifted gears, making sure he sounded happy that she'd called him at work - again.

"Good morning, my sweetheart. How are you?"

Michelle Burkhart smiled. Vic was such a honey and she was the luckiest girl on earth.

"I'm fine, darling. Did you make it in okay? This rain is just awful, isn't it?"

"Yes, it is, and I hope you're staying home. I don't want you out driving around in this mess. Can't have anything happening to my best girl."

Michelle giggled. "I won't, I promise. Oh my, I almost forgot why I called. Isn't there a woman named Sadler who works at The Depot?"

Vic's gaze immediately slid toward Poppy.

"Yes, there is. Why do you ask?"

"Oh, it's all over the news and it's just awful. You heard about them pulling a body out of the Little Man this morning, right?"

Vic frowned. "No, I didn't. Why? What does that have to do with Poppy?"

"Oh. Is that her name? Anyway, about that body they found. They said the man was murdered but they hadn't given out his name until just now. They identified the man as Jessup Sadler. I wondered if they were any relation?"

Vic's gut knotted. "That's her father."

"Eww, how awful. I thought I should let you know since she works for us. Maybe we should send flowers or something, whatever you think best."

"Yes, yes, I'll make sure to take care of that. Thank you for calling, honey. I'll see you this evening."

"I can't wait," Michelle said, and then giggled again before she hung up.

Vic slipped the phone back in his pocket, debating with himself about what to say to Poppy. She had to know. The cops would have already told her before the name was released. He couldn't believe she'd still come to work. Why hadn't she told him straight out what had happened? And the minute he thought it, he knew.

Money.

In Coal Town, it was always the first word on the worry list.

He guessed they were already struggling because of her mother's cancer and now this. He couldn't imagine what she must be thinking.

He watched, waiting until she headed into the kitchen with a tray of dirty dishes before he followed her inside.

"Uh...Poppy, we need to talk."

She turned around, saw the pity on his face and knew he'd heard.

"Why didn't you tell me?" he asked.

No, no, no, we're not having this discussion. "Tell you what?"

"About your dad."

"What about him?"

Vic felt sick. *Oh hell, maybe she doesn't know.* "Have you talked to the police this morning?"

She leaned against the sink, giving herself time to think. Once she gave life to these words, there would be no taking them back. The reality of what happened would become fact. Finally, her shoulders slumped.

"Yes, I talked to them."

Vic's relief was instantaneous. "Oh. Thank God, I thought... anyway, never mind what I thought. Dang it Poppy, you should have told me. What kind of an ogre do you think I am? I would have understood. I would have expected you to stay home."

Poppy's eyes welled, but she wouldn't cry.

"What good would it do to stay home and watch it rain? I can't do anything. I can't change anything. They haven't even found our car. I need the money and I'm in limbo. The best place for me to be is here. I just can't talk about it, okay?"

Jewel walked in on that line and realized she'd interrupted something. But since no one told her to get lost, she stood her ground as Vic continued.

"But honey, now that it's been on the news everyone is going to know what happened to your daddy. They're going to know he was murdered. When the lunch crowd arrives, the people who know you will either be watching to see if you break into tears or they'll want to talk about it. Surely you'd rather be with your Mom at the hospital today. Does she know?"

Poppy started to shake. “She’s not there.”

Vic frowned. “But I thought-“

Poppy took a deep breath. *Help me Jesus.*

“She died this morning. The hospital called right before the cops showed up at the door.” She tried to focus but her words sounded like she was talking down a well. “When they said Daddy was dead, that they’d pulled his body from the Little Man, I thought he’d probably gotten drunk and drowned.”

She glanced up. Everyone in the kitchen was listening and the expressions on their faces were almost her undoing. She blinked then looked away.

“But I was wrong. Someone shot my daddy three times and threw his body in the Little Man and I don’t know why. So they’re dead. They’re both dead.”

Jewel wasn’t the kind for emotional displays, but she felt guilty on so many levels for how she’d treated Poppy this morning that she reached for her without thinking.

“Oh honey! I’m so sorry. If I’d known I-“

Poppy flinched and pulled back. “Don’t! You didn’t care this morning before you knew, so you don’t get to care now. Don’t touch me. Don’t anybody touch me.”

All of a sudden the walls started to move. She had to get out. She had to get out now before they came any closer. She staggered toward the break room to her locker, grabbed her purse and slung it over her shoulder, pulled on her raincoat and headed for the back door.

“Wait, Poppy! Wait damn it! I’ll take you home,” Vic yelled.

Poppy stopped. “No. I don’t want your pity. Am I fired?”

Vic threw up his hands. “Hell no, you’re not fired! Just call when you’re ready to come back, okay?”

“Yes.”

“Will you at least let me call a cab for you?” he asked.

She shook her head and opened the door. There was a moment when she was silhouetted against the rain and the wall of graffiti on the other side of the alley then she walked out into the downpour, slamming the door behind her.

Jewel was ashamed and left the kitchen.

Vic felt like a heel.

Sonny started shouting orders, making everyone get busy.

"God damn it," Vic muttered, and followed Jewel back into the dining area.

Detective Harmon was on his way to Caulfield #14 to talk to the foreman who'd fired Jessup Sadler. They needed a break in the case. Whatever evidence might have been left on the riverbank when Sadler's body was dumped had been washed away with the rain and the same for the forensic evidence that might have been on Jessup Sadler. It disappeared when he went into the river.

However, he knew Bonaventure and Sadler had some bad blood between them and Bonaventure better have a damn good alibi or he was going to be the first name on the suspect list.

The road up to the mine was blacktopped, but the runoff from the rain was like driving on a water slide. Once he even hydro-planed but managed to regain control before he went off the road.

"God damn rain," Harmon muttered as he steered the car out of a slide.

He'd made the last payment on it less than three months ago. The last thing he needed was to wreck it and glared at his surroundings. The road leading to the mine had been cut through what must have once been a heavily forested area. Now it was raw and denuded from the mining, like a half-dressed woman slowly stripping for whoever paid to watch.

The damage throughout West Virginia from both strip and mountain top mining would have been painful to see for anyone who loved nature, but that did not include Harmon. He'd grown up in a city and did not love the great outdoors. He did not appreciate how much destruction had occurred, or the amount of years and money in reclamation it would take to put it back. All he knew was that the mine he was going to today was the kind that gave him the creeps. He couldn't imagine working inside the belly of a mountain and sucking in coal dust while knowing at any time that a pocket of poison gas or a cave-in would be what ended your life.

According to his GPS he was less than a mile from the mine. He began watching for the sign that would show him where to turn when all of a sudden something darted out of the bushes and across his path. He stomped the brakes, but not in time. There was a heavy thud, the familiar sound of crumpling metal, and then the sudden cacophony of an animal in mortal pain.

"Well, son-of-a-bitch!" he muttered, and shoved the car in park.

He got out, immediately soaked despite the raincoat he was wearing, and moved around to the front of his car just as a teenage boy came flying out of the trees with a rifle in his hand.

Between the mangled dog on the road and the look of shock on the boy's face, Harmon knew his day was about to get worse.

The boy leaped across the bar ditch and knelt by the redbone hound that was yelping and writhing in pain.

"Oh Mister, what did you do?"

"Look son. I'm real sorry, but the dog ran out in front of me. With this rain and all, I didn't even see him until it was too late. If he's hurt bad we can load him up and take him back down to Caulfield to the vet."

"Easy Sam, easy old boy," the boy murmured as he ran his hands over the dog's body, although the obvious wounds were already visible to the eye.

The dog's yelps and cries of pain had diminished to an occasional whimper. There were broken bones piercing the dog's flesh in several locations and two of his legs lay in the opposite position to the way God had meant them. Basically, the dog was dead and just didn't know it yet.

"He's ruined," the boy said. "His ribs are all broke up. There's blood coming out of both ears. His legs, oh God, his legs... he'll never run on them legs again, even if nothing else was wrong."

"I'd be happy to pay the vet bill," Harmon said. "You pick him up and we can go back-"

Before he could finish what he'd been going to say, the boy stood, put the barrel of his rifle against the dog's head, and pulled the trigger.

Harmon jumped like he was the one who'd been shot. It was obvious the boy was heartbroken, and yet he'd been man enough to do what had to be done so the dog would not suffer.

"Is there anything I can do?" Harmon asked.

But the boy was through talking. He slung the rifle strap over his shoulder, picked the big hound up in his arms and crossed the road into the trees.

Harmon stood in the downpour while his eyes burned and his stomach rolled. He started back toward the car then stopped and threw up until his ribs were aching. Finally, he dragged himself into the car and shut the door.

The engine was still running and the rain hammering on the roof of the car was almost deafening.

He glanced at the GPS.

He was less than a hundred yards from his turn-off. Five seconds difference one way or the other and the accident would never have happened. He wouldn't let himself think about the years of that dog's life or of his own daily routine, and why the universe decided that today was the day they would meet and one be the reason for the other one's death.

He started to put the car in gear and then stopped, crossed his arms on the steering wheel and dropped his head. Before he knew it he was sobbing.

It took almost five minutes before he got himself under control, and another five minutes before he trusted himself enough to drive. When he finally took off, he was shaking.

By the time he got to Caulfield #14, he was in one hell of a mood.

He parked, killed the engine, and then looked at the muddy expanse he was going to have to cross to get to the trailer house that served as an office. He reminded himself it was part of the job, but when he got out and lost both shoes in the mud before he'd gone five steps, he got pissed all over again.

He stomped past the truck yard with his shoes in his hand while the mud slowly pulled the socks off his feet. By the time he reached the office he was barefoot. There wasn't a rational thought left in his head as he knocked on the office door.

The door opened abruptly, as if the man inside had seen him

coming and had been waiting for the knock.

"Come on in here out of that miserable weather," the man said.

"Are you Tom Bonaventure?" Harmon snapped.

"Why, yes sir. Yes, I am."

All Harmon saw was the man's black eye and busted lip before his mind slid to how that might have happened, like maybe two men fighting on the banks of the Little Man before one of them pulled a gun and ended the fight.

"We need to talk," he stated, and pushed his way inside.

Bonaventure had been a little anxious before, but now he was nervous.

"Detective Harmon, right? Here you go, have a seat right here and I'll pour you up a cup of hot coffee to break that chill."

Harmon shed his raincoat by the door, dropped his shoes on the floor and threw his socks in a trash can. His bare muddy feet made little splat-splat sounds as he walked across the cheap green linoleum and wondered why they hadn't laid down a color in some shade of brown. It would have at least matched the grime on top of it.

Bonaventure politely ignored the man's condition as he poured coffee to within an inch of the rim. "How do you take your coffee, Detective?"

"Black," Harmon said, and managed to nod a brief thank you as the man put it in his hands.

It was hot and bitter and at least a day and a half old, but it had caffeine, and for now that was enough. He took a quick sip, set it on the desk between them, then opened his notebook and fixed Bonaventure with a hard, angry stare.

"I understand you fired Jessup Sadler less than a week ago. What was your reason?"

"Why, drinking on the job," Bonaventure said. "It's against strict policy, you understand. Can't have a drunk down in the hole. Makes him a danger to more people than himself."

Harmon made a quick note.

"How did he take it?"

"Well sir, he was mad. He was real mad, but he knew the rules."

"Did he mention anything about the fact that it would cost him his pension - a pension he was only months away from drawing? Or that losing his job would end his health insurance and put his dying wife's care in jeopardy?"

Bonaventure felt like a trapped rat. This wasn't going well. The way the detective sounded, it made it seem as if he was the one at fault, not the man who'd come drunk.

"He mentioned all of that," Bonaventure said.

"And you weren't persuaded that he might have a second chance? Like sending him home and docking his pay instead of firing him just before his thirty years were up?"

Bonaventure frowned. "A rule is a rule, Detective and I didn't make none of them. I was just hired to follow them."

"So who has the final word here?"

"Why, that would be Mr. Caulfield. Of course it didn't come to that. Jessup took his firin' like a man and left after he'd said his piece. I didn't hear from him again."

"How did you get that black eye and busted lip?" Harmon asked.

"Um... well, I think I got a little tipsy at the bar last night and fell on my way out the door, but I'm not real sure."

"You're sure you didn't run into Sadler last night and get into a fight? Then someone pulled a gun and the fight was over, right? Maybe he was the one who'd brought the gun and you were just protecting yourself. Is that how it went down?"

Bonaventure felt like he'd just been sideswiped. He had not seen this coming.

"No, sir it is not! The only gun I own is a huntin' rifle, which I damn sure don't carry around to no bars. And, I did not get into a fight with anyone last night, especially Jessup Sadler."

"So you got drunk off your ass last night with a clear conscience, yet had no compassion for Sadler?"

Bonaventure was getting pissed. He'd tried to be nice, but he didn't like the way this was going.

"I never said I was a teetotaler. I just don't come on the job drunk, mister, and neither does anyone else who works here. Is there anything else I can do for you?"

"Yes. I need a list of people who work on the same shift that

Sadler worked, and the names of anyone who can verify your whereabouts from sundown last night until sunup this morning."

Bonaventure's eyes widened in sudden panic. For the first time in the five years since he and Mayrene had gotten a divorce, he wished it hadn't happened. At least she would have been waiting up for him like she'd used to when he'd dragged his sorry ass home. He got up and pulled a list from the filing cabinet, ran a copy for the cop and handed it over.

"There's your list. I don't know what time I left Doobie's Bar, but I'm sure he can tell you. However, I live alone, and there ain't no one who can say what time I got home or what time I left the house until I clocked in here at six a.m."

Harmon was writing fast and furious.

Bonaventure was sweating.

"Did Jessup ever have any arguments or disagreements with the men he worked with?"

Bonaventure thought for a moment. As much as he would have liked to point the finger of guilt at someone else, he couldn't think of a one. "None that I knew of."

Harmon stood abruptly. "I don't need to tell you not to leave town, do I?"

Bonaventure belly rolled. "Are you insinuating I had something to do with Jessup's murder?"

"I didn't insinuate anything. I'm just telling you not to leave town. Do we understand each other?"

Bonaventure wanted to punch him. Instead he managed to nod in what he hoped was an accommodating manner.

"Yep. Yep, we do."

Harmon put his raincoat back on, picked up his shoes and left as abruptly as he'd come in, shutting the door behind him with a slam.

Bonaventure started to call the boss then stopped. If he told Justin Caulfield he was now a murder suspect because he'd been drunk last night and woke up with a black eye and a busted lip, he was likely to be the next one fired. He didn't want that to happen.

What he needed was a drink, but after what had just gone down, he didn't have the guts to indulge. Instead, he locked the office door and headed for the back of the trailer. If he couldn't get a release one way, he'd get it another. So he locked himself into the bathroom and proceeded to jack himself off.

CHAPTER THREE

Detectives Amblin and Duroy were at the police precinct going over the hospital security footage. Earlier, they'd combed the parking lot for Jessup's car, but hadn't found it. So, either he'd never made it to the hospital, or he'd been murdered after he left. They were still waiting for a time of death from the coroner's office and without a crime scene or witnesses, they were at a loss. Hopefully they'd get an answer to one of the questions from the tapes.

They'd been at it for nearly an hour when Mike suddenly hit Pause and leaned forward, staring at the image frozen on the screen.

"Hey, Kenny, isn't that our guy?"

Duroy compared the photo they had from the DMV to the face on the screen. "Looks like him. What's the time stamp?"

Mike glanced down. "7:40 p.m. So the daughter was right. He did go see his wife. What floor was she on?"

Duroy scanned the list of info they had on the Sadler family. "Uh, third floor."

Mike flipped the video feed from the first floor to the third floor, matching the time and date. Within seconds they saw the elevator doors open and Jessup Sadler walk out. His steps were slow and plodding and his shoulders slumped.

"Poor bastard," Duroy said. "Wife's dying. Got his ass fired and still keeping the secret. Wonder what he was thinking? It's for damn sure he wasn't thinking that he'd never see another sunrise."

Mike eyed the man as he walked, noting absently that

Poppy Sadler must have taken after her mother because she looked nothing like this man, except maybe for the height. Sadler was a big man and Poppy was at least five foot nine, maybe even five-ten. But since thinking about her was immaterial to what they were doing, he set the thought aside and kept making notes of their findings. When Mike saw Jessup pause and then enter a room, he pointed.

"Okay... he's inside."

"Fast-forward to when he comes out," Duroy said.

Mike watched the occasional relay of nurses going in and out, noting a doctor who went in and exited less than three minutes later. But Jessup remained.

"There! There he comes," Mike finally said. "Time is 10:33. He's walking toward the elevator. Now he's making a run for it... ah... he didn't make it. Gotta wait for the next car. Okay, now he's getting in." Mike flipped video again to the ground floor, waiting to see Jessup appear, which he did, walking out the same way he walked in. "...and there he goes. Damn it! Do we have footage on the parking lot?"

Duroy shuffled through the stack and then handed Mike a tape. They fast-forwarded to coincide with the time stamp showing Jessup Sadler leaving the building.

"That's him," Mike said, then paused. "No, my bad. That's not him. Just another big man in a raincoat. It would start to rain when we needed to confirm this."

"Stop!" Duroy said, pointing the man in the raincoat. "Who is that guy? He looks familiar."

Mike hit pause, again focusing on what they could see of the face.

"Well it's definitely not Sadler and that car is not a 1999 Ford."

Duroy frowned. "I should know who that is."

"It could be anyone and it wouldn't matter. Why do we need to know who's coming and going? Sadler is who we're looking for."

"I guess," Duroy said, and gave up the notion as Mike hit Play.

A few moments later they saw Sadler come into camera view.

"There he is!" Mike said. When Jessup paused and unlocked an old car, he added. "And there's the 1999 Ford with one black fender."

The footage wasn't great, but the faint glow of light in the parking lot helped ID him. Even though the rain had already begun, there was no mistaking his broad shoulders or the slump in his posture as he moved. What they did note was he was almost running – they assumed to get out of the rain.

They watched him start the car and turn on the lights then were startled by the sudden spurt of speed as he took off out of the parking lot, almost like he was chasing someone.

Duroy frowned. "Wait. What the hell is that all about? Before when he was running I thought it was to get out of the rain. Now he's out of the rain, so what's the hurry? What are we missing?"

"He's either trying to follow someone, or maybe he got a phone call that caused him to leave in such a hurry," Mike said. "Do we have his phone records?"

"I'm not sure. Bonaventure is doing follow-ups on Sadler's contacts and whereabouts for the last week."

"Go see what he knows," Mike said. "I'm going to go back through the video and see if we can identify who and how many people left just ahead of Sadler."

"Will do," Duroy said.

Mike hit rewind on the first floor video and then began watching it again, hoping to find something they'd missed.

Poppy didn't know how long she'd been walking because she'd left her wristwatch at home. She had no way of knowing the time it would take to walk from the restaurant in downtown Caulfield to her house, because she'd never done it. All she could do was keep putting one foot in front of the other until she was home.

As she waited for a light to change, she glanced down at the trash rushing down the flood-swollen gutter and flashed on a memory from her childhood.

It was summer - the best time of the year when school didn't happen and days were twice as long and twice the fun. The sun was brutal, but she and Johnny were oblivious to the heat. They were playing outside when a sudden clap of thunder rattled the heavens. They looked up into a sky turning darker by the moment and when a flash of lightning struck near the bridge, their mother came running out of the house to call them in, although there was really no need. They were already in flight.

At first they were disgruntled about having to stop in the middle of their game, and then Mama appeared with a tablet of paper, a box of crayons and some tape, and sat down in the floor beside them. All of a sudden, it was fun again.

Curious, they watched as she tore a sheet of paper from the tablet and began folding it one way and then another until she'd turned it into a paper boat. She folded boats until the pad was all used up and gave them crayons to color the sails. When the storm finally passed, Poppy and Johnny had an armada. They took off like puppies turned out of a pen and began sailing their tiny, boats through the rain swollen ditches until the paper soaked through and the armada was defeated by saturation.

Someone honked.

Poppy jumped back to keep from being splashed by the backwash from a passing car, then wondered why it mattered. She couldn't be any wetter.

And just like that, the memory was gone.

When she realized she'd missed her chance to cross, she just pulled the hood of her raincoat a little tighter around her face and waited for the next light.

She lost all track of time as she kept walking south. Somewhere along Dupont Street she looked down and realized she was walking in water. Her shoes were full and spilling over with each step that she took, and she couldn't even register dismay. She thought about taking them off then decided it was too cold to be barefoot, and too late to save the shoes, so she kept on walking while her head was spinning. The bottom line was that her daddy's murder made no sense. The only thing that had changed in their lives, besides her mother's cancer, was the fact that Daddy had been fired. Yes, that would have made him mad and it would have scared him, too. He wouldn't have been able to provide.

So who would he have challenged? The foreman at the mine? Justin Caulfield himself? Even if all those things had happened, killing him still made no sense. He posed no threat to anyone.

The only other thing she could think of was that someone had killed him for the car, which was crazy. The car was old and on its last legs. Why murder for something that might not even make a getaway from the scene of the crime? Poppy was at a loss. She needed to make sense of a senseless act and it wasn't happening.

As she came around the corner, she quickly realized someone else was afoot in the rain. When she recognized the old homeless man, her heart skipped a beat. She didn't think she needed to be afraid of him, but he was unsettling. She put her head down and kept moving without making eye contact, but it didn't help. As soon as he saw her, he started to shout.

"The devil is alive. I seen him. You gotta hide!"

Poppy lengthened her stride, trying not to stumble, but her feet and legs were so cold she could barely stand upright.

"You!" Prophet shouted. "He'll get you next! Run girl! Run! The devil's in the house!"

When he reached for her, she panicked. All of a sudden she was running, tearing through the rain-soaked streets, taking shortcuts through the alleys just to get away.

By the time she got to the bridge over the Little Man her heart was hammering against her chest and she was shaking so hard it was difficult to put one foot in front of the other. Just as she stepped up on the foot path to take her across the bridge she caught a glimpse of the roiling flood waters below. It was yet another mistake in a day filled with errors.

She couldn't look down without thinking of her daddy being thrown in there like so much garbage. She tried to look away, but it was too late. The river swallowed her up just like it had taken her daddy until she was leaning over the railing, drawn to the power of the water rushing past.

The sound of a car horn broke the spell. Startled, she pulled back, and then moaned. Overwhelmed by the distance and growing weaker by the minute, she tried to talk herself across.

Move, damn it! You're freezing. Get over yourself and start walking. Just don't look down. Don't look down.

She made it two steps further before another horror popped into her head. What if Daddy hadn't been dead when he fell in the river?

Oh Jesus.

Had he struggled against the storm and the current, bleeding and in pain? He would have been frantic, thinking about her and Mama, knowing what a mess he would be leaving behind.

Again she forced herself to look away from the river and focus on the other side of the bridge. From where she was standing she could almost see the roof of her house. So close, and yet it might as well have been a thousand miles.

All of a sudden her legs buckled and she was on her knees, shaking too hard to get up. It was a bitch, coming this far and then coming undone. She slumped against the railing, then threw her head back and screamed. Assaulted by the downpour and the harsh sobs burning up her throat, she curled up into a ball and prayed to God to just let her die. The bridge was vibrating beneath her as the flood waters slammed against the pilings below. She wondered if it would collapse and take her with it.

She didn't hear the screech of brakes or see the man who jumped from the car. All she felt were hands pulling her up and a voice near her ear telling her to lean on him.

So she did.

When Mike Amblin learned Jessup Sadler's missing car had been located in the parking lot of an all-night gas station, he took off to the site, leaving Duroy with Harmon. Because of the rain, the possibility that they might find evidence anywhere outside the vehicle was unlikely, but they could get lucky and find something inside.

There were already two patrol cars on the scene when he

pulled into the station. A large area around the vehicle had been blocked off with crime scene tape. A couple of uniformed officers were walking the area searching for evidence while another was directing traffic. As usual, everyone wanted to see what was going on. Even though he doubted this was the actual scene of the crime, they had to go through the motions.

He parked and got out, flashing his badge as he approached. "What do we know so far?"

The officer recognized Mike and began relaying information.

"The car is locked but here's a weird one. The keys are still in the ignition. A passing patrol car spotted it. The clerk's name is Roy Parnell. He said it was there when he came to work at 6:00 a.m."

"Have you found any bullet casings or anything that would lead us to believe this was where the shooting occurred?"

"No, and honestly, even if there had been anything here, it wouldn't have lasted long. Look at the slope. The run-off is going straight into the gutters and then into the city sewers."

"What about security cameras?"

The officer pointed to the corner of the building. "There are cameras. Don't know if they're operational or not. There's a wrecker on the way to tow the car to the crime lab."

"Thanks," Mike said, and headed into the station to talk to the clerk.

The door chimed as he entered. He scanned the store for the clerk, spotting him behind the counter. Mike flashed his badge again.

"I'm Detective Amblin with the Caulfield police department."

"Roy Parnell," the clerk said, eyeing the water making a puddle around the big cop's feet.

"Nice to meet you, Roy. You got a minute?"

"Yeah sure, anything I can do to help. Is this about the man who was murdered? The one they pulled out of the Little Man this morning? I heard it on the news."

"Yes. That car belongs to him. I understand you didn't come to work until 6:00 a.m. this morning. Was the car already there?"

Roy nodded.

Mike pulled out the DMV photo of Jessup Sadler.

"Have you ever seen this man before?"

Roy took the photo and studied it for a few moments before handing it back.

"I don't know him. If he's been here before I don't remember him. We get a lot of customers through a day and the majority of them are regulars, but he's not one of them."

"Who was on duty last night?"

"Two different men, depending on your timeline. Hank McGowan worked until ten p.m. Then Billy Joe Fossey came on at 10:00 and worked until I came on at 6:00 a.m."

"I'll need phone numbers for both of them."

The clerk scanned his cell phone, then read them off as Mike made note of them in his notebook.

"Do your security cameras work?" Mike asked.

"Yeah, but even on a good night the images are shitty. I can't imagine what they'll show what with this damned rain and all."

That wasn't what Mike wanted to hear. "I still need the tapes."

"Be right back," Roy said, and went into a back room.

The wrecker arrived as Mike waited. He watched them winching Sadler's car onto the flatbed and thought of Poppy Sadler again. They'd found her car. She would be happy about that. At few moments later, the clerk was back.

"Here you go. I put them in a plastic bag so they wouldn't get wet."

"I appreciate that," Mike said, then ran back through the rain to his car.

His intention was to head back to the department to view the tapes, but the least he could do was put Poppy Sadler's mind at rest about the missing car, so he made a call to The Depot.

Vic Payton answered. "This is the Depot, home of the best homemade pies in West Virginia. How can I help you?"

"This is Detective Amblin. I'd like to speak to Poppy Sadler please."

Vic knew Mike from their years in high school together. "Hey Mike, it's me, Vic. Poppy's not here."

Mike frowned. "I dropped her off less than four hours ago. What happened?"

"Once the news got out about who the murdered man was, we thought it best that she go back home. You know, so she wouldn't be hammered with stares and questions."

"How long has she been gone?"

"Almost an hour and a half now, maybe more."

"Then I'll catch up with her there. Thanks," Mike said.

"Oh, hey, you might want to give her a little more time before you try."

"Time for what?"

"She might not be home yet. She wasn't acting herself today. Didn't tell any of us what had happened. We just found out like everyone else when the news broke on TV. Then she wouldn't accept any help. Didn't want a ride and wouldn't let me call her a cab. She just took off out the back door."

Mike stared through the windshield. Even though he was less than thirty feet from the building across the street he could barely make it out.

"Walking? You let her walk home in this shit?"

Vic's guilt resurfaced as he began to defend himself. "Look. You don't know her. She keeps to herself. She isn't easy to talk to or anything."

"I don't have to know her to know she was in shock. That's why she wasn't talking. She was in shock, damn it."

Mike dropped the phone in the console. He had no idea which streets Poppy Sadler would have taken to get herself across town to go home, but he was by God going to make sure she was there before he did anything else. He took off out of the parking lot, leaving rubber as he went.

Anxiety grew as he drove. It would be a long miserable walk in good weather. On a day like today it would be grueling. He was pissed at Vic for letting her go, and pissed at himself for even taking her to work in the first place. His first instincts were to go to straight to her home. If she wasn't there, then he could backtrack.

Urgency grew as he continued south. It was all he could do not to turn on the siren and lights and run hot through the streets, but it would be a recipe for disaster to speed in this weather.

Every car that slowed him down made him antsy. No one was afoot, which worsened his concern. Even the people who lived on the streets knew enough to take shelter.

It took nearly fifteen minutes to get through the city and by the time he saw the bridge in the distance, his belly was in knots.

At first his focus was on traffic, and then he glanced at the bridge, saw a figure standing on the footpath and knew it was her. When he saw her go down, his heart slammed against his ribcage. This time he didn't hesitate as he hit the lights and siren and went flying through the last traffic light, leaving a rooster-tail of water spray behind him.

He braked as he reached the bridge, slammed the car into park, and jumped out running. She was sobbing so hard she didn't even see him. He didn't bother trying to talk to her. When he bent down to pick her up, she didn't fight him.

"I've got you. Lean on me."

She went limp.

CHAPTER FOUR

For Poppy, the next few minutes were a blur of images.

The face of a man she thought she should know.

A scream in her head that wouldn't stop.

Windshield wipers rocking to the rhythm of the rain.

Questions she couldn't answer.

Blessed warmth on her hand.

It was the warmth she held onto, and the warmth that ultimately pulled her back to reality.

The scream was actually a siren.

The man was the detective from this morning.

And the windshield wipers were still at battle with the goddamned rain that continued to fall.

This time when she heard the detective speak, the words actually registered.

"Miss Sadler, you're going to be okay. I'm taking you home."

Poppy looked down at her lap. The warmth to which she was clinging was his hand, and the death grip she had on it was turning his knuckles white, yet he'd said nothing or tried to pull it away.

"I'm so cold."

Mike gave her a quick glance as he sped over the bridge. That she finally spoke was reassuring. He tried not to think about the blue tinge around her lips or the fact that she was shaking so hard she couldn't sit still.

"We're almost home. Just hang on a couple more minutes."

She didn't think about how he'd found her. She was too

grateful to be out of the rain to care.

Mike turned off the siren as he came off the bridge and when he turned down her street he killed the lights. No need advertising their arrival and sparking a string of visitors she wasn't ready to face. He pulled up in the driveway as close to the house as he could get then killed the engine.

"Sit tight a sec." He jumped out and rounded the car to help her out. "Easy does it," he said, but when she stepped out, she staggered.

He slid an arm around her waist to steady her as they splashed through the rain and puddles, and wound up all but dragging her onto the porch. The moment they were beneath the roof he heard her sigh. That he understood. This was sanctuary.

She was trying to find her keys, but her fingers were trembling too hard to find them in the depths of her purse.

"May I?"

She handed him the purse and within moments he had the keys in his hand.

"Blue cap," she mumbled, pointing at the color-coded keys.

Mike opened the door then paused to drop his raincoat and step out of his shoes.

"No need making a bigger mess than I have to," he said. "Here, let me help you with yours."

Before she knew it, her raincoat was off and he was on his knees helping her out of her shoes. When he started to bring them inside, she shook her head.

"Leave them, they're ruined," she said, and then stumbled as she took another step.

Again, Mike steadied her as they entered the house. The warmth enveloped them as he closed the door. Then he took her by the shoulders - scanning her eyes – taking note of her breathing - checking for anything that would indicate a serious problem while she kept swaying and stumbling in his grasp.

"Are you dizzy, Miss Sadler?"

Poppy was physically and emotionally numb. It took her a few moments to even process the question.

"Um...no. It's my feet. I can't really feel them."

She heard him curse beneath his breath and then once again

she was in his arms.

"Where's your bathroom?"

"What... uh... down the hall, first door on the left."

"You need to get warm. Quickest way is in a bathtub."

Poppy panicked, thinking he intended to strip her. "I'll do it. I don't need help."

His eyes smiled before his lips, but for some reason it was all the reassurance she needed.

"I don't intend to give you a bath. I just want to make sure you and the tub are in the same room before I leave."

She noticed a drop of water running out of his hair and down behind his ear as he carried her down the hall. It was a nice ear, as Mama would have said - lying flat against his head. His hair looked black. She didn't remember it being that dark this morning, but of course now it was wet.

Mike sat her down on the toilet seat and then turned around to start the water. As the tub was filling, he backed up to the door.

"I came to tell you that we found your father's car. It was parked at a gas station over on Nichols Avenue. Do you know anyone up that way?"

Poppy was surprised. All along she'd been expecting them to tell her they'd found it stripped and burned, or that they would eventually pull it out of the Little Man. Parked hadn't been part of the scenarios.

"Parked? Really? Was it... could you tell if-"

"It was locked. We towed it in. The crime lab will go over it, but at first glance I'd say that's not where he died."

The hot water was making steam, fogging up the mirror and warming the room even more. There was a sense of relief and at the same time, even more confusion for Poppy. If her daddy hadn't been killed there, then where? Now there was a whole new set of questions without answers.

"When can I have it back?"

"Not sure, but I'll hurry up the process as fast as I can. Do you have other family? Or some friends that you can call on to help you until we can release the car?"

She shrugged. "I have a brother. I'll call his cell. He might answer. He might not."

"Aren't you two on speaking terms?"

Poppy thought how odd it was that she was sitting on the closed lid of her toilet, having this conversation with a cop who'd just run her bathwater. Then she realized he was waiting for an answer.

"It's not that. He couldn't face watching our mother die, so he left. I can't imagine what he's going to do or say when he finds out about all this."

"That's tough. People take death and show grief in all kinds of ways," Mike said, then glanced behind him. "Looks like your tub's about full. You still have my card. Feel free to call if you need anything."

"I haven't thanked you for bringing me home."

Mike turned off the bath water then turned to face her. There was a question that had been bugging him ever since he'd talked to Vic.

"Why didn't you let Vic bring you home when he offered?"

A frown creased her forehead. "I have no idea. I don't even remember leaving the restaurant."

He sighed. It was just as he'd thought. Delayed shock from the whole fucking day.

"I'll lock the front door on my way out. When you get warmed up, get something warm in your belly as well."

"I will. Thank you, again."

"You're very welcome, Miss Sadler. I'll be in touch."

He closed the bathroom door behind him.

She heard his footsteps as he walked up the hall. Once she heard the car driving away, she stripped and stepped into the tub, groaning softly as the hot, steamy water rose around her.

The warmth was painful, but as she soaked, full circulation slowly returned. It wasn't until she could feel her fingers and her toes again that she began to cry.

But it wasn't the primal scream from before - just the first welling of true grief for the acceptance of what she'd lost, coupled with a good dose of fear that the worst wasn't over yet.

Amelia Caulfield wiped her eyes as she exited her

granddaughter's room. The nurse had come in to change IV bags and take Callie's vitals. She'd used her appearance as an excuse to go to the waiting room to get a cold drink, when in truth she just needed a moment to compose herself. With every passing day, she was more convinced they weren't aiding in Callie's recovery, and that she was, instead, witnessing a slow, miserable death.

She and her husband, Adam, had only had the one child, their son, Justin. And Justin and Deborah had only had the one child before Justin developed an infection that left him sterile.

All of a sudden, the Caulfield dynasty that had been a strong and thriving bloodline for so many generations had been relegated to one last child and a girl at that. There were no more males to continue the family name.

She'd grieved with Justin when Deborah died in a fiery car crash, but she'd never heard him as devastated as he'd been when he'd called to tell her about Callie.

While she'd been horrified and then saddened beyond measure as she'd heard the news, there had been a selfish moment when she'd resented being asked to come back to West Virginia to help. She'd nursed Adam through seven long years of diminishing sanity before he'd finally died from Alzheimer's disease and it had nearly killed her. To get away from the bad memories, she'd moved away from West Virginia to Florida, and over a period of years finally made a new life for herself. It wasn't perfect, but it was peaceful.

And then Justin called, and guilt and duty brought her back just to watch it happen all over again. She wondered from time to time what it was the Caulfield family had done that was so awful they would be punished in such a way, and then reminded herself that isn't the way God worked. They had made a good run of it for over a century. Maybe their time was just running out. She patted her pocket to see if she had money then started down the hall.

It was after five p.m. before Justin could get away from the office to go to Saint Anne's to see Callie. The worst of the thunderstorm had passed, although it continued to drizzle. It was too damn cold for September. At any time if felt as if that drizzle could turn to snow.

His mother had been at the hospital most of the day, sending him hourly updates of Callie's condition either by phone or by texts.

Over the past few days he began to realize they were measuring the failure of Callie's body in the same increments as they'd measured her progress in infancy. Now they marked her deterioration by whether or not she was able to eat - how much pain meds she'd had to have – and if the bleeding in her lungs was any better than it had been the day before, just as they had marked her progress as a baby by the first burp, her first smile, and how many ounces of formula she got down in a single feeding. How could God give you a child and then take her back just like that and make her suffer in the process?

It was fucking obscene.

By the time he got parked he had control of his emotions. The last thing he wanted was for Callie to sense how he felt. If she knew how tenuous her condition really was, she might quit fighting.

Almost every day he brought Callie a treat. Sometimes it was a flower, sometimes a book she'd wanted to read. Today it was an angel - a small porcelain figurine with wings outspread, hands folded and head bowed, as if in prayer. The word FAITH was written in gold script on the hem of the gown. Callie collected angels, so he knew it would be a hit.

He strode through the lobby, nodding courteously to the employees and staff that he passed. They were all used to seeing him here on a daily basis, and more than one called out a greeting and to tell Callie they said hello. He waved and smiled and kept on walking, when in truth he resented them all. They went home to their families and had dinner and went to bed, confident that when they woke, their world would still be in order. He wanted to tell them all it was a façade; that life was just waiting for them to be really happy before it threw them for a loop, but he didn't. He was Justin Caulfield and therefore always circumspect.

As he exited the elevator onto the third floor he saw his

mother emerge from Callie's room and pause in the hall with a tissue in her hands. It occurred to him then how elegant she appeared despite her seventy-plus years. She was tall and slender in dark slacks and a yellow blouse, set off by her crown of snow-white hair, although he remembered that same hair had been dark – almost black – when he was a boy.

When he realized she was crying his heart dropped. God in heaven! Was it over? Had Callie taken a turn for the worse and died before he could even say goodbye?

Before he could react, he saw Oral Newton, his mother's driver, jump out of a chair down the hall and head for Amelia at a fast clip.

Back when Adam Caulfield had been alive, Oral Newton had been Amelia Caulfield's personal chauffeur/bodyguard. His devotion to her stemmed from more than thirty years of service to the family, and when she'd come back from Florida to help care for Callie, he'd taken himself out of retirement and come back to the family residence to make certain she was not inconvenienced in any way by her daily visits to Saint Anne's. Newton's expression of empathy on seeing Amelia's tears only added to Justin's panic as he lengthened his stride.

Oral caught up with Amelia before she reached the waiting room, ever ready to serve her in any way she needed.

"Can I get you anything, Mrs. Caulfield?"

Amelia smiled. "I was going to get myself a cold drink."

"I'll get it for you, ma'am. Seven-up or Sprite?"

She smiled. "I can't believe you still remember what I like to drink. Yes, please."

As Oral stepped into the waiting room where the snack machines were located, someone grabbed her by the arm.

"Mother! What's wrong? Why are you crying? Has something happened to Callie?"

"Nothing is wrong. You're hurting me, Justin. Calm down."

Her dismissive tone was a slap in the face. After the crap he'd been dealing with at the office and Callie's situation, he didn't need to be talked to as if he was a child.

"Calm down? How do you calm down, Mother? Tell me, because I haven't been able to do that. My child is dying and no one, including that damned God you pray to, seems inclined to stop the process."

Amelia frowned. "Don't blaspheme. I raised you better than that." Then she slipped a hand over his arm and gave it a quick squeeze. "Let's don't take our fears out on each other, dear. We're both worried sick and we're tired. But it's Callie we have to focus on, not ourselves."

Justin had always disliked the fact that she rarely showed emotion. Even in the face of discord, she never raised her voice. But she was right. Fighting solved nothing.

"You're right. I'm sorry. It's been a hellish couple of days."

She made a face then patted his cheek. "Poor dear. Trouble at the office?"

"Nothing I can't handle. Don't worry. It's not worth mentioning."

"Of course you can handle it," she said. "I never doubted you, just as I never doubted your father. He could always figure a way out of trouble. You got that from him."

Justin pointed toward Callie's room. "What's going on in there?"

"Just the usual. I took the time to take a break. Do you want something cold to drink? I was going to the waiting room to get a soda but Oral is getting it for me. Would you care for something, too?"

"I guess. I'll be right back."

Amelia eyed her son as he strode away. There were actually wisps of gray in his dark hair and faint lines at the corners of his eyes. He was showing his age. Funny, she'd never noticed that before. But he was still her tall, handsome boy – so like his father. She chose to forget what a trial he'd been to the family through his teens and college years. That was then and this was now.

She watched him stop to speak to Newton then take the cold drinks he was carrying, leaving the bodyguard standing in the hall with a disgruntled look on his face.

Justin handed her the cold can that had been wrapped with a napkin and already opened for her convenience.

"Thank you," she said, and drank thirstily.

"You're welcome, Mother. Why don't you go home and get some rest? It's almost stopped raining."

She took another sip and then set it aside. "I believe I will. Let me tell Callie goodbye and get my bag. She'll be thrilled you're already here. You're her favorite, you know."

Justin smiled. He knew his daughter idolized him. The feeling was mutual.

As they walked into Callie's room, he couldn't help hoping one day they would all look back on this time as nothing but a bad memory and that she would grow up and grow old, giving him grandchildren to spoil.

"Daddy! You're here," Callie said, and then grabbed a washcloth to cover her mouth as she coughed. When she pulled it away, he could see tinges of red. The bleeding still hadn't stopped.

Amelia picked up her bag and then wiggled her fingers in what passed for a wave. "Callie, darling, since your daddy is here, I'm going home for the evening. Sleep well and I'll see you tomorrow."

Callie managed a wan smile. "Okay, Nana, see you tomorrow."

Justin swooped past his mother and the nurse who had just changed Callie's IV, ignored the dialysis machine and kissed his daughter on the forehead.

"Good evening, beautiful. I brought you a surprise," he said, and pulled the angel out of his pocket.

Callie beamed. "A new angel! Oh, look, her name is Faith! Just what I need to remind me I'll get better! Thank you, Daddy! I love her."

"And I love you," Justin said. "So tell me what's been going on. Did you eat your lunch? Have you been out of the bed today?"

Justin listened with one ear as his daughter began to talk, but he was focused on something more pressing. The shadows beneath her eyes were deeper – even darker. Her skin was almost translucent – as if she was already teetering toward the other side. He felt like crying. Instead, he laughed at something she said and tried not to think of how many sunrises she had left. Tomorrow would take care of itself. It always did.

After receiving a phone call from the funeral home regarding her mother's body, Poppy made herself eat a bowl of soup. The relief of learning Jessup had already paid for the funeral was overwhelming. They gave her a list of things they needed her to bring to get her mother's body ready for the viewing, and in an odd way, having purpose gave her strength. She hadn't been able to help Mama die, but she could do something positive to help her get buried.

It didn't take long for the word to get out, because the phone had been ringing with sickening regularity. The first few calls were difficult and before they were over, both Poppy and the caller were in tears. But then they began to get easier. It wasn't that Poppy was growing callus about the losses, it was just that she had no more tears to cry. The ache was still there in the pit of her stomach. The words were still as bitter on her tongue, but for now, she'd cried herself out. Everyone knew what to say about Helen. She'd had cancer. Cancer was a socially acceptable reason for dying. The sad thing was that no one knew what to say about Jessup. Murder did that to a family. It was as if by blood alone, the death had tainted them all.

The first one to finally mention him was Hannah Crane, the wife of one of the men Jessup had worked with. She voiced her sympathies about Helen Sadler's passing, and then eased into what happened to Jessup without mentioning the actual crime.

"Poppy honey, do they know yet who hurt your daddy?'

Poppy frowned. Whoever 'they' were had done more than cause him pain.

"Nobody hurt Daddy, Mrs. Crane, he was murdered, and no, the police don't have anyone in custody, if that's what you mean."

"Yes, well, of course that's what I meant, I just didn't want to say-"

Poppy sighed. "I know. I appreciate your thoughtfulness. I haven't been to the funeral home, so a date and time have yet to be set for Mama's service. You can call them tomorrow around noon to get details."

"I'll do that, for sure," Hannah said. "If there's anything you need, you just let us know. We'll be praying for you, sugar. Take care."

The call disconnected so fast it made Poppy's head spin. That was lip service if she ever heard it. Hannah Crane didn't want to help. She just wanted something to gossip about with the claim that she'd gotten it straight from the orphan's mouth.

Poppy hung up the phone. "God give me strength."

It was later in the day when the phone finally stopped ringing. She couldn't put off calling her brother any longer. She had no idea how he was going to take the news or what he'd do about it, but he deserved to know.

She pulled the phone into her lap and made the call, then curled up at the end of the sofa as it began to ring and ring and ring. Just when she thought it was going to voice mail, she heard a click, and then the deep husky timbre of her brother's voice.

"Hello."

"Johnny, it's me, Poppy."

There was a long silence and then she thought she heard a sigh.

"Is it over?"

His lack of communication irked her. He hadn't been home in six months and now this. No hello – no how have you been? His, just-get-to-the-point-and-get-my-misery-over-with, attitude hit her wrong.

"It all depends on what you're talking about. Mama's dead, if that's what you meant. She died this morning."

"I'm really-"

"Shut up, Johnny. I'm not done. Only minutes after the hospital called, two cops showed up at the front door with the news Daddy was dead. Sometime last night, someone shot him three times and threw his body in the Little Man. He was murdered."

She heard John gasp, and then words spilled out of him like marbles hitting a hard floor and rolling in different directions.

"No, no... God no! What..., do you... has anyone been arrested? Are there any suspects?"

"No arrests. No suspects. I'm going to the funeral home in the morning to set a date and time for Mama's funeral. The cops still have Daddy's body so I can't bury them together. His funeral will have to be later."

"I don't understand. Why did this happen?"

Poppy wanted to scream. "I couldn't begin to tell you, but that's pretty much what I've been asking myself all day. I will tell you that Daddy got fired a week ago and never told anyone."

"Fired! What the hell?" Then he sighed. "Shit. That was as stupid a question as the first one I asked. Chalk it up to shock. I'm sorry, Poppy. I'm so sorry. Hang on, sister, I'll help. It'll take a while for me to get there, but I will be home by tomorrow night."

The knowledge she wouldn't have to make all the decisions on her own was all it took to resurrect tears. Just as she thought she'd cried herself out, her brother's voice brought new pain.

"Are you crying?"

"Yes."

"Cry for me, too, sister, and hang on. I'll get there as fast as I can."

"I love you, Johnny."

She heard another sigh, and this time when he spoke, his voice was shaking. "Ah, Poppy, I love you, too."

The line went dead.

She was trembling violently by the time she hung up. The inability to control her emotions was shaking the foundation of the woman she'd believed herself to be. Outside the world was still grey and overcast. Exhausted in every cell of her being, she stretched out, pulling Mama's pink Granny Square afghan from the back of the sofa up over her body, and cried herself to sleep.

When she woke up, it was dark. Night had fallen on Coal Town. Though the rain had finally passed, the sky had stayed overcast and the wind was getting colder. Her first thought was that Daddy would be home soon and she needed to start supper, and then she remembered. The shock was fresh, like hearing the news for the first time all over again. Loss swelled until she felt she might choke.

Desperate to shift focus, she threw back the afghan and headed to the bathroom. As she was returning to the living room, she began hearing footsteps up on the porch and then someone knocking on the door and calling her name.

"Poppy, Poppy, it's me, Gladys."

Gladys was a neighbor from a few houses down and one of her mother's best friends. Girding herself as she went, she turned on the porch light and opened the door.

Gladys Bailey was standing on the threshold holding a foil-wrapped dish. Her eyes were red-rimmed and swollen.

Poppy looked for the car then realized Gladys had walked. "You must be frozen. Come in."

Gladys set the dish down as Poppy shut the door, shucked out of her coat then wrapped Poppy in a warm, enveloping hug.

"Honey, honey, I can't tell you how sorry I am. Me and Mel were bracin' ourselves for your mama's passin', but what happened to your daddy has done knocked us off our feet. What do you need? How can we help?"

The offer took Poppy unawares. She hadn't heard from even one of the people she'd grown up with. So far all of the calls had been from her parents' circle of friends. And not one person from the restaurant had called to see if she'd made it home. It spoke volumes about her personal life. She had none.

"You are so sweet to ask," Poppy said, and patted Gladys's hand while wondering what had possessed the woman to start out walking in the dark in this weather wearing those bell-bottom pants and open-toe clogs, then chided herself for the thought.

"Please take a seat. Can I bring you some coffee? You have to be chilled."

"Do you have some made?" Gladys asked as she plopped down at one end of the sofa and began fluffing her hair.

"Yes, if you don't mind it being reheated. I made it at noon."

Gladys smiled. "I don't mind a bit."

Poppy hurried into the kitchen, popped a cup of coffee into the microwave and then waited for it to reheat. While she was waiting, she put a handful of cookies on a plate then carried the hot coffee and the cookies back to Gladys.

"I didn't ask. Do you want sugar or milk?"

"This is fine," Gladys said. "Sit yourself and talk to me."

Poppy felt cornered. This was the conversation where Gladys began talking about how much she loved Helen and how she didn't know what she was going to do without her. She tried to steer it away to something safer – something that might keep her from crying.

"I don't know what to say. Do you mind if I ask you some questions instead?" Poppy asked.

"Course not," Gladys said. "Ask me anything you want."

Poppy watched her dunk a cookie into the hot liquid, then purse her lips and suck it like a baby pacifier before she took a big bite. It was a strange habit, but then Gladys was unique in a number of ways.

"About Daddy..."

Gladys frowned as she chewed. "What about him, honey?"

"Did he tell Mel he got fired last week?"

Gladys gasped, nearly choking on the food in her mouth. "Lord no! At least I don't think he did 'cause Mel would have surely told me. Why did he get fired?"

"I don't know all the details yet," Poppy said. "Had he said anything to Mel about having trouble with someone at the mine, or anywhere else for that matter?"

Gladys paused, as if searching her memory, then shook her head. "No. All he ever talked about was a new treatment for Helen and how she seemed stronger every time he saw her, although I'm sure in his heart he knew better."

Poppy slumped. This wasn't helpful. She'd been hoping for something that would make sense of what had happened.

Gladys set her coffee aside and then folded her hands in her lap and leaned back. Poppy felt like she was being measured for something more. Her instincts had been right.

"I need to tell you something," Gladys said.

Poppy tensed. "Okay."

"I visited your mama four days ago," Gladys said.

"You did? She never mentioned it, but I'm grateful. Mama loved you so much."

Gladys's eyes welled as she took a tissue out of her pocket and blew her nose, but when she spoke, it was very matter-of-fact.

"You do know she was ready to die."

Poppy shrugged. Even though she'd sensed more than once that her mother had wanted to talk about it, Poppy had never been willing to go there. Now it was too late.

"Well, she was," Gladys said. "She was plain wore out from the sufferin' and you need to accept that. Everyone dies and it was your mama's time. She made me promise to tell you and make sure you understood that if a doctor had come in and told her there was another treatment to try, she was gonna tell him no."

Poppy was shaking. It took her a few moments to realize that it was from a feeling of relief.

"I think I'm most upset that she died alone, without any of her family there," Poppy said. "It's something that's been weighing on my mind."

Gladys waved her hand as if she was shooing away a fly. "Honey, I can't tell you how many times in my life I've heard Helen say, 'there are only two things in life you have to do alone, getting yourself born, and figuring out how to die.' Ain't no one on this earth who can help you through it or do it for you. Understand?"

Poppy bit her lip in the hope she wouldn't cry again. There were still things she needed to say and bawling all over the place wouldn't help.

"Can I ask a favor of you?"

Gladys beamed. "Anything."

"I need a ride across the bridge tomorrow. I saw a pink dress in Bolton's window display that I want to get for Mama's viewing, and I need to take it to the funeral home so they can get her ready."

"I'll do better than that," Gladys said. "When you're ready to go tomorrow, you just come down to the house and get my car. Do all the running around you need to do tomorrow and bring it back when you're done."

Poppy sighed. Huge problem solved.

"Thank you, Gladys. Thank you, so much."

"It's the least we can do." Then she remembered why she'd come. "I swear, I almost forgot. I brought you some of my chicken pot pie. All you need to do is pop it in the oven for about twenty minutes to heat it back up and it'll be good to go. Now I need to be gettin' on home to see to Mel's dinner. He don't like to be kept waitin'. "

"I appreciate your thoughtfulness and help," Poppy said, and then followed her to the front door.

Gladys stopped long enough to put on her coat and give Poppy a kiss, then she stood in the doorway watching Gladys hurry down the steps, waiting for Gladys to turn around and wave, which she did. Predictability was oddly comforting.

Poppy waved back then took the pot pie into the kitchen to reheat. Once it was in the oven, she got the notepad out of the junk drawer and wrote down the first name.

Gladys Ritter – chicken pot pie.

She knew the rules of the house for when someone died. Keep track of the food and flowers for thank you notes later. She'd just never thought about being the one on the sad end of the situation.

The aroma was beginning to fill up the small room. On any other night, she would be waiting anxiously for it to come out of the oven. Tonight, the last thing she wanted was food, but again, she knew she would eat.

Only the strong survive.

CHAPTER FIVE

Early the next morning, John Sadler notified his boss he was going home. For the most part, he was a self-sufficient man. He was twenty-eight, fairly solvent, and women thought he was good-looking, but he knew something the rest of the world didn't. He was an emotional coward.

The guilt of what he'd done to his mom was overwhelming. She'd literally wasted away and died without seeing him again. He couldn't even use the excuse that she wasn't his birth mother as a reason, because she'd loved him without boundaries.

He'd just turned eight, and had no memory of a mother when his Dad married Helen. Never once had she made him feel less important than Poppy, who was born less than a year later. And because he was loved, he knew how to love the new baby, too. There were no words to explain his act of cowardice. All he could do was get home and start over with his sister – if she'd let him.

He crammed the last of his shirts into the suitcase, zipped it shut, and within minutes was out of the apartment and in the midst of Atlanta traffic. Thirty minutes later he was eastbound on I-85 heading toward North Carolina. From there he would hit I-77 north and take it all the way to West Virginia. After that it would be small roads and back roads, but it didn't matter. John Sadler was going home.

Mike Amblin came into the precinct carrying a box of doughnuts and a to-go cup of black coffee. When Kenny Duroy saw the Franny's Bakery logo on the side he started to grin.

"Did you get any bear claws?"

"Good morning to you, too," Mike drawled, as he opened the box and took out two doughnuts, then passed the box. "Help yourself and then put the box in the break room, will you?"

"Glad to," Duroy said, as he fished out a giant, sugar-glazed bear claw and laid it on a napkin, licking his fingers as he walked away.

Mike was downing the last bite of his first doughnut when Kenny returned.

"What did you find out from Harmon?" Mike asked, as Duroy took a big bite of his sweet roll.

Kenny talked around the bite he was chewing. "He's in a shitty mood. Yesterday on the way to the mine where Sadler worked, he ran over some kid's dog. He says he doesn't want to talk about it, but then brings it up every time there's a break in the conversation."

Mike grimaced. "That's tough."

Duroy nodded. "He said he went to Caulfield's office to ask him why Sadler had been fired. Caulfield admitted he didn't know the man or the situation, which I suppose is understandable considering how many aspects there are to Caulfield Industries and the number of people he actually employs. However, once he learned where Sadler worked, Caulfield hooked Harmon up with the foreman, a man named Tom Bonaventure, who happens to be the man who fired Jessup Sadler. Bonaventure said Sadler got fired because he came to work drunk. I have a list of names of the men who worked the same shift Sadler worked. That's your copy." He tossed a sheet of paper on Mike's desk and took another bite of his sweet roll.

Mike scanned the list, recognizing several names, but knew talking to them wasn't going to be easy. Since they worked the day shift at Caulfield #14 they were, at the moment, somewhere deep inside a mountain. He'd have to catch them at home after dark.

"I'll take the top half, you take the bottom, okay?"

"Sure," Kenny said, circling the names on the list.

Mike took a sip of coffee as he sorted through a stack of new reports. He paused then picked one up from the coroner.

"Did you see this?"

It was a report listing Sadler's time of death between 11:47 p.m. which was when his wrist watch stopped, presumably when he went into the water, and no later than 2:00 a.m. with an addendum that he couldn't be more specific due to the cold temperature of the water in which Sadler had been found.

"Yeah, I did. Did you get any security footage from that quick stop?" Kenny asked, licking sugar off his thumb.

"I have some, but the clerk wasn't all that positive about us being able to see anything on it. He said the quality of the footage isn't good, even when the sun is shining."

Kenny frowned. "I never understood that. Spend money to put up security but use shoddy equipment. Then you're screwed if you ever really need it because you can't see a damn thing."

"I think a lot of people believe just the appearance of having security cameras is enough to do the job."

"It's still stupid," Kenny said.

Mike shrugged. No need to argue with the truth. He grabbed the last bite of doughnut and shoved it in his mouth, then picked up his coffee.

"I'm going to get the security tapes from the evidence locker. I'll be in the tech room if you need me."

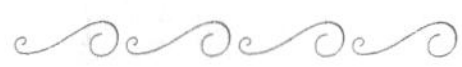

It didn't take long for Mike to fast-forward through the footage from the gas station to the time when they knew Sadler had left the hospital. But it took a little more than two hours watching seriously shitty footage before he finally saw Sadler's car arrive at the station.

He leaned forward, watching intently to see who emerged from the car. What he wasn't expecting to see were two skinny white boys. They looked like kids, but it was hard to judge age when he couldn't make out a face. They jumped out and ran off into the downpour without ever looking toward the station. There was no way he would be able to identify them from this, but at least they knew they were looking for two killers, not one. He reached for the phone and called his partner.

"Kenny, come look at this."

"On my way."

Mike played the tape again for his partner.

"It is seriously bad footage, but now we know there were two of them," Kenny said.

Mike picked up the phone again, this time to call the crime lab.

"Crime lab. Bonnie Kirk."

"Hey Bonnie, this is Mike Amblin. Where are you on the Sadler car they towed in yesterday?"

"We're just starting on it, but I can tell you for certain Sadler was not in this car when he got shot. No blood or broken glass like you would expect to find."

"So I still don't have a crime scene," Mike said. "Do you have any prints on file for the daughter? The family only had the one car so there would be hers for sure, and possibly even her mother's prints, although I don't know how long it's been since she was well enough to drive."

"The only prints I have are for Jessup Sadler. You need to send an officer to tell the mother and daughter to come in so we can print them for elimination."

"Nix the mother. She died of terminal cancer the same morning Jessup's body was found. You'll have to send someone to the funeral home to get her prints."

"Wow, that's tough on the daughter."

Mike thought about Poppy Sadler. "Yeah, it was a bad day for her yesterday and I doubt today will be much better. Since we have the family's only car, I'll get a print kit and go get her prints myself. I'll drop them by the lab afterward."

"Thanks."

"If you get any hits, give me or Duroy a call."

"Will do," Bonnie said, and hung up.

Kenny had been listening. "So nothing yet, I take it?"

"The car was not our crime scene."

"Well hell. So, unless those two men killed him inside some

building then dumped the body in the river afterward, we're not going to have a crime scene to process. Not after yesterday's rain."

"Possibly, which means we need an ID on those two. Maybe they weren't wearing gloves and we'll get lucky," Mike said.

"So you're going to Sadler's residence to print the girl?"

"I'll call first to make sure she's there, but yeah. What about you? Are you coming?"

"Might as well. We can't interview any of the miners on Sadler's shift until late this evening. Until we get IDs on the guys who drove that car we're on hold."

"Hang on a sec and let me see if she's home," Mike said, and called Poppy's number.

Poppy woke before daylight and couldn't get back to sleep. She started a pot of coffee but as she walked through the house, was lost by how empty it felt. Before her mama's illness, her parents would have already been up. Mama would be in the kitchen making breakfast and packing Daddy's lunch, with the television playing in the background to catch the morning news and weather. Daddy would have been in the shower, or reading what he could of the newspaper before he had to leave to catch his ride to the mine. She had taken it all for granted until it was gone.

While the coffee was brewing, she headed for her parents' bedroom. She hadn't been in it since their passing, and was met with the aroma of Jessup Sadler's aftershave when she opened the door.

"Oh Daddy."

Tears quickened, but she blinked them away. She had to go in. There were things that needed to go to the undertaker and no way to get them but to go through their things.

Since she intended to buy her mama a new dress, she didn't have to go through her clothing, and it didn't take long to find the needed undergarments. The funeral home had already told her not to bother with shoes because the lower half of the body was never shown during a viewing. Still, Poppy added a pair of white socks to the pile. After Mama got sick, her feet had always been cold and she wasn't going to bury her with bare feet.

She moved from the clothes to the jewelry box to get the wedding ring. It had finally fallen off Helen's finger after three months of chemotherapy and she'd worn it on a chain around her neck until her final hospitalization. It was a simple gold band with one tiny diamond – an unassuming ring that had been symbolic of their lives.

She started to put the ring in her pocket then was afraid she would lose it, so she slipped it on her finger. It felt a little strange to be wearing something so intimate that didn't belong to her, but she wouldn't have it on long. Satisfied she was choosing everything Mama would have wanted, she closed the lid and gathered up the lingerie. The phone rang on her way to get dressed. She ran to answer, dropping the lingerie on her the bed as she picked up.

"Hello?"

"Miss Sadler, this is Detective Amblin. I hope I didn't wake you."

"No, I was up. Do you have more news?"

He thought about the grainy footage from the gas station and then decided against mentioning it. The less she knew about the investigation until it was solved, the less she would have to worry about.

"We're still waiting on a report from the crime lab. If you're going to be home for a little while, I need to fingerprint you so the crime lab can eliminate your prints from what's gathered inside the car."

"I'll be here for about another hour or so. I have to wait until at least 9:00 before the stores open."

"Great. I'll be there shortly and promise not to delay your plans."

"Alright, see you soon."

The minute she hung up, she began stripping off her pajamas and grabbing some clothes. By the time the police car pulled up in front of her house, she was properly dressed, hair brushed, and a half cup of coffee in her system.

She watched the two cops get out and tried to remember the

older one's name but couldn't. She did, however, remember the other one – Detective Amblin – Detective Mike Amblin. He was tall like John, and had a good face. Strong chin, high cheekbones, steady gaze from really nice blue eyes – the kind of face that would grow even better looking with age.

She waited until they knocked then let them in.

"Good morning, Miss Sadler. Sorry about this," Mike said, and just as he apologized, realized he wasn't sorry because it meant seeing her again.

"It's all right. I'm willing to do anything it takes to help find out who killed Daddy. Where do you want to do this? Is the kitchen okay? There's more room on the kitchen table."

"Yes, the kitchen is perfect," Mike said and followed Poppy out of the room.

Kenny eyed his partner's face and rolled his eyes as he trailed the pair. Damned if it didn't look like Mike was half-way attracted to the vic's kid. That spelled all kinds of trouble. They'd have to have a little chat about conflict of interest on the way back.

Poppy watched curiously as Mike set out everything he'd brought.

"Does it matter which hand?"

"We'll do the left one first," he said, and then saw the ring as he reached for her hand. "Nice ring."

Poppy flinched. "Oh. Sorry, I forgot it was there. It's Mama's wedding ring. I'm taking it to the funeral home. She would want to be buried with it."

She slipped the ring off her finger and laid it aside. Mike felt a slight tremble as he took her hand and knew she was girding herself for another tough day.

"This won't take long," he said quietly, and proceeded to print her thumb then each of her fingers before switching to her right hand and repeating the process. "You can go wash now," he said, as he packed everything back up.

Poppy went to the kitchen sink and picked up the bar of her daddy's Lava soap and started to scrub. It was a harsh, abrasive soap favored by mechanics and people who worked with their hands. He had used it each night to wash the coal dust from his skin and out from under his nails, but she'd never imagined she'd be using it to wash off fingerprint ink.

"There's coffee if either one of you want a cup," Poppy said. "Cups are in the cupboard just above the coffee maker."

"I'm still working on one I left in the car, but thanks," Mike said.

"I wouldn't mind half a cup," Kenny said.

"Help yourself," Poppy said, and turned to reach for a towel only to find Mike standing beside her with the towel in his hands.

"Here you go," he said, and smiled.

Poppy smiled back before she thought and then took the towel and turned away. She dried quickly, anxious for them to be gone, and hung the towel on a door handle. Once more, when she turned around Mike was there, this time holding her Mother's ring.

"I would hate to be responsible for making you forget this," he said, and dropped it into the palm of her hand. "How are you getting down town?"

"I can promise you I'm not walking," Poppy said.

He almost smiled again, and then realized there wasn't any reference to yesterday that could be misconstrued as humorous.

"If you need a ride-"

She shook her head. "A neighbor has offered me the use of her car for today. She lives at the end of the next block down."

"Do you want us to drop you off?" Mike asked.

Kenny stifled a snort and then downed the last bit of coffee he'd begged and set the cup in the sink.

"No, but thank you anyway."

Mike realized he was dragging out something that should have ended five minutes ago and knew he was going to hear about it when they got in the car.

"Then we'll get out of your way. Again, sorry we had to bother you."

Poppy slipped the ring on her finger as she led the way back to the living room, then opened the door. It occurred to her that the gesture might appear as less than hospitable, but then decided it didn't matter. They were the police and they hadn't come for hospitality.

"Thank you for saving me a trip to the police station."

"You're welcome," Mike said.

All of a sudden they were on the porch, shut out of the house and out of her sight.

Kenny arched an eyebrow.

"Shut up, Kenny. Just shut up and get in the car."

"I don't know what you're talking about," he said, but as soon as they got in the car, he gave Mike a look. "She's part of a case we're working on. Remember that."

Mike already knew that, but it didn't keep him from thinking he needed to protect her, even though there was no indication that what had happened to her father had anything to do with her. He glared at his partner and drove away without bothering to answer.

CHAPTER SIX

Poppy was about to leave the house when she saw Gladys drive up. She stepped out onto the porch as Gladys honked and waved, then a shudder suddenly ran through her. She would have sworn her mama had just stepped out onto the porch beside her. It was becoming painfully clear there would be many moments like this before the reality of death soaked in.

"Good morning, sugar!" Gladys said, as she came up the steps, rocking a seventies look in bright green patio pants and an even brighter orange top. She'd pulled her hair up into a wad on top of her head and fastened it with a giant banana clip, which made her look a little like a bleached blonde cockatoo, although it was already coming down in more places than not. She dropped the keys in Poppy's hand.

"Let's go inside a minute. We need to talk."

Poppy's heart skipped a beat as she followed her back into the house. "Is something wrong? Did Mel know something about Daddy?"

Gladys rolled her eyes. "Oh, no, I shouldn't have said it like that. It's just that I've been getting calls from your mama and daddy's friends all morning, wanting to know what they can do, and wanting to bring food and the like. I knew you needed to be gone for most of the day so I thought, if it was okay with you, I'd just stay here at your house and take in the calls and the food that comes. If it makes you uncomfortable to have a stranger in the house, just tell me, no thank you. It won't hurt my feelings a bit, so what do you think?"

Poppy hugged her. "Oh Gladys, you're not a stranger.

You're proving what a good friend you are, and I so appreciate it. I've already started a list. It's on a pad in the kitchen. Please feel free to make yourself coffee or food anytime you want. I promise not to be gone any longer than I have to be."

"Go. Do what you gotta do and don't worry about anything here."

Poppy picked up the little bag with her mama's things and slung her purse strap over her shoulder. She was out the door before Gladys could change her mind, and minutes later, driving over the Little Man, completely focused on the day ahead of her.

John Sadler stopped in Charlotte, North Carolina just before 8:00 a.m. to get fuel and breakfast. The day was overcast, adding to the somber mood he was in. Guilt colored every thought he'd had since Poppy's call, which made the urgency of his trip that much worse. He was already closer to home, but it still felt like the other side of the world. All he could think about was his little sister and what she was going through alone.

As soon as he'd gassed up his truck he drove through a McDonald's, got some breakfast to go and a large coffee and hit the I77 northbound. As he ate, he kept going over the last few phone conversations he'd had with his dad, trying to remember if Jessup had mentioned anything that might lend a clue as to who would want him dead, but nothing came to mind. All he had wanted to talk about was a new treatment for Helen, or how he thought she'd taken a turn for the better. Now it was too late to ask if anything more had been going on. He finished his coffee and tossed the cup in the floorboard of his truck and kept on driving.

The miles and the time were passing while the yellow line separating the two lanes of traffic on the interstate became John's yellow brick road. All he had to do was follow it to get to Oz. Only there wasn't any wizard waiting with answers at the end of this road – just a police department with a whole lot of questions.

The knot in his belly grew tighter, increasing the urge to cry, but guilt wouldn't let him release the pain. After what he'd done to his family, he deserved misery.

His head was spinning with questions when he suddenly thought of Aaron Coulter. During John's high school years, Aaron was the star quarterback of the high school football team. Then during his senior year he'd blown his knee, lost his chances for an athletic scholarship, and gone into his daddy's line of business instead. That it was mostly illegal hadn't bothered Aaron, since it was all he knew, but it had been the beginning of the end for the circle of friends he'd once had. However, John knew that if his dad had been in trouble, or pissed off the wrong people, Aaron would know.

He called information for Aaron's number then made the call. Just when he thought it was going to go to voice mail, Aaron answered in a gruff, sleep-husky drawl.

"It's too fuckin' early for chit-chat, so you better have somethin' good to say."

John grinned. Aaron never had been one to temper his words.

"Hey, Aaron, it's John Sadler. Sorry I woke you."

Surprise shifted Aaron's focus as he threw back the covers and sat up on the side of the bed.

"John. Heard about your mom and your old man. Sorry as hell that happened."

"Yeah. Thanks. Poppy called me last night. I'm on my way home."

Aaron rubbed the sleep out of his eyes then put the call on speaker phone, grabbing a pair of jeans as he talked.

"I know this ain't no social call, so what's up?"

"Poppy said Dad got fired last week but he didn't tell anyone. As far as we knew, except for my mom's health, nothing was wrong. I got to wondering, if he was in trouble because he'd borrowed money from someone then couldn't pay it back… maybe you might have heard something about it."

"No man, this was a big shock to everyone. Your dad was a straight arrow. Everyone liked him."

"Someone didn't," John said. "Someone pumped three bullets in his body and threw him in the Little Man and I want five minutes alone with the bastard who did it."

"I hear you, man and I'd feel the same. Look. I'll drop a few questions and see what turns, but I can't promise anything."

"I appreciate it, Aaron. You know I do."

"Yeah, sure. I guess I'll see you around when you get back. Tell Poppy I'm real sorry."

"Yeah, see you around," John said. "If you hear anything, call me back at this number. Sorry about waking you up."

"No biggie. Later, dude."

"Yeah, later."

The call ended. John dropped his phone in the console and accelerated. He needed to be home.

According to the advertisement at Edison Funeral Home, they'd been in the business of burying since 1933. Poppy had seen the building plenty of times but had never been inside. There was a first time for everything.

Her gut tightened as she entered the lobby. An overpowering scent of too many flowers with an underlying scent of something medicinal went up her nose. It left her feeling somewhat uneasy, as if it was there to mask a more offensive smell.

Logically, she knew her mama's body was here being prepared for viewing, but there wasn't anything the undertakers could do to it that cancer hadn't already destroyed. As sad as she was, she wouldn't wish her mama back to suffer one second more. She had Mama's things in the bag and the wedding ring on her finger. This was the last physical act she could do for her and she wanted to do it right.

The sound of footsteps alerted her that someone was coming, and then recognized Truman Epperson, one of The Depot's regular customers. It occurred to her that this was the first time he'd be serving her needs rather than the reverse.

"Miss Sadler. Please accept my condolences for your loss," he said.

"Thank you, Mr. Epperson."

"Please, call me Truman. I see you've brought a bag. Let's

see what dress you've chosen, okay?"

Poppy handed it over and waited as he sorted through the things.

Truman pulled out the dress, shaking it gently to straighten out the skirt. "May I say that pink is a beautiful choice. And the other things in this bag... the under garments, I assume?"

Poppy nodded. "Yes, and I added socks. I know you said shoes weren't necessary, but her feet were always cold. I know it doesn't matter to anyone but me, but I want the socks on her feet. Is that okay?"

"Absolutely," Truman said. "Anything else? Any jewelry or mementos you want with her?"

"Oh, yes! And this, too," she said quickly, pulling the ring from her finger. "It's Mama's wedding ring. She got so thin that it wouldn't stay on, but she would want to be wearing it. Is there a way you can-"

He touched her shoulder in a brief gesture of understanding.

"Of course, Miss Sadler. That won't be a problem."

"Is there something I need to sign, or-"

"Not a thing, my dear. Your father was most thorough in his preparations. Everything is paid for, including a large floral spray to go on your mother's casket. And, you'll be pleased to know that the flowers Jessup chose were pink. Your father had already spoken to your pastor, so he was forewarned about holding the service at your church. He's just waiting for you to set a date and time.

The knot in Poppy's throat began to swell. Daddy had thought of everything, including Mama's favorite color.

"Today is Thursday. My brother, John will be here by tonight and he's the only person we would be waiting on. So if it's all right, I would like to hold the service Saturday morning at 10:00 a.m."

"Certainly. I'll let the pastor know and I'll notify the newspaper."

Poppy gasped. "Oh no. I completely forgot about the obituary. It's going to be too late to get it in the paper in time."

"My goodness. Your parents kept you in the dark about a lot of things, didn't they? You don't need to worry about that either. It's already been turned in."

"You mean Daddy had already written it?"

"No, your mother wrote it and her eulogy months ago and brought them to me, herself."

Poppy felt like she'd been side-swiped and left bleeding on the side of the road. She'd failed. She'd failed both of them by always changing the subject when the issue had come up at home. She couldn't imagine what had been going through her mama's mind as she wrote her own obituary but it made her sad.

"Well then. I guess that's that," she said. Her lips felt numb and the room was beginning to spin. She didn't know if she was going to get through this or not. "When can I... I mean, I want to see her before... before-"

"I can assure you we will not begin public viewing until the family has been here first." Truman glanced at the clock. "It's a quarter to ten. If you can be back here after two, we'll have her ready, okay?"

Poppy didn't trust herself to speak, so she nodded.

"Is there anything else I can do for you?" he asked.

Tears were burning at the back of her throat.

"Before Mama got sick, she was a pretty woman."

"Yes, I remember," Truman said.

Poppy took a deep breath, but it didn't help. Despite her best intentions, she began to cry.

"Make her pretty again."

Justin was in a meeting with shift managers from the Caulfield paper mill, trying to define a policy issue when his secretary knocked on the door.

"I'm sorry to interrupt, but the hospital is on line two for you."

Justin tried not to panic, but when it came to Callie, there was reason.

"Gentlemen, you must excuse me. I need to take this," he said, and headed for his office to take the call in private.

The scent of fresh coffee and the banana nut muffin he'd eaten at his desk less than an hour earlier still lingered. His hands were shaking as he picked up the phone.

"Justin Caulfield."

"Mr. Caulfield, this is Dr. Summers. I have some good news for you."

The relief was so great he felt weak. He sat down in his chair with a thump.

"We could do with good news. What's happening?"

"Callie's lungs are no longer bleeding. We think we've turned a corner."

And just like that Justin went from despair to disbelief.

"Oh my God, that's wonderful news! Does this mean she'll begin to get stronger now?"

"Eventually. It's going to take time to rebuild her immune system and strength. I wish we could say the same about the renal tests we ran again this morning, but I'm sorry to say that the facts were conclusive. Her kidneys don't function in any capacity and there's no chance of reversal."

Rage hit him like a fist to the gut. That was just like that elusive God his mother was always quoting. Hand him a miracle with one hand and slap it away with the other.

"So, we're talking kidney transplant, right?" Justin asked.

"Yes. With your permission, we will enter her name on the list."

Justin frowned. "Of course you have my permission. I'll sign anything that needs signing when I get there this evening, but how long do you think it will be before a kidney will become available?"

"Since you can't donate, your mother is too old, and you've assured me there are no relatives left who might come forward as a match, this means she goes to the transplant list like everyone else. There's just no way to predict a time line. As you know, usually someone has to die first, and the family of the deceased has to be willing to donate organs before the option even arises. It's a sad situation for all concerned. We'll do all the proper testing to get her registered. Beyond that, it's wait and see."

"If it's a matter of money, you know-"

Summers interrupted. "Justin, in this case, I'm sorry but it's not. If you had a family member who was willing to be tested and was a match, then the question would be moot. But anonymous transplants are done on a highest-need basis. In other words, the patients who are the sickest are at the top of the list. The ones who have time to spare are farther down."

"And you're saying Callie is farther down?"

"I'm saying she won't be in danger of dying tomorrow from kidney failure. She's on dialysis now. It's a hassle for any patient to be hooked up so often, but if it keeps her alive, then that's all that matters, right?"

Justin frowned. It wasn't what he wanted to hear but he couldn't be resentful, not when they were licking half the problem.

"Yes, of course. That's all that matters. Thank you for calling," he said.

"Of course. See you later."

Justin disconnected then shoved his hands through his hair in frustration as he walked to the windows. Whenever he was in doubt, or needed space to think, the sight of the ever-flowing river seemed to center him.

But this thing with Callie – this illness that no amount of money or determination could fix was kicking his butt and he didn't like it. There had to be a way to circumvent the wait.

He was still looking at the river when he remembered the meeting he'd abandoned and headed back into the conference room with a smile on his face.

"Gentlemen! Good news! My daughter's health is improving. She's turned a corner in her treatment and things are looking up."

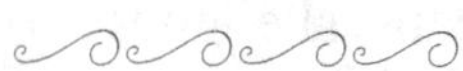

For the first time since Amelia Caulfield's return from Florida, she was beginning to believe her granddaughter might survive. Knowing Callie's healing had begun was what they'd been praying for, but her joy was soon tempered by the cold, hard facts of her granddaughter's perspective.

"Is it good news, Nana?" Callie asked. "Am I better?"

Amelia clapped her hands as she leaned over the bed and gave Callie a hug.

"Yes, my darling, you are getting better."

"When can I go home? I'm so tired of this place and these machines. I can't wait to get back to school and spend the night with Sheila and-"

"Wait, wait," Amelia said. It was obvious Callie didn't grasp the enormity of what had happened to her. "Yes, you're getting better, but you won't be able to do a lot of that until we work out a schedule for your dialysis."

The look on Callie's face was nothing short of pure horror as she stared, first at the dialysis machine, then back at her grandmother.

"What do you mean? You said I was better."

"Your lungs appear to be healing, but your kidneys will not."

Callie's face registered her shock. "What's going to happen to me? Will I always be hooked up to that machine until I die?"

Amelia was disconcerted. Justin needed to be the one dealing with this, not her. But he wasn't here and the questions were coming faster than she could think.

"No, no, that won't happen. You'll get a kidney transplant and then things will be different. You'll see."

Callie's heart was beating very fast like it did when she was afraid.

"Nana, do you believe in heaven?"

Amelia brushed a bit of hair from the corner of Callie's eyes and then smiled.

"Yes, I do. Do you?"

Callie frowned. "I'm not sure. I think so, but it's scary to think about dying."

"You're not going to die," Amelia said firmly.

"Everyone thought I would. I heard them talking. Something could still go wrong. What if they can't find a new kidney for me?"

Now Amelia was angry. How dare anyone speak negatively where the girl could hear? She was going to have to have words with Justin about this.

"But they will find a kidney, my darling, they will. I promise. You need to stop worrying, okay? Dr. Summers and your Daddy and I are going to take care of everything. All you have to do is keep getting stronger."

Callie looked past her grandmother's face to the windows beyond.

Amelia felt as if she was looking at a stranger. Callie's face was pale and her eyes so sunken it was almost like looking at a corpse.

"But Nana, if I get a transplant, doesn't that mean someone has to die first in order for me to live?"

Amelia blinked. Dear lord, but they had been living in a bubble, thinking Callie was unaware of the implications. She had to be careful not to scare her, but help her understand the seriousness of the situation.

"Not necessarily. People have two kidneys, but they can live a long normal life with just one, so sometimes people donate a kidney to someone else. Okay?"

"Can you donate one to me, Nana?"

Amelia sighed. "No, and it breaks my heart. I'm too old and not so healthy. You wouldn't want one of mine. It wouldn't last long enough to make you better. I'm so sorry, my love. I'm so sorry."

"It's not your fault, besides, don't worry. Daddy can give me one of his."

Amelia shook her head. "No, he can't. Remember when your daddy got sick when you were little and spent all the time in the hospital?

Callie nodded. "That was before Mommy died."

"Yes, before your mommy died. So when he got sick, it made his kidneys sick too. When he began to get well, one got well but the other didn't. Now he only has one, which he has to keep."

She watched Callie's eyes widen as the seriousness of the situation sunk in. Her chin began to quiver.

"Maybe I'm not supposed to live to be an old woman. Maybe I'm supposed to go live with Mommy in heaven."

Amelia wanted to weep. Instead, she wrapped her arms around Callie's shoulders and pulled her close. Callie had enough courage. All she needed was strength.

"We're not going to worry about this. This is out of our hands. God is good and He will take care of you. I have faith that is so."

"Don't worry, Nana. Whatever happens, I'm not afraid."

Poppy parked in front of The Depot, then smoothed down the front of her blouse before going inside. Since she wasn't on duty, she wasn't going to slink in the back door like a step-child.

Vic saw her within moments of her entrance, and waved.

Two of the waitresses stopped long enough to stare then looked away.

Poppy frowned. What the hell? She hadn't done anything wrong, so why was everyone treating her like a pariah?

"Poppy, it's good to see you," Vic said. "We're all worried about you, you know."

"How would I know that?"

Vic blinked. "Why, I just assumed some of the girls had given you a call."

"No one from work has called. I came to pick up my paycheck."

Immediately, he was on the defensive. "Sorry. Did you get the flowers? We sent you flowers and everyone signed the card. No, what am I thinking? I only called that in this morning. They probably haven't been delivered yet."

Vic didn't know what else to say and she wasn't helping the conversation with her silence. He needed to get her out of the restaurant. He felt sorry for her. It was hell to lose a parent to an illness, but to have one murdered tainted the whole family. It wasn't fair, but it was what it was.

"So, give me a sec. Your check is in the office."

She sat down at the counter. Both waitresses walked past her twice before Vic came back. One gave her a nervous look and muttered something about being sorry, while the other flashed a brief smile.

"Here you are," Vic said, as he handed her the envelope with her paycheck inside. Have you set a date for your mother's service yet?"

"Saturday morning. 10:00 a.m. at the Church of Angels."

"I'll let everyone know," Vic said. "Remember what I said, when you're ready to come back, just give me a call."

"Yes, I remembered, and thank you."

"Oh, hey, have you heard from John?"

Poppy nodded. "He's on his way home."

Vic felt as if he was leaving something out – that there was some kind of social protocol that he was missing. But all he could do was smile.

"That's good. Tell him I said hello."

"I will," Poppy said.

Vic watched as she got in the car then went back to work. At least in here he knew what to do without making a faux pas.

CHAPTER SEVEN

The Caulfield police department was unusually quiet as Mike escorted one of the clerks from the convenience store into an interrogation room to view the footage from the night Jessup Sadler had been killed.

Billy Joe Fossey was a scrawny, forty-something man with bad teeth and a fear of cramped spaces, which explained why he was working at a quick stop rather than down in the mines.

"Thank you for coming in, Mr. Fossey. Have a seat. This won't take long," Mike said.

"Yeah. Glad to help."

Mike pointed to the screen near Fossey's elbow. "If you'll just turn your chair a little you'll get a better view of what I'm about to show you."

Fossey shifted his chair. "Is this the tape of them men leaving Sadler's car?"

Mike nodded. "As you know, the footage isn't good, but I want you to watch closely and see if you recognize anyone."

He hit Play and the grainy, black and white images popped up on the screen.

"Just take your time. You can't really ID them by their features, so pay attention to the way they stand, the tilt of their shoulders, their stride as they run away."

Fossey leaned forward, staring intently at the screen.

Mike played it over for him seven times before Fossey finally gave up.

"I'm real sorry, but I don't recognize neither one of them, and they don't bring no one to mind."

Mike turned it off. He knew it had been a long shot, but they'd had to take it. "It was worth a try. I appreciate your help. I'll walk you out of the building."

Their trip through the department was silent. Mike gave Billy Joe a pat on the back at the front door.

"Well, thank you again. Have a nice day, Mr. Fossey," Mike said.

"Yeah sure, I'll see you around," he said, and left the building as Mike went back upstairs.

Mike's frustration was growing. He'd dropped Poppy Sadler's fingerprints off at the crime lab several hours ago and wondered if they'd found any prints other than those belonging to the family.

"How did it go?" Kenny asked, as Mike slid into the chair behind his desk.

"Like everything else connected to this case...nowhere."

"Have faith partner, things are looking up. The crime lab got a hit on two separate sets of prints out of Sadler's car. They belong to two young perps named James Thomas Walters and Marlin Barnett. They're being brought in for questioning as we speak."

"How young?" Mike asked.

"We have two eighteen-year old neighbors with almost identical rap sheets. They've been in and out of juvie for crimes ranging from shoplifting to selling weed."

Mike frowned. "Their juvie days are over since they turned eighteen, and if they're good for this murder, they've just moved themselves up into the big time."

"As always, they're coming into the station in separate cruisers which will keep them from getting a chance to coordinate their stories. It will be interesting to see what they have to say about stealing a dead man's car."

Poppy was sitting on a bench in Maypenny Park watching mothers pushing their toddlers in the swings. The mothers' voices of caution were drowned out by the toddlers' squeals and shrieks, although it didn't seem to matter to anyone concerned that one was canceled by the other.

The breeze was brisk, but the sun was warm. For Poppy, it seemed a bit obscene to be sitting in the sunlight in the middle of a beautiful day amidst so much life and laughter as her own world was crumbling around her. It was past time to go to the funeral home and yet she couldn't bring herself to move.

Suddenly, an acorn dropped onto the ground near her feet. She looked up just as a small squirrel disappeared into the upper branches of the old oak, then she looked beyond, to the intermittent rays of sunlight unraveling through the leaves and spilling down into her eyes. She took a deep breath then closed them, feeling the warmth of the sun and the swift kiss of the breeze upon her face.

God help me get through this.

A happy shriek suddenly turned into a cry of pain. Poppy turned just as one of the mothers scooped up her child in a comforting hug and then walked away.

Taking that as a sign it was time to go, she reluctantly got up and began walking across the grass to where she'd parked her car. She was more than halfway there before she realized that crazy homeless man, Prophet Jones, was standing in her path.

The last time she'd seen him had been the day her mama and daddy had died. Then, he'd been soaking wet and standing between her and the way home. Now here he was again, standing between her and her only means of escape.

He was taller than she remembered, and looked like a scarecrow wearing too many clothes. The breeze was flying his thick gray beard at half-mast, while even bushier eyebrows gave his eyes a hooded appearance. To her horror, he began to wave his arms and mutter under his breath. When he began to shout, Poppy started backing up.

"Heed my word. The devil is in this world. He's in the mines. He's in the cars. He's on the streets."

Poppy felt trapped. The more she backed up, the closer he came. Just as she was about to turn and bolt, an older woman who'd been watching, got up from the bench where she'd been sitting and introduced herself to Poppy.

"Hi honey. I'm Lucy. I've seen you at The Depot. Don't

worry about Prophet. He won't hurt you. He's just sad."

"The devil steals lives. I know it. I've seen it with my own eyes!" Prophet yelled, and then stomped his feet and turned in a little circle.

Poppy was shaking. "I've seen him on the streets for years and never saw him act like this. What's the matter with him?"

"It's hard to say. He used to be a preacher, but he hasn't been right since his wife and three little boys were killed in a wreck years ago. Here, you just give me a minute. I'll calm him down," Lucy said, then called out. "Good afternoon, Prophet. How have you been?"

The old man's beard was still flapping in the breeze, but the question stopped him cold. He squinted against the sun then all of a sudden he smiled.

"Why, good afternoon, Lucy. I'm fine. How about you?"

"I can't complain," she said, then tugged on Poppy's hand, pulling her closer. "I know you didn't mean to, but when you started preaching, you didn't realize you were scaring her, did you?"

It was a bit difficult to tell what with all the hair on his face, but it appeared that Prophet Jones was appalled.

"Oh my! I never meant anyone harm. You know that." His gaze slid to Poppy's face. "Do I know you?"

"No sir," Poppy said.

"Do I know your people?" he asked.

Lucy slid an arm around Poppy's waist. "Her parents were Jessup and Helen Sadler."

Prophet threw up his hands. "Jessup Sadler is dead! Lord, lord, the devil is on the streets!"

Lucy sighed. "Prophet, Miss Sadler needs to go about her business. Would you step aside so that she could be on her way?"

To Poppy's surprise, the old man bowed and stepped aside.

"It's okay," Lucy said. "You can go now."

Poppy didn't have to be told twice. "Thank you," she whispered, and then tried not to run as she passed him by.

"God be with you," Prophet yelled, as she reached the street.

She jumped into the car, but didn't breathe easy until she'd started the engine and backed away from the curb. It was only two blocks from the park to the Edison Funeral Home, but it would be the longest two blocks of her life. She didn't want to see her mother laid out in that casket, but today wasn't about what she wanted. Today was about duty, and it was her duty to make sure that Caulfield's last glimpse of Helen Sadler was one of serene repose.

Truman Epperson was watching for Poppy Sadler's arrival. He'd known her and her family for a good number of years and was saddened by what had happened. As soon as she entered the funeral home, he stepped out of a nearby office to meet her.

"Good afternoon, Miss Sadler. We have your mother ready for viewing. If there's anything you want changed, or something you're uncomfortable with, please let me know. Our purpose is to give the family of the dearly departed some peace and closure, and we want you completely satisfied with her appearance."

Poppy's stomach rolled. She took a slow breath to calm herself, bracing for what lay ahead.

"Are you ready?" Truman asked.

She nodded.

"This way," he said, then cupped her elbow and led her across the lobby, pausing at a small table outside one of the viewing rooms. "Visitors will sign this guest book and at the end of our services, you will receive it, along with all the sympathy cards that accompany the flowers."

Poppy heard him, but most of her focus was on the casket in the room beyond.

Truman followed her gaze, then folded his hands and then stepped aside.

"I'll be waiting out here for you. If you want something changed, just let me know."

He closed the door behind her as she walked in, and the first thing she noticed was the dark blue carpeting and pale gray walls with dozens of tiny shelves affixed to the surfaces. It took her a few moments to figure out that's where floral arrangements and potted plants could be displayed.

There was a pearl gray casket against the back wall with tall palm fronds in massive silver urns at either end. The assortment of gray, wing-back chairs were for the mourners, and there was church music playing softly in the background, but her heartbeat was so loud against her eardrums that all she heard was a buzz. Her hands were shaking as she moved closer.

"Help me, Jesus," she said, and then found herself looking down at the body inside.

There was a moment when she thought they'd made a mistake – that this couldn't be Mama, and then she began to focus.

Helen's hair - hair that had been so limp and lifeless was curled and shiny. The hollows in her mother's cheeks from the many months of suffering had somehow been miraculously filled. Her lips had a brush of pink and her fingernails had been painted with clear gloss.

They'd done as she asked.

They'd made her mama pretty.

Poppy set aside her grief to make sure everything was as it was supposed to be. The pink dress she'd chosen looked nice against the white satin of the inner lining, and the wedding ring she'd been so worried about was in its proper place on the third finger of Helen Sadler's left hand.

Tears welled as her voice dropped to a whisper.

"Oh Mama, I don't yet know how I'll live my life without you, but I will learn. I'm not sure how any of this works, but I think you're somewhere close and that you've been waiting for me to come say goodbye. I hope Daddy's with you. I don't want the two of you hanging around worrying about me and all the stuff that's going on because of Daddy's murder. Johnny's coming home. I won't be alone. Go be with God, Mama, and know that I'll love you forever."

She staggered backward, then dropped into one of the chairs and began to sob.

Truman Epperson had been waiting for the sound. Even though those left behind were never ready to accept it, tears were healing.

J.T. Walters swagger ended the moment the cop handcuffed him to a table fastened to the floor and shut him inside an interrogation room alone. He stared up at the mirror on the opposite wall and knew from watching TV that the other side was like a window, and that whoever looked in, could see him. He wanted to act tough, but he was worried. This was the first time he'd been busted since he'd turned eighteen and the laws were no longer in his favor.

He wondered what Big Boy was thinking and hoped he had the good sense to keep his mouth shut, although that was hoping for a lot. Big Boy wasn't all that bright and J.T was worried he wouldn't remember about the age thing and that it would change how they might be charged.

It never occurred to him to wonder what it was they'd been picked up for because they'd done enough in the past to get arrested for most anything. Still, just to make himself feel better, he looked straight up into the mirror and gave himself the finger, well aware he'd just 'told' whoever was looking at him to 'fuck off'.

"Look at the little bastard," Kenny muttered.

Mike nodded. "I see him. So let's go take that smirk off his face. What do you say?"

"Hell yes," Kenny said. "You're the lead on this case, but anytime you want me to scare him, just nod."

Mike grinned. "It's too bad you don't enjoy your job."

Kenny shrugged. "You gotta take it when you can get it. Let's go rattle his cage."

They walked around the corner and then into the room. Kenny slammed the door behind him.

J.T. Walker flinched then glared as the two cops took seats on the other side of the table. He knew how this worked. Good cop/bad cop. The taller younger cop would play good cop. The shorter older one the bad cop. He lifted his chin and stared in their faces without comment.

Mike slid a file onto the table in front of him.

"I'm Detective Amblin. This is my partner, Detective Duroy. Did the officers read you your rights when they brought you in?"

"I know my rights," J.T. muttered.

"Answer the question," Mike snapped.

J.T. frowned. So maybe his IDs were off. Maybe this one was playing bad cop.

"Yeah, they read me my rights."

"Do you know why you're here?" Mike asked.

"Cause I'm a bad boy?"

Mike leaned forward. "Your fingerprints were found inside a car that did not belong to you. Want to explain how they got there?"

Understanding dawned and if he was smart, he just might talk his way out of this.

"It was raining. We needed wheels. It was there on the banks of the Little Man with the door open and the engine running. Yeah, we took it. But it's not like we stole it. It had been abandoned. And we didn't take it far. We left it at the station where it would be found."

Mike's instincts told him that had come freely and with a ring of truth. He glanced at Kenny then looked away.

"What time was that?" Mike asked.

J.T. frowned, thinking back. "It was late. After midnight but other than that, I ain't sure."

"What were you doing at the river that time of night?"

They could see the kid weighing his options when he suddenly shrugged.

"We was smoking weed under the bridge, okay? No big deal. Then it started to rain."

"And you needed a car to get home and didn't want to walk all that way in the rain so you took one that didn't belong to you? Is that right?"

J.T. shrugged.

Mike glanced at Kenny who jumped into the conversation with both feet.

"So you yanked a drunk out of his car, pumped his belly full of bullets and drove yourself home, is that how it went down?"

The kid's eyes widened. His mouth went slack. That was definitely the bad cop.

"No, man. We didn't kill no one. That car was empty like I told you. I don't even own a gun."

Kenny slapped the table. "So your buddy was the shooter. But you had to help throw the body in the river, because the man you murdered was a real big guy. If you're not the shooter now's the time to say so. It will keep you off death row. You better talk now because when we go talk to your friend and he rolls over on you, your chance is gone."

"No! No! We didn't shoot no one. No one, I tell you."

Mike stood up and headed for the door. Kenny followed.

"Hey! Where you guys goin'?" J.T. asked.

"To talk to your friend," Mike said, and shut the door behind them.

They paused out in the hallway and looked back into the room through the two-way mirror. The kid was in full-blown panic.

"We should have known they wouldn't own up all that easy," Kenny said.

"Do you think he could be telling the truth?" Mike asked.

Kenny snorted lightly. "I don't think that boy's told the truth since he learned to talk."

They moved down the hall to another interrogation room where Marlin 'Big Boy' Barnett had been stashed. There was no two-way mirror in this room and when they walked in abruptly, the skinny teenager handcuffed to the table actually jumped.

"Man, like what's goin' on?" he asked. "This situation is whack. You guys just show up and slap me in handcuffs without no explanation whatsoever. You can't fuckin' do that."

"And yet it happened," Mike said shortly, and sat down across the table, thinking Big Boy's nickname was overrated. He wasn't much over five feet tall and so skinny his pants wouldn't stay up. "My name is Detective Amblin and this is my partner, Detective Duroy. Why do you think you're here?"

"I ain't got a clue," Marlin said.

"Did the officer who brought you in here read you your

rights?"

"Hell yes, and wouldn't tell me why."

Mike leaned forward. "If I told you that we found your fingerprints inside a stolen car, what would have to say about that?"

Marlin's eyebrows arched then his lips went slack.

Mike could almost hear the wheels turning in the teenager's head. If he admitted to it, then it linked him to a dead man. The trick was to explain away the fingerprints without linking them to a murder.

"I ain't got nothin' to say," Marlin muttered.

Mike glanced at Kenny. "I told you this one would be the dumb one. You owe me five bucks."

Rage spread across Marlin's face. "I ain't dumb."

"That's a matter of opinion," Mike said. "I'm standing here telling you we found your fingerprints inside the car of a murdered man and all you decide to do is clam up."

Like J.T., the word murder sent Marlin into a tailspin.

"What the hell you talkin' about, man? We didn't murder no one. We just took the car. I swear!"

"Oh, so you did take the car?"

"Yes. Hell yes, we took the car but we didn't kill no one."

Mike shook his head. "That's not what your friend, J.T. is telling us. He's pointing the finger at you as the one who pulled the trigger. But why did you do it? Did the man come at you? Were you scared? Did he come at you and you two panicked? Is that how it went down?"

Sweat began running out of Marlin's hairline, down the back of his neck and into his eyes. He swiped at the sweat with the back of his hand as the tone of his voice rose an octave.

"No, sir. No way. We didn't see no guy. We didn't shoot no one."

Mike kept pushing. "And yet your fingerprints are in his car."

Marlin started to cry. "Me and J.T. were under the bridge smoking pot, man. Mindin' our own damn business and smokin' a little weed. That's all. I swear."

Now Marlin was wiping away sweat and tears. The only thing left was for Kenny to draw a little blood to go with it.

"No! That's not all," he shouted. "You killed a man just so you wouldn't have to walk home in the rain!"

Marlin started to sob. "No, no, that's not how it went down!"

Mike's heart skipped a beat. Here it comes, he thought.

"Then how *did* it go down?" Kenny said.

"We was smoking weed like I said. It started to rain but we thought we'd just wait it out under the bridge. Then the storm got worse and we figured we was just gonna have to get wet to get home. It was thunderin' and lightnin' and the wind was blowin' something fierce. I told J.T. we was gonna get struck by lightnin' but he said it was either take our chances with the storm or drown in the river so we come up out from under the bridge."

Kenny tapped the table. "And that's when you saw the man sitting in his car, right?"

Marlin was shaking his head so hard he was slinging sweat across the table.

"No, no. I keep tellin' you. We didn't see no man. We was comin' up the slope when some crazy old homeless guy come runnin' through the rain tellin' us to run, that the devil was comin, that he was on the bridge and we were gonna die."

Kenny blinked.

Mike took a deep breath. Okay. It wasn't the confession he'd expected.

"So now you're claiming a homeless guy was the killer?"

"No, man, no. I'm sayin' we didn't see nobody die and we damn sure didn't see no body layin' around. Just that homeless guy wavin' his arms and yellin like a mad man."

Mike suddenly flashed on Prophet Jones coming out of nowhere on the bridge the day of the downpour and how he'd nearly run him down. He'd been yelling something about the devil, too. What the hell?

"That doesn't explain your fingerprints," Mike said.

Marlin yanked at the handcuff around his wrist in frustration. "The crazy man scared us. We was runnin' away when we saw that car. The door was open, the engine was runnin' and nobody in sight. We jumped in and drove away, then left it at that all-night gas station. We didn't steal it, man.

We just borrowed it to get away from that crazy man." The kid shuddered, as if a huge weight had just lifted off his chest. "And that's the truth, so help me God."

"So, the fact that J.T. fingered you as the shooter doesn't change your story?" Mike asked.

"You're lyin'," Marlin shouted. "J.T. wouldn't say that cause it didn't happen. I'm done talkin'. If you're gonna accuse me of murder, I want a lawyer."

CHAPTER EIGHT

They headed back to the interrogation room where they'd left J.T. stewing, and paused at the window to look in. The kid was laying across the table with his buried his head in the crook of his arm. His shoulders were shaking.

"Looks like this one's bawling, too," Kenny said. "What do you make of all this?"

"I want to hear the last half of his story again before I make a call," Mike said. "He didn't mention anything about a homeless man before."

Walker's head came up as the door opened. When he saw the cops, he began swiping the tears off his face.

Mike sat and leaned back in the chair, balancing it on the back two legs as he eyed the teenager.

"You boys didn't get your stories straight. Marlin's got a different story to tell."

"Like how?" J.T. cried. "I didn't lie to you."

"Then tell me again," Mike said. "You were under the bridge smoking weed and it started to rain, right?"

The kid nodded. "Yeah, yeah, man. That's right. Smokin' weed. It started to rain. We thought we'd wait it out but it just kept getting worse. Thunder was so bad sometimes it would thunder one right after the other... and lightning was bad, man, and the water was rising."

"Thunder doesn't come in multiple rumbles. It thunders. Then it will lightning. But thunder doesn't go boom boom boom boom," Kenny said.

"Well it fuckin' did. It thundered three times in a row cause

I heard it," J.T. said.

His hand was shaking as he reached up and scratched his head. The blue Mohawk was so weighed down with hair gel that it all moved in one piece.

Mike struggled with the urge to lean back, hoping there weren't any lice in it, too. It wouldn't be the first time they'd had to delouse an interrogation room but it always gave him the creeps for days afterward.

"We won't quibble about the thunder," Mike said. "So the water was rising. Then what?"

"So we ran out from under the bridge toward the river bank. The lightning was striking all around us and I thought we'd get hit and-" J.T. paused. "Oh hey, wait. I almost forgot about that crazy man."

"What crazy man," Mike asked.

"You know, that old homeless guy. Sometimes he preaches in the park. I think they call him Preacher or something like that."

"Are you talking about Prophet Jones?" Mike asked.

"Yeah, yeah, Prophet. That's the one."

"So you saw Prophet. So what does he have to do with you boys killing a man and stealing his car?"

Mike saw J.T.'s eyes begin to water. He was scared and that was good. Scared meant he still wanted to talk his way out of it. When they got pissed or knew they were caught, that's when they lawyered up.

"We didn't kill no one," J.T. cried. "That crazy man was shouting at us, telling us the devil was on the bridge or something like that. He was yelling 'run, run, run," and so we did. We came up on that car and just like I told you before, it was abandoned. The door was open with the keys in the ignition and the engine running. We just got in and drove away."

Mike kept a hard edge in his voice as he fired back at the kid. "You've told us two different stories now. The first one didn't have a homeless man in it. Now this one does. What's the truth?"

J.T. hit the table with his fist. "I didn't lie. I just forgot about him the first time. It's all still the same story. We didn't kill anyone and we didn't really steal a car. It was abandoned and we needed to get out of that storm."

Kenny glanced at Mike and then nodded.

Mike stood.

"So do you believe me? Are you gonna let us go?" J.T. asked.

"Oh hell no," Kenny said. "Your fingerprints were inside a dead man's car. You're going to jail, and unless someone tells us otherwise, you and your buddy are going to be charged with theft and murder. Sit tight. There's an officer coming to take you to booking, after which he will show you to the jail cell of his choice. You have a nice day."

J.T. Walker was too shocked to move. He was still staring at the mirror when Mike and Kenny passed by outside the interrogation room.

"What do you think now?" Kenny asked.

"I think we need to find Prophet Jones," Mike said.

Kenny frowned. "You can't take anything he says as fact. He's crazy, man."

"Still, if he saw something no one else saw, it might point us in another direction," Mike said.

"You don't think those boys are guilty, do you?" Kenny asked.

Mike shrugged.

Kenny sighed. "I thought I taught you better than that."

"My instincts tell me to keep looking, that's all, and I don't ignore my instincts."

"So where are we gonna find a crazy homeless man?" Kenny muttered.

"On the streets," Mike said. "We'll put out a BOLO. Maybe we'll get lucky and someone will spot him and bring him in, which means he won't be transported in our car. He smells to high heaven, not to mention the fleas and lice."

Kenny shuddered. "Shit. I wasn't thinking of that."

"I always think of that," Mike said. "It's a holdover from when I was a little kid in grade school. I got lice in my hair in second grade because the kid who hung his coat next to mine had them. My Mom shaved my head and the crap she put on me to kill all the nits and eggs was something I'll never forget."

Kenny laughed. "Gives new meaning to the word, egghead, doesn't it?"

Mike jabbed Kenny's arm. "Very funny. So let's go find us a prophet. I have a sudden need to hear God's truth."

Caulfield Industries was unusually calm. One of Justin's afternoon appointments had cancelled and he found himself with a couple of hours to spare. His first thought was to go see Callie, but when he called the room to check in with his mother, he found out Callie was in x-ray, which meant even if he went, he'd spend more time waiting in her room for her to come back, than actually getting to see her, so he decided to wait until later. Still, the idea of getting out of the office was too enticing to dismiss. On impulse, he buzzed his secretary.

"Yes, Mr. Caulfield?"

"Frances, I'm going to be gone for awhile. What do I have on the calendar for later this afternoon?"

"A conference call was tentatively scheduled for 4:15 but we never got confirmation."

Justin glanced down at the list on his desk, and noted he had one last issue pending.

"Did you get through to the company lawyer about confirming Jessup Sadler's retirement?"

"Yes sir. He said he'd contact the family on your behalf, let them know that the pension will begin immediately, that any extra medical expenses for Mrs. Sadler not covered by the insurance will be picked up by the company, and that the company will be paying for Mr. Sadler's funeral services, as well."

Justin glanced up and then out the window toward the river, then looked away.

"That's perfect. Thank you, Frances. If there's nothing else pressing, I'm taking the rest of the afternoon off. It will give me some extra time with Callie."

"Yes sir. I'll call the necessary parties and make sure they know you're unavailable in case they were still trying to pull it off."

"Thank you, Frances. Have a nice evening."

"You too, Mr. Caulfield, and give Callie my best."

"I'll do that," Justin said.

He hung up the phone, grabbed the morning paper he had yet to read, and headed down to the parking lot with a bounce in his step. It felt a little like skipping school, but Justin was in the mood for rebellion. He'd missed lunch thinking he would be in that meeting and was in the mood for something good. He thought of The Depot's famous chicken and dumplings and made a quick turn at the corner and headed downtown.

Vic Payton was having a rough day. His fiancé called constantly demanding his undivided attention, while his boss/future father-in-law was riding him about rising costs and leaner profit. Vic was up to his eyeballs in paperwork trying to trace the cause. He couldn't remember any of their suppliers upping costs on anything specific, so it had to be on the customer side. The lady who did their books was off this afternoon and Vic wasn't the best when it came to numbers, but he was quickly learning that headaches like this were just part of the new job description.

When his phone rang again, he almost let it go to voice mail then saw it was from Michelle again, cursed aloud, then took a deep breath and answered.

"Hi honey, what's up?"

"Tony and Myra want us to go with them tonight to that new place out on highway 10."

Vic frowned. "Are you talking about The Blue Duck?"

She giggled. "Yes, that's the one. Isn't that the funniest name? But I hear the food is amazing and I want to go."

The whine in her voice cut straight to his bones. If she'd been standing in front of him, it would have taken everything he had not to slap her silly.

"I can't baby, I have to work until close tonight."

"No Vic. I'll talk to Daddy. He won't-"

"You do not talk to Daddy," Vic said shortly. "This is my

job. I don't own this place. Your father does. If I don't do my job well, he won't be happy with me. Do you want him to be pissed at me, or what?"

"But Vic, I want to go so bad and Tony and Myra are so much fun. Why can't you be more like Tony?"

It was the worst thing she could have said and he reacted without thought – spitting out words in short angry bursts.

"Because I was born in Coal Town and Tony was born on the other side of the bridge, that's why. His daddy owns two blocks worth of businesses in downtown Caulfield. My daddy died in a mine when I was eleven. If you don't like who you got engaged to, all you have to do is say so. I got pride, Michelle. I worked hard to get where I am and I'm not gonna piss it away."

There was a long, uncomfortable silence. Vic couldn't believe he'd just said what he'd said, then realized he wouldn't take one bit of it back. And since she decided not to comment, he finished up with condescending permission she wouldn't like.

"If you want to go with Tony and Myra, you have my blessing. Tell them I said hello. I have a problem here that your father wants resolved and I need to get back to work. Talk to you later... or not. It's your call."

The moment he hung up, he groaned. God. What the fuck was he thinking? If Michelle gave back his ring, would her old man fire him? Fucking hell, why couldn't Poppy Sadler have given him the time of day? She was the woman he'd wanted, but when she hadn't been interested, he'd dropped his pursuit. She seemed satisfied with her lot in life and he wanted to be a mover and a shaker like Michelle's old man. So he'd sold his soul to the devil's daughter and now he was paying out the ass for someone he no longer wanted.

He frowned at the stack of invoices and in a fit of disgust pushed away from the desk. He wasn't a damn bookkeeper. He belonged out front, mingling with the customers, and that's where he was going.

Moments later he was back on the floor, weaving his way through the tables, eyeing what needed busing and how the plates looked as they came out of the kitchen. That's what he knew. It's what he did best. When he saw Justin Caulfield coming in, he moved past the hostess, grabbed a menu and greeted him personally.

"Good afternoon, Mr. Caulfield. Are you meeting anyone, or dining alone?"

"Alone," Justin said. "And somewhere near the windows, please."

Vic smiled. "Certainly sir! Right this way!" and seated Justin at a table for two with a window view.

"Perfect," Justin said. He laid his unread newspaper on the table, took the menu Vic offered, then looked up, scanning the room.

Vic caught the move. "Are you looking for someone in particular, sir?"

"Yes. I like that young waitress who works your day shift. You know... the tall slender one with dark hair, but I don't see her."

Vic fidgeted nervously. He hated to disappoint a man of Caulfield's stature.

"I'm sorry, sir, but she's off for a few days. She had a death in her family. Two actually. It's quite the tragedy."

Justin frowned. "That's too bad, but now that I think of it, I don't think I ever knew her name."

"Her name is Poppy Sadler. Her father was the man who was murdered just yesterday. The one they found in the river."

Justin frowned. "How unfortunate. Yes, that is a tragedy."

"But not the entire story," Vic said. "Her mother died of cancer the same morning her father's body was found. But I'm sure that's more dismal news than you care to hear. I'll send Jewel right over. She'll take good care of you and enjoy your meal."

"Fine. Thank you," Justin said, and then reached for the paper. Curious, he opened it to the obituaries and then began to scan the page, looking for a Sadler obit then found it.

Helen "Sunny" Roberts Sadler – born October 4th, 1974 – deceased September 12th, 2011.

Justin read the name, and then read it again. Sunny Roberts.

He read the entire obituary three times, folded up the newspaper and set it aside.

The waitress appeared with water, coffee and a menu. He ordered the chicken and dumplings he'd come for and then reached for the sugar as she walked away, only to realize his hands were shaking.

It was nearly 4:15 when Poppy got home. She was exhausted both physically and mentally, and walking into a warm house filled with enticing smells and a half-dozen pots of colorful chrysanthemums was a welcome she hadn't expected.

Gladys came out of the kitchen wearing one of her mama's aprons and for a moment Poppy couldn't think what to say beyond 'take that off'. Thankfully she refrained and handed Gladys the keys to her car.

"It's back in one piece, safe and sound and full of gas. I can't thank you enough for the loan, not to mention staying here for all this."

"Oh sugar, I was happy to help," Gladys said. "You have quite a list on the kitchen table and I made a second list of all the people who've called. They don't expect you to call back. I just thought you'd want to know."

"I do. I really appreciate it."

Gladys untied the apron then laid it in Poppy's hands. "I'll be getting on home now. Give you some time to yourself and maybe get you some of that good food in the kitchen. Didn't you say John was coming?"

"Yes, ma'am. He'll be here some time tonight."

"Good. I don't like to think of you here all by yourself. Now if either of you need anything at all you just give us a call."

"I will."

Gladys patted Poppy's cheek, grabbed her jacket and purse and was out the door. Poppy locked it behind her, then, for a moment, stood in the silence and closed her eyes.

She could hear a faint sound of running water and realized the plunger on the toilet was probably stuck again. Sometimes you had to jiggle it to make it shut off. She recognized the scent of freshly brewed coffee, but there were other more enticing scents of something hot and sweet. She could almost hear her mama's voice, calling out.

Baby? Is that you? We're in the kitchen. Come on in.

Poppy pinched the bridge of her nose to stop a fresh set of tears, headed for the bathroom to check the toilet then went into her room to change.

A few minutes later she entered the kitchen wearing a pair of faded jeans and a long-sleeved t-shirt. Her house shoes were old fleece-lined moccasins. After being on her feet all day, she craved comfort and familiarity, and maybe a piece of pie to hold her over until supper.

It was a little like potluck dinner at church as she sorted through the foil covered bowls to see what was here, but she didn't stop until she found the desserts. After poking her finger in a couple to test for taste, she settled on a piece of coconut cream pie, poured a glass of milk, and headed for the living room to eat.

Gladys had been watching the movie channel, and although the sound had been muted, the movie was still playing. Poppy sat then upped the volume as she took her first bite. The pie was sweet. The milk was cold. When she realized it was an old John Wayne movie, the food suddenly stuck in the back of her throat. Daddy's favorite movie star had been John Wayne. Even though the actor had been dead for years, his movies lived on. Her vision blurred as she set the food aside. Now Daddy was gone, too. Was there enough love left between her and Johnny to keep their family alive, or would Johnny disappear on her like he had on Mama? She was afraid to be alone.

Gunshots rang out. Poppy jumped then realized it was the movie. A poor choice considering the way Jessup Sadler had died. She muted the western, then leaned back against the sofa and closed her eyes.

Less than a minute later, there was a knock at the door.

She wiped away tears as she went to the door, expecting to see someone she knew, not a stranger with a briefcase.

"Yes?"

"My name is Graham Ring, of Ring and Padgett Law

offices. I need to speak with the Sadler family."

"That would be me," Poppy said.

"May I come in?" he asked.

She hesitated, then shrugged and stepped back. The way she was feeling, if he was an axe murderer and did her in, he would be doing her a favor.

"Have a seat," Poppy said.

He sat at one end of the sofa. Poppy sat at the other.

"First, I would like to offer my condolences to your family at this most tragic of times."

Still in the dark as to why the man was here, she folded her hands in her lap.

"Thank you."

The lawyer took a folder out of his briefcase, removed a check, and handed it to Poppy.

"As of today, your father's pension is in full effect. Ordinarily a pension would have been paid to the widow of the deceased for the rest of her life, but since she has sadly passed on the same day as Mr. Sadler's death, Mr. Caulfield has very generously instructed us to pay it out to you for as long as you are a resident of Caulfield."

Poppy stared at the check in disbelief. As much as she needed it, she knew this was a mistake. She handed the check back.

"I'm sorry, but you've made a mistake. Mr. Caulfield fired my father a week ago which was before his death, ending not only his chance for a pension, but his health insurance as well.

The lawyer handed the check back to Poppy.

"Mr. Caulfield has been made aware of the circumstances, but was in deep sympathy for your situation and rescinded the act. He is also taking care of the outstanding debts for your mother's medical bills, as well as any costs you will accrue for the two funerals."

Poppy was in shock. "Why?"

"I can't speak for Mr. Caulfield personally, but I'm sure this was his way of expressing his sympathies."

Poppy stared at the numbers on the check, and then back up at the lawyer.

"This would have been the amount of Daddy's monthly

pension when he retired?"

"Yes, ma'am."

"And I'm getting this same amount every month as long as I maintain residence in this city?"

"Yes, that is correct."

Poppy was stunned, and at the same time furious. This felt like blood money. Caulfield was acting out of guilt, not sympathy.

Graham Ring knew what this money would mean to someone who lived in Coal Town. Considering what this young woman must have been going through for the past forty-eight hours, he was glad to be the bearer of some good news. When she had no further comment, he decided his job was done.

"I won't bother you any longer," he said as he stood. "Again, I'm so sorry for your loss."

Poppy walked him to the door. She doubted that their paths would ever cross again, but there was something she felt compelled to ask before he left.

"Mr. Ring, before you leave, may I ask you something?"

"Why, certainly."

"If Daddy had not been murdered, do you think this would be happening?

Ring felt a flush coming up his neck. There was no way to answer that truthfully and still keep his job.

"I have no way of knowing that, Miss Sadler."

Poppy saw the red spots on the lawyer's cheeks. The fact that he suddenly shifted his gaze to the toes of his shoes was answer enough.

"That's what I thought," she said.

Ring started to leave and then stopped again. "It is what it is, Miss Sadler. You need it. You have it. I'm happy to have been the bearer of a bit of good news."

Once he left, Poppy looked back at the check - a single piece of paper with a few lines of words and numbers – an inconsequential item bearing the weight of someone's guilt. She didn't know which was worse – that Justin Caulfield had basically just paid them off to assuage his conscience, or that she'd let him do it.

She put the check in her purse and then carried her uneaten pie into the kitchen and put it in the refrigerator. Maybe she'd eat it another day when the bitter taste in her mouth was gone. She glanced at the clock. It was nearly 6:00. Where was Johnny?

CHAPTER NINE

Coal Town - 7:30 p.m.

It was dark and the houses in Coal Town were lit from within as families went about the business of their daily lives. Dark was kind to this side of town, shrouding the wear and tear of the neighborhoods while the lights inside the homes made them appear warm and festive.

But it was a thin façade between the truth and the rest of the world. Men still fought with their wives, as the addicts shot up or snorted the drug of choice behind dingy gray curtains. Children sat down hungry to meager sustenance and got up from the table the same way. Some of them were already alone for the night as the single parent in the household went off to a second job.

It was into this world that Detectives Amblin and Duroy went calling, working their way down the list of men on Sadler's shift at the mine, hoping one of them would have an answer as to who might have wanted him dead.

They had intended to divide the list and each go their own way, but the Lieutenant had ordered otherwise. It wasn't wise for a cop to go into Coal Town alone, especially after dark. During the last hour and a half they'd gone to the houses of seven of the twelve men on the list, and only two of them had been forthcoming. The others had clammed up and glared at the detectives without having anything helpful to say.

"That went well," Kenny said, as the eighth man also claimed ignorance.

Mike shrugged. "Did you think it would be otherwise?"

"I guess not, but you would think if you'd worked with a guy for all those years and then he gets murdered, you'd want to do anything you could to help find the killer."

"Unless you're the killer, or you just don't want to get involved," Mike said.

Kenny slid into the passenger seat and buckled up as Mike started the car.

"Who's next?" Mike asked.

"Carl Crane. 774 South Bellwood. Give me a sec. I'm putting it in the GPS."

With their directions in place, Mike drove off. He didn't realize until he turned a corner that they were coming up on the Sadler residence.

"Hey, isn't that Sadler house?" Kenny asked, pointing to the only house on the block with a porch light burning.

"Yes, I guess it is," Mike said, and fought the urge to stop as they drove past.

"She's got the porch light on. Probably had a steady stream of visitors all day."

"Probably," Mike said.

He glanced down at the GPS, took the next right. A few minutes later they pulled up at the residence. The lights were on inside the house and there were two cars in the yard. At least they were home.

As soon as they parked, a dog started barking.

"Damn dogs," Kenny muttered. "I don't want to get bit."

Mike glanced over his shoulder. "It's the dog across the street and it's on a chain."

"Whatever," Kenny said, and followed Mike to the front door.

Someone had been grilling. The scent of charcoal and cooking meat still lingered in the damp night air. The sky was dark and overcast - the quarter moon hidden behind a bank of slow moving clouds.

"Feels like fall," Mike said, as he knocked, then stepped back.

"Football weather," Kenny said.

Mike grinned. Kenny did love his sports.

They kept waiting for someone to answer the door, but the television was so loud inside that they could hear it word for word.

"Whoever's inside has to be half-deaf. Knock again," Kenny said.

Mike pounded a little harder, and within seconds, the TV was muted and they could hear footsteps, then the porch light came on. The door swung inward, revealing a short, stocky man with a tuft of graying hair around the back of his head and a greasy comb-over.

"Good evening, Sir," Mike said, flashing his badge. "Are you Carl Crane?"

"Yep, that's me," Carl said.

"I'm Detective Amblin and this is my partner, Detective Duroy. We're investigating Jessup Sadler's murder. We've been making the rounds tonight trying to talk to everyone he worked with. You worked the same shift at the Caulfield mine, correct?"

"Yep, yep, I did."

"May we come inside for a minute? I only have a few questions."

The little man stepped aside. "Sure, sure, come on in. Jessup was a good friend. We're all tore up about what happened."

Finally, someone who cared about the man, Mike thought.

"This here's my wife, Hannah. She was friends with Jessup's wife, Helen. It's almost more than a body can imagine that them two would die on the same day, but not together... like in a wreck or something. Know what I mean?"

"Nice to meet you, Mrs. Crane. Yes sir, it was a tragic occurrence."

"Ya'll take a seat," Hannah said.

"Thank you, ma'am," Kenny said. At least this couple was friendly, whether they knew anything or not.

Mike waited until Carl sat down.

"I'll get straight to the point," Mike said. "Did Jessup Sadler have any enemies at the mine, or someone he'd had a recent fight with?"

Carl shook his head. "No sir, not to my knowledge. We all got along on that shift."

"We were told he got fired for being drunk on the job."

Carl hesitated then shrugged a little, as if to say this was no big deal.

"Plenty of men have come to work a little hung-over and the like. Jessup used to drink in the old days, but he hadn't had a drink in years."

"Had he been drinking the day he got fired?"

"I guess. Maybe a little, but he wasn't falling down drunk or nothing like that. Hell, even the shift boss drinks some."

Mike scanned his notes. "Are you talking about Tom Bonaventure?"

Carl's eyes narrowed angrily. "Yeah, the weasel. Course, he don't go down below anymore, but the rule oughta apply to everyone or no one at all. Right?"

"Did Bonaventure have a grudge against him?"

"Not that I knew of," Carl said. "Bonaventure is a pussy. He used to work a regular shift like the rest of us and then he got promoted. He's been a pain in the ass ever since, but I never saw him single anyone out and give them a hard time."

Mike kept making notes as Carl talked. When he paused, Mike took the questions in a different direction.

"On Jessup's last day at work, did he say anything to you when he arrived that would explain why he'd started drinking after such a long dry spell?"

Carl shrugged. "We figured it was just because of Helen. She was barely hanging on and it was killing him to watch her die like that."

"So he didn't say anything... anything at all about having a run-in with someone, or being hassled?"

"No."

Hannah had been silent, but Carl was leaving out all kinds of stuff and she couldn't be still any longer.

"Now Carl, what about the last time he was over to the house?"

Carl frowned. "What about it?"

Hannah rolled her eyes. "Carl is so hard of hearing that he probably missed that whole conversation. He can't hear thunder you know, but he doesn't like to admit it so he pretends he's following the conversation right along with everyone else then blows his cover by bringing up the cost of gas or something when we've all been talking about a neighbor's new baby."

Mike hid a grin. That explained the loud TV.

"What about his last visit, Mrs. Crane?"

"His daughter was working late at The Depot so we had him over for supper. He was upset when he got here and I thought it was because Helen had taken a bad turn. But when I asked, he said no, she was holding her own. Then later, I heard him say something to Carl about the old days, like back when we were all in high school together. You see Jessup was older than the rest of us. He'd already been married, had a son, and buried his wife before Sunny graduated high school. Anyway, he asked Carl if he knew anything about what happened to Sunny the night of our senior prom."

"Wait. Who's Sunny?" Mike asked.

"Oh, sorry. That was Helen's nickname. We called her that pretty much through all twelve years of school. It wasn't until she graduated and went to work at the paper mill where her folks were employed that she began to go by her given name, Helen."

Kenny glanced at Mike and arched an eyebrow, as if to say where the fuck is all this going?

Mike ignored him and let Hannah talk.

"So, did something happen to Sunny at your prom?"

Hannah pursed her lips and then quickly looked away. "I don't know."

Mike knew better. "Please, Mrs. Crane, whatever you tell me could help us catch the person who murdered Jessup."

Carl cleared his throat.

Hannah frowned. "It's not right to speak ill of the dead."

Kenny was tired of all the chit chat and abruptly entered into the conversation.

"Ma'am, if you know something, it's your duty to tell. Just quit talking in riddles and spit it out."

Hannah glared at him and set her jaw. She didn't let any man tell her what to do.

"Mrs. Crane, what does the prom have to do with Jessup Sadler's murder?" Mike asked.

Hannah turned away from Kenny as if dismissing him from the conversation and focused her attention on Mike.

"I don't know that it has anything to do with it, but you asked if something had happened that might make Jessup take up drinking again and his behavior that night was not normal."

"You're right. I did. Please continue," Mike said.

"Sunny was so pretty, but she didn't have a date for the senior prom. Even though a bunch of us girls went solo, Sunny never lacked for partners at the dance. We were all having a grand time and then all of a sudden she was gone. We never saw her leave and I have no idea who she was dancing with before she left, but she didn't come to school afterward for nearly a week. We were told she'd had food poisoning. She didn't say anything different when she came back."

"Why, after all these years, would Jessup suddenly become interested in something that happened over twenty years ago?"

"I don't know. I'm just telling you what I heard Jessup ask Carl, okay?"

Mike was frustrated. This complicated everything. Either this had nothing to do with Jessup's murder, or they had to look back to the past to find a reason for someone wanting him dead.

"Is there anything else you can remember about that evening?"

"Only that Jessup was unusually quiet, which again, I just chalked up to Helen's condition."

Mike stood, and Kenny followed suit, anxious to finish the names on the list and get home.

"Thank you both for your time. Here's my card. If you think of anything else please give me a call," Mike said.

Hannah slipped it into her apron pocket. "Yes sir, we will."

The dog across the street barked again as they made their way to the car.

"Unlock the door," Kenny said, and lengthened his stride.

Mike grinned as he hit the remote. The car lights blinked as the doors unlocked, which set the dog into a frenzy.

"That was a bust," Kenny said, as he buckled up.

"Maybe, maybe not."

"Seriously, partner. It's getting late and I'm hungry. We

have three names left on the list. Let's get this over with and get home, okay?"

"Then give me an address," Mike said, entering it into the GPS as Kenny read one off.

As luck would have it, they drove back past the Sadler residence and this time there was a late model pickup parked in the drive.

"Looks like she's got company," Kenny said.

Mike caught a glimpse of the plates. "Out of state. Probably the missing brother."

"I didn't know there was a missing brother," Kenny said. "What else don't I know that you do?"

"Yes, you did and stop being an ass," Mike said. "When we get to the next house, you take the lead. Maybe it'll release some of your pent-up hostility."

Poppy was checking to make sure there were clean sheets on John's bed when she heard a car pull up in the drive. She glanced at the clock. It was too late for company. Please God let it be Johnny.

The thump of footsteps sounded on the porch as she came hurrying down the hall, but it wasn't until she heard the key in the lock that she knew he was home.

The front door swung inward just as she entered the living room.

Johnny!

He was thinner than the last time she'd seen him, which made his shoulders look wider than ever. He stood in the doorway, as if waiting for an invitation to come the rest of the way in.

"Hey, Poppy."

"Johnny. Thank God, thank God," Poppy said, and then she was in his arms.

He kicked the door shut behind him as he swept her off her feet. "I'm sorry, sister, I'm so, so, sorry."

"It doesn't matter. You're here now," Poppy said, and then began to sob.

John thought he had his emotions in check until he'd seen the dark circles beneath her eyes and the look of terror on her face. Tears burned the back of his throat as he choked on what he'd meant to say. Moments later they were weeping in each other's arms.

Amelia Caulfield had always loved the dining room in the family mansion. It was one of the few rooms she'd never redecorated during her years here with Adam.

The wallpaper was gold flocked with a wine-red diamond pattern. Adam had hated it, saying it reminded him of argyle socks. But Amelia loved it, so it had stayed. The elongated crystals dangling from the chandelier glittered like strands of diamonds, and at her bidding the maid had set table tonight with the Paul Revere silver and Waterford crystal.

She sat in the captain's chair like a queen residing over her dominion, while Justin sat just to her right. Proper etiquette would have had Justin at the head of the table since he was now the 'man of the house', but when Amelia came back from Florida to help with Callie, she had claimed age over propriety and chosen the seat in his stead.

She delivered a different, but witty conversational subject with each course that was served, and by the time they got to dessert, she was on an emotional high.

The only downside to the evening was Justin's non-committal attitude and his lack of appetite. She'd gone through the entire meal, watching him poke at his food. After having spent the better part of the afternoon and evening together at the hospital with Callie before coming home to a late dinner, he was obviously too distracted to eat.

"Justin."

He looked up. "Yes, Mother?"

"What's wrong? Are you worried about Callie? Is it something at the office? Talk to me. I may be getting old, but I'm not senile and I am a good listener."

He looked away, giving his fork a good deal of introspection before putting it on his plate and then shoving it aside. Amelia could tell he was weighing a decision as to whether to confide in her or not.

"Well, for God's sake spit it out," she said.

His nostrils flared as he lifted his head. "I don't care for the tone of your voice."

The resemblance was so strong that for a moment, it was as if Amelia was facing her husband and not her son, then she frowned.

"I'm just trying to help. What's on your mind, son?"

He laughed. "You don't want to know."

"But I do. I'm your mother. What bothers you, bothers me."

Justin smiled, but it did not reach his eyes.

"No, impropriety bothers you, Mother. Not my feelings. But since you insist on probing my psyche, I have a question. How does that saying go about the sins of the fathers being visited upon the children?"

"I'm not sure of the exact wording myself, but I know what you mean," Amelia said.

"So, do you believe one generation pays for the sins of another?"

It was an odd question, but she had no problem answering. "No, I don't. I think each person follows a pre-destined path that has nothing to do with another, but that's just me."

The corner of his mouth turned up just enough that would lead one to think he might but be amused, except he wasn't.

"Of course you would think like that. If that's your belief, then it allows all kinds of leeway without having to claim a responsibility for your choices. Living life your way, you can never be faulted for making a bad decision or be deemed cruel because what you did was not intentional. It was just the path you were destined to be on."

Amelia didn't know whether to be concerned or offended. This confrontational behavior wasn't like him. In fact, it was completely foreign. He was a natural leader – a man who never exhibited stress. This had to be because of Callie.

"Callie needs a kidney transplant, but neither of us qualify as donors," Justin said.

Amelia relaxed. Her instincts had been right. This was about Callie.

"Don't worry. Transplants are done daily all over the country."

"I do worry. I will continue to worry. I cannot imagine why you don't. Dr. Summers put her on a waiting list, but she's nowhere near the top."

Amelia frowned. "Really? I would have thought-"

Justin stared into his mother's face. "Money can't buy us out of this."

Amelia lifted her chin – not much, but just enough for any observer to realize she'd gone from amiable table companion to formidable host.

"Now I don't like the tone of *your* voice. If I didn't know better, I would think you're implying that the family goes around committing sins and then buying their way out of the messes they cause."

A muscle jerked at the size of Justin's jaw but his gaze never wavered.

Amelia felt the accusation, but she wasn't going there. Not now. Not ever.

He watched her expression shift. Between one breath and the next it was as if their conversation had never happened.

"You know what dear, I'm very tired this evening. Callie was particularly bored today and demanded a lot of my attention. I believe I'll turn in for the night."

Justin stood, momentarily looming over his mother's chair.

"You do that, Mother. I know you'll rest well. You gave your conscience to the devil years ago."

Amelia's lips parted in shock, but whatever volley she'd been about to deliver was nullified by her son's angry exit.

Justin couldn't calm down and knew it would be impossible to sleep. Without thinking about the time, he stormed out of the house.

The sky was overcast, but security lights triggered by motion detectors came on one by one as he strode to the garage, elongating his shadow and turning it into a child's version of a monster. The faster he walked, the more it appeared as if he was being chased.

By the time he got to the garage his heart was pounding. As he drove down the driveway and then out into the city, he felt as if he was making an escape, but from what? A man could not outrun his past no matter how far or how fast he went, but he needed to put distance between himself and his mother before one of them said something that couldn't be taken back.

Traffic was steady in the entertainment side of the city, especially around the mall and the movie theatre. His fingers tightened on the steering wheel as he drove past the mall parking lot. He couldn't remember the last time he'd been to the movies and he'd never been inside that mall because a Caulfield should not mingle with the masses. He'd had that beaten into him early on and never forgotten, and if his behavior at the dinner table was any indication of the grudge he still carried, he'd never forgiven it either.

There was no purpose to his route. He drove up and down streets in one neighborhood after another - wondering what it would be like to be one of *them* - worrying about the economy and maybe a kid who was failing in school or smoking weed. Wondering how it would be to have had a wife who'd married you for love instead of the size of your father's bank account. And then looking at the other side of the coin and wondering if they ever wished they were him.

Right now, he would trade places in a heartbeat, trade his mother for a wife who loved him and a kid who was healthy as a horse.

He drove out of the residential area and back into the downtown part of Caulfield, but didn't realize where he was until he stopped at a stop sign. That's when he saw the floodlights shining on the sign on the front lawn of Edison's Funeral Home.

His skin crawled. All this time - all the driving – and this was where his subconscious had led him?

As he watched, the front door of the funeral home opened. A couple emerged hand in hand, their heads bent in obvious grief. He drove through the intersection, then up into the parking lot and found himself unwilling to move.

What the fuck was he doing? What would this prove?

Then his attitude shifted to one of defiance. He didn't have to prove anything to anyone but himself and he wanted to go in. He strode up the sidewalk without hesitation, his steps long and sure. There was a moment as his fingers curled around the doorknob and he felt the cold metal beneath his palm that brought him to a halt. The flash of reality almost made him go back to his car, but he stopped. He'd been running from this moment for over twenty years. The least he could do was say goodbye. He turned the knob and walked in.

Truman Epperson was on duty, and got up from the desk.

"Mr. Caulfield. How can I be of service?"

"I've come to pay my respects to Jessup Sadler's wife. He was one of my employees and I was given to understand that she had passed."

"Helen Sadler. Yes, yes, right this way," Truman said, and then moved toward a viewing room at the end of the central lounge.

Once they reached the doorway, everything began happening in slow motion. Justin saw Truman's mouth moving, but he could no longer hear what he was saying. When Truman paused and gestured to his left, Justin saw the guestbook and signed his name without thought, then entered. The room was empty of mourners, with only a couple of green plants and one basket of flowers to mark her presence.

Justin kept walking all the way up to the casket before he would allow himself to look inside. Once he did, the knot in his gut turned into a full-blown ache.

Sunny.

He'd been through this once with Deborah, now Sunny was dead, too?

He'd never thought of Sunny Roberts as growing older. In the back of his mind she'd always stayed the same pretty, happy girl who liked hot fudge sundaes and making love in the rain. It was shocking to see what the cancer had done to her body. Even though the dress she was wearing was pretty enough, it was evident that she was skin and bones beneath. When he saw the ring on her finger, it served to remind him it was his own damn fault she'd been another man's wife.

But he hadn't come just to walk away. Not until he said what he needed to say, but discreetly, of course. She'd kept their secret all these years. The last thing he needed was for someone to overhear him and soil her memory.

He reached inside the casket, hesitating but a moment before he cupped her hand. Even though it was cold and stiff, a part of him remembered how eagerly she would have returned the caress.

"Sunny, I'm sorry. You don't know how many times in the past twenty years that I wished I'd made a different choice. I never expected you to forgive me. I never expected you to understand. I traded you for a birthright, and just between the two of us, it was a really bad deal."

There was a lump in the back of his throat. Tears were burning to be shed, but not here.

"Rest well, Sunny girl. If there's such a thing as heaven, I hope to see you again."

He touched her chin, traced the curve of her cheek then walked out of the room.

"Goodnight Mr. Caulfield," Truman said.

Justin nodded and kept on moving – all the way down the sidewalk, then into his car. He started the engine, backed away from the curb, then pulled over to the dark side of the parking lot and laid his head down on the steering wheel.

Tears came swiftly, but when he tried to draw breath, he choked. He moaned, then he raged, pounding the steering wheel until his hands were numb while the wind rose and the clouds rolled in.

By the time his grief was spent, it had begun to rain. He put the car into gear and drove away, once again putting distance between him and his Sunny girl. It occurred to him as he left the area that in a symbolic way, the rain was washing away the tracks of where he'd been. It was only fitting he hide this last visit, since their entire relationship had been a secret, as well.

CHAPTER TEN

"Do you want some more fried chicken?" Poppy asked.

"No, but I'll help you clean up," John said, as he scraped the chicken bones into the trash. He frowned as he watched her running dishwater into the sink. "You didn't eat."

"I know. It feels like I'll choke when I put food in my mouth."

"I'm sorry, sister. What can I do?" The look she gave him was one of relief, which only added to his guilt.

"You're here. That's enough."

"Is there room for all this food in the refrigerator?" John asked.

"There should be now. I already put the casseroles in the freezer in the back room. They'll be easy enough to reheat the day of the funeral. The rest of the stuff to be refrigerated should fit. Don't worry about the cakes or the fruit pies. They'll be fine sitting out."

"Got it," he said, and began covering up the uneaten food and putting it away.

They worked in silence for a few minutes, but as soon as they were finished John led her into the living room and sat down on the sofa.

"Talk to me," he said.

There were so many things they needed to discuss that Poppy couldn't choose a topic.

"You first."

He didn't hesitate. He might not like what she had to say but needed to know where he stood.

"Do you hate me? Tell me the truth. I can take it. Lord knows I hate myself enough for the both of us."

Her eyes welled. "No, Johnny, I don't hate you. I couldn't. Gladys says everyone deals with grief their own way. You did what you had to do to survive."

Shame turned the food he'd just eaten into a knot in his belly. He shook his head and looked away.

"It's okay, Johnny. Really."

"No it's not. I sacrificed you to save myself and never once thought what my leaving would do to you until it was too late."

"It's not too late. I managed. Besides, I'm not a baby anymore. I don't need anyone to take care of me. I can take care of myself."

"It wasn't about taking care of you, sister. I hurt you and I hurt Mom and Dad because I couldn't face the ugly truth. I was a coward and I'll have to live with that for the rest of my life."

Poppy's heart was breaking. She'd never seen her big brother so defeated – so shamed, and the worst part of it was there was nothing she could say that could make it better.

"Can I ask you something?" John asked.

"Anything," she said, as she watched his eyes well with tears.

"Did she suffer?"

Poppy's shoulders slumped. "I won't lie. Probably. Yes, some for sure. But Dr. Summers was wonderful and toward the end they kept her comfortable. The thing about Mama was that she was always upbeat. Every time I visited I'd have to psych myself up to go into her room, but I'd walk out feeling better. I don't know how she made that happen, but looking back, I think it was just her love filling me back up."

Tears slipped down the sharp angles of his face. He didn't bother wiping them away.

"What about Dad? Do the cops have any suspects? Have they found his car?"

Poppy pulled a handful of tissues from the box near her elbow and handed them to him without comment.

"No suspects, but they did find the car. It was at an all-night gas station with the keys in it and the doors locked."

"You're kidding! I thought they'd probably find it stripped

and burned or in the river," John said.

"So did I," Poppy said.

"What are the names of the cops in charge of the case? I want to talk to them tomorrow."

"Detective Amblin and Detective Duroy."

"Amblin? Mike Amblin?" John asked.

"Yes, do you know him?"

"He's a couple of years older than me, but yeah. Star quarterback his last two years of high school. I heard he'd played some college ball too, but I lost track of all that once I graduated. And you know how I hated the mines. Once I got into trucking, I was only in and out of Caulfield long enough to see family."

Poppy flashed on strong arms picking her up off the bridge - carrying her into the bathroom and running a hot bath to warm her because she was too cold to stand.

"Detective Amblin has been very kind," she said.

John nodded. "I want to thank him for that, too. I've lost touch with most of the friends I had in school." *Except for Aaron Carter who is playing snitch for me.*

Poppy picked at a hangnail without thinking, then looked surprised when it started to bleed. She wrapped a tissue around it and then put her hands in her lap.

"I see mine now and then, but they don't see me. Most of them are already married. Some with a baby or two."

He frowned. "You're only twenty. Plenty of time for all that."

"Now you sound like Mama and Daddy. I'm almost twenty-one. Every time I talked about getting an apartment they both had a fit. And I didn't push the issue all that much either. I don't make much waiting tables and it costs a lot to live on your own."

"Tell me about it, although I can't complain about my salary. I do okay as a long-haul trucker and with no wife and kids, I don't have that feeling of guilt some do that they're missing out on the best years of their lives."

Poppy eyed her brother, trying to see him from a prospective girlfriend's point of view.

"Do you have a girl, Johnny?"

He smiled. "I have lots of girlfriends, but not one special one. What about you?"

She thought of Vic Payton. He'd wanted her, but the spark between them just wasn't there, at least for her. He'd chased her for nearly a year before he'd finally given up.

"No. No one special."

"So we're both flying solo for now. It's all good. Whatever is meant to happen will happen, but not until it's time."

"I guess."

"Okay, another tough question. Can you handle it or are you too tired to keep talking?" John asked.

"We need to talk. What do you want to know?" Poppy asked.

"Have you seen Dad's body?"

Her voice began to shake. "In my mind every time I look at the river - in my sleep every time I close my eyes, but no, not in the sense that you mean. He's still at the morgue."

"Then I'm going there tomorrow. Do you want to come?"

"No, and I don't know if I want to view his body at all." She shuddered. "He was in the water most of the night. It's a miracle he didn't wash downriver because the storm and the downpour were awful. His body probably caught on something. I don't want a bad image locked in my memory."

"It's okay, honey. I just didn't want to leave you out of the loop if you wanted to go."

Poppy needed to change the subject. "Your bed is all ready, clean sheets and everything. You know where everything is, but if you need something I didn't think of, just ask me."

John cupped the side of her face. "Thank you. It's been a long drive getting here. I'm going to shower and then hit the sack. I won't take too long so you can get to bed, yourself."

"I think I'll watch TV for a bit. Sleep well, Johnny."

"You too, Poppy," he said, then kissed the top of her head and left.

Poppy turned on the television because she'd said that she would, but she couldn't concentrate on anything except the days ahead. She wondered if the murder investigation was progressing, which brought Mike Amblin to mind. It was disconcerting to try and merge what Johnny said about the detective having been a local football star with the soft-spoken, hard-eyed man who'd come into her life at such a terrible time.

She hoped he was as good at his job as he had been playing football. She wanted her father's killer behind bars. Well, that wasn't exactly true. Actually, she wanted to watch him die, but she would settle for putting him behind bars for the rest of his miserable, cowardly life.

Amelia Caulfield was restless. The conversation she'd been having with Justin during their dinner had ended on such a terrible note that she'd couldn't sleep. She wound up in her bedroom, pacing the floor. She didn't understand why he was so angry, but he obviously was, and – although it didn't make sense, he seemed angry with her – which prompted a surge of indignation.

She'd done nothing but love him and do everything within her power to make his life perfect from the day he'd been born. The best toys, the best clothes, the best schools, the best education money could buy. She'd been the one who'd set him up with Deborah, who turned out to be the perfect wife, and when he'd called in desperation about Callie's health, she'd dropped everything to do his bidding. He had no reason to be angry with her and every reason in the world to be indebted.

The longer she paced, the angrier she became. This wasn't fair and she'd put up with it long enough. She glanced at the clock. It was nearly eleven p.m. If he was already asleep, then it was just too bad. He should be awake and miserable like she was, but when she caught a glimpse of herself as she passed a mirror, she hesitated. No makeup and a dark hairnet over her steel-gray hair. Ah well. It's not like he'd never seen her face this naked, but maybe it would be a good reminder that she was an old woman who deserved the respect her age demanded.

She tightened the tie on her robe, slipped her feet into her house shoes, and strode out of her room. The nightlight in the hallway was bright enough that she had no problem navigating the distance without turning on lights. As she passed the door to Callie's bedroom, out of habit she almost stopped to peek in, then remembered her granddaughter was still in the hospital.

By the time she reached Justin's bedroom she had worked herself up into a snit. She'd raised him better than this. He was going to wipe that sarcastic tone from his voice or know the reason why. Anger fueled the power of her knock as she rapped four times on the door in rapid succession.

"Justin! It's me. I want to talk to you."

She took a step back, expecting the door to swing inward at any moment, but when she got no response it made her angrier. This time she doubled up her fist and pounded on the door.

"Justin! Open the door or I'm coming in."

Indignation was in every line of her body - in the expression on her face - in the tone of her voice as she opened the door and strode inside.

"Justin! How dare you ignore my-"

The room was empty. The bed was still made. As far as she could tell he hadn't been here since he'd left for work early this morning. She frowned.

"What the-"

All of a sudden she heard footsteps coming down the hall at a fast clip. She stormed back out of his room with an accusation on her lips, but it wasn't Justin, it was her bodyguard, Oral Newton.

"Are you all right, Mrs. Caulfield? I was making the rounds downstairs before retiring and heard noises and shouting. Is something wrong?"

Amelia sighed. If only Justin was as accommodating as Newton.

"No, Newton, everything is fine. I wanted to speak to Justin and was knocking on his door, rather loudly I suppose. I'm sorry I startled you."

Oral eyed her attire and quickly looked away. "Then I'll be going to my room, unless there's something I can do for you."

"I don't suppose you know where my son has gone?"

"No ma'am. He left the house right after dinner and hasn't returned, but I can find him if you need him."

"That won't be necessary. We can have our conversation tomorrow."

"Yes ma'am, then I'll say goodnight," Oral said, and turned

away.

"Newton!"

He pivoted sharply. "Yes ma'am?"

"Thank you. You are not just a faithful employee. You are a true and trusted friend."

Oral stood a little straighter. "It's been my honor to serve you, ma'am, and I'll be here as long as you need me... for whatever you need me to do."

Amelia's eyes narrowed as she lifted her chin. "Hopefully the worst of our days are behind us, isn't that so, Newton?"

"Yes ma'am. All is well, and with Callie getting better, there should be nothing left to cause you distress."

She watched him go downstairs, waiting until she could no longer hear his footsteps before she returned to her room.

Despite her frustration with Justin's bad attitude, the interlude in the hall had been enough to settle her. She kicked off her shoes then crawled between the covers and quickly fell asleep.

She never knew when Justin came home, and by the time morning came, he had his emotions under control. When Amelia came down for breakfast, he had already finished and was on his way out the door.

"Good morning, Mother. I have early meetings. Have a nice day," he said, kissed her cheek and was gone before she could gather herself enough to call him back.

Mike Amblin got up tired and somewhat pissed at himself. It had been difficult falling asleep and when he finally had, had dreamed of Poppy Sadler - dreams that had no place in a murder investigation. He ate breakfast with reruns of Carl and Hannah Crane's conversations in his head, trying to make sense of what they'd said, but such was the life of a homicide detective.

Yes, the cops put the bad guys in jail when they could, but usually after days of investigations and interviews and running down leads that went nowhere – always waiting for that one good tip that would blow a case wide open. It was like solving a puzzle and Mike liked puzzles, and with any kind of encouragement, he'd be liking Poppy Sadler, too.

All the way to the precinct, he kept a running scenario of things that could happen to a high school girl at her prom that would be dire enough to bother her husband twenty years later, and none of them were good.

If Sadler had been a jealous man, finding out his wife had a serious lover he'd never known about would piss him off.

If something violent had happened to Helen and she'd never told, then that might be a reason for him to seek justice on her behalf.

What he needed was more research on Helen. If she came up clean, then he'd be convinced this was the wrong angle to pursue, but he had to be sure. If there had been any witnesses to Sadler's murder, they weren't talking, and no one had phoned in any tips that could give them a new lead to follow.

Kenny didn't agree with him, but Mike would bet money the two teenagers they had under arrest were guilty of nothing more than swiping an abandoned car.

The one man who might be able to corroborate that story had suddenly gone to ground. For whatever reason, Prophet Jones had become a scarce commodity. He was hoping the coroner had finished the autopsy on Jessup Sadler and found some evidence they could use.

As he passed The Depot, he saw Vic Payton standing outside in what appeared to be a heated argument with a young woman. Since he was the manager, Mike didn't think he would behave that way with a customer, so he was guessing it was the new fiancé Poppy mentioned.

"Better you than me," Mike muttered, remembering his one fling in college and the girl who'd dumped him when she found out he wanted to be a cop, not a professional athlete.

When he reached the precinct he had his head on straight, ready to face the day.

John Sadler was up early, but Poppy still beat him to the kitchen. One look at her face and he was wondering if she'd ever gone to bed.

"Coffee's made," she said, pointing to the coffee maker. "How many eggs do you want?"

"Two if you fry. Three if you scramble," he said. "I'll do toast."

And just like that, they picked up where they'd left off years ago, sharing the work and the food beneath the same roof. The only thing different now was the absence of their parents.

"Did you get a date set for the funeral?" he asked.

"Yes, tomorrow morning, 10:00 a.m. Gladys and some of the ladies from Mama's Sunday school class will take care of serving the dinner afterward at the church. She and Mel will be by here around 8:30 in the morning to pick up whatever food that was delivered here we can't eat and add it to what will come in at the church."

John eyed her curiously as he slid bread into the toaster slots and turned it to medium brown. One moment she could be so matter-of-fact about the business of dying, and then the next she was crying like she'd been shattered. It never ceased to amaze him how women could departmentalize themselves like this and still function.

"Is there anything you need to do today? Do you have something to wear? If you need a new dress, I've got money."

Poppy's head came up. "You said the word money, which reminds me. I forgot to tell you what happened before you got here last night."

"What?"

Poppy cracked eggs into a bowl with a steady rhythm as she recounted the visit.

"A lawyer named Graham Ring, who represents Caulfield Industries, came by. To make a long story short, he said Mr. Caulfield heard about what happened to Daddy and how Mama had passed the same day. Despite the fact that Daddy had already been fired, he put Daddy's pension through to the family. He said normally the pension would have gone to the widow, but because Mama died the same day as Daddy, he wanted to give it to me. As long as I live in Caulfield, I will receive the full amount of what would have been Daddy's monthly pension."

John reacted just like Poppy guessed.

"That's weird. Dad gets fired, and then the boss gets a conscience. Why does this feel like blood money?"

"That's exactly how I felt, and yet I took it because, damn it, Daddy earned it. Was I wrong?"

"No. Hell no, you weren't wrong. Don't ever think that," John said.

"That's not all. The lawyer said Caulfield is picking up the outstanding debts for Mama's care at Saint Anne's, and he's offered to pay for both funerals, although Dad already had Mama's services paid for."

"That's weird," John muttered. "I mean... the pension I can see, because Dad already had put in more than thirty years with the company, but the other I don't get. It's almost like... like-"

"Hush money?" Poppy said.

"Yeah. Exactly. But why?"

"I don't know, but I didn't refuse it either, so I guess I let him buy us off."

"Don't think like that. He's the one with the guilty conscience or it wouldn't have happened, right?"

"I guess," Poppy said. She whipped the eggs with a fork, poured them into a hot buttered skillet and began to stir. "At any rate, I don't need a dress to wear, but if I did, I would have the money to get it, okay?"

He nodded. The toast popped up. "Butter and jam?"

"In the fridge. Get some milk, too. I don't like my coffee black."

She dished up the eggs as John set the table, and then they sat down to eat.

"Are you still going to talk to the police this morning?" she asked.

John nodded as he chewed. "Which reminds me, I forgot to pack socks. Do you think you could find me a pair of Dad's to wear until I can buy some?"

"You don't need to buy any. He isn't going to be wearing them again."

He smiled. "That sounded just like something Mom would have said."

It still hurt Poppy to think of her in past tense, but it was what it was.

"I guess that's not so hard to understand. I am my mother's daughter."

"And I am my father's son, so I will wear his socks and be glad we both had big feet."

Poppy giggled then seemed embarrassed she'd been frivolous at such a sad time.

"Don't do that," John said.

"Don't do what?" she asked.

"Feel guilty because you laughed. This used to be a happy house. Hopefully one day soon it will be again."

They finished the meal in an awkward silence. Poppy carried her plate to the sink.

"I'm going to get the socks. Just put your stuff in the sink when you're through eating and I'll clean up after you're gone. It will give me something to do."

"Okay," John said, and got up to top off his coffee and put another piece of bread in the toaster.

Poppy walked down the hall with a lighter step. It felt good not to be alone in the house.

She entered her parents' bedroom with socks on her mind, and once again, was met with faint scents of the pine-scented aftershave Jessup Sadler always used and the much fainter smell of her mama's perfume.

She could almost believe one of them was about to step out of the closet and ask her what she wanted, but then she shook her head and headed for the dresser.

She opened the middle drawer in Jessup's dresser, wincing as it squeaked, then remembered there was no longer a need to maintain quiet on her mama's behalf. She dug into the stack of socks, looking for a pair with the right weight that would work with John's boots.

Her dad had always been fussy about his socks. He'd wanted them matched in pairs, then turned one into the other until they looked like little fat tubes. When she was a child, she used to sneak out a pair of his heavy winter socks and use it for a pillow for her doll. Even now, this felt like trespassing, digging into his things like this, but knew she was being silly. He would have given John whatever he needed without thought.

As she thrust her hand into the drawer, feeling for a mid-weight knit, she felt something hard and flat. Curious, she dug down then pulled out a book. It wasn't until she looked inside that she realized it was actually a diary, and according to the flyleaf, had once belonged to her mother when she was a girl.

Poppy started to put it back and then stopped. This didn't make sense. If this was Mama's diary, why was it in Daddy's dresser? It's not where her mother would have kept it. And if her daddy had put it beneath the socks, he'd intended to hide it. Something wasn't right.

Normally, she would have put it right back and been embarrassed she'd found it, but their lives were in limbo with a question hanging over their heads. Suddenly there were secrets in this family that didn't make sense – like someone having a big enough grudge against Jessup Sadler to want him dead. So she took the diary and the socks and met John coming down the hall in his bare feet.

"Here are the socks, and when you need more there's a whole drawer of them in Daddy's dresser."

"Thanks, honey."

"You're welcome."

"Sure you don't want to come with me this morning?" John asked.

"I'm sure," Poppy said, and kept on walking with the diary tucked under her arm.

A short while later John left, but not before making her promise if she needed a ride anywhere to give him a call.

CHAPTER ELEVEN

John was still struggling with his conscience as he drove through the streets of Coal Town. There was no way he would have ignored Poppy's plea to come home, but he couldn't get past the feeling that he'd come back too late. One night he'd gone to bed and the next day half his family was dead. If it wasn't for her, he would officially be an orphan - grown, but nevertheless, alone in the world.

He was angry - sick in the deepest part of his soul angry – for not coming back, but the rage he had for the coward who killed his father was another kind of anger. The kind that could get a man into all kinds of trouble, and he couldn't give in to that rage. His days of indulgent behavior had to be over. He'd walked out on his mother when she needed him most, but he couldn't do the same thing to Poppy, so there would be no heroic gestures to try and avenge his father, or anything else that might get his ass thrown in jail.

He was shocked as he drove past the park where he and Poppy used to play. It looked as derelict as the rest of Coal Town. Only one swing set left, but with all the seats broken and dangling, and a large capped pipe that was once the base for a teeter-totter. Calling it a park now was a joke. The only activity that went on here now was probably drug deals after dark.

It was the thought of drug deals that led his thoughts straight to Aaron Coulter. It had barely been twenty-four hours since he had called him. He was anxious for Aaron to call back, and at the same time, reminding himself not to put too much hope in a man on the wrong side of the law.

Someone honked as he stopped at a stop sign. He turned to look, recognizing the man in the passing car as a member of their church. He waved, and as he accelerated through the intersection, a warning light and a repetitive chime suddenly sounded inside his truck. He glanced down. The gas gauge was sitting on empty, which prompted him to turn right at the next corner. It took him straight to Millwood's Gas and Grocery. As he was pulling up to a pump his cell phone rang.

"Hello?"

"Hey, Johnny. It's Aaron. Where are you?"

"Millwood's getting gas."

"Stay there. I'm on my way."

John's heart skipped a beat. "I'll be waiting," he said, and then the line went dead.

He fueled up while waiting for Aaron to show, then pulled away from the pumps, parked on the north side of the station and rolled down the windows to wait.

Less than five minutes later, a big white Hummer pulled into the station. The driver paused as if to get his bearings then headed straight for John's truck.

The passenger window rolled down. It was Aaron.

"Get in," he yelled.

John locked up his truck and got in, pausing to eye the driver who was checking him out, as well. They gave each other the once-over, noting the changes life and time had done to their faces, and grinned.

Aaron punched John on the shoulder. "Damn, man! Did you grow some more after we got out of school? You are one big son-of-a-bitch."

John rolled with the punch and then held up his hands in a gesture of defeat as he pointed to Aaron's tats.

"Barbed wire and skulls? Seriously, dude?"

Aaron's smiled widened. "Women love 'em, man. You oughta check out a little ink for yourself."

"And mess up this perfect body? No way."

The bullshit broke the ice as they both laughed.

"Got time for a little ride?" Aaron asked.

And just like that, the fun was over. "Am I gonna like the

destination?"

"It's not about the destination. It's about the chit-chat on the way, man," Aaron said.

"Then hell yes, my friend. I've never ridden in a Hummer."

Aaron grinned. "A virgin! My favorite."

John laughed.

And just like that, the years fell away. They didn't talk about anything pertinent until Aaron passed the city limit sign.

"Should I have packed a bag?" John asked.

"We're not going far. I just figured you didn't need to ruin your reputation by being seen with me."

"I don't roll like that," John said.

Aaron's glance was quick but telling. "I know that, or I would have hung up on your ass when you called. So, I won't keep you in suspense. I don't have much to give you. For the most part, everyone, and I mean everyone is pretty shocked by what went down. Your old man was a straight arrow, Johnny. There was no hidden funny business."

It wasn't until Aaron said it that John let go of the fear he'd been hiding - that the cops would discover his dad had been involved in something illegal that got him killed.

"Thanks for that," John said. "But I guess that means no one knows anything."

"I didn't say that," Aaron said. "Depending on who you want to believe, there might be a witness."

The news was a shock. "You're serious? Who? Why haven't they come forward?"

Aaron pulled off onto a mountain overlook and parked.

"Well, that's just it. He's been telling it all over Caulfield, but no one's listening."

John frowned. "What the hell are you talking about?"

"Prophet Jones. Remember him?"

"That crazy old homeless man?"

"I don't think he's crazy, Johnny. He and God have just been having a difference of opinion."

"Don't talk in riddles, Aaron. We're talking about murder, here."

"Yeah, I know, but to understand where I'm coming from, you have to know Prophet's story. Did you know he used to be a preacher who lived by the Word and did everything right? Then his wife and kids are in their car on the way to church one morning and get t-boned by a truck from Caulfield mines. They die and the cops ruled that the driver was not at fault and walked away without a scratch. Prophet lost it. He couldn't believe God would let someone as pure as his wife and kids die, and let the man who killed them go unpunished. He began preaching in his church about the devil in the city. Everything connected to Caulfield Industries was 'the devil'. You've heard him. He did it for so long that it got his ass tossed out of the church. That's when he went postal. They took away his church and pulpit, so he took it to the streets."

John's frown deepened. "Yeah, but you can't believe anything he says. He's crazy, Aaron."

"No, not crazy. He believes to this day that Adam Caulfield bought off the cops so Caulfield Industries wouldn't have a wrongful death suit on their hands. So in his mind, anyone associated with the company is in cahoots with the devil."

"But what does that have to do with Dad's murder?"

"All of Prophet's latest sermons have a single theme, which is that the Devil was on the bridge the night your daddy died. He says he saw him."

"I don't get it," John said.

"You haven't been paying close enough attention. The only devil in Prophet's world is associated with the name Caulfield. And that's not all. I was told that he has something from the crime scene. He calls them the Devil's footprints."

"What the hell?"

Aaron shrugged. "I don't know what he's got, but if it was me and this was my old man who'd been killed, I would follow up on any and everything I heard that might lead me to the killer."

John's head was spinning. "I don't know what to think."

"You don't have to think, man. That's all I got. Just take what I said to the cops and see what happens."

Aaron put the Hummer in gear, made a u-turn on the highway and headed back to the city. They were mostly silent on the drive back but when Aaron pulled up to Millwood's and stopped by John's truck, John extended his hand.

"Thanks, Aaron. I owe you."

Aaron clasped it, felt the calluses and the strength and knew a moment of regret for the path he'd taken, but then it was gone.

"You don't owe me anything, Johnny. We were friends."

John frowned. "We still are, Aaron."

Aaron shook his head. "No, man. It's not in your best interests to be friends with me, but I appreciate what you're saying, okay?"

John's heart was heavy as he got out of the Hummer. By the time he got back in his truck, Aaron was gone.

He didn't know what to make of Aaron's news, but he would tell the cops what he'd learned. It remained to be seen what they would do with it, but time was passing. It was already close to 10:00 a.m. and he had yet to figure out who he needed to see to get permission to view his father's body. His best guess would be the Caulfield P.D., and since he intended to talk to them anyway, there was no time like the present.

The precinct was in something of an uproar. Someone smelled gas in one of the offices, which prompted an evacuation of the entire building, and now the fire department and people from the gas company were on the scene. The parking lot was standing room only and spilling over onto the back lot of the local community center with employees from the building.

Amblin and Duroy were on the other side of Caulfield, unaware of what was happening back at the department. They had been running down another lead on Prophet Jones that had gone nowhere and their frustration level was at an all-time high.

"I don't get it," Kenny muttered, as Mike braked for a red light. "Prophet was always on the streets or in the park. You couldn't go anywhere without seeing him. The crazy bastard was all over the place and now he's suddenly AWOL. What's that all about?"

"I don't know," Mike said, and then heard a spate of frantic traffic on their radio. "Listen to that," Mike said. "Something big is going down at the precinct."

The listened a few moments more, then Kenny slapped the dash in sudden disbelief.

"Holy shit! They're evacuating the building because of a gas leak! We better get back."

Mike ran hot all the way back, with flashing lights and siren screaming to find the building had already been barricaded and the parking lot and adjoining properties full of employees, waiting for the all clear sign.

"That sucks," Kenny said.

"It's still in one piece. It could be worse," Mike said.

They parked about a block away then walked back to find the lieutenant from homicide in street mode, directing traffic along with a couple of uniformed officers.

"Look at that," Kenny said. "He hasn't lost his touch."

Mike was eyeing the building when he heard someone call his name.

"Hey, Detective Amblin."

He turned toward the crowd as a tall, broad-shouldered man stepped out and walked toward him. The man looked familiar, but he couldn't place him.

"Yes, I'm Amblin."

"I'm John Sadler, Jessup Sadler's son."

Poppy's brother. What surprised him was that he recognized him.

"You were a couple of years behind me in school, right?"

John nodded. "Poppy said you're in charge of my dad's case. Can we talk?"

Mike looked around for his partner, but he was on the other side of the street.

"Yeah, sure. Want to walk back down the street to my car so we'll have a little privacy?"

"My truck is right there. Will that do?" John said, pointing to a dark, late model truck only two cars down from where they were standing.

"Absolutely," Mike said.

They walked without talking, waiting until they were inside the truck.

"I'm sorry about what happened to your father," Mike said.

John nodded. "Poppy said you've been really kind to her. I want to thank you for that."

Mike flashed back on her collapse at the bridge. "No problem. She's had a rough two days. It's good you're here now. How can I help you?"

"I have something to ask you, and something to tell you," John said.

"Ask away."

"I want to see my father's body."

John nodded. "That can be done. He's still at the morgue, but I'll take you there myself."

That was easier than expected, which left John with the story about Prophet Jones.

"Now as to what I have to tell you. I have a friend here in Caulfield, a friend who knows the kind of people who don't talk to cops, and I asked him if he'd heard any street talk about who killed my dad."

Mike's interest shifted from Poppy's brother to business. He'd take a lead, no matter where it came from.

"And?"

"He said there's someone in Caulfield who's been talking about the killing ever since it happened, but no one's listening."

Mike frowned. That wasn't possible or they would have heard it. "If someone is talking, they're not talking to us. Who the hell is this witness supposed to be?"

"Prophet Jones."

The skin crawled on the back of Mike's neck. Once again, the old man's name had come up regarding the murder, and from yet a different source. What if this actually backed up the two car thieves' claim?

"Who's your source?" Mike asked.

John shook his head. "It doesn't matter who told me. It's what he said that matters. Do you know Prophet Jones' story?"

"What do you mean?"

"Do you know how he got the way he is?"

Mike frowned. "Yeah, he went crazy after his family died, right?"

"The guy I talked to said Prophet isn't crazy. He's just on a mission to see justice done. As for his family, do you know how they died?" John asked.

"A wreck I think. Why? What does all this have to do with your father's murder?"

"Let me lay it out for you, then you do what you will with the information, okay?"

"I'm listening."

"So here's what I know," John said. "Prophet used to be a preacher. His family was killed by a man who drove a truck for Caulfield Industries. The man was never charged. Basically walked off a free man. Prophet believes Adam Caulfield bought off the cops at the time so that the company would not be sued for wrongful death."

"That's not-"

John held up his hands. "Look, this is all before our time. Just let me tell the story the way it was told to me."

Mike frowned. "I'm still listening. So Prophet blames Caulfield. Then what?"

"Being a preacher, when the law let him down, he took his grievance to the pulpit, calling Caulfield and anyone associated with him, the Devil. That cost him his church and so he took to the streets, still preaching the same message. And, according to my source, Prophet Jones is saying he saw the Devil on the bridge the night Jessup Sadler died. He says the Devil killed him. Prophet took something from the crime scene that he calls the Devil's footprints. I don't know what that means, but it could be evidence. The old man could have seen it happen and took something afterward for proof."

Mike felt blindsided. He'd seen Prophet on the bridge during that rainstorm and even then the old man had been saying the Devil was on the bridge. He'd ignored the rant. But now-

"Are you implying that Justin Caulfield murdered your father?"

"I'm not implying anything, damn it. I'm just telling you what I heard. Besides, Adam Caulfield did not kill Prophet's family, but he blames him for getting the killer off, so, I guess in his mind, anyone associated with the family could be the

Devil."

"Okay, I see what you mean. We'll definitely check out what you've told us. As soon as we can locate the old man, we'll bring him in for questioning."

John sighed. "Thanks."

"It's our job," Mike said. "Listen, let me go tell my partner where we're going, and then I'll take you to the morgue, okay?"

"If you don't mind, I'll just follow you in my truck."

"Yeah, sure. Give me a sec."

John watched him get out and jog back across the street to talk to his partner, then head to the next block to get his car. A few minutes later he drove past and honked. John pulled out into traffic and followed the dark, unmarked car to the city morgue.

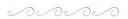

As soon as John left the house Poppy got a fresh cup of coffee and settled into the living room in Jessup's recliner. The chair had taken on the shape of Jessup's body. It was as close to a hug as she would ever have from him again. After a sip of the hot, steamy brew, she opened the diary to the first page.

This diary belongs to Sunny Roberts, age 17.

It hurt Poppy's heart to think of her mother at that age – how happy she must have been with her life stretching out before her. She wondered what that Sunny might have done differently if she'd known her life would be cut so short.

She flipped through page after page of childish entries, most of which dealt with who she was mad at, and who was in trouble, and how stupid a certain teacher was, and why she would never go out with someone named Tommy if her life depended on it.

The phrasing made Poppy smile. She could almost hear her mother's voice just by the way she turned a phrase. There wasn't anything in the diary entries which would have given Jessup a reason to hide the fact that he was reading it. She was beginning to believe that he'd hidden it simply because he was reading something that belonged to his wife without having asked her permission. He'd probably found it looking for articles of her clothing to take to the hospital, just as Poppy had found it while looking for socks for John.

Still, Poppy wasn't going to stop reading. This was like getting to know a completely different side of her mother and she intended to treasure it along with the memories she would keep. Poppy read some more, noting the passing of time by the dates of the entries. It was, after all, her senior year – a remarkable time in any girl's life. Then just after school resumed from Christmas break, the tone of Sunny's entries began to change.

Monday, January 4th.

He's been watching me for days. I run into him everywhere I go, like he's making that happen. Oh I wish he would say something. Anything. Even just hello.

Tuesday, January 5th.

It happened! It happened! He stopped me in the hall at school and said hi. I thought I would die. Everyone was looking at him. I know what they were thinking. What's a cool dude from the north side of Caulfield doing talking to a nobody from Coal Town?

Thursday, January 7th.

He caught me after school to ask if I was going to the basketball game. When I said yes, he said he'd see me there.

Friday, January 8th.

It's late. I don't want Mom to catch me still up and writing. I can't tell anyone what happened tonight without getting both of us in trouble, so I'm writing it here. That's almost like telling my best friend, only I can't tell Gladys because she can't keep a secret. It finally happened. HE KISSED ME!!

Poppy laid the diary in her lap and leaned back. She could almost feel the excitement in the words. This was Sunny before she was anyone's wife or mother - just a teenage girl in high school on the verge of a great adventure. And in an odd way, it seemed like a story about someone else – someone she didn't know. She didn't remember her mother ever being this light-hearted and giddy. She couldn't help but wonder what had happened between her and this fellow that had ended the young love.

Outside, a car sped past on the street in front of the house, which broke her concentration. When she realized how much time had passed, she was surprised, but had no need to panic. Thanks to the generosity of their neighbors, there was already plenty of food prepared. She wouldn't have to cook for a week.

After John got home, she wanted to go back to the funeral home and see her mother again. The funeral was tomorrow. It was going to take all the strength she had to get through it.

She took the diary with her when she went into the kitchen to get something for lunch, and read it while she ate. The thing between Sunny and her secret boyfriend seemed to be heating up. Poppy could almost guess what the next big revelation would be and wondered how she would feel when she read it. She and her mama had never talked about her first time to have sex, although Mama had drilled it into Poppy's head plenty of times about the dangers of having sex and then losing regard for your own reputation. Poppy had called it the 'once you lose it, you begin to abuse it' speech. She knew it by heart, but now she was wondering if something had happened to Sunny that had turned Helen into a guard dog for her own child.

By the time Poppy finished eating, she'd read the diary posts all the way through spring and according to the diary, it was little less than two months to graduation.

April 3rd.

I snuck out last night after everyone else was asleep and met him at the bridge. We drove out of town and up into the mountains to a place where we could be alone. We have talked about this for weeks and he keeps telling me I have to be sure before we do it. (That's how I know he loves me). I am sure. I'm still a virgin, but I want him to be my first.

April 4th.

Last night I became a woman. It wasn't exactly how I

thought it would be. The first time it hurt and I cried. He cried, too, telling me he was sorry, that he didn't mean for it to happen. But then we did it again and I felt my body take flight. This is the most beautiful thing that can happen between two people who love each other.

Poppy didn't know until she stopped reading that she'd been crying. The joy in that single entry alone was a physical burn. For the rest of her life she would remember those words. *I felt my body take flight.*

She put the diary aside and walked away, needing space to remember that this was something that had happened over twenty years ago – something that Sunny had experienced and Helen had filed away with the rest of childhood's memories.

The phone rang as she was getting herself a cold soda and noticed it was Johnny.

"Hey, you."

"Hey honey, are you doing okay?"

"Yes, I'm fine. When are you coming home?"

"In about an hour or so. I'm on my way to the morgue then I'm going to see Mom. When I get home I'll fill you in on what's going on. Do you want to go to the funeral home with me?"

"No, I think you need to go by yourself the first time, Johnny. You can take me back tonight, okay?"

"Sure I will, Poppy. I told you. You're not alone in this anymore. Do we need anything at home?"

"No."

"Okay, see you later."

Poppy hung up, then grabbed her cold soda and carried it out onto the back porch with the diary. Even though the day was a little chilly, the sun was warm on her face. She sat down in the porch swing and then pushed off with the toe of her shoe before she took a drink.

This was her favorite place – the place where she'd come as a child to do all her thinking. It was as good a place as any to absorb what she'd been reading and remember that, while it was new to her, it was all in the past. Then she picked up the diary and once more, fell into Sunny Roberts' world.

April 12th.

It's almost time for Senior Prom. Three boys have asked me to go, but I'm going solo. He said he wanted to take me but we both knew what that would cause. I didn't want to get him in trouble with his family. They wouldn't like him dating someone from Coal Town. But if we both go solo, then it won't matter who's dancing with who during prom.

April 14th.

The prom was supposed to be fun. It was the worst night of my life. His family found out about me and they're sending him away after graduation. He didn't fight for me. They told him what to do and he just did it. He's not the man I wanted him to be – just a figment of my imagination. I wish I was dead.

May 22nd.

I'm pregnant.

At this point, Poppy gasped. The feeling in her chest was the same desperate, out-of-control feeling she'd had when she'd gotten the call from the hospital that her mama had died.

May 25th.

Daddy knows. He's going to see the family and make them pay for everything. I told him if he did I would jump off the bridge into the Little Man and drown myself. He reminded me I wouldn't be just killing myself. I would be killing my child.

Poppy's hands were shaking. She looked back at the entry date on the diary and flipped through the pages only to realize there were no more entries.

She stood abruptly and staggered into the house. The diary fell from her arms as she headed into the bathroom. Once there, she paused to look at herself in the mirror. The woman she saw had become a stranger. The dark eyes were wide with shock. The skin on her face was the color of ash. Not pale, but gray, like she was already dead.

And that's exactly how Poppy felt. Mama and Daddy weren't the only ones who had died this week. Poppy Sadler, daughter of Helen and Jessup Sadler, had just suffered an abrupt and unexpected death on the back porch of her home.

Cause of death – ceased to exist.

She glared at the woman in the mirror as if she'd just committed some unforgiveable sin, then stepped back and covered her face. The blood was racing through her body in a dizzying rush. The need to vomit was overwhelming, but nothing would come up. The betrayal of what she'd just read was overwhelming. She'd lost her anchor to her world.

Disbelief was swiftly followed by panic, then rage as she grabbed the closest object, which happened to be her hair dryer, and threw it at the mirror. It shattered, splintering her reflection. Now she was as broken on the outside as she felt on the inside.

Poppy staggered backward, her head still spinning. So, Sunny Roberts got pregnant and had herself a baby girl. This definitely meant Jessup Sadler was not her real father. She knew this because Jessup was years older than Helen. He'd been out of school, married, become a father, and widowed before she even graduated. Sunny wouldn't have been seeing him in the halls at school and he certainly hadn't come from the north side of Caulfield. Jessup was a native of Coal Town, just like her.

Poppy's heart was racing. Had Daddy known?

Something told her he had not known before, but he found out, or he wouldn't have hidden this diary in his sock drawer.

In that moment, Poppy understood her mother's words. *I want to die.* Everything was coming undone and she couldn't do this again on her own.

"Johnny... I need Johnny."

She staggered down the hall, back into the living room where she picked up the diary. She dropped onto the sofa then reached for the phone. Twice she tried to dial the number but dropped the receiver both times before the call could go through. By the time she was successful, she was also in tears.

It began to ring.

The room was spinning.

She put her head between her knees to keep from passing out.

One ring, then the second, then *thank you God* her brother's voice.

"Hello, Poppy?"

Her fingers tightened around the receiver. "Johnny, I need you." She wanted to scream, but it hurt too much to breathe.

Panic was in his voice now. "Poppy? What's wrong? What's happening, honey?"

"Come home. Just come home."

The diary fell out of her hands. She dropped the phone as the room began to spin and then all of a sudden, her world turned black.

CHAPTER TWELVE

The medical examiner's office was in a gray two-story building circa 1920. With the pair of gargoyles perched on either end of the building, it looked more like something out of a horror film than it did a municipal building, but certainly suited the location of a morgue.

John was filled with a huge sense of dread as he followed Mike Amblin into the building. He didn't want to see his father like this, but he had to. No more hiding from the truth.

Amblin flashed his badge as they passed a security guard then crossed the lobby toward a bank of elevators. When they got in and started down, John's nerves began to fire.

"Why are morgues always in the basement of a building?"

"It probably has to do with the availability of space and the amount of refrigeration needed," Mike said.

It made sense, but didn't make John feel any better. It felt like a trip down to hell and when the elevator doors finally opened, he shuddered.

The cold day in hell had just arrived.

"You okay?" Mike asked.

"Let's get this over with."

"This way," Mike said, leading him through a wide hallway to the double doors at the far end. "I called ahead to let them know we're coming."

"Thanks again for helping me through this," John said.

Mike stopped short of the doors. "It's part of the job. Are you ready?"

John nodded then straightened his shoulders as he followed

Amblin into a long, cold room with gray floors and gray walls. He shuddered again. Stainless steel tables were lined up in a row like candles on a birthday cake. The lab equipment looked impressive – far beyond the capabilities of a man who drove trucks for a living. But it was the scents of formaldehyde and an overpowering smell of commercial cleanser that was the slap in the face he needed to focus.

When a tiny bald-headed man slid off a high stool, separating himself from the microscope he'd been using, John stopped. Moments later, Mike introduced them.

"Doctor Wheeden, this is John Sadler."

"Yes, yes, Detective. Nice to meet you, Mr. Sadler. I have the body ready," then he gave John a nervous glance. "Sorry, it's your father. I'm sorry. I don't do well with the living. At any rate, he's here."

The doctor scurried to the back wall to the bank of drawers where the bodies were kept and opened door number six. The tray rolled out quietly and efficiently with a sheet-covered body on the rack.

It was offensive to John that his father had been filed like a sheaf of papers, then shifted the anger to where it belonged – at the foot of the man who'd put him here and not those who were tending his murder case.

Mike lifted the sheet off of Jessup Sadler's face and folded it back across the broad expanse of his chest.

"When you're done, we'll be waiting outside the doors."

The sight of his father's face was like a fist to the gut. How could a big, vital man like Jessup Sadler be reduced to a mound of cold gray flesh? He kept staring at the body and trying to find his father, but he wasn't there.

His hands were shaking, touching first his father's face, then his shoulder, delaying the inevitable. Finally, he reached for the sheet and lifted it all the way up, needing to see the extent of the wounds - and they were obvious.

Jessup had been shot twice in the belly and once in the leg. The moment John saw the location of the wounds, he felt sick.

God damn it. Gut shot. He'd bet a year of his life that his father was still alive when he'd hit the water.

John's voice was shaking, both in shock and rage. "Who did

this Dad? Rise up like Lazarus and talk to me."

But there would be no miracles in this morgue - just an acceptance of the cold hard fact that his father was dead.

Tears welled. "I'm sorry. We'll make it right, no matter how long it takes."

He pulled the sheet back over the body, pausing to smooth down a wild hair in Jessup's eyebrow before he let it settle over his father's head and face.

Mike and the M.E. were only steps away as he exited. He went straight for Wheeden.

"Doc, I have a question. Was my father still alive when he hit the water?"

Wheeden answered in a calm, matter of fact manner. "There was water in his lungs, which indicated he was still breathing."

John's fingers curled into fists. "Son-of-a-bitch."

The M.E. hastened to add. "His wounds were mortal, though. He would not have survived them, regardless."

John's voice was shaking. "That's not why I asked. My father was deathly afraid of water. He couldn't swim. So when he hit the water, he knew exactly what was going to happen, regardless of the wounds."

It was a shocking revelation that only added another layer of tragedy to the murder, but before anyone could comment, John's cell phone began to ring.

He glanced at Caller ID as he answered.

"Hello Poppy."

"Johnny, I need you."

He could hear her crying. "Poppy! What's wrong? What's happening, honey?"

"Come home. Just come home."

When the line went dead, he panicked. "I've got to go. Something's wrong at home."

Immediately, Mike Amblin moved into cop mode. He didn't like to think she might be in trouble again, but the possibility existed. "What's happening?"

"I don't know, but I'm going to find out."

"I'm going with you," Mike said, and ran to catch up. "Someone murdered your father and until we know who it was, we have no way of knowing how far-reaching the reason can be."

That scared John even more. By the time they cleared the building, they were both running.

"Follow me. I'll get us there fast," Mike said.

John jumped into his truck.

As soon as Mike started up his car, he hit the lights and siren.

John was on his bumper all the way through Caulfield. He kept imagining one bad scenario after another, and was in a full-blown panic by the time they crossed the bridge over the Little Man.

Mike notified Kenny what was happening on the way over. When they drove up, he was relieved there no other cars in front of the house. The fact that the front door was not standing ajar was also a good sign, but not enough to stop the adrenaline rush as he slammed the brakes on his car and slid to a halt in front of the house. Her brother was right behind him.

John had the key in his hand, shouting Poppy's name as he ran. When they entered, they saw Poppy's body lying on the floor.

John panicked. "Poppy! Poppy! Can you hear me, honey?"

"I'll get a wet cloth," Mike said as John lifted her onto the sofa.

"The bathroom is down-"

"I know where it is," Mike said, and bolted down the hall.

It occurred to John then that there might be more to Poppy's statement about the cop being kind to her than he'd imagined, then forgot about it when she moaned. She was coming to.

"Poppy? Honey... it's me, Johnny. I'm here, sister. I'm here."

Mike came back carrying a cold wet washcloth. "The bathroom mirror is broken," he said, and handed the cloth to John.

"What the hell?"

Mike shrugged.

She moaned again, shifting John's focus. "So you know

where the bathroom is."

Mike realized what his familiarity with the place implied, but he was defensive enough on Poppy's behalf to answer in his cop voice, which was just shy of pissed.

"The first time I met your sister was when my partner and I came to notify her of your father's death. She fainted. The second time I was here was after I found her on the bridge over the Little Man. She'd tried to walk home in the rain from The Depot and collapsed. She was so goddamned cold she couldn't feel her feet. The third time I was here was to fingerprint her as a means of print elimination after we located your family car. This makes the fourth time. To my regret, all the visits have been a series of tragedies. Put the cloth on her forehead."

John blinked. Message received. He did as he was told. Within moments, she began coming around.

Poppy jerked. Something wet was on her face.

"It's okay, honey. It's me, Johnny."

Panic subsided when she heard his voice, then she tried to sit up.

"What happened?"

John sighed. "You tell me, sister. You called me crying and told me to come home."

Everything came flooding back. "Oh my God, you won't believe-" She realized they were not alone. "Why is he here?"

"We were together at the morgue," John said. "He got me here faster."

"Did someone hurt you?" Mike asked.

Poppy's gaze swept across the detective's face as she realized why he'd come. "Ever my knight in shining armor, aren't you?" Then she shook her head slowly. "Not like you mean."

Poppy tugged at John's hand, pulling him down beside her. "I found Mama's diary."

Mike held up a hand. "Whoa. I think this is my cue to leave you two alone to talk."

"No. Wait," Poppy said. "It may have nothing to do with

Daddy's death, but secrets can rot a family from the inside out, especially one like this. Please stay."

Mike sat.

John saw the book on the floor near his feet and picked it up.

"Is this it?"

Poppy nodded.

"So what's the big secret?" he asked, flipping idly through the pages.

Poppy felt sick. Once these words were said aloud, there would be no going back.

"The diary was written during Mama's senior year in high school. I didn't think it amounted to much until I got to the entries she wrote after Christmas break. Without going into a lot of repetitive detail, the bottom line is that Mama had a boyfriend from the north side of Caulfield. They hid their relationship, and you know why. No one from the north side dates anyone from Coal Town."

"That's for sure," John said.

"So according to the diary, they got serious. They were having sex and she was head over heels in love with him, then the night of the senior prom he dumped her. A few weeks later she finds out she's pregnant, but by then he's off to college and out of the picture. The last entry was about her father going to demand the boy's family pay for her expenses and she was threatening to jump off the bridge over the Little Man if he did."

John put his arm around Poppy and hugged her. "Honey, that's tough to hear, but it's not the end of the world."

Poppy glanced at Mike. There was sympathy in his gaze, but something more that gave her the guts to continue.

"Actually, it's the end of mine."

"What the hell are you talking about?" John asked.

"I was born seven months after that entry."

John jerked as if she'd just slapped him. "Oh my God. Oh honey." Then he reached for her, pulling her close. "It doesn't matter. Not a damn bit of it. You're still you and I'm still me. We're all that's left of our family and nothing is going to change that."

Mike frowned. "I'm slow. Help me, here."

Poppy leaned back in her brother's arms. It was somewhat easier to say leaning on someone else's strength.

"Daddy was years older than Mama. When he and Mama married, he was a widower and his son, my brother Johnny, was eight. She did not go to school with him. He was born and raised in Coal Town. He could not, in any way, be my father. I think he came across Mama's diary while looking for something she probably wanted him to bring to the hospital, read it and hid it. I found it beneath his socks in his dresser. I don't know if this has anything to do with what happened to him, but I won't hold back anything that might find his killer."

Mike's thoughts were spinning, bouncing from the interview with Carl and Hannah Crane telling him Jessup had been asking about the prom, to the video they'd seen of Jessup entering and leaving the hospital the night that he died. He'd looked like hell and they'd attributed it to his wife's condition, but what if it was more? What if he confronted her and knowing she was on her deathbed, she told him the truth.

"Damn. Just like that, another piece of the puzzle falls in place," he said.

John frowned. "What?"

"We know your father was asking some of your mother's friends if they'd known about anything specific happening to her the night of her senior prom. I'm curious. Did she ever identify the boyfriend in the diary?"

Poppy's heart began to pound. "When she wrote about him, it was always he and him, never a name."

Mike nodded. "And Jessup probably wanted to know who dumped her."

John was stunned. "Son-of-a-bitch! Are you saying my father was murdered over something that happened before Poppy was even born?"

"I'm not saying anything definitive, but people have killed for less. I need the name of the boy who dumped her. If you find anything more, call me."

Moments later he was gone.

John locked the door behind him then looked at his sister. To hell with blood. In his mind they were as related as two people could be, but the dejection on her face was stark.

"Poppy. Look at me. You're my sister. I don't ever want to hear you say you're not."

She shook her head. "I keep thinking about what Daddy must have thought when he read that. How hurt he must have been. How betrayed he must have felt. I wonder if he and Mama fought about it?"

"We'll never know," John said. "Now, what can I do?"

"You can't fix this."

"You're not listening. There's nothing to fix. So what if Dad wasn't your birth father? He was the only father you had, just like Mom was the only mother I had and she wasn't mine. We're family forever, regardless of blood."

"You aren't seeing it from my standpoint. I don't know who I am anymore. The Poppy Sadler I knew doesn't exist and I have no information to replace her."

John sat back down beside her and gave her a hug. "I'm sorry, honey. I didn't think. So for the moment we have questions. Time will take care of that, right?"

"I guess, but do you think this could have anything to do with Daddy's murder?"

"I don't know but that's not for us to solve. That's Detective Amblin's job. We have our own set of things to tend to, including Mom's funeral tomorrow."

She nodded. "You're right. Did you get a chance to go to the funeral home?"

John shook his head. "No, but-"

"Then go, Johnny."

"Not unless you come with me."

She sighed. "If I come, will that make you feel uncomfortable?"

He frowned. "Hell no. I have to apologize to her and I don't care who hears."

"I need to change."

"Then do it," John said.

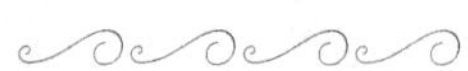

Mike was driving over the bridge when he saw a dark figure

on the far end go scurrying off the walkway and disappear below. Sunlight reflected on the hood of his car and into his eyes, momentarily blinding him. When he looked again, the man was gone, but he was almost certain it was Prophet Jones. If it hadn't been for the traffic, he would have hit the brakes and followed up to see for sure. He filed the site away for future investigation and kept driving to the precinct. The dispatcher had assured him the gas leak had been dealt with which meant they were back in business. He needed to fill his partner in on what he'd learned. He made the call as he drove, then waited for Kenny to pick up.

Kenny answered on third ring.

"Homicide. Duroy."

"Kenny, it's me. I have some interesting information that may or may not play into Sadler's murder. Is Harmon there?"

"Yeah, what do you need?"

"Have him get a list of graduating seniors the year Helen Roberts graduated. She was Jessup Sadler's wife. Went by the nickname, Sunny. I think it will be the class of 1991, but not sure. From that list I need the names of all the boys who lived on the north side of the river. No Coal Towners, okay?"

"Yeah, okay. Got it. Anything else?"

"Meet me out front. We're going to the hospital."

"What the hell is happening?"

"I'll fill you in on the way."

Justin went through the workday on automatic pilot. He'd answered questions, signed contracts, dealt with a strike threat at one of their companies in upstate New York, and managed to check on Callie without interacting with his mother, who had stayed home sick. He didn't know what to say to her. Something along the lines of, 'I'm still pissed at you for ignoring my feelings twenty years ago, but even angrier with myself for knuckling under,' seemed futile. It was twenty years too late to change his mind.

But life went on – or at least his did.

Sunny's was damn sure over and his daughter's future was

shaky.

Today thoroughly sucked and he was tired dealing with it. He buzzed his secretary.

"Frances, I'm through for the day and heading to the hospital. You know how to reach me if the need arises."

"Yes sir. Give my best to your daughter."

"Thank you, I will."

Moments later he was on his way down to the parking lot.

Callie Caulfield was in her hospital room, standing at the window overlooking the parking lot and wishing there was a way to change the last twelve months of her life.

The friends she'd had then were all weird when she talked to them now – like what she had might be catching, even though she kept telling them she was getting well. They were growing up and moving on – changing best friends and boyfriends as often as they changed their clothes, while she was caught in this time warp where nothing changed but the sheets on her bed.

Very little happened to her between the times when she wasn't hooked up to dialysis. Even though she knew its purpose, on those days she was hooked up, she imagined the machine as her own personal vampire, sucking all the fluids out of her body and leaving behind nothing but a shell of her former self.

It wasn't fair that this was happening to her and she was sick and tired of pretending it was. Nana kept telling her to pray and all would be well. Callie didn't argue, but she didn't believe it anymore. She'd been praying for a year and look what happened. In a really secret part of her head, she actually wished that the doctors had just let her die. Then she'd be with her mother and not living like some awful zombie, waiting for someone to die so she could live.

Something crashed out in the hall. She turned toward the sound, half-expecting someone to come in, but the door stayed shut and the noise was short-lived.

Nana hadn't come to see her today. She'd called with

regrets, telling her that she wasn't feeling well and wasn't allowed to visit for fear she'd bring her germs to Callie. Callie had told her it was okay and to get well soon. What else could she say? But it wasn't okay. She didn't have anyone to play cards with and nothing to do, and television without cable sucked eggs.

Frustrated and feeling extremely sorry for herself, Callie pushed away from the window and went to find her robe and house shoes. Even if she couldn't leave this floor, at least they were finally allowing her to leave her room.

Kenny Duroy was waiting when Mike drove up.

"What the hell's going on?" he asked, as he slid into the passenger seat.

"Poppy Sadler found an old diary that belonged to her mother when she was in high school. Remember when we interviewed the Cranes? The wife told us Sadler had asked if they knew anything about something happening to Helen on the night of her senior prom?"

"Yeah? So the diary tells all?"

"And then some," Mike said. "Helen, who went by Sunny back then, had a boyfriend from the north side of town. They got serious. Then he breaks up with her the night of the prom and a few weeks later, after he's off to college, she finds out she's pregnant."

"So what's that-"

"Jessup Sadler did not go to school with Sunny, remember? That's why he was asking the Cranes about it. So the kid Sunny was pregnant with was Poppy, and Jessup Sadler was not the father. He obviously figured it all out and wanted answers, only his wife was dying."

"Holy shit."

"Pretty much," Mike said.

"How's the daughter taking it?"

"Not good, that's for damn sure."

"So why are we going to the hospital?"

"I got to thinking about that video from the hospital that we watched the night Sadler died. Remember how dejected he looked? We were chalking it up to his wife's condition. What if he was going to confront her about what he'd learned? What if she told him what he wanted to know?"

A slow grin slid across Kenny's face. "You know, you just might turn into a half-ass detective before I retire after all."

Mike shrugged. "I just thought there might be a chance they'd had some kind of argument and one of the nurses on duty could have overheard something we can use."

Kenny rubbed his hands together. "I love it when a plan comes together."

"Don't jinx it. Nothing is together yet," Mike said. "Oh, and one other thing, I think I saw Prophet Jones on the bridge but then he ducked off and headed down toward the river. If it was him, he might have a hidey-hole somewhere underneath."

"That would explain how he'd come to witness Sadler's murder, if that really happened," Kenny said.

"Right," Mike said, and then they were at the hospital.

He pulled into the hospital parking lot. Once inside they checked the information desk for the critical care floor and started across the lobby.

"Hey, that's Justin Caulfield," Kenny said, pointing to the man waiting at the elevators.

Mike nodded. "I heard his kid is sick with something serious."

They reached the elevators just as the doors opened and followed Caulfield inside.

"Good afternoon, Mr. Caulfield," Kenny said, as he pressed the button for the third floor. "What floor do you need?"

"Good afternoon, gentlemen. Three please."

"Ah. We're all going the same direction then," he said.

"You two are with the police department, right?" Justin asked.

"Yes sir."

"I hope there's not a problem on three. That's the floor where my daughter is being cared for."

"No sir, nothing like that," Kenny said. "We're just following up on a case. How's your daughter doing?"

Justin actually smiled. "Thank you for asking. She's

beginning to heal from the disease that nearly killed her, but she suffered renal failure. She'll need a kidney transplant before she's back to her normal self, and we're hopeful that will come soon."

"We're glad to hear she's on the mend," Kenny said.

"Absolutely," Mike added.

The doors opened.

"Have a good afternoon," Justin said, and turned left as the detectives went right toward the nurses' station.

CHAPTER THIRTEEN

As Mike and Kenny reached the nurses' station, the duty nurse looked up. Mike pulled his badge.

"I'm Detective Amblin and this is my partner, Detective Duroy. I'd like to speak to the nurse in charge."

The short thirty-something red-head with lavender scrubs and a serious case of sunburn got up from her chair.

"That would be me, Victoria Glenn. How can I help you?"

"Helen Sadler was on this floor, right?"

"Yes, she was."

"We need to talk to the nurses who were on duty the last night she was alive."

She frowned. "Why? Has someone complained about her care?"

"No, ma'am. This is in reference to her husband's murder."

Her expression shifted from reticence to regret. "Ah. That was such a shock, and of course a horrible tragedy for the family. He was certainly a devoted man. I don't think he missed a night coming to see her."

"I believe she passed away early in the morning, correct?"

"Yes, she did."

"I need the names of the nurses who worked that last night shift before her passing."

"That was the night we had that really bad storm, right?"

"Yes, ma'am."

"We had some nurses unable to get here due to flooded roads, so a few of us pulled double shifts. Give me a few minutes and I can find out who worked that night. There may even be a couple of them here."

"Thanks," Mike said. As he waited, a frail blonde teenager in a pink robe and house shoes came walking down the hall.

She caught Mike's eye and smiled.

He smiled back. "How's it going?"

"Good, but even better when I get a new kidney. Got one you're not using?" And then she giggled.

It dawned on him this must be Caulfield's daughter. Before he could answer, he saw Caulfield come around the corner at the far end of the hall. The expression on his face was anxious until he spied the girl.

Mike pointed. "I think someone's looking for you."

She made a face. "Uh-oh, caught again. That's Daddy. Ah well, back to jail I go."

The giggle was gone, as was the twinkle in her eye. Even her shoulders slumped as she began to retrace her steps. As soon as Caulfield reached her, he slid an arm around her waist to steady her and they disappeared around the corner.

"That's tough, a young kid like her being that sick," Kenny said.

Mike nodded.

Moments later the head nurse was back with two other nurses at her heels.

"This is the list of names you wanted as well as two of my nurses who were on duty that night. The blonde is Erin Morgan. The brunette is Loretta Fisher."

"Is there someplace private where we could talk for a bit?" Mike asked.

She pointed to the small office behind the desk. "You can use my office. Just close the door and you'll have all the privacy you need."

"Thanks," Mike said as he nodded at the two nurses. "We won't be long."

The women led the way into the office. As soon as they were all inside, Mike shut the door.

"I'm Detective Amblin. This is my partner, Detective Duroy. Did Nurse Glenn tell you why we're here?"

"You wanted to talk to nurses who were on duty for Mrs. Sadler's last night. We were both here."

"Our questions are regarding Mrs. Sadler's husband. Did either of you see him come to visit her that night?"

They both nodded as Loretta spoke. "He always came about the same time every night. Probably after he got off work and ate. He worked at one of the Caulfield mines."

"I need you to think back carefully. Did you hear or see anything unusual happen between them that night?"

"What do you mean?" Erin asked.

Mike didn't want to lead them into an answer, but it was obvious his questioning wasn't specific enough.

"Anything that was out of the ordinary for them, like, did you happen to overhear an argument, or did one or both of them act upset?"

Loretta shook her head. "No sir."

Erin hesitated before she answered. "No, I didn't either."

Mike caught the look on her face. "Please. This is important. You're not telling anything out of turn. You're not breaking any code of secrecy. We're trying to find out who murdered her husband. If you know anything, no matter how unimportant you think it might be, please tell us."

Erin glanced at her friend and then back at Mike. "I didn't hear it personally, but I overheard Susan talking about it on break that night."

"Who's Susan and talking about what?" he asked.

"Susan Ellison. She's an LPN who pulled a double that night. This is her day off."

Mike checked the list. The name and contact info was on it. "Okay, exactly what was Susan talking about?"

"When she went into the room with Mrs. Sadler's meds she walked in on an argument. She said Mr. Sadler was crying and asking her the same question over and over. What's his name? What's his name? She said Helen was crying, too. Susan excused herself, gave Helen the meds and left."

"I'll be damned," Kenny muttered.

"Did either of you happen to see Mr. Sadler leave?"

"I did, but he didn't say anything. He just left her room as usual then about halfway down the hall he started to run, like he wanted to catch the elevator before the doors shut, but he didn't make it. He had to wait for the next one."

Mike glanced at Kenny and guessed they were both remembering the same thing – watching Jessup Sadler take off out of the parking lot like his tail was on fire.

He took a card out of his pocket. "Thank you, ladies. If either of you remember anything else, give me a call."

They left the office.

Victoria Glenn eyed them curiously, as if expecting them to share what they'd learned.

"Thank you for your help," Mike said, and then they were gone, leaving Glenn with her curiosity still intact.

Justin's heartbeat was finally settling as he got Callie back into her room. It had been unnerving to walk in and find the room empty, and he could tell she was irked that he'd gone looking for her as if she was a runaway toddler. He'd seen that same expression a thousand times on her face when she was little and hadn't gotten her way.

"It's great to see you up and walking around. I just don't want you to overdo it," he said.

"I only made one loop around the floor before you showed up. That's not overdoing it," she said, as she crawled up into bed.

He ignored the comment by throwing out a suggestion he knew she would like.

"Want to play some cards?"

Her eyes brightened. "Uno! I love Uno." She got the deck of cards out of the table beside her bed. "You shuffle, Daddy. My hands are too shaky."

He tweaked the end of her nose. "Oh yeah, I'll shuffle. I'll put the Caulfield shuffle on this deck."

Callie giggled.

Justin smiled at the delight on her face. It had been too long since either one of them had anything to rejoice about. As he began to shuffle, Callie plumped her pillows and settled cross-legged on the bed with the tray-table between them.

"How's Nana feeling?" Callie asked, as Justin continued to shuffle.

"I don't know. I haven't talked to her today."

Callie frowned. "You should call and check on her. It will hurt her feelings if you don't."

"I was afraid I might wake her up if I called. I'll be home later and check on her then."

"What if she needs to see a doctor?" Callie asked.

Justin began to deal. "Mr. Newton is there. He'll look after her just fine. If she thinks she needs a doctor, he'll get her there."

"Oh right, I forgot about him." Callie began smiling as she sorted through her cards.

"What are you grinning about?" Justin teased. "Don't tell me I gave you good cards already?"

She giggled again and wiggled her eyebrows at him.

Justin laughed out loud.

Callie played her first card and then gleefully whooped when Justin had to draw from the deck right off the bat.

"You are such a card shark," Justin said, as he had to draw twice more before he could play.

She pursed her lips. "I play like a Caulfield, don't I, Daddy?"

Justin paused. "How does a Caulfield play?"

"Nana says Caulfields' always play to win, no matter what it takes to make it happen."

Justin felt like he'd just been slapped. It took all his control not to get angry.

"Well, Nana's not one hundred percent right. We play to win, but not at any cost. We play fairly and obey the rules, right?"

Suddenly Callie was serious. "Yes, we do. Always. I don't want to make God mad. He might not find me a new kidney."

Justin blinked. What the fuck had his mother been teaching his child while she'd been 'helping out'?

"Honey. God isn't punishing you. And your kidney transplant does not hinge on how good God thinks you are. I don't know where you got that, but that's a crock of shit."

Callie giggled. "Daddy. You said a bad word."

Justin sighed. "Yes, I did, and I may say a few more before the night is over if you wind up beating me again at this blasted game."

The moment passed as the game continued, but Justin had a whole other set of issues to discuss with his mother besides her health when he got home.

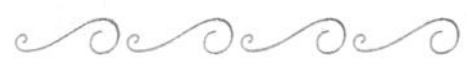

Poppy didn't have much to say on the way to the funeral home and John wasn't in the mood to strike up a conversation. He was sick to his stomach just thinking about the task ahead. By the time they pulled into the parking lot he was shaking.

"Johnny?"

He killed the engine. "Yeah?"

"She wasn't mad at you. Ever."

"Well, she should have been," he said, then glanced at her expression and realized a new level of despair had been added to Poppy's situation. "Are you okay? I mean, after what you found out, are you mad at her?"

"I'm numb, Johnny. I don't know how I feel. Are you ready?"

"Yeah."

They walked hand in hand up the walk and into the funeral home.

Truman Epperson greeted them as they came inside.

"Good afternoon, Poppy. Hello John, I'm very sorry for your loss."

"Thank you," John said. "We'd like some alone time with Mom. Is anybody in there?"

"No. There's no one in the viewing room with your mother at this time and I'll close the door and make sure you're undisturbed until you're ready to leave."

"Thank you," John said.

He felt a rush of anxiety as Poppy's grip tightened. This whole thing was a nightmare, but they would get through it together. As soon as they entered the viewing room, Truman promptly closed the door behind them.

Poppy gasped. The room was still cold, but Helen's casket was no longer the only thing in the room. It was awash in flowers. John's gaze went straight to the casket at the end of the room, but she couldn't quit looking at the array of floral tributes. Yesterday the shelves had been empty. Now there wasn't a space to be had and some were sitting on the floors and against the walls.

"Go on," she said, urging John forward.

He moved toward the casket. Poppy followed a few steps behind. She waited, expecting him to speak, but his eyes were closed and his face was streaked with tears.

"Johnny, just say what's in your heart."

He reached into the casket, touching her cheek with the back of his finger then stifled a shudder, unprepared for the absence of life.

"God Mom, I'm sorry. I'm so sorry I didn't come back when you were still here. You were the best mother a kid could have and when you needed me most, I wasn't there for you. If I could, I would do everything different, but I can't. I know you and Dad are together. It's the only thing that makes this disaster bearable. I'll take care of Poppy and I'll make sure the police don't quit until we find out who killed Dad. I promise."

Poppy laid her cheek against his shoulder. "She looks pretty, doesn't she, Johnny?"

Tears were streaming down his face, but his heart was lighter, the way it used to feel when he was a boy and he'd finally confessed to some misdeed.

"Yes, she does. The dress is her favorite color. Did you do that?"

Poppy nodded.

"You're the best," he said softly.

Poppy pulled a handful of tissues from the box on the table and put them in his hand. He wiped his eyes and blew his nose and then turned around and hugged her in what felt like desperation. It took a few moments for them to gather themselves, and when they did, she began pointing out the flowers.

"When I was here yesterday, there weren't any flowers. Now look. Mama would be so touched to know how many people cared about her like this."

"Can you tell who they're from?" he asked.

"Usually the cards are pinned on the bows somewhere, or

somewhere within the leaves." She began to search, and to her surprise, only a few had cards. The rest of the arrangements and potted plants had none. "I'll ask Truman. He'll know."

John turned to the casket for a final look then turned away. "I'm ready when you are."

They left the viewing room, pausing briefly to scan the guest book.

"Look at who's already been here," John said, running a finger down the list of names. "Guys from Dad's shift at the mine, women from Mama's Sunday school class, people she worked with at the paper mill, even some of your friends from The Depot. Here's Vic Payton's name. Didn't you tell me he's the manager now?"

"Yes. Engaged to the boss's daughter, too," Poppy whispered.

"Hey. Here's a name I didn't expect to see," John said.

"Who?" Poppy asked.

"Justin Caulfield. Can you believe it?"

Poppy frowned. "Probably still riding that guilt trip from firing Daddy. Oh... wait, here comes Truman. I'm going to ask him about those flowers."

"Is there anything I can do for you?" Truman asked.

"There are a lot of flowers in the room without cards. Were they already removed?"

"Oh, no, they came that way. But the deliveryman said that they were all purchased at once by the same person."

John frowned. "Really? Did they say who?"

"I believe Caulfield Industries. There were no flowers to speak of the night Mr. Caulfield came by the viewing room. I suppose he was concerned there would be none. It was quite considerate of him."

Poppy stifled a gasp. This was going too far. First the pension, picking up outstanding bills for Mama's care and the funerals, and now this?

"Yes, considerate," Poppy echoed.

John frowned at her, but said nothing.

"Well, thank you for your kindness, Truman," John said.

"Yes, of course. I'll see you both tomorrow at the church."

They left the funeral home in silence and got into John's

truck before they let feelings fly.

"What is going on with Caulfield?" John asked.

"I don't know, but I'm beginning to feel like he views us as his personal charity case, and I'm trying not to be insulted."

John grinned. "Easy, sister. Let the big man throw his money around if it makes him feel better. It's just one more bill we won't have to worry about."

"Whatever," she muttered.

John glanced at his watch. "I missed lunch and now it's after 4:00 p.m. How about we go by The Depot and have an early dinner?"

"We have all that food at the house."

"So, we'll take it to the church tomorrow."

Poppy almost smiled. "I've never eaten at The Depot as a customer before."

John frowned. "Then it's about damn time you did."

Her smile went viral. "Yes, about damn time."

John winked, started the truck and headed uptown.

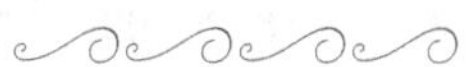

Vic Payton was trying to smooth the ruffled feathers of a cantankerous diner when he saw Poppy and John walk in. Anxious to seat them himself, he ended the conversation quickly by comping the customer's food.

"I'm sorry you were disappointed by the meal, Mr. Wyman. Please consider this our treat."

The diner frowned, but Vic could tell that was what he'd been waiting for. He smiled, patted the man on the back and then made a u-turn and headed for the front.

"Hello, Poppy. John, it's good to see you again. I hope you're here for some food. It would be my honor to treat you both to a meal."

"That's not necessary," John said.

"I know. That's why I want to do it," Vic said. He grabbed a couple of menus and then flashed a brief smile at Poppy before he led them to one of the tables with a good location.

He seated Poppy, then smiled as he handed her the menu.

Poppy felt a little obligated to converse, even though she

didn't want to. Without thinking, she picked what she thought would be a safe bet.

"Have you and Michelle set a date yet?"

"We're no longer engaged," Vic said. "I'm lucky I didn't get fired in the process."

"Oh, my gosh. I'm sorry. I didn't know," Poppy said.

Vic shrugged. "I'm not sorry. It was a mistake from day one, and you have nothing to apologize for. Now, I'll send a waitress right to your table. The fish tonight is salmon and the rib-eye steak is the Chef's special. Poppy can attest to the quality of both. Enjoy."

He walked away, leaving John in no doubt as to why they were getting a free meal.

"He's still got a thing for you," John whispered.

Poppy frowned. "Sssh! For Pete's sake, Johnny!"

John shrugged. "So, what's good here?"

Glad he'd dropped the subject, she began pointing out things that she knew he would like. By the time their waitress appeared, they were ready to order.

As luck would have it, Jewel was their waitress. Instead of her usual rancor, she appeared anxious to please.

"Good evening, you two." Then she paused. "Poppy, John, I'm very sorry for your losses. I just wanted to say that before we started."

"Thank you. We appreciate it."

Jewel smiled and took their orders. "I'll be right back with your drinks," and left.

"She's nice," John said.

"No, she's not," Poppy said, and then laid her napkin in her lap.

John grinned. "Wow, sister. Don't be shy. Tell me what you really think."

Poppy shrugged. "I work with her, remember?"

"Yeah, I get it. Different story if I wasn't here, right?"

"She was an eternal bitch to me the day Mama and Daddy died and then found out afterward what happened and felt guilty. The guilt has yet to wear off, but it will."

He frowned. "I'm sorry. I didn't know you didn't like where you worked."

"I like the place. Workers come and go. Some are nice. Some aren't. Maybe she'll leave."

"I'll write Santa about her," John said.

Poppy's eyes widened. "You remember that?"

"I always wrote to Santa about the kids who were mean to you at school. I think the process should still work."

Poppy reached across the table and laid her hand on her brother's arm.

"I love you, Johnny."

The trust in her eyes was difficult to see. When he thought about what a burden she'd carried all alone, it was a miracle she was still talking to him.

"Love you, too, honey."

Vic watched from across the room, wishing it was him she was reaching for, and then looked away. Some things were too painful to bear and being in love without having the feelings returned was nothing short of hell.

Mike and Kenny returned to the precinct. They needed the list Harmon was gathering on Sunny Robert's classmates but he was still scrambling with some of the addresses. While they waited, they filled Lieutenant Green in on where they were in the investigation including Mike's sighting of Prophet Jones.

"You know we've been looking for Prophet Jones? So, I think I finally saw him today," Mike said.

Green's interest shifted. "Where?"

"Under the Little Man bridge."

"Under it?"

"I think so. He was on the bridge and then I saw him bolt off and head down toward the river. It's been years since I've prowled along the riverbank, but I'm thinking there are places up under it where someone could hide."

"I'll send a car and a couple of officers to check it out."

Mike grinned. "Good. If he's there, it will be their car and not mine he contaminates."

Green chuckled. "Yeah, stink is one thing. Vermin is another."

Kenny shuddered and scratched his head. "Makes me itch just talking about it."

Mike continued his briefing. "In the meantime, I want to go back over the hospital tapes. Maybe now that we know more, we'll spot something new."

Green nodded. "If we find Prophet, I'll let you know."

They left the office.

"So we're off to the movies again?" Kenny asked.

Mike nodded. "I want both of us watching the same film at the same time. Two sets of eyes and all that."

"Agreed," Kenny said. "I'll set it up if you'll get snacks. I'm starved."

"Why is it that my donation to the party costs money and yours doesn't?"

Kenny smirked. "I assure you that never occurred to me."

Mike rolled his eyes. "Like hell. Sweet or salty?"

"Both," Kenny said. "Something chocolate and any kind of chips."

"Back in a few," Mike said, and headed to the break room as Kenny went back to Evidence to pull the tapes.

By the time Mike had drinks and snacks in hand, Kenny was ready and waiting.

"Knock yourself out," Mike said, as he slid two bags of chips and a couple of candy bars toward his partner.

Kenny caught the cold can of Pepsi Mike slid toward him, ignoring the wet trail of condensation it left on the table.

Mike popped the top on his Coke. "I'm ready."

They settled in, making separate notes as they watched who came and went through the hours before Jessup Sadler's arrival, then paid even closer attention when Sadler, himself, first appeared on the scene.

Mike licked nacho cheese powder off his fingers and then pointed to the screen.

"Pause this a minute, will you?"

Kenny nodded. The screen froze with Jessup Sadler in mid-stride as Mike continued.

"Okay, knowing what we know now about the daughter not being *his* daughter, watch his demeanor. See the stoop of shoulders and the drawn, sad expression on his face. It's no longer just about his wife's health. And, we also know they had a confrontation at the hospital."

"But we don't know for sure if Helen gave him a name," Kenny said.

"Yeah, okay," Mike said. "I was just thinking out loud. Play the rest and we need to pay particular attention to who leaves the floor ahead of him, although it's my feeling that he was only rushing because he had a name and was going in search of him. Not that he was following someone in particular."

Kenny hit Play and opened his last candy bar.

Mike stretched his legs out in front of him as he watched, trying to look at the footage with new eyes. Every glance Jessup made, every person he passed, they made note of. After he went into his wife's room, they later saw the nurse emerge who'd reported the fight they'd been having. From the expression on her face when she exited, it was obvious she'd been upset.

Once Kenny glanced at his watch, then hit pause and went to the bathroom. Mike took the time to check in on Harmon to see if the list had been completed.

"Hey, Harmon, it's me, Mike. How's it going?"

"I'm running one more check through military files and then I'm through," he said.

"Military?"

"Yeah," Harmon said. "I'm pretty sure we're going to have one name that's since been deceased while in service and another one still serving Uncle Sam and due for retirement this Christmas."

"Then we can certainly rule them out as possible shooters," Mike said. "Anyway, I know you've heard this before, but I need it ASAP."

"This is one of those cases where I sure don't mind doing extra leg work. Losing both parents on the same day in such startling circumstances must be hell on the rest of the family."

"Pretty much," Mike said, remembering Poppy Sadler's look of disbelief. At that point, Kenny returned. "Hey, gotta go. Thanks for the update."

"I'll be in touch," Harmon said.

He disconnected. Kenny hit Play, and they slipped back into

view mode. About an hour later, they caught sight of a man passing by the camera and Mike hit Kenny's arm.

"Pause it. Isn't that Caulfield?"

Kenny squinted. "Yeah, I think so. But his kid's on that floor, remember?"

Mike nodded. "Okay... resume."

They watched for another ten minutes before Jessup Sadler came out of his wife's room. Again, they took special note of his demeanor.

"He looks pissed," Kenny said.

"Yeah, I think you're right. Do you think she told him?"

Kenny shrugged. "It's hard to say. He could just be angry because she didn't. Or it could be because he finally found out who fathered the girl he thought was his."

"There he goes toward the elevator. You can see it at the end of the hall. Oh hell! Wait. Someone's getting in the elevator. Look at Sadler! He's running."

Kenny paused the tape. "But is he running to catch the car, or catch who's getting on?"

"Can you tell who it is?" Mike asked.

Kenny rewound it, then they watched it again, but the view was still blurred and he never turned around.

"What do you think?" Kenny asked.

"It's impossible to say if Sadler was running toward the man or the car. Don't we have video of him exiting the building?"

"Yeah, hang on. It's this one, I think," Kenny said. He fast-forwarded it to the right timeline. "It'll be right around this time. Too bad it was dark and raining so hard, it makes the images blurry."

Within a few moments they made the same mistake they'd made before. "There he is," Kenny said.

"No. It's not. Remember, we did this before. It's someone else, remember?"

Kenny leaned closer. "Oh yeah. I said then he looked familiar." He hit Pause and then studied the image on the screen. "I know who that is. It's Caulfield, isn't it?"

Mike leaned closer. "We saw him earlier on the floor. I guess he was leaving, too."

Kenny frowned. "So, he's obviously the guy who got on the

elevator just ahead of Sadler because he gets all the way to his car and drives off before Sadler makes it to the parking lot. See, there he is, running. Again, we assume because of the rain, but what if it's not?"

Mike shook his head. "We could make suppositions all day, but until we have solid evidence to tie one thing to another, this gets us nowhere."

Kenny began packing up the tapes to return to Evidence while Mike began cleaning up their trash. They were on their way out when Harmon showed up.

"Here are the names you wanted. If you need anything else from me, save it for tomorrow, will you? Wife just called. Oldest son is in ER getting stitches. Don't know details but it's probably from doing something stupid." Harmon rolled his eyes. "He takes after the wife's side of the family."

"Thanks, man. Hope he's okay," Mike said, and then glanced at the list, paused in mid-step and whistled beneath his breath.

"What?" Kenny asked.

"Probably just a coincidence, but check out the fourth name down."

CHAPTER FOURTEEN

It was just after 6:00 p.m. when Justin pulled into the driveway of his home. He circled the house and parked in the garage, then walked into the back door with an angry stride. It was too damn bad his mother was not feeling well, because he was about to make her feel worse. As far as he was concerned, she'd been brainwashing Callie with 'a Caulfield is better than the little people' mentality just like she'd done to him and he wasn't having it.

Newton was sitting at the kitchen table having his supper and talking to Lillian when Justin walked in, surprising them both.

The cook gasped.

Oral stood up.

Justin lifted a hand. "Sorry I startled you. I'm tired. Thought I'd take a shortcut. Where's my mother?"

"She's in her room. Still not feeling well," Oral said.

"Did she go to the doctor?"

"No sir. She didn't want to go," Oral said.

"She's so goddamned important she can heal herself," Justin snapped, and strode through the kitchen in long, angry strides.

Lillian glanced at Oral who shrugged and sat back down to his meal. The help was used to being in the middle of family turmoil without having to cope with the outcome. However, Oral shifted his focus as he continued to eat, keeping one ear on the rest of the house – just in case he might be needed.

Justin strode up the stairs and then down the hall to his mother's room. He started to barge in and then withheld the urge and knocked.

"Come in," Amelia called.

He walked in wearing his attitude with barely disguised civility. Amelia was lying on her bed, but hardly an invalid. Her hair and makeup were in place, she was fully dressed, and thumbing through a magazine.

"I see you're feeling better."

Amelia let the magazine fall to her lap. "Actually, I still feel a bit shaky. I don't know what's-"

"Then you should have gone to the doctor this morning. At least you would know why instead of commenting about your ignorance of the situation."

Amelia's eyes widened. Whatever had been wrong the other night was still there between them.

"What's wrong with you? This is the second time you've challenged me in a very rude manner and I don't appreciate it."

"Welcome to the club. I don't appreciate the crap you've been feeding Callie either. A Caulfield wins no matter what it takes? Seriously, Mother? That's like saying we'd do anything to get our way and mow over whoever it takes to make it happen."

"When your father was alive, he-"

"I'm not Dad! I will never be. I don't want to be. In my opinion, he was a hard, ruthless man who loved money more than family."

Amelia was shocked, not only by what Justin was saying, but at being challenged in such a manner.

"You don't know what you're talking about. He kept Caulfield Industries afloat during several very rocky times in our country's economic history! You are reaping the benefits of the birthright he left you, and have no right to criticize how he made it happen!"

"I have every right, because I paid the price to follow in his footsteps and I know exactly what it cost me to do it!"

All the color suddenly faded from Amelia's face. "You can't seriously be holding a grudge about all that nonsense! You were little more than a boy and that's all water under the bridge."

He flashed on Sunny's wasted body lying in that casket and

lost it.

"Water under the bridge? Fuck you, Mother! When you get to feeling better, I want you out of this house. You have just been discharged from any further duties regarding me and my family. Whatever Callie needs, I will deal with it myself or hire someone who can."

Amelia gasped. She threw the magazine aside and was out of the bed and in his face before he had time to move, but he'd already prepared himself for the slap. It was the calling card for her anger.

"That was a pretty good blow for someone who's a little shaky," he drawled.

Amelia threw up her hands in disgust. "Fine! I lied! I needed some time to myself and I took it. You don't know what it's like at my age to watch another member of my family wasting away. I had a life in Florida and I gave it up to come back and help you with your daughter and this is how you repay me."

Justin was so pissed he was shaking. It took everything he had not to double up his fist and knock her on her ass. But instead of stepping back, he moved forward until he was right in her face.

"You're right. I don't know what it feels like at your age, but I know what it feels like at mine. And just for the fucking record, my daughter is not going to waste away. Not anymore. As soon as she gets a transplant, she'll be on the road to a full recovery. I'll give up my own life to keep her alive before I'll let her die."

"Then you'd be dying for nothing because nothing in your body would be a match!" she screamed, and the moment she said it, all the blood drained from her face.

Justin jerked as if he'd just been punched in the gut. "What the hell do you mean by that? She's my daughter. Of course it would be a match."

Amelia was in a serious state of panic. All these years she'd kept the secret then blurted it out in a fit of anger.

"Nothing. I meant nothing. Now leave me alone. I have packing to do."

When she started to turn away, Justin grabbed her by the

arm. "No. You're not going anywhere until you tell me-"

There was a knock on the door and then it opened before either of them could speak.

Oral Newton stood on the threshold with his shoulders back and his chin up, as if bracing for a fight. It was as if Justin wasn't even there as his gaze went straight to Amelia.

"Ma'am, are you all right?"

Justin's cheeks burned from a rush of angry blood. "How dare you interfere in personal family business? Get out!"

Oral didn't budge. "Ma'am?"

Amelia sighed and waved him away. "It's all right, Newton. You may leave. I'll be fine."

Oral gave Justin a look. It wasn't much more than a glance, but Justin felt the warning as surely as if it had been voiced. Then the door shut.

Justin spun toward his mother. "That was a little above the call of duty. What's going on there?"

Amelia's shock that anyone might assume she would toy with the hired help was obvious.

"You're disgusting, you know that?"

"You don't want to talk about your business, fine! You will answer my question. Why would you say my DNA and Callie's would not be a match? Are you insinuating that she's not my daughter, that Deborah was fucking someone else and you knew it and let it happen right beneath my nose?"

Amelia's heart was hammering so hard that she feared it might burst.

"Let it be, Justin."

"Tell me now or I'll order a blood test and find out for myself."

Suddenly she was aghast. "You'd hang our dirty laundry out for all the world to see?"

Justin felt sick. She'd just confirmed it without saying the actual words. Callie wasn't his.

"When did you learn about this?"

Amelia shrugged. "Her family had an impeccable bloodline while the man she was seeing was not only an unsuitable match, but was already married with a family of his own."

Justin's stomach rolled. "Well we've all heard that story

about unsuitable bloodlines before, haven't we?"

Amelia ignored him. "Deborah's family was Catholic and didn't believe in abortion. You needed focus. She needed a husband. Both your father and I, along with Deborah's parents decided it would be a good match."

Justin couldn't believe what he was hearing. "Deborah was in love with someone else, was pregnant with his child, and still agreed to marry me?"

Amelia shrugged. "And it worked out, didn't it? A marriage of convenience is often a good thing. You can fall in love later."

"You disgust me. Out of curiosity, does that man even know he has another child?"

Justin's rage was frightening. Amelia was over her head and tried bluffing her way out.

"I don't know and don't care. It has nothing to do with us."

"Oh my God, Mother. What if the situation had been reversed and Sunny and I had made a baby I didn't know about? Would you care then?"

It was the twitch at the corner of her mouth that stopped his heart – that and the fact that she immediately shifted her gaze to a painting over his left shoulder.

"You're not serious?"

"Serious about what?" Amelia muttered.

"Sunny was pregnant when I left Caulfield? Why wasn't I told?"

"For the same reason Deborah married you. They wanted someone decent to raise her child."

Justin grabbed her by the shoulders and shook her until the anger in her eyes was replaced with mortal fear.

"I'm someone decent! What was wrong with me raising my own child?"

"But that girl wasn't decent. She was from Coal Town," Amelia shouted.

Justin paled. "Who raised mine, Mother?"

"I don't even know there ever was one. Her father showed up about a month after you were gone claiming she was with child. We didn't believe him. You know how people are, always wanting to scam the rich for easy money. Your father paid him off. If it had been me making the decision, I would have disposed of her like you do any cur with a litter you don't want. Into the Little Man and good riddance, I say."

Justin stared. He couldn't believe what he was hearing. He'd never seen this hard, ruthless side of his mother. When he realized she was still talking he refocused his attention.

"Anyway... he got what he'd come for, which was the money. If she had been pregnant, she probably aborted it and moved on."

Justin swiped his hands across his face and then turned on his heel, reached for the nearest thing he could find which happened to be a Tiffany lamp, and threw it across the room. It shattered into irreplaceable pieces.

"What have you done?" Amelia cried. "That was a priceless piece of Tiffany."

Justin hands curled into fists as he started to yell. "What have I done? What have *I* done? Are you fucking crazy?" Then he shoved his hands through his hair in complete frustration and started to laugh.

Amelia took a step back. This was a side of Justin she'd never seen and it was frightening.

"Stop laughing," she said.

It only made him laugh that much harder.

Amelia darted to the other side of the room, keeping the king-sized bed between them as she reached for the phone.

"Stop laughing. Stop it, I say. If you take another step toward me I'll call the police."

By now, tears were running down his face, but he couldn't have stopped laughing if he'd tried. "Call the police? I dare you," he said, then sat down on the floor because his legs would no longer hold him.

"Justin, why are-"

"Shut up. Stop talking. You are an evil, selfish bitch. If only I was the cuckoo's child in this mess and not my Callie. At this moment, it would give me great satisfaction to know there wasn't a drop of Caulfield blood in my body."

Amelia sank onto the mattress with her hand pressed against her chest. Their lives would never be the same. She'd just lost a son and a granddaughter. If only Adam were here to make

Justin see the wisdom in what they'd done.

"You don't mean that," she said.

"Actually, I do," Justin said, and then dragged himself to his feet and started to walk out of the room when a thought occurred. He pivoted sharply. "Who is Callie's father?"

She shrugged. "I'm sure I don't know."

"I don't believe you. You and Dad would have made it your business to know everything. What's his name?"

"Why? What do you think you can accomplish by facing him now?"

"I think I can find a kidney donor for my daughter. That's what I think. What makes me sick to my stomach is that you would have let Callie die before you'd told me this truth."

Amelia paled. "It wouldn't have come to that."

"I want a fucking name by tomorrow morning or I will hire a private investigator and get the information for myself. And you know if it comes to that, the whole city will eventually find out what a conniving pair of unnatural parents you and my father actually were."

Amelia grabbed her chest as she began to sway. "I feel faint."

"Then lie down or die. Right now I don't give a damn which turn you take," he said softly, and walked out of the room.

He met Oral Newton lingering at the head of the stairs.

"My mother will be leaving within a few days. At that point, your services will no longer be needed. In the meantime, you might go check on your bitch. She was threatening to faint."

Justin watched shock on Newton's face turn to rage. The man was torn between punching him and tending to Amelia.

Concern for Amelia won out.

Newton bolted down the hall as Justin went to his room to pack. He needed to get away from this house and everything it stood for. There was a small apartment on the top floor of his office building where visiting businessmen sometimes stayed. It would serve his needs until his mother got her sorry ass out of the house.

Prophet Jones liked the way small places made him feel – the way he'd always felt being cradled in his mother's arms. It was also quite freeing to no longer live by the rules of polite society. He didn't have bills to pay. He didn't go to a job. He ate what others threw away, and when his garments became too rank or rotted and came apart, there was always a church charity closet to fix him right up. His only possessions were his bible and the clothes on his back, which made moving quite easy.

For the past few weeks he'd been sleeping in a spot under the bridge he called the nest. It was a nice water-proof niche about five feet wide and five feet deep within the under-structure of the bridge. He'd dug into the dirt embankment years ago and made himself a cozy little hidey-hole. The noise from the overhead traffic was somewhat muted by the depths in which he slept, but if the river was in flood stage it wasn't safe to use. However, at this time, such was not the case.

He pulled the old quilt a little tighter around his shoulders and rolled over onto his side. Later after the sun went down, he'd run his route through the alleys behind the restaurants and find himself some dinner. For now, he needed to rest. One never knew when the Devil would show up again, and he wanted to be ready in case he needed to fight.

This was where he'd been the night the Devil came down to the Little Man. Even though it had just begun to rain that night, he'd witnessed it all - from the argument, to the gunshots, to watching the man fall backward into the river. A flash of lightning was all it took for Prophet to see the Devil's face.

When the Devil drove off, he climbed down from the under-structure and raced through the rain, but not in time to save the man. He was already floating face down in the water and the rain had turned into a deluge. Prophet said a prayer for his soul then glanced at the dead man's car. It was sitting on the bank with the lights on, the door open and the engine still running.

He kept looking back toward the city, afraid the Devil would return, but knew he needed something to prove what he'd seen. He didn't intend for him to buy his way out of this evil deed like he'd done the time before. That's when he saw the empty shells lying in an ever-growing puddle on the ground.

That was it! Footprints! The Devil had left his footprints. Prophet grabbed the empty shells and stuffed them deep inside an inner pocket. He needed to think about who he should tell. It had to be someone he could trust - someone who couldn't be bought off like before. But he'd think about later, after he got out of the rain. He was running back toward the bridge when two men came out of nowhere.

"Go back! Go back! The Devil's on the bridge!" he shouted, but they acted like they didn't hear him and ran past, and now here he was, days later with proof of the evil deed in his pocket.

A siren sounded somewhere off in the distance, rousing him just as he was at the point of drifting off to sleep. The sound made Prophet antsy. He didn't trust the cops. He threw his covers back and crawled to the edge of the nest to peer out and saw a black and white cop car pulling up to the riverbank.

"Too little, too late," he muttered, thinking they should have been here three nights ago to catch the Devil in the act.

When he saw them getting out and looking toward his location, he panicked. After all these years, his first instinct was to run. He slipped out of the hidey-hole and went out on the opposite side of the bridge before disappearing into the brush and trees along the riverbank. The cops never saw him leave, and even though they eventually found where he'd been, he was nowhere in sight.

Poppy needed to sleep. Tomorrow was the funeral and all it entailed, but every time she closed her eyes, her thoughts went straight to Jessup, wondering if he'd quit loving her when he'd found out she wasn't his. Her mother's shame was seeping into every living pore of her body and she didn't know how to make it stop. Even though Helen had been a good and loving wife, Poppy was living proof of Sunny's lie.

Exhausted and heart-heavy, she finally got up and went to the kitchen to warm some milk. It had been Mama's cure-all for restless sleep. Adding some chocolate syrup made it even better.

The floor was cold beneath her feet as she sat at the kitchen table waiting for the milk to warm. She should have gotten her slippers, but she didn't want to go back now for fear of getting the milk too hot. She caught sight of the little brown mat in front of the kitchen sink and brought it back to her chair to keep her feet off the cold floor while she waited.

The quiet and the familiarity of the house enveloped her as she sat. This was home. She'd never lived anywhere else, and as simple as it was, right now there wasn't another place on earth she would rather be. By the time she'd downed her warm chocolate milk, something within her had settled. She rinsed the glass and pan she'd used, replaced the mat in front of the sink and then ran back to her room.

The weight of covers against the chill of the night was comforting – warming both her feet and her heart. She thought she heard the clock in the living room begin to strike, but she was too near asleep to count the chimes.

John had fallen asleep easily, but was a long way away from resting. He was caught in a nightmare, watching his father's murder from the opposite bank of the Little Man - catching glimpses of the act in progress through intermittent flashes of lightning.

Rain.

Thunder.

Lightning snaking across the sky as John saw his daddy drive his car up to the Little Man.

In another flash of lightning, Jessup was out and standing on the riverbank.

The rain was deafening. John tried to shout, but his daddy didn't hear him, and in the darkness, couldn't see him.

In the blinding flash of the next lightning strike a second man had entered the scene.

Before John could tell what was happening, they were swallowed back up by the night and the storm.

There were other flashes - the flash of repeated gunfire – and then one lightning flash lasting just long enough for John to see Jessup staggering, falling backward in the Little Man.

John was screaming as he ran toward the river.

Suddenly the light was in his eyes and Poppy was standing beside his bed, shaking him awake.

"Johnny! Johnny! Wake up! You're having a bad dream."

John sat up in bed and touched his cheeks. They were wet. In the dream he'd felt the rain on his face and all the time it had been his tears.

Poppy sat down on the side of the bed. "Are you okay?"

He swiped his hands across his face, wishing he could wipe away the memory as well.

"Hell of a dream. I'm sorry I woke you."

"You were screaming at Dad, saying his name over and over."

John leaned back against the headboard and closed his eyes.

"Talk to me, Johnny. Once you share the burden, it's never as heavy, remember?"

Their mother's words were all too familiar, but telling what he'd learned about Jessup's death was horrifying. He kept thinking he needed to protect Poppy from the burden of anything else.

"Please," Poppy said. "No more secrets in this family."

He reached for her hand. "Dad was still alive when he hit the water."

Poppy jerked as if he'd just punched her. "No! Oh my God! How do you know?"

"I went to the morgue, remember? I talked to the doctor who did the autopsy."

"Daddy couldn't swim."

"I know."

Her voice broke. "He was so scared of the water."

"I know, sister."

He expected her to cry. He had not expected anger. Within seconds the expression on her face went from sad to fury.

"The day the killer is sentenced, I will be in the courtroom facing him down and wishing him a slow journey to hell."

"Well, I have to say that's a damn healthy way to look at it," John said.

"Would you like me to make you some hot chocolate to help you get back to sleep?"

John smiled gently as he ran his thumb along the curve of her cheek.

"No, honey, I think I'll be fine. I'll just cover myself up with a corner of your sweet revenge and sleep like a baby."

Poppy sighed. "It's 3:45. I set my alarm to go off at 6:30. Is that early enough for you? Remember the service is at 10:00 a.m. and Truman said the family car from the funeral home will come pick us up at 9:30."

"Yes. Sleep well, little sister, and thank you for rescuing me."

"That's what family is for," she said, and blew him a kiss as she left the room, turning the lights out behind her.

John slid back down beneath the sheets and then closed his eyes. There was a moment when he feared the dream would come back, but in his mind, all he saw was Poppy's face.

CHAPTER FIFTEEN

Mike had been dreaming of a tall slender girl with long black hair and dark eyes who couldn't stop crying. He kept wanting to hold her, but she was always two steps away from his reach. He woke up, frustrated and feeling like he'd never gone to bed.

There was no getting around the fact that he'd taken a big step beyond police protocol in letting himself get this attached to Poppy Sadler, especially since the entire range of their relationship was based on nothing but a murder investigation.

He didn't know how her future was going to play out, but there was a part of him hoping he was still in it. The detective in him wanted answers to the things he didn't know about her – like her favorite food – or her favorite color. He knew what made her cry, but he wanted to know what made her laugh. The longing to be closer to her was growing, but this wasn't the time, and it might never come.

Mike was a man who accepted the facts which included his shortcomings, and learning she had no interest in him whatsoever might be the biggest hurdle he would ever have to face.

He ate his standard peanut butter and grape jelly sandwich in front of the television, still in the gym shorts he slept in, and washed it down with re-heated coffee.

On his way to the kitchen to put the dirty dishes in the sink, it occurred to him that she was probably doing something similar. She'd be up by now and making breakfast for her and her brother. Either they'd be talking too much to ignore what lay ahead, or not at all as they faced burying their mother.

A quick glance at the clock was all it took to make him focus. He needed to get to work.

A short while later he pulled into the parking lot, anxious to get inside and play catch-up with new info on the case. But once inside, he wound up going through the morning with a bit of frustration. Kenny had called in sick, a case of food poisoning from the take-home food he'd had last night, which left Mike on his own.

The lead he thought he'd had on Prophet Jones hadn't played out. The officers had found what appeared to be one of his hidey-holes, but he wasn't there.

What he did have was the list of names Detective Harmon had worked up. There were a dozen names on the list of people who still lived in the area, including - Tom Bonaventure, Jessup Sadler's boss at the mine, and Justin Caulfield.

Seeing Bonaventure's name had been something of a surprise. Even though Tom had grown up on the north side, he lived in Coal Town now. They already knew Jessup had been angry at Bonaventure for firing him. Harmon had a notation next to Bonaventure's name as a reminder to Mike that the man had no alibi for the night Sadler died, and had shown up at work the next day with a black eye.

There were also other names on Harmon's list for which he could not account. One man had been diagnosed as bi-polar, and despite family care and medical help had opted to go his own way. According to the family, he came and went without notice.

Another had recurring drug issues and only intermittent contact with his family. Unfortunately for the police, he was, at the present, missing.

A third was a repeat of the second, but with a rap sheet longer than Kenny Duroy's arm and had served time in prison. There was no current address for him although he was reported living in the area.

And while they still had the two teenagers who'd stolen Sadler's car in custody, after learning about the diary, Mike was of the opinion they'd had nothing to do with Sadler's murder, just the theft of his car.

He'd been thinking that he might make a low-key appearance at Helen Sadler's funeral just to see what happened. It paid to cover all the bases where murder was concerned.

After clearing it with Lieutenant Green, he headed across the bridge to the Church of Angels where Pastor Louis J. Harvard preached the word of God with all the fervor that a Pentecostal preacher could bring.

Justin woke with a sense of confusion that quickly morphed to a grim understanding. He was in the apartment above his office. A glance at the time sent him into overdrive as he threw back the covers and headed for the shower. Less than ten minutes later he was getting dressed. The first of his earliest employees would be arriving soon and he had no intention of letting anyone know where he'd spent the night. Within a few minutes he was out the building and on his way to pick up some breakfast at a fast-food drive-thru.

Although there was a full day of work on his schedule, he had only two things on his mind – finding out the date of Poppy Sadler's birthday and getting the name of Callie's father.

If it turned out that Poppy was his child, then he had another problem - whether to share the news with her or not. Today she was burying her mother and after her father's body was released she would be burying him, too. Now was hardly the time to let her know he'd knocked her mother up then chose his father's money over his first love.

And then there was Callie. He didn't care what anyone thought or what a cuckold he became if people learned she was not his, as long as she got her chance at a new life. But he had to go through Amelia to get that info, and after a night to think about their fight, knowing her, she was probably out for blood - his in particular.

Amelia hadn't fainted last night. In fact, it was quite the contrary. The shock of hearing her own child tell her he didn't care if she lived or died had fueled anger, not despair. Once she'd gotten past Oral's outrage on her behalf and calmed him down into lapdog submission, she'd begun to make plans.

The only drawback in making them work was that everything hinged on Justin's desire to keep Callie's well-being at the forefront. The Caulfield estate had been her home before Justin was born, and he was not going to kick her out like the poor relative looking for a handout. Even though she hadn't wanted to come back, she was the one who would make the decision as to when she would leave, and she wasn't above using a sick child to make her point.

She got up at her usual time and dressed for the day at the hospital, making sure to take the new card games she'd purchased, as well as another angel figurine as a surprise gift for Callie. She went down to breakfast with her chin up and purpose in her step, ordered a waffle and fruit along with her usual café au lait, and began to read the paper.

It was a name in the obituaries that caught her eye. Once she began to read, everything about Justin's behavior was suddenly clear.

Sunny Roberts was dead.

She scanned the rest of the obit, noting Sunny's husband has passed on the same day, and that she was survived by two children – step-son John Sadler of Atlanta, Georgia, and daughter, Poppy Sadler of the home.

Amelia's heart skipped a beat. So she'd had a child. That didn't mean it was Justin's. More likely, it belonged to the man she had married. Still, she had to tread lightly. What she needed was information, and she knew where to get it. The family lawyer was a font of information. What he didn't know, he could find out.

When she heard Lillian coming from the kitchen with her food, she calmly turned the page to an EPA study on water contamination and strip mines. In their line of business it paid to stay on top of the new regulations.

"Good morning, Mrs. Caulfield," Lillian said, as she set the food and coffee at her place. "Is there anything else I can get you?"

Amelia glanced at the plate. "No, it looks fine. Would you tell Newton that I'll be ready to go to the hospital as soon as I've eaten?"

"Yes, ma'am."

Amelia took her first bite. "Delicious."

Lillian smiled. "Thank you, ma'am. I'll be back in a few minutes to refill your cup. In the meantime, enjoy your breakfast."

Amelia did just that, right down to the last bite of strawberry and waffle, finished off her coffee and went to get her things.

Newton was waiting by the limo as she left the house. He opened the back door.

"Good morning, Mrs. Caulfield."

"Good morning, Newton. It's a beautiful day."

"Yes, ma'am, that it is. Do you need to stop anywhere else before we go to the hospital?"

"I think not."

He shut her door as she got inside, and they were soon on their way to St. Anne's.

As soon as Amelia buckled up she called the company lawyer on her cell, using his private number to bypass the secretary. It rang twice before he picked up.

"Graham Ring."

"Graham, this is Amelia Caulfield."

"Good morning, Mrs. Caulfield. How are you this fine morning?"

"I'm well, thank you. I'm on my way to the hospital to visit my granddaughter."

"I hear she's better, which is such a blessing. So, what can I do for you?"

"Yes, it is a blessing. What I need is a little information. There's a young woman here in Caulfield named Poppy Sadler, daughter of recently deceased Helen Roberts Sadler. I need to know Miss Sadler's place of birth and birthday. And call me back on this number."

"Oh. Yes, ma'am, Poppy Sadler. I've already met her. Sweet girl."

Amelia frowned. "Really? In what capacity, may I ask?"

"Just company business. Her father's murder struck a chord of sympathy with your son, Justin. He ordered me to make Miss Sadler the beneficiary of Mr. Sadler's pension rather than her mother, who had died that same day. Peculiar circumstances, then both dying on the same day like that, wouldn't you say?" "Yes. Peculiar. I'll be waiting for your call."

"Of course," Graham said, and hung up.

Amelia's gut knotted as she dropped her phone back in her purse. So Justin had gone all soft and doled out a pension to a family member other than a spouse, and that was before she'd let the cat out of the bag.

He was already tying himself to the girl just because she'd been Sunny's child. Now that he knew she might be his, she wouldn't be surprised if he tried to insinuate himself into her tawdry life – or even worse – bring her into theirs. She quickly shoved the thought aside. There would be time to deal with that issue, if and when it happened.

By the time she got to the hospital, she was gearing herself up for the day ahead.

Justin swallowed the last bite of his second sausage and egg biscuit and then washed it down with a big gulp of coffee. He tossed the refuse in a drive-by trash can and then put in a call to the company lawyer on his way back to the office. Like his mother, he bypassed the secretary, using Graham's personal line.

"Graham Ring."

"Good morning, Graham, it's Justin."

"Justin! I suppose this is my morning for the Caulfield family!"

Justin frowned. Damn. His mother had called the lawyer? He couldn't help but wonder what was she up to now, but wasn't going to ask and have it appear something was happening that was out of his control.

"I have a task for you," Justin said.

"Certainly. What do you need?" Graham asked.

"Remember the Sadler girl I had designated as the recipient of her father's pension?"

"Poppy Sadler?"

"That's the one. What I need is her official date of birth as well as where she was born."

Graham laughed. "Obviously you and your mother didn't cross paths this morning."

Justin's frown deepened as he braked for a red light. "What do you mean?"

"She's already called in the request. I just spoke to her about ten minutes earlier. I believe she was on her way to the hospital."

"I see," Justin said. "When you get the information, you call me, not her. I'm the one who needed to know. I suppose she was trying to help."

"No problem," Graham said. "In fact, I already have the information right here. She was born December 9th, 1991."

"December 9th, 1991?"

"That's correct," Graham said.

"Thank you," Justin said. "No need to call Mother. I'll do it myself."

"You're welcome. Have a nice day," Graham said.

The line went dead in Justin's ear, but it took a few moments for the fact to soak in. His head was spinning as he sat at the intersection, counting backward from the date of her birthday. Sunny had been pregnant before the prom, which meant the child had to be his. It wasn't until someone honked a horn, urging him to drive through that he realized the light had already changed.

He felt blindsided by the news, and at the same time an overwhelming sadness for what he'd missed. Sunny had been pregnant. He wouldn't let himself think about what she'd gone through alone, or the hell her family must have given her. It was too late to apologize to her. All he could do was make things right for the child - their child. It wasn't until he felt tears on his cheeks that he realized he was crying.

The parking lot at the Church of Angels was in overflow. Arriving cars were now parking up and down the streets. The pews inside were already full, and extra seating had been set up along the sides of the sanctuary and some out into the hall. Helen Roberts had been a well-loved member of this church, as well as the community, but it was her husband being murdered on the same day she died that had caused the influx. Morbid curiosity was a big draw. Would the family grieve more at this service, knowing there was another soon to follow? Suspicious whispers went back and forth throughout the church while they waited for the services to begin. What if Jessup's killer was among them? What if it was someone they knew?

When Pastor Louis J Harvard got the nod that the family was coming into the church, he stood.

"All rise," he said, as the family, which consisted of only John and Poppy, were seated.

Confident of his role in this gathering, he opened the service with a prayer.

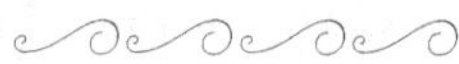

Poppy was trembling. She had been ever since the long black car had pulled up in front of their house that was to bring them to the church. This was it. The last act needed to render her mama into the realm of what people referred to as 'the dearly departed.'

She looked up at the pulpit without focusing on the casket - to the sunlight coming through the stained glass window above Pastor Harvard's head.

So beautiful.

So peaceful.

And the flowers - all the flowers Justin Caulfield sent were on the railings, and on the floor, and sitting on little pedestals so that it almost appeared that Helen's casket was sitting in a field of flowers. At that moment, all of her resentment about the flowers slid away. This was no longer about Poppy's indignation. This was for Mama, and she would have loved it.

The preacher was talking, but her only focus was the grip John had on her hand. Today he was her anchor and she was afraid to let go. As if sensing he was the source of her thoughts, John gave her hand a gentle squeeze. She laid her head against his shoulder, and when someone began to sing, she closed her eyes against the tears running down her face.

Mike Amblin had slipped into the church and was standing against a wall in the corner of the room. He'd known the minute he entered the church that he'd come because of Poppy, not because he thought he could magically finger someone in this crowd as a killer.

He'd never been in this church before, but he recognized a lot of familiar faces – some of whom were people he and Kenny had interviewed during their investigation, like Mel and Gladys Ritter, and Carl and Hannah Crane. He saw Tom Bonaventure, the manager at Caulfield #14 sitting at the end of a pew and remembered from the info in their case file that the man was divorced. Bonaventure kept eyeing John and Poppy instead of the preacher. Mike guessed he was suffering some guilt at having been the one who fired their father from his job.

Or he could consider Kenny's theory that Bonaventure could be Poppy's father and that he was the one who Jessup had fought with, and the man who'd ultimately killed him. Of all the ones they'd interviewed, Tom was the only one who'd turned up the next day with wounds from a brawl.

When someone began to sing, Mike saw Poppy lean against her brother's shoulder. To his surprise, his eyes welled with tears. He took a deep breath, trying to calm the swell of his emotions. He couldn't imagine what she was thinking, but he knew that she was sad. It was enough to hurt his heart.

Vic Payton was at the service, sitting four pews from the front and paying little attention to the service. His gaze was fixed on the back of Poppy's head and on the slight slump of her shoulders. He felt her sadness all the way to his bones. He knew what it felt like to lose a parent, but the pain he was feeling now had to do with losing her. Even though he'd never had a relationship with Poppy, it didn't mean he hadn't wanted one. It was hell loving someone who didn't love you back. When all the chaos in her life subsided he was going to give it one more try, and then if she still wasn't interested, he would look elsewhere.

John sat in stoic silence beside his sister, but he felt all eyes were on him, judging him and finding him lacking for what he'd left undone. It would be years, if ever, before he got past the guilt. He'd apologized to his mom. He'd apologized to Poppy. He'd even made a vow to his dad to help find his killer. But what he really needed was absolution from the all-knowing, all-seeing God. He looked up at the preacher, then beyond to the stained glass window bearing the image of a bleeding Jesus hanging from the cross.

Forgive me.

He didn't expect to get an actual answer, but oddly enough humbling himself enough to ask seemed to help.

All of a sudden he heard Pastor Harvard begin to pray and was shocked the entire service was coming to a close and he couldn't remember a single word that had come out of the preacher's mouth.

A few moments later they opened the casket.

Poppy moaned.

He caught her as she bent double, afraid she was going to topple out onto the floor. Her shoulders were shaking, but she wasn't making a sound.

"Sister," he said softly, lifting her up.

Poppy fell into his arms. She couldn't face the sympathy and pity on the people's faces and not lose her mind. Like a coward, she let John bear the burden while the congregation began to file past the casket on their way out of the church. She felt their presence - the gentle touches on her shoulder - the whispered words of comfort - but she wouldn't – she couldn't look up.

Both the trip to the cemetery and the trip back to the church were all a blur. Poppy remembered coming in out of the cold and feeling warm air on her feet, then looking down and seeing the petal from a flower stuck to the skirt of her dress. Someone thrust a plate in her hand, herded her toward a table and she hadn't moved since, letting the conversation flow around her while she stirred through the food and sipped her drink.

John was more at ease visiting with everyone, but he was never far away. She just wanted the day to be over. She wanted to go home. She needed to get past the sight of her mama's casket being lowered into that hole, of hearing the first clods of dirt falling onto the lid and knowing all she had left of her now were the memories. Sunny Roberts had been dead for years. Helen Sadler finally caught up.

CHAPTER SIXTEEN

Justin arrived at the cemetery with flowers for Deborah's grave, but the visit was all a ruse. Today his dearly departed wife was getting a little pay-back. He was using her as an excuse to be on site when the hearse arrived with Sunny's casket. It seemed fair, considering how she'd used him.

It was one of those crisp fall mornings when the air was still and the sky was so blue and clear it appeared to go on forever. It was a good day to lay a sweet soul to rest.

He rolled the windows down in his car then leaned back and closed his eyes. The faint screech of a hawk sounded somewhere high above him, and off to the right he could hear the distant thump of one of the powerful engines down at the paper mill. Nature and progress, always at odds in the world.

He sat without moving, absorbing the quiet and gathering strength for the battle with his mother that lay ahead. She was a strong, conniving woman who had always gotten her way, and just because she'd aged, did not mean she'd grown weaker.

He couldn't change the past, and there was the chance he could lose one daughter while trying to make amends to another. It would mean airing dirty laundry and giving up his pride. It was a small price to pay to give Callie a kidney and better Poppy Sadler's life.

By the time the procession of cars from the funeral began to arrive he was braced. As they pulled up on the next path over and began to park, he got out with his flowers and began walking toward the place where Deborah was buried.

He knew there were enough mourners already gathering for Sunny's service that his presence would not be noticed, and even if it was, the assumption that he was there for his wife rather than someone else's would be automatic.

When he reached Deborah's grave, he looked back. There was a moment of real physical pain when he saw the pallbearers carrying Sunny's casket to the open grave. A part of him was dying, too.

Then he saw her children. He'd never seen the stepson before, but quickly recognized the bond between them as they clung to each other in shared despair. It was strange to realize he'd seen Poppy Sadler off and on for years without knowing who she was. He'd admired her manner and the quiet confidence with which she carried herself as she worked. It was daunting now to look at her and know that she was also his – and that she'd been made from the young love and passion that he and Sunny had shared. Before he'd only seen her as another young woman, but now he was looking for shared similarities. He wanted her to turn around. But when she sat down beside her brother, the crowd of mourners moved between them and she disappeared from view.

He glanced down at Deborah's grave then gave the flowers he'd brought with him a toss. They landed slightly askew up against her tombstone.

"So Deborah, I thought you might like to know your naughty little secret is finally out. I'd like to be pissed, but it appears I am not one to be casting stones. Rest assured that Callie is still my beloved daughter in every sense of the word, but I am not committed to lies as the rest of you were. I will walk over as many bodies as it takes to find the other side of her family, and I will, by God, get her well."

With that, he turned on his heel and walked away. Preacher Harvard was saying a prayer as Justin drove away, and by the time the first clod of dirt landed on Sunny's casket he was back in the office.

It was after 5:00 p.m. by the time Justin got to the hospital.

He'd taken Callie's IPod home the night before and was bringing it back with new uploaded songs, via the list she'd given him, along with a pint of her favorite ice cream and extra spoons. The urge to take every day as a gift and ride it all the way to sundown had been made all too clear on this day. Since tomorrows came with no guarantee, today was about music and ice cream.

He got off the elevator and headed down the hall toward her room knowing his mother was there. He was ready for battle and walked in without knocking to find Callie and Amelia playing cards.

"Hey, pretty girl! I hope you're trouncing your Nana good."

Callie smiled. "Daddy! Nana said you were too busy to come in today. I'm so glad you're here."

Justin glanced at his mother and smiled. He'd just caught her in yet another a lie. At least she had the grace to flush.

"Oh, Nana doesn't know everything about me," he said, then laughed, knowing Amelia would get the inference without anyone else being the wiser. "I brought your IPod back with all the new uploaded songs, and..." He held up a sack. "Guess what else?"

Callie laughed. "I don't know, but I hope it's not a puppy 'cause the bottom of the sack is getting wet."

Justin laughed. Even Amelia was forced to smile.

"No puppies. Just your favorite ice cream!"

"Yay!!! Cookie dough with chocolate chips?"

"Yep, and three spoons. One for you and two for me."

She laughed again. "You are such a pig, Daddy. One for me, one for you, and one for Nana."

"Oh. Okay, it's your treat. I'm just the delivery boy."

He took the lid off the pint then grabbed a clean washcloth from the shelf by the sink, wrapped it around the carton and handed it to her, along with a spoon.

He made a production of bowing toward Amelia to give her the plastic spoon as if he were a page at court presenting silver to a queen.

"Mother dear, your spoon."

Amelia met his gaze with a show of bravado, although it was obvious she was at a loss as to what was going on. She'd expected anger, not this.

"Thank you," she said.

As soon as he'd forced her to meet his gaze, he immediately shifted focus and ignored her.

"Is it good, baby?" Justin asked, smiling at the joy on his daughter's face.

Callie rolled her eyes, nodding slowly as she let the first bite melt in her mouth.

Justin winked as he dug his spoon into the carton and scooped out a big bite, leaving Amelia to her own resources. As far as he was concerned, she could use it to eat ice cream, or shove it up her ass.

Amelia took a small bite and then slipped it between her lips, but it might as well been medicine. There was a sick feeling in the pit of her stomach that the other shoe was about to drop. She listened to the continuing chit-chat between father and child, well aware she was an obvious outsider to their funny banter. She was debating with herself about calling Newton to come pick her up when her cell phone suddenly rang.

Finally.

She'd been waiting for Graham Ring to call her back all day. But when she saw Caller ID and realized it was just her hair stylist, she let the call go to voicemail.

Justin saw her frown. "If you want another bite, Mother, you'd better dig in. Looks like Callie's about to finish it off."

"Yes, here Nana, get another bite," Callie said.

Amelia shook her head. "Thank you, darling, but I'll pass. I've been expecting a call all day. Now that your father is here, I'm going to step out for a bit and check in."

Justin waved his spoon in the air for punctuation. "Oh, hey! Was it a call from Graham Ring? I'm sorry I didn't mention it sooner. It seems we both had the same idea this morning. He filled me in. I told him I'd pass the info along."

Then he smiled.

Amelia froze. The smile. The only reason he would be happy was if Poppy Sadler was actually his.

God in heaven. What do I do now?

Justin tossed his spoon in the trash and then turned so that

Callie couldn't see his face. Although the tone of his voice light, there was no mistaking the warning on his face.

"Don't worry," he said. "You've done more than enough. I'll take it from here."

Her chin went up in fighting mode as her eyes narrowed angrily, but she too, maintained a normal tone of voice.

"Fine. I'm going to give Newton a call. I believe I'm ready to call it a day." She gave Callie a quick smile. "You don't mind, do you, darling? Nana is still a bit shaky from yesterday."

"It's okay, Nana. Besides, I've got my new tunes to listen to and my tummy is happy."

"That's my girl," Justin said. "Then I'll leave you to rock out on your own and I'll give you a call before I go to bed tonight. Okay?"

"Sure, Daddy," Callie said, as she dug her ear buds out of the drawer and plugged them into the IPod. She waved goodbye to them both and settled back against her pillows with her foot bouncing beneath the covers in time to a song only she could hear.

Justin turned to Amelia. "So, Mother. It seems we're excused. I'll walk you down."

She shrugged, refusing to admit defeat. "If you wish."

"Oh, I wish," Justin said, as he gripped her firmly by the elbow and all but shoved her out of the room.

They maintained their courtesy to each other all the way down the hall and until they boarded the elevator. Then the moment the doors went shut, Justin had his mother in the corner.

"I want his name and where he was from."

"Wade Lee Tiller. Newport."

The elevator doors opened. Justin walked off, leaving Amelia behind.

"Wait," she called. "This isn't the lobby."

"The air is foul in there. I'm walking the rest of the way down."

Amelia blanched.

The doors went shut – a symbolic ending to a relationship already in ruins.

John parked his truck in the driveway and killed the engine. They were home, but Poppy couldn't think what to do next. Today had shattered what was left of her sanity. If she moved, she was afraid she would collapse.

John glanced at her profile then got out and opened the passenger side door. Without speaking, he physically lifted her out, then put his arm around her shoulders and walked her into the house.

While they were still at the church Gladys had come down to the house to let the florist drop off all the potted plants. Everything else had been left at the cemetery. The room looked like the mortuary, but without all the weird smells.

"Oh man," John mumbled. "I didn't know they would bring this stuff here."

Poppy looked down at her clothes. The black dress she was wearing had been one of her mama's. It hadn't fit particularly well, but it served its purpose. Only now it was over and she wanted it off.

"I have to change."

"Yeah, me, too," John said, and headed for his room while Poppy went to hers.

As soon as she was alone, she stepped out of her shoes, unzipped the back of the dress, let it fall to the floor, then crawled between the covers and closed her eyes. If God was merciful, she would die in her sleep. If not, when tomorrow came, she was going to have to face going through this all over again when Jessup was buried.

A short while later John knocked on her door.

"Poppy. Are you hungry? Would you like something to eat? You haven't eaten all day."

When she didn't answer, he peeked in. "Poppy?"

"I want to sleep, Johnny. Just let me sleep."

He closed the door gently then headed for the kitchen in his sock feet. He needed to think, and he thought better without an empty stomach.

Hours later, and after fielding a dozen phone calls from

acquaintances extending their condolences because they hadn't been able to attend the service, he finally turned off the ringer, locked up the house and went to bed. Like Poppy, he'd had all he could take of today.

Surely to God tomorrow had to be better.

Prophet Jones had a burden he needed to share. He'd witnessed a crime. He considered it his legal, as well as God-given duty to tell what he'd seen. But since he didn't trust the police, it had taken him a few days to figure out what would be right. It wasn't until he'd seen the funeral procession taking Helen Sadler's mortal remains to the cemetery that he figured it out. It was logical. It was all about telling the proper people in the right order. He prayed about it all night, and when the sun came up over the Little Man, he headed for Coal Town.

It was after 8:00 before John woke. He lay without moving, listening to see if he could hear anything that would tell him Poppy was up. He didn't want to go banging around in the kitchen when she needed to sleep. He got up to go to the bathroom and as soon as he opened his door, he smelled coffee, which meant the answer was yes.

After a quick trip across the hall, he went back to get dressed, then joined her. He half expected to see her still in her robe and gown, but she was dressed – granted in old jeans and a faded long-sleeved shirt, but it was proof enough that she was willing to face the day.

"Hey, sister."

Poppy turned. He saw shadows under her eyes, but her gaze was steady.

"Hi Johnny. How do you want your eggs?"

"Two over easy."

"You do the toast."

He smiled. "One or two?"

"One for me. Two for you and one to grow on."

He pulled the end of her long ponytail. "Some things never change, do they, honey?"

"That's what Mama always said to Daddy when he made toast."

John nodded. "I remember."

She cracked eggs into the skillet and for a few moments reverted to silence. It wasn't until she was taking up his eggs and adding bacon to the plate that she spoke again.

"What do we do now?" Poppy asked, and handed the plates to John.

"What do you mean?" he asked, as he added toast and carried them to the table while Poppy went for the butter and jam.

"Mama's been buried. Daddy's in the morgue." Poppy sat down and covered her face with both hands.

Just when John thought she was going to burst into tears she looked up. There was a small, crooked smile on her face.

"Sorry. That sounded like the beginnings of a really bad country song."

He laughed. "Oh my God, you are good for my soul."

Poppy couldn't laugh, but she felt better as she buttered her toast. "I guess what I really want to know is when are you going back to Atlanta?"

"Not until I help you bury Dad, that's for sure."

"I know... but after that. Do we just get on with our lives and hope the police find out who killed Daddy? Do I try to find out who got Mama pregnant? What do we do?"

"Pass the salt and pepper."

She scooted the shakers toward him. "Well?"

"I don't know what you want to do, but I'm eating breakfast. Then we're gonna move those damned flowers and potted plants out of the living room, at least most of them. We'll figure it out as we go, okay?"

It was better than what she'd been thinking, which was nothing. Every rational thought in her head had gone missing.

She didn't want to know who had donated the sperm that made her. She wanted to go back to the beginning, when all she'd had to do was deal with finding a killer. She wasn't ready to deal with the fact that they could be one and the same.

They ate in silence for a few minutes until John got up to put his third piece of bread in the toaster.

"I don't know why you don't just make three to begin with when you make the others," Poppy said.

"Cause then it would get cold and the butter wouldn't melt. Do you want one?"

She shook her head. "Did you look to see if the paper was on the porch yet?"

"No."

"I'll check," she said, and strode through the house to the front door.

She swung the door inward then took a quick step back.

"John. John!"

"Yeah, what do you want?" he yelled.

"Come here, please."

He eyed the toaster and then jogged out of the kitchen to see what she needed, only to come to an abrupt halt behind her.

"What the hell?"

Prophet Jones was standing on the steps.

Even though it was nothing more than the morning sun at his back, he appeared to be glowing.

Prophet pointed at them. "You are Jessup Sadler's children."

John put his hands on Poppy's shoulders. "Yes we are."

"I saw your father struck down by the Devil's hand. I have his footprints in my pocket."

John flinched. *I'll be a son-of-a-bitch, Aaron was right.*

Poppy was stunned. "You witnessed my father's murder?"

Prophet pointed to the heavens. "As God is my witness, yes I did."

"Why haven't you gone to the police?" John asked.

The old man threw up his hands and began to dance around on the porch as if his shoes were on fire.

"They are corrupt. If I tell, they will do what they did before. They will let the Devil buy his way out and justice will not be served."

Poppy's heart began to hammer. If this was true, this was exactly what Mike Amblin needed to hear. But how to convince the crazy old man was another issue.

"Have you eaten this morning?" Poppy asked.

Prophet's rage settled so fast it was almost as if it had never happened.

"Why, no, ma'am. I have not."

"I can make you an egg and bacon sandwich, if you like."

"I would appreciate that," Prophet said, then looked nervous that they might expect him to go inside. He hadn't been inside a building in so long he wasn't certain he knew the rules any more – but he did remember there were rules. "I will set out here to eat."

"That's fine," Poppy said. "My brother, John will wait with you."

She gave John a look, as if to say, don't let him get away, and then flew back into the house. Within three minutes she was back with the food and a hot cup of coffee laced with cream and sugar in the biggest mug they owned.

She handed him the food and then stepped back, expecting him to wolf it down like the animal he appeared to be. But he surprised her. Instead he seated himself on the top step, put the plate on his knees, and then bowed his head and said a blessing. That's when they remembered he'd been a preacher. Maybe he wasn't so far from God after all.

Poppy waited until he'd gotten down a good half of the sandwich before she spoke.

"Mr. Jones, I'm very grateful that you came. I understand your concerns, but I want you to know that my brother and I have a very good friend on the police force who is honest, diligent, and hard working. His name is Mike Amblin."

"I don't like cops," Prophet repeated.

"You would like Mike," John said, adding to Poppy's praise. "He's our friend. He's trying very hard to find out who killed our father."

Poppy was so anxious to convince him that she had to fold her hands in her lap to keep them from shaking. "What if we call him to come here? Then you can tell him what you saw in front of us. That way no one can deny what you said because we'll be witnesses." She could tell he didn't like it, but before he could argue, she fired another question at him. "Do you like pie? I have pie. I have chocolate and apple. Would you like a piece of each?"

Prophet looked at her as if she'd just told him she wanted to give her soul to God.

"I do like pie. A piece of each would be fine since you offered."

"I'll be right back," Poppy said, and flew back into the house and went straight to the phone. The detective's card was lying beside it. Her hands were still shaking as she made the call, then it rang three times before she heard his voice.

"Homcide, Detective Amblin."

"Detective Amblin… uh, Mike... Prophet Jones is sitting on my front porch eating an egg sandwich and I'm about to give him two pieces of pie. He said he witnessed Daddy's murder. He says he has the Devil's footprints in his pocket. I don't know what that means, but I think it might be important. He doesn't trust police. I don't know why, but I think he'll talk to you if John and I are witnesses. Can you come?"

Mike's head was spinning. They'd been looking all over for the man and then Poppy offers him up with an egg sandwich and a piece of pie.

"We're already on the way and if he has anything good to say, save a piece of that pie for me."

The line went dead. She raced to the kitchen, cut two pieces of pie, grabbed a fork, and ran back.

Prophet was swallowing the last bite of his sandwich when she traded one plate for the other.

"How about some more coffee?" she asked, and then grabbed the cup before he could answer and flew back into the house.

Prophet was too entranced by the pie to answer.

"This is a fine sight," he said, and picked up the fork.

"A fine sight, indeed."

"Yes sir," John agreed.

Poppy returned within moments, slid the cup down beside Prophet, then sat down in one of the old metal lawn chairs and looked toward the bridge. She wasn't certain how long it would take to get from the precinct to her house, but she hoped they hurried. She didn't know how often this old man ate, but she was sure it wasn't regular and nothing like what he'd just polished off. If she fed him anything else, she was afraid that he'd be sick.

John glanced at her over his shoulder.

She nodded.

He gave her a thumbs-up and then continued to talk religion with Prophet while he ate.

Within a couple of minutes Poppy began to hear a siren and suspected it was Mike. She hoped he didn't drive up to her house like that and expect the old man to stay put. The sound got closer and closer and she caught a glimpse of flashing lights from a car driving onto the bridge and then all of a sudden the sound ended. Less than a minute later, she saw Mike's dark sedan turn the corner at the end of the block and come flying down the street. That was when her anxiety disappeared. In her mind, Mike would fix it, just as he'd been doing ever since they'd met. In the worst of times during the past few days, Mike Amblin had been her savior.

"Are they cops?" Prophet asked, pointing his fork at them as they came up the walk.

"Yes, but just our friend, Mike and his partner," John said.

Prophet frowned, but there was still pie on the plate and he wasn't leaving that behind.

Poppy walked to the edge of the porch.

"Hi guys. I'm really glad you could stop by. Do you know Mr. Jones?"

Mike caught on immediately that she was playing down their arrival. "Well, I know who he is, but I've never had the pleasure of an official meeting," Mike said, and immediately extended his hand. "Mr. Jones, you know me, right? I'm Detective Amblin and this is my partner, Detective Duroy. I understand you have some valuable information you need to share. You don't know how happy we are that you were willing to come forward."

It was the straightforward approach that won Prophet over.

"I considered it my legal, as well as God-given duty to stand as witness for a man who cannot speak for himself."

"Admirable," Mike said, and gave Kenny the eye, making sure he was on board.

"Yeah, good job," Kenny said. Just looking at the old man made him itch and he had to shove his hands in his pockets to keep from scratching.

"I am having pie," Prophet said. "As soon as I finish, I will give you my information, is that all right?"

Mike eyed the pie. "Absolutely. Pie that good needs not to be wasted."

Now that the cops were here, John didn't feel the need to stand guard.

"Mr. Jones has requested to stay outside, so I'm going to get some folding chairs. I'll bring a couple out so you guys can be comfortable while you talk."

Prophet finished off his pie then handed the dishes to Poppy with a good deal of formality while the detectives took a seat on the porch.

"It has been some time since I've been treated so kindly. It is my opinion that your parents did a fine job raising the pair of you."

"Thank you," Poppy said.

Prophet took the paper napkin that Poppy had given him and wiped his mouth and hands as carefully as if he was a clean-shaven man, and then resumed his seat on the top step and faced the cops.

John moved over to where Poppy was sitting for moral support. He had a feeling this wasn't going to be an easy thing for either one of them to hear.

"I am ready," Prophet said.

Mike leaned forward, resting his elbows on his knees. "I would like for you to tell us what you saw and if we have questions afterward, would it be all right to ask?"

"Yes, that will be fine. I will begin by telling you I have a place under the bridge I call the nest. It's a nice place and it's private and that's where I was the night the Devil came to the Little Man. That's where I was when it got dark. Later it started to rain. Do you remember that it was raining?"

Mike nodded. "Yes, we remember."

"Well then, I will continue," Prophet said. "I heard noises so I looked out. Two cars were on the riverbank. Two men arguing, waving their arms and shouting while the rain kept getting heavier. I never saw the gun, but I heard the shots. Three of them. As lightning struck, I saw Mr. Sadler stagger and fall backward into the river."

Poppy moaned, then doubled over and hid her face.

John felt the shock, but it was swiftly turning to rage.

Prophet looked anxious, as if he'd just realized he was talking about their loved one.

"I'm sorry," he said.

"It's okay," Mike said. "They want the bad guy caught as much as we do."

Prophet nodded. "So just after Mr. Sadler fell into the river, another bolt of lightning struck the south side of the river bank, which I considered a sign from God. It lit a spotlight on the evil that had been done, and that's when I saw the Devil's face. I saw it as clearly as I'm looking at you, but he didn't see me. He got in his car and drove away. I ran to the riverbank to see if I could help, but Mr. Sadler was already floating face down and I couldn't reach him."

He glanced over at John and Poppy. There were tears on his face. "I'm sorry. I'm so sorry I couldn't help."

"You are helping," Mike said. "You're standing witness for Mr. Sadler when he cannot. So what happened next?"

Prophet gathered himself then paused. For a moment they thought he was through, and then he thrust his hand into the depths of the rags he was wearing and pulled out three empty cartridges. He dropped them in Mike's outstretched hand.

"I found his footprints. I knew the police would not believe me unless I had proof."

Kenny pulled an evidence bag out of his jacket. "What have we got?"

"45 caliber. We're gonna be looking for a revolver," Mike said as he dropped them inside, then sealed, dated it and put it in his pocket.

"Great job, Mr. Jones. We'll log this in as soon as we get back to the precinct. This is the first piece of real physical evidence we have from the crime scene. Could you show us exactly where this took place?"

Prophet got up and then pointed north toward the river.

"See those three pines grouped up together just to your

right? The ones barely showing over the house with the green roof?"

"Yes."

"One of the men parked to the left of the trees. The other parked to the right. The shooting took place between the cars and Mr. Sadler fell off the bank right where they stood. Only the car's not there anymore. Right after I picked up the footprints, two young men came running up out of the dark. I told them to get away, that the Devil was on the bridge. They took Mr. Sadler's car but maybe they were just scared. I know I was. The Devil is a frightening sight. I went and hid just in case he came back but I didn't see him again."

"You keep calling him the Devil, but we need a name."

Prophet slapped the top of his head with both hands and then the sides of his face. It was hard to tell if he was angry or frustrated, but he wasn't happy with the question.

"The Devil has many names. Beelzebub. Satan. Fallen Angel. It is not my place to name him."

Mike sighed. This is just what he'd been afraid of. The old man was rambling. Still, they had the empty cartridge, which was more than they'd had before they came.

"If you saw a picture of the Devil who shot Mr. Sadler, could you identify it?" Mike asked.

"Of course, of course," Prophet said. "You find the minion, I'll say yea or nay."

All of a sudden Mike understood. "Minion? Are you telling me that the killer is just one of the Devil's helpers?"

"The Devil is legion. He has many guises... not the least of which are those he chooses to do his works."

Mike glanced at Kenny, who rolled his eyes and looked away.

"Do you know where the Devil lives?" Mike asked.

Prophet pointed across the river. "He dwells in the same place he's always been ever since the city began."

Mike kept remembering John's story about Adam Caulfield supposedly buying off the police so that no one was held guilty for the deaths of Prophet's family. But Adam was dead. So were they looking for someone who worked for Caulfield, or was this just the rants of a man bent on revenge?

He couldn't ignore the fact that Justin Caulfield's name was on the list of Helen Sadler's classmates and he'd been the person who'd left the hospital just ahead of Jessup the night he died. Had he and Jessup caught up with each other? Was the shooting a result of the confrontation? So far they had nothing but theories, and police work was all about facts not guesswork.

The only thing he knew for sure was that J.T. and Big Boy's alibis had just been verified. They would be charged with car theft, but nothing more.

"Is that all you need?" Prophet asked. "I have an appointment I need to keep."

"Unless you have something more to add, I think that does it," Mike said. "I said it before and I'll say it again, thank you for coming forward. I promise your testimony will not be wasted."

"Then I will be off," Prophet said, and got up with a flourish. It was a fact that his gentlemanly speech and manner were at odds with his appearance. But it was noticeably poignant that he paused to brush off the back of his pants, as if it was actually possible to shed the years of accumulated dirt with which he lived.

Poppy stood up, as well. "Thank you, Mr. Jones. Johnny and I will be forever grateful to you. Whenever you want something to eat, just knock on my door."

Prophet beamed. "You are a good woman and a fine cook and I thank you for the open door invitation."

He walked off the premises with a bounce in his step and never looked back.

Poppy caught Mike looking at her. "I have pie."

Mike smiled. "You're not trying to bribe an officer of the law, are you?"

"Certainly not. Just a bite of something sweet to send you on your way."

"I'll take some and Mike's share too, if he doesn't want it," Kenny said.

"Come inside," John said, and held the door for them as they followed Poppy into the house, then into the kitchen.

Poppy pulled three pies out of the refrigerator, set three

plates and forks on the kitchen table and handed John a knife.

"Would you cut the pies while I make some more coffee?"

"Sure." He waved the detectives toward the table. "Take a seat, guys. We're trying to eat our way through the generosity of our neighbors."

Kenny grinned. "Happy to be of service."

Mike had yet to sit. He wanted an excuse to help Poppy, but it wasn't happening. He finally sat down just to keep from calling attention to himself then wound up watching her as she worked. She caught him staring again, but this time she smiled.

Mike was verging on making a fool of himself and realized he didn't care. He made a vow that when this case was over, he was going to come back and knock on her door for an entirely different purpose.

CHAPTER SEVENTEEN

Poppy was at loose ends. Her father's body had yet to be released and she was too unsettled to go back to work, although she would have to go soon. It wasn't as if she could afford to stay home much longer. She dreaded going back and facing Vic knowing he was no longer engaged. He was a good guy but, for her, the magic wasn't there.

She'd done all the laundry and John was out running errands. She was still avoiding her parents' bedroom, which was prolonging the inevitable. It wasn't like the place was haunted by anything but memories and it would give her something to do.

As she entered, she left the door ajar then pulled up the blinds and opened a window. The air was chilly, but she wanted lingering scents of aftershave and perfume gone. It made her sad that a scent could survive the people who'd worn them.

She hesitated only briefly before moving to the closet. Money was too hard to come by to waste something that could be reused. John might want some of his father's shirts, but the pants would never fit. Jessup had been a good fifty pounds heavier.

Poppy moved hangars back and forth, checking Helen's clothes and knew, because she was much taller than her mother, they just wouldn't work. The logical thing would be to have a yard sale and get what she could for the clothes, but she couldn't bring herself to hawk their clothing for nickels and dimes on the dollar. Her other option was donation, and that's the way she would go.

The black dress she'd worn to Helen's funeral had worked only because it had been an extra-long style. As soon as John came back, she'd have him go through the shirts he might want and pack up the rest for donation.

Satisfied by the decisions she made, she scanned what was left of the room. There was the dresser where she'd found the infamous diary, a couple of chairs, and Mama's vanity. The furniture stayed, and she would pack up the drawers when she packed up the clothes.

Her gaze went back to the drawer where she'd found the diary and couldn't help wondering where it had been hidden or how her father had come to find it. She wondered if anything else might be hidden that she needed to find.

The property had been in the Roberts' family since her great-grandparents time and she'd heard stories of the old-timers in the family no longer trusting banks after they failed in the 1930s. There were bound to be hidey-holes in this house where they'd kept money and important papers. Although she'd lived in this house her entire life, she'd never thought about looking for secrets. It might be something she should do.

Now that the notion was in her head, she couldn't let go. The logical places to begin were in closets. Since she was still in her parents' bedroom, she started with theirs.

She pulled everything from the bottom of the closet out into the room, shoved all the hangars to one end of the rod and got down on her hands and knees. An hour and three closets later all she had found were dust bunnies and the occasional spider.

The grandfather clock at the end of the hall struck the hour as she walked past on her way to the linen closet. She paused to check her watch against the time and then stopped, suddenly struck by the clock, itself.

It had been sitting in the same place for as long as she could remember. She knew there was nothing behind it, or in the floor beneath it, but the glass door on the front opened up when the pendulum needed to be reset.

She had a moment of 'what if' and opened the door. She stopped the pendulum, then knelt and began running her fingers all along the inside.

The base of the clock's interior was a good fifteen inches above the floor. If the base wasn't a solid piece of wood, it would leave plenty of room to stash stuff – if, in fact, the little floor came up.

There was only one way to find out.

It didn't take long to find a thin, fingernail-size groove at the back of the base. She felt a kick of excitement, thinking she might be onto something, so she dug in her nails and pulled. The floor came up, revealing a deep pocket beneath.

"Oh wow," Poppy said, but excitement quickly faded when it appeared to be empty.

As she leaned in for a closer look, she saw something up against the front corner wall. She pulled it out, then rocked back on her heels.

An old tobacco tin?

She eyed the faded red paint and the Prince Albert logo, remembering her Granddaddy Roberts had rolled his own cigarettes. Still, it seemed odd to hide something so ordinary. She opened the lid, tilting it toward the light and saw what appeared to be a piece of paper inside. When she turned the tin upside down, the paper fell out.

Her eyes widened, and then her heart skipped a beat. It was a check - made out to Helen Roberts - for the sum of fifty thousand dollars – and it had never been cashed.

When she saw the signature, her stomach rolled. She had a sick feeling she'd just found the identity of Sunny's first love. Her pulse began to race from the weight of new fear.

She put the check in her pocket, dropped the floor back in place and set the pendulum into motion. Her legs might be shaking but her thoughts were clear. She had to call Mike.

Kenny Duroy was at the dentist having a root canal. Detective Harmon was doing follow-up on Tom Bonaventure out at Caulfield #14.

Mike was stuck at the desk catching up on paperwork, the only part of his job he disliked. When his phone rang, he was glad for an excuse to stop.

"Homicide, Detective Amblin."

"I know who got Mama pregnant."

And just like that, his heart was racing. "Poppy?"

"I am going to talk to him. You can go with me, or I'll go on my own."

Panic set in. "Wait! You can't go on your own. It could be dangerous. He may be connected in some way to your father's death."

"Then I guess you better come get me, because I'm going, one way or the other."

The line went dead in his ear.

"Oh shit."

He headed for the Lieutenant's office on the run, then knocked once and poked his head inside.

"We may have a break in the Sadler case. I'm going to pick up the daughter now."

Green frowned. "Why do you need her? I don't like getting citizens involved in police procedure."

"Because she's the one with the information and all she told me was that she knew who got her mother pregnant and that she was going to see him, with or without me. I can't stop her when I don't know where she's going."

"I don't like this. Get the info and leave her at home."

"Sorry, sir, but you don't know her. The woman has a mind of her own."

"Then make damn sure no one gets hurt. And take Duroy."

"He's at the dentist, remember?"

"Call him to meet you."

"Yes sir," Mike said, and left the room running.

All the way across town he kept wondering what condition she'd be in when he arrived. She'd sounded mad and determined which, for him, was far better than hysterical or on the floor in a flat-out faint.

He had no sooner pulled up to the house when she came out. Her chin was up, her long hair flying, and the length of her stride was nothing short of forceful.

Yeah. She was pissed. That he could handle.

She opened the door and got in, then fumbled for the seat belt before she finally got it buckled.

"Well?" she said, when he still sat there with the car in park.

"I don't know where we're going, remember?"

She sighed, shoved her hands through her hair in quiet frustration, then took the check out of her pocket and handed it to him.

"I found this hidden in an old tobacco tin."

"Son-of-a-bitch, so it *was* Caulfield."

Poppy flinched. "You suspected him? You never said anything about it."

"It was part of our ongoing investigation. We had the list of boys your mother graduated with. It was a case of simple elimination to figure out who was from the high side of the city and who lived in Coal Town, then find current addresses. There weren't all that many who would have been present the night your father died. And there's still no proof that the person who killed your father was connected to the boy who got Sunny pregnant."

Poppy frowned. "That's not true now! You heard Prophet Jones yourself. You heard what he said. If he considered anyone connected with the Caulfields the Devil, and Justin Caulfield's name is on the graduate list, and his father's name is on that check you are holding, and he said the Devil's minion killed my daddy, what else could you possibly want?"

"We have to have more than Prophet's eye witness testimony. Remember the time and the weather when Prophet claimed he was the witness to the murder? He was a good distance away under the bridge, in the dark, and in a torrential downpour. Any lawyer worth his pay would excuse all that away as nothing more than the crazy ramblings of a man with a grudge against one family."

"But you have the shell casings."

"Yes, but we don't have the gun. Casings can't prove ownership, and frankly, neither can a gun unless it's been registered or used in a prior crime that might be traced back to a specific person during the commission of that crime."

Poppy was angry. She wanted justice and all she was getting was the run-around. She unbuckled her seat belt.

"Give me back the check."

"But-"

"If you aren't interested in finding out the truth then I don't need you. Give it back."

Mike sighed. "That's not what I said and you know it. Besides, I didn't say it never happened, I just said right now we can't prove it. You are not going to confront a suspect on your own, regardless."

He started to hand over the check and then stopped.

"Oh. Wait. Son-of-a-bitch. She never cashed it. Talk about a statement. There was no doubt that she took it as the insult it was meant to be."

Somewhat mollified by what he'd just said, Poppy nodded. "Ever since I found it, I've been thinking about that last entry in her diary."

Mike nodded. "Where she threatened to kill herself if her father went to the family, and he reminded her she'd be murdering her own child?"

"Yes, and obviously, Grandpa Roberts did go because here's the evidence. But Adam Caulfield didn't pay him off. Mama was the one he wanted gone. He made the check out to her. He wanted her to know *she* was the one who was unsuitable. I can only imagine how frustrated Grandpa was when he saw it, and I am guessing there was one great big fight when she refused to cash it. It was her way of telling all the men in her life that she couldn't be bought."

Mike handed the check back to her. "What are you going to do with this?"

"Make sure he knows his dirty little secret isn't a secret anymore. I hope it gives him nightmares. After that, he's all yours."

"I'll make some calls. Find out for sure where he's at before we start what could turn into a wild goose chase, okay?"

"I don't care how you do it."

"Where's your brother?"

"Running errands. I left him a note."

"Sit tight. I'll see if Caulfield is at work," Mike said. He found the number for the company headquarters and called it first.

"Caulfield Industries, Frances speaking. How may I direct your call?"

"This is Detective Amblin with Caulfield P.D. It's imperative that I speak to Mr. Caulfield."

"I'm sorry, but he's already left the office for the day." "Then I need the number to his cell phone."

Frances hesitated. "We don't give out the number to his private phone."

"Look, Frances, I'm not selling tickets to a raffle. This is police business. The number. Please."

Startled, she quickly gave it up.

"Thank you for your cooperation." He hung up then before the secretary had time to think about what she'd done and call Caulfield herself, he made the call.

Justin answered on the second ring.

"Justin Caulfield."

"Mr. Caulfield, this is Detective Amblin with Homicide. It is imperative that I speak with you, but your secretary said you'd already left for the day."

Justin was a little curious, but nothing more. "Actually, I haven't left the building. I've been staying in the apartment on the top floor for the past couple of days. Do you want me to meet you, or are you okay with coming here? All you have to do is go to the guard in the lobby. I'll tell him to send you up."

"We'll come there," Mike said, and hung up just as John pulled into the driveway. "Hey, looks like your brother is back."

"Wait here," Poppy said and got out.

Mike saw the frown on John Sadler's face when he realized the police were back. Then he remembered Kenny needed to know where they were going and quickly sent him a text.

Mike watched their conversation without hearing it, but it didn't take her long to state her case. When she started back to the car, John was behind her.

"He's going with us," she said.

John got in the back seat without speaking.

Mike put the car in gear and drove away. When they got to the office building of Caulfield Industries, Kenny was waiting.

"You made good time," Mike said as they approached the building.

"Mouff's numb. You talk."

Mike frowned in sympathy then glanced back at the Sadlers. John's hand was on Poppy's shoulder. She was standing as close to him as she could get. He got the message. Whatever happened, they were in it together.

"Let's get this over with," he said, and led the way into the building and flashed his badge at the guard. "We're here to see Mr. Caulfield. He's expecting us."

"Yes sir, he already alerted me to your arrival. Follow me."

The guard led the way to the bank of elevators, then paused at a single elevator door and used a key to open it.

"As soon as the door closes, just press the button. There's only one. It will take you straight to the penthouse."

"Thank you," Mike said, and within moments they were on their way up.

He looked at Poppy. She was pale and tense, but her head was up, her shoulders back. She didn't appear nervous so much as braced for a fight.

The car stopped suddenly. When the door opened, Justin Caulfield was standing on the other side. Mike watched the expression on his face go from congenial to shock as the car emptied. He glanced back at Poppy. She wore anger well. Her skin was pale - her chin was up - her shoulders back. Then she separated herself from the others to face Justin alone.

Poppy felt the impact of this full-circle moment. From Sunny's betrayal to Jessup's murder to coming face to face with a child he had denied, Justin Caulfield had run out of places to hide. And then something happened that she wasn't expecting. He started to cry.

"I didn't know about you. I swear to God, I didn't know," he said.

She wanted to shoot him herself. "Ignorance is no excuse," she snapped, and when he reached toward her, she slapped the check in his hand. "I believe this is yours."

Justin's stomach rolled as he recognized his father's handwriting. If he had a snowball's chance in hell of ever having a relationship with her, he had to dump his pride at her feet.

"I loved Sunny with every pore of my body and when I should have been a man and stood up to my father's threat, I buckled instead. I was a fool. I've lived with the shame of that ever since. But I didn't know anything about what happened in her life after the break-up. I went away to college and didn't come back. Not for visits. Not for holidays. Nothing. I was angry at my parents and that was my juvenile pay-back for what they'd demanded. I didn't know she was pregnant. I didn't know my father paid her off. I didn't know about you, about any of it until just before your mother's funeral."

Poppy was so mad she was shaking. "I don't believe you."

Justin felt sick. "I don't blame you, but it's why I'm here instead of in my own home. Would you please come sit? All of you? I ask because I don't think my legs are going to hold me much longer."

"I don't need to hear this," Poppy said.

John walked up behind Poppy. "Yes, you do, sister."

"No, Johnny, I don't want-"

"It's to your advantage to know all there is to know about how you came to be."

He took her by the elbow and led her toward the sofa while the others followed.

It never occurred to Justin that a police presence was unnecessary for this revelation. He was just grateful the secret was no longer an issue.

As for Mike and Kenny, they were curious as to where this was going. They had a better chance of gaining new information if Caulfield didn't know he was a murder suspect.

Justin was transfixed by Poppy's presence. She dominated the room with her righteous indignation and he applauded her for it. She had not come to insinuate herself into his moneyed world. She'd come to annihilate the man who betrayed both her and her mother.

"It is painful to me that I have seen you off and on ever since you began working at The Depot and not know who you were. By that, I meant, not know you were Sunny's child. I would have never imagined you were mine as well. As for your father's death, I heard a body had been found in the river when

I got to work. My office overlooks the Little Man. I could see police and rescue vehicles on the river bank but didn't know what was happening or that the victim they found had been murdered. Even after I learned the victim's name, I had no way of knowing he was your father or Sunny's husband. I didn't know your mother by any name other than Sunny. If someone had walked in and told me Helen Sadler died the same day her husband was murdered, I would have thought it a tragedy, but nothing would lead me to believe I was in any way connected to the family."

"So it was just pity that caused you to give Daddy's pension to me?" Poppy snapped.

Justin shrugged. "Compassion is a better word, but yes. He'd given thirty years of his life to Caulfield Industries. One error on a job lasting that long deserved a break. If that's wrong, then I'm guilty."

Poppy didn't buy it and the tone of her voice gave it away.

"So, paying for the rest of Mama's medical bills, all the flowers you sent to her funeral, and offering to pay for Daddy's were just more gestures of compassion?"

"Yes and no. At the risk of making this sound insulting, your family lived in Coal Town. It costs a fortune to bury one person. I couldn't imagine how a family from there could come up with the money to bury two. The outstanding medical bills would have not been an issue if Mr. Sadler had not been fired, so I considered it a company problem that had to be fixed. But the flowers were a different matter. I went to the funeral home. There were no flowers. Sunny loved flowers. It was too late to apologize to her. The flowers were a sop to my conscience, not a ploy to gain some kind of points from you. And you need to remember, at that point, I didn't know of any connection to you."

Poppy folded her arms. She'd heard him out. She was ready to leave then Mike changed her mind.

"If I may, I'd like to ask a few questions," Mike said.

Justin was so overwhelmed that it still had not registered as to why there were actually police on the premises for what amounted to a very personal revelation.

"Ask whatever you want," he said.

"When did you find out about Sunny's pregnancy?"

The expression on Justin's face shifted to one of anger. "Right after I found out Callie was not my daughter."

Mike's first thought was 'where the hell did that come from' and then sat back and waited to see what came after.

Justin sighed as he shoved a shaky hand through his hair. "Considering what I'd caused, fate dealt me a good dose of payback, don't you think?"

"I don't follow," Mike said.

"Look, for now, what I'm going to tell you needs to stay in this room. My fourteen-year-old daughter Callie is very ill and still knows none of this. The disease she's been suffering from over the past year nearly killed her. She's finally on the road to recovery, but it destroyed her kidneys. She needs a transplant to save her life. My mother and I were having an argument, which is nothing new, when something I said scared her into saying something she would never have revealed."

"And that was what?" Mike asked.

Justin looked at Poppy. "I only have one kidney. But I said I'd do anything to save Callie's life, including dying so that she could have mine."

Poppy blinked. That didn't fit in with the cheating, lying killer she believed him to be.

Mike frowned. "And that angered your mother?"

Justin nodded. "I guess she was afraid I'd do something crazy to make that happen. Basically, she said I'd be killing myself for nothing because I wouldn't be a match. That's when it hit the fan. Long story short, I found out my deceased wife had been pregnant when she married me. I made some kind of remark about fate and irony then said at least that hadn't happened to Sunny. It was the look on my mother's face that gave her away. I lost it. She finally admitted Sunny's father had come demanding compensation after I'd left for college, that they didn't really believe him about her pregnancy, but in any case wanted her paid off and out of their lives. I told her they'd had no right to keep that information from me, and that they were merciless in the way they'd treated her. Of course she disagreed, but that was that. I told her to get out of the house and not to come back, but she's still there, which is why

I'm here."

Mike glanced at Kenny who shrugged and looked away. Once again, if they believed this story, their theory of how the murder could have happened just tanked.

Justin caught the look. "What? What am I missing here?"

Mike knew what he was about to do was risky, but the whole case was full of holes. Might as well put another one in it and see what leaked out.

"There's a witness to Jessup Sadler's murder," Mike said.

Justin waited, when no one said anything else, he frowned, then leaned forward.

"Isn't that a good thing?"

"It is for us," Mike said.

Justin glanced at Poppy. "I'm sure that's good news for you and your brother, as well."

John squeezed her hand to keep her quiet. Poppy got the message and leaned back against him. This was overwhelming on so many levels.

Justin frowned. Everyone was staring at him, like they were waiting for a lit fuse to blow.

"Look, I may be a world-class louse, but I'm not stupid. What aren't you saying?"

"Where were you Tuesday night?" Mike asked.

Justin leaned back. "At the hospital with Callie."

"Jessup Sadler was at the hospital that night, too. A few days prior he'd found out Poppy wasn't his child, but that's all he knew. We know nurses on duty heard him he and his wife arguing about it that night."

Poppy suddenly moaned then covered her face as John pulled her close.

Mike sighed. Damn. He'd forgotten the family knew none of this, but it was too late to take it back.

"I'm still not following," Justin said.

"We have reason to believe Helen Sadler gave up your name, and that you and Jessup might have met up and had words. You left the hospital only minutes ahead of Sadler, who sped out of the parking lot right behind you."

Justin's eyes widened. "You think I had something to do with his murder? You can't be serious? Why would I kill him for news like that? My God, if I'd known it then, I might have had a chance to make my peace with Sunny before she died."

"So you're saying he didn't show up at your house, that you two did not argue, and that you did not follow him to the river?"

"I didn't go home from the hospital. I drove straight to the office and was almost late, at that. My secretary, Frances, can vouch for my arrival. I had an overseas conference call that lasted until just after 1:00 a.m. The records will reflect that. I don't know what Mr. Sadler did when he left the hospital, but if he thought he would catch up with me at home, he would have soon realized he was mistaken."

"What do you mean?" Mike asked.

"He would have had to deal with Mother. If he had gotten loud or pushy, she would have had Newton send him packing."

"Who's Newton?"

The tone of Justin's voice was nothing short of sarcastic.

"Mother's driver-slash-bodyguard, as if she needed one. It gives her a false sense of entitlement to think she's so damn special she needs to be sheltered from the masses. He worked for us for years when I was growing up, then retired after Dad died and Mother moved to Florida. He came out of retirement at Mother's request when she came back to help me with Callie."

"Would you consider him capable of murder?"

Justin's expression went blank and then a muscle suddenly jerked at the side of his jaw.

"I don't suppose I ever thought about it."

"So, now that you are thinking about it, do you consider him capable of murder?"

All of a sudden, Justin remembered the fury on his mother's face when she'd told him if it had been left up to her, she would have had Sunny and her baby tossed into the Little Man like an unwanted cur and her litter.

He stood abruptly. "I need a drink."

CHAPTER EIGHTEEN

Justin headed for the mini-bar, then suddenly diverted and made a dash for the bathroom.

They heard the door slam, then the sounds of retching.

"Is he lying?" Poppy asked.

"Right now there's no way of knowing for sure," Mike said.

"What's your instinct telling you," Poppy persisted.

"That he's telling the truth."

Poppy glanced up at her brother. "Johnny?"

John threw it back on her. "It doesn't matter what I think. What do you think about what he's said so far?"

"That I don't want to be related in any way to people who behave like this."

Moments later, Justin came back carrying a wet washcloth. He paused at the mini-bar, but instead of getting liquor, he got a bottle of water, took a drink then carried it with him as he sat back down.

"I apologize," he said softly, took another sip of the water, then leaned back and closed his eyes.

"You never did answer my question," Mike said. "Do you think this Newton fellow capable of murder?"

He swiped the cold cloth across his face and then sat up. The calm in his voice was out of context with the upset he'd just suffered.

"Given the right set of circumstances, I think some people are capable of doing almost anything to achieve what they want."

"What does that mean?" Mike asked.

Justin shrugged as his focus suddenly shifted from reaction to action.

"I have an offer to make."

Mike frowned. Just when he thought the guy was on the up and up, it appeared he was suddenly ready to make a deal. The knowledge was somewhat disappointing.

"What kind of offer?"

"I am going home. Obviously, I have Poppy's check to return to my mother, and some things that need to be said to her as well. Put a wire on me. If anything is said during that conversation that will, in any way, aid you in finding out who murdered Jessup Sadler, I am willing to do it." Then he looked at Poppy. "I'll do anything it takes to make this right."

Poppy was shocked by the offer. She didn't want to feel anything for him – not empathy for his daughter's health or regret for what he and her mother had lost, or that he might be offering to do something noble.

"The only thing that would make this right is if Daddy hadn't been murdered," she snapped.

"I didn't do it, but I will help you find out who did," Justin said.

Again, the man surprised Mike. He still didn't know who killed Jessup Sadler, but he would bet his pension it wasn't Caulfield.

Two hours later, with the police surveillance van in place one block over, they were ready to monitor the latest confrontation between Justin and Amelia.

That's when Justin Caulfield drove home.

His gut was in knots. His heart was pounding. He couldn't let himself think about what he was doing or he'd back out. If God was ready to give him a break, the police would hear nothing but another fight between mother and son. But he wasn't hopeful. There was a very sick feeling in the back of his mind that he already knew what the outcome would be.

He knew Poppy was in the van with Duroy and Amblin. She would be a witness to whatever was said and that was okay with him. She deserved to know the truth – all of it – no matter how ugly. But he hadn't let himself think of how the outcome might impact Callie. He'd deal with that as it unfolded.

As he turned up the drive, a strange thing happened. Instead of growing more anxious, a calm suddenly came over him. If he'd been a more religious person, he might have thought it was God reminding him he was not alone. But what it did do was reassure him what he was doing was right.

He parked in front of the house and got out just as the sun was beginning to set. The sky toward the west was awash in long, feathery plumes of purple laced with streaks of cotton-candy pink and popsicle orange. The beauty of the sky was definitely at odds with the ugliness that sheltered beneath his roof. His hand strayed to the front of his shirt as he felt the microphone taped to his chest then he unlocked the door and went in.

The security alarm beeped twice, signaling the door had been opened, then went silent, but it brought Oral Newton out into the hall. When he saw it was only Justin, he made a u-turn to go back to the kitchen.

"Newton, where's my mother?"

"I believe she's in her room."

"Would you please tell her I need to speak with her. I'll be in the library."

Newton was still pissed that Justin had alluded to some kind of personal relationship between him and Amelia Caulfield, but silently acquiesced.

Once Justin entered the library, he went straight to the bar and poured himself a shot of whiskey, downing it neat. It lit a quick fire in his belly that he couldn't afford to flame, which meant stopping with one. He set the glass aside and moved to the windows overlooking the back grounds. It was a beautiful scene that he'd taken for granted. Matching the luxury with which he'd been raised against the poverty in which Poppy had grown up made him sick. It was just one more nail in the wall going up between him and his mother.

When he heard her footsteps coming down the hall, he pulled the check Poppy had given him out of his pocket and turned toward the door. What he had to say, he would say to her face.

Amelia didn't know what was up, but she was not happy that she'd been summoned in such a manner and intended to let Justin know it. She hadn't seen him since they'd met in Callie's room and supposed he'd come to gloat about that illegitimate bitch down in Coal Town. If he thought she would ever accept her, he had another think coming.

By the time she got to the library, her indignation was at an all-time high. Her chin came up as she crossed the threshold then saw her son silhouetted against the windows overlooking the grounds. For a moment she thought it was Adam, and then remembered her husband was dead.

"Do not ever summon me in this manner again," she announced.

"Your behavior has nullified courtesy. You've been filling my daughter's head with appalling advice. You've kept secrets from me that were nothing short of inhumane. You've already been asked to leave and you're still here. It has become increasingly obvious to me that I've never really known you. The mother I thought I knew is really nothing but a vicious, lying fake."

Amelia's jaw set as she crossed the room to where Justin was standing. The rage was still there. Something had fueled it, but what? She waited until she was so close she could count the three freckles still on the bridge of his nose, and then smirked.

"What happened? Did the reunion with your little bastard not go as well as you'd hoped? What happened, did she try to milk you for a bundle of money, too?"

Justin wouldn't let himself think about what Poppy was hearing. He'd come for a specific purpose and that was what held his focus.

"Actually, she came to see me before I got the chance, and as you said, it *was* about money. Oh, by the way, she brought something for you when she came."

Before Amelia could react, Justin grabbed her hand and slapped the check into her palm.

"She found this in her mother's possessions, and needless to say was not only shocked but disgusted. Finding out I was her natural father was not high on her list of happy moments. You will notice Sunny never cashed it and Poppy didn't want it either, which says a whole lot about their morals and backs up my opinion of my dear parents."

Amelia was stunned. Fifty thousand dollars would have been a fortune to someone from Coal Town. "But-"

"But what, Mother? Why didn't she cash it? I'd be guessing, but the Sunny I knew wasn't the kind of girl who could be bought. She wasn't impressed with who I was. She just loved me. I seem to remember you saying that her father was the one who'd come after money, not her, but you notice Dad made the check out to her, not her father. Her father couldn't cash it and she wouldn't. She got back at all of us. She wouldn't be bought."

Amelia tossed the check onto the desk behind her.

"Fine! So she was a saint, but as I've already stated, it's all water under the bridge."

"At least you got your money back, which proves Sunny wasn't the cur you said she was. The one you said should have been sacked up and tossed over the bridge like an unwanted litter of pups."

Out in the van, there was a collective gasp. Mike glanced at Poppy, who sat in stony, tight-lipped silence. He couldn't take anymore and curled his fingers around her hand.

"I'm sorry," he whispered.

Poppy's eyes were flashing. She didn't respond, but she didn't pull away. A few moments later, her fingers curled into his, and she leaned forward, her gaze focused on the receiver, as if she could see as well as hear what was being said.

Amelia shrugged. "Just let it go, Justin. It would never have worked, and for the record, I resent being called a liar."

"Then how else do I define you, Mother? Every day things go on that you choose not to tell me."

"Like what?"

"What about the man who came to the house the other night when I wasn't here? He raised all kinds of hell and you chose not to tell me. This is my house, Mother. It's my responsibility to make sure it's a stronghold against such things as this. What if Callie had been here and she'd been in danger? Do you think I wouldn't want to know this?"

Amelia blinked. "How did you find out about that?"

Justin's stomach knotted. *Damn it to hell. Sadler was here after all.* He threw up his hands in pretend disbelief. "How do you think? This is *my* home, now. The people who work here work for me, not you."

"Fine, so you know. So what? Nothing happened. It's over. He's gone."

"It's not over. I need to know who it was and make sure it doesn't happen again."

Amelia was caught and Justin could tell she was struggling with how to say it without giving herself away. Finally, he saw her expression set. It was an expression he'd seen countless times before – the one that said she was in charge.

"It won't happen again, I can promise you that."

Now was the time to push her. He raised his voice, knowing how much she hated that.

"That's ridiculous. You have no way of promising any such thing. I demand to know his name so I can deal with him in my own way."

Amelia's cheeks reddened. "All you need to know is that he's already been dealt with, and, for a change, in my way."

He frowned. "I don't know what you mean."

Her hands curled into fists. "I'm sick of people taking advantage of this family. I am appalled at how much money we have lost over the years at having to pay people off to keep them quiet. And no matter how many times we do it, they just keep coming."

"Pay off? What the hell are you talking about? I'm talking about a man invading our home."

"And I'm talking about another man wanting to trade his silence for more money!"

"The man who came to the house wanted money? What on earth for?"

"It doesn't matter, I told you. It's over. It's dealt with and he won't be back."

"You don't know that. You can't know that. I want a name," Justin yelled. "I want a fucking name."

"I do know that!" Amelia screamed. "I know it because he's dead. He's dead and this is the end of the discussion!"

Justin didn't have to pretend shock. Even though he'd suspected it, just hearing her say it had been the death knell to what was left of his family.

"He's dead? What the fuck are you saying? Who's dead? How did it happen?"

He watched her shift from defiant to that of a victim.

"He threatened me. He threatened our family. He said he would tell everyone the truth. I had to stop him."

Justin was numb. Even though he knew what had happened, he knew the police needed to hear her say it. And so he pushed one more time. He would deal with the guilt later.

"You stopped him? You killed a man? Tell me that didn't happen?" he begged.

Amelia shook her head. "No, no, I didn't do it. When he left, I sent Newton after him. I had no choice. You understand, don't you, Justin? I had no choice."

"You told Newton to kill him."

"Actually, I didn't use those words. I said, stop him at any cost."

Justin groaned. "That's called a death sentence, Mother. You gave the order which makes you as guilty as the one who pulled the trigger."

Amelia's eyes narrowed. "I did what I had to do to protect this family, just as your father used to do when he was alive."

Justin's vision blurred. "Who was it, Mother?"

"Jessup Sadler, the man Helen Roberts married. I don't know what happened, but after all these years he somehow found out the child wasn't his. He said you'd fired him, that his wife was dying of cancer. He wanted his job back so he would have insurance for her bills or he was going to tell."

Justin staggered, then sat down with a plop in the nearest chair.

"You killed a man who just wanted his job back?"

"And if we'd given him his job back, then what would he want next? He'd hold that over us for the rest of his life. It was his fault for threatening me like that."

Justin didn't answer. There was no need. He knew the police had heard all they needed to hear. He was just waiting for the doorbell to ring.

"So now you know, and in a way, you have yourself to blame. If you'd never gotten mixed up with such trash, none of this would have happened."

Justin shook his head, too heartsick to respond.

And just as he expected, the doorbell did ring.

Amelia frowned. "Who on earth could that be?" She glanced down at Justin. "Are you expecting anyone?"

He got up and walked out of the room, pulling off the wire as he went. When he met the police coming toward him up the hall, he handed it to Duroy and kept on going.

The bright light of day was startling as he exited the house. He paused to look around, wondering how everything could still be ordinary when his world had just exploded.

Then he saw Poppy standing by the van.

Their gazes met, but he had nothing left to say. He got in the car and drove away, knowing he'd sold his mother down the river. The upside to it was he didn't have to stay and watch her drown.

The minute the name came out of Amelia Caulfield's mouth Mike shifted into action.

"Did we get all that?" Mike asked the tech who'd been manning the equipment.

"Yes sir, and backed up," the tech said.

Mike glanced at Kenny. "How far away are the arrest warrants?"

"They should be here soon," Kenny said.

The Lieutenant had been waiting at the courthouse with the warrants. Once they'd given him the names, he'd hand-carried them straight to the judge's chambers for signature.

Mike nodded, although he still couldn't believe what just happened. Caulfield had come through for them in a very big way, but Poppy didn't seem all that impressed.

"He did it, Poppy. He kept his word to you at great expense to himself and his family."

"As he should have. His family has already annihilated mine."

Mike sighed. She was a tough one, but it all came from love and loyalty. He wouldn't mind being loved like that.

"When we pick them up, you will stay in this van, understood?"

"I hear you," she muttered.

"Damn it Poppy, I need your word."

"I will not cause a scene. I will not follow you into the house. I promise."

He noticed she'd said nothing about staying in the van, but short of handcuffing her to a chair, which he wasn't going to do, he would settle for the reluctant vow.

At that point, the officers pulled up with the arrest warrants and they proceeded up to the house in a quiet procession.

Mike waited until they were all congregated at the door before he rang the bell, then glanced back at the van. She was nowhere in sight. Then the door opened.

"Oh my! What's going?" Lillian asked.

"Caulfield P.D. We need to speak with Mrs. Caulfield. Is her driver, Oral Newton on the property?"

"Yes, he's in the kitchen."

"We need to speak to him, as well."

"Mrs. Caulfield is in the library with her son."

"We need to speak with her now."

Lillian looked startled, but moved aside for them to enter. "Follow me. I'll show you to the library then send Newton in as well."

"Officer Chandler will go with you and escort Mr. Newton."

"Yes sir," Lillian said nervously, and shut the door.

As soon as they were inside, Poppy got out. She didn't intend to cause trouble, but she wanted to see their faces when they emerged.

Suddenly the door opened again. It was Justin. She hadn't expected him to be the first person out.

She'd heard everything, from the opening conversation, to the way he'd lead his own mother into a confession of murder. The behavior depicted strength of character far beyond what she'd expected. She couldn't read his expression, but she saw the tears on his face

So he was crying.

She'd done nothing but cry since this whole nightmare began. It seemed only fitting that the people at fault should cry, too.

She was still standing by the van when he drove away. The part of her bent on revenge needed to see Amelia Caulfield come out in handcuffs. She wanted the cold-hearted killer to know who'd been part of taking her down.

Amelia watched her son leave without a qualm. The sooner Justin realized this was the way of the world, the better off he would be. Blackmailers got what they deserved. She smoothed a hand over her hair, brushed a fleck of lint from the front of her blue dress, and then started to go back to her room when she heard the sound of footsteps – many footsteps – coming up the hall. She paused. Moments later a half-dozen policemen walked in, followed by two officers in plain clothes.

"What is the meaning of this?" she cried.

Mike flashed his badge and took the warrant out of his pocket.

"Amelia Caulfield, we have a warrant for your arrest." He began to cite the Miranda warning, which shocked, then enraged her. She began shouting over his voice, demanding to be heard.

"What is this about? Are you people out of your minds? I'll have your badges for this!"

"You're under arrest for the murder of Jessup Sadler."

All the color faded from her face. "I don't understand. How-"

"Your son was wearing a wire. We heard everything."

The handcuffs around her wrist were shocking, but it was the distinct click they made when they locked that sent a wave of panic throughout. This was happening. It was really happening. She'd been betrayed by her own flesh and blood.

"I demand the right to call my lawyer. I need to call Graham Ring."

"You'll get a phone call... after you're booked and jailed."

Lillian reached the kitchen only to find it empty. The police officer frowned.

"Where is he at?" Chandler asked.

"Probably in his room. I'll show you."

She led the way to the servants' quarters and knocked on the first door.

Oral answered quickly, making Lillian think he'd been waiting.

"Yes?"

Lillian pointed to the officer. "The police are here. They want to talk to you in the library."

All the color faded from Oral's face. For a moment Lillian thought he might pass out, but he seemed to gather himself and just nodded.

"Yes, of course," he said.

Lillian scurried back into the kitchen as Newton came out of his room. He gave the officer a brief nod. When Chandler's focus momentarily shifted, Newton hit him squarely in the nose with his elbow. The cop dropped, unconscious to the world with his nose crushed against the side of his face.

Oral rolled him over onto his side so that he wouldn't choke to death on the blood, then headed for the library with a military-swift stride.

By the time he reached the main hall he could hear Amelia's voice shrill with anger, then panic. He quickened his pace. He already knew what he needed to do. No matter the cost, he would not let her suffer.

When he strode into the room it was to see Amelia in handcuffs and begging. Rage swelled. Disgrace! Utter disgrace to treat her in such a manner. If he saved her, there wasn't much time.

"Let her go!"

His voice rang out, startling everyone, including Amelia, as they turned toward the door. It was all he needed.

"You're not taking her anywhere!" he shouted.

From the corner of his eye he saw three uniformed officers coming at him. His arm came up.

Mike caught a glimpse of the weapon in Newton's hand.

"Gun!" he shouted, and was reaching for his own when Newton fired one shot into Amelia Caulfield's head, hitting her right between the eyes. Then he swung the gun beneath his chin and pulled the trigger. He was dead before her body hit the floor.

The silence after the gunshots was startling. It had happened so quickly. Even though parts of Amelia's brains were on the wall where she'd been standing, Kenny knelt to check her pulse.

"She's dead," he said.

"So's this one," an officer said, who'd checked Newton's pulse as well.

"Well shit," Mike said, looking around for the officer who should have been with him. "Somebody go look for Chandler."

Two of the officers took off out of the library on the run.

Kenny eyed the two bodies. "Now that's what I call true devotion. Save her the embarrassment of facing the world as a murderer, and save the county the cost of a trial."

One of the officers was back.

"Chandler's down."

Mike's heart sank. "Call for an ambulance. Kenny, call the M.E. and tell him we've got two to pick up."

He reached for his own phone. It wasn't supposed to have happened like this. He hit redial, then waited for Lieutenant

Green to answer.

"This is Green. Are they in custody?"

"No sir. They're dead. Newton came to the library with a gun. Before we could stop him, he shot her and then himself. We had an officer with Newton. Unknown to us, Newton took him out then came after her."

"God damn it, Amblin. This isn't going to look good in the papers."

Mike thought of Poppy. "Then you give the papers the hook you want to sell. The P.D. solved the murder of Jessup Sadler. In the process of arresting the killers, one killed the other then shot himself. You can mention names at the end of the damn story, rather than at the first. A killer is a killer, no matter what the pedigree.

CHAPTER NINETEEN

The moment Poppy heard shots she jumped back inside the van. Her heart was pounding as she grabbed her phone and dialed John's number. He'd been uneasy about letting her go on her own and this wasn't going to make it better.

"Hello? Poppy? How did it go?"

"Justin got his mother to admit she'd sent her bodyguard to follow Daddy and kill him."

"Oh my God, so Dad really did go there? Why?"

"He wanted his job back. He said if they didn't give him his job back he was going to tell everyone Justin was my father, which in her mind was grounds for murder."

"Did they arrest her?"

"I don't know what's happening. Everyone went inside a few minutes ago and that's when I heard gunshots. I'm outside in the van."

"I'm going to come get you."

"No. I am hearing more sirens, which means it's about to become a madhouse here. There are already police cars all over the place. If more are coming they wouldn't let you get near, even if you came. I'm not in danger."

"I don't like it," John said.

"The other police are here. I've got to go."

She disconnected before he could argue, then sat down on the floor in the far corner of the van and waited for Mike to come find her.

Justin drove straight back to the office apartment and told his secretary, Frances, that he was not to be disturbed. His head was pounding and there was a knot in the pit of his stomach. As soon as he got inside, he called Graham Ring.

"Hello."

"Graham, it's me, Justin."

"Justin! How are you?"

"I've been better. I want to give you a heads up about something. My mother and her driver, Oral Newton, were arrested for the murder of Jessup Sadler."

"What? You can't be serious?"

"I wish I wasn't, but I am. She admitted it to me and the police heard it all."

"I'll get down to the jail as soon as I can and let you know what's happening. If they set bail, I'll soon have her out."

Justin swallowed past the knot in his throat. "Don't bother. Do what you have to on her account, but I've washed my hands of her."

He disconnected, then sat down on the sofa and put his head in his hands. The lump in the back of his throat was so big he couldn't cry. This was a nightmare that kept getting worse.

A few moments later, his cell phone rang. He started to let it go to voicemail then noticed it was from Mike Amblin.

"What?"

Mike sighed. "I have bad news."

"I don't see how it could get any worse," Justin snapped.

"We sent an officer to get Newton out of his room. He took out the officer and went to the library on his own. I'm sorry, Mr. Caulfield, but he shot your mother and then himself. They're both dead."

Justin inhaled sharply. The carpet pattern beneath his feet was suddenly going in and out of focus.

"I did not see this coming."

"Neither did we. I'm very sorry for your loss."

"Thank you for calling."

He dropped the cell phone onto the sofa then leaned back and closed his eyes. He was numb. Maybe tomorrow he could cry for his mother, but not today. Today he was in mourning for Sunny and the man who'd loved her – the man who'd needed his job so badly he'd been willing to beg for it, only to die at his mother's hand.

She was reaping a bloody harvest of what she'd sown.

The elegant grandeur of the Caulfield mansion had undergone a rude transformation with EMTs and crime scene techs traipsing in and out.

Lillian was in something of a state. She kept trying to sweep up after the people coming and going while keeping track of where they went, as if she was afraid they were going to carry off the family silver. She stayed diligent right up until the two body bags were wheeled out on gurneys. Knowing Amelia and Newton were inside sent her into a decline. Kenny sent an officer to escort her to her room and told her to stay there until they were gone.

The good news was, except for a broken nose and a slight concussion, the officer Newton downed was going to be alright. The EMT remarked it was fortunate for Chandler that he'd fallen onto his side or he might have drowned in his own blood before he was found.

It was also noted that Amelia Caulfield never knew what hit her. Mike kept going through the sequence of events in his mind, trying to figure out what they'd missed. It wasn't until Kenny showed him what had popped up on the background check they ran on Oral Newton that gave Mike the answer.

They'd seriously underestimated the man. Not only was he ex-military, but he was ex-Green Beret. Had two meritorious combat medals from Vietnam, and done a stint in a psych ward for PTSD. Then Adam Caulfield hired him to be his wife's bodyguard and driver. That explained his skill and his aim. It didn't make them feel any better but it was something to add to the report.

When the Medical Examiner finally arrived, Mike turned the crime scene over to him and headed outside to check on Poppy. He glanced at his watch and could only imagine what she'd been thinking. It had been over forty-five minutes since they'd gone inside for what was supposed to have been a simple arrest. Who the hell could have seen this coming?

He paused as he exited the house, but didn't see her. There were police units at the bottom of the drive and more stringing crime scene tape, but no sight of Poppy.

He headed to the van at a lope with the sun in his eyes and a sick feeling in the pit of his stomach. The day had already gone to hell and he needed her to be okay. He'd told her to stay in the van but he hadn't expected her to comply.

Then he opened the door and breathed a quiet sigh of relief. She was sitting on the floor in the back of the van, hugging her legs with her head down on her knees.

"Hey, Poppy."

Her head came up. She was pale as a ghost, but her voice was surprisingly calm.

"What happened?"

He stepped up in the van and headed toward her. "It didn't go well. Newton surprised us. He shot Amelia and then himself."

Her eyes widened in surprise. "Are they dead?"

"Yes."

Then just as quickly, her eyes narrowed suspiciously. "Are you going to hide what happened or is the truth going to come out?"

The insult was harsh and unexpected – after all they'd been through together she still didn't trust him.

"Hell no, we're not hiding anything. Your father's murder has been solved. It will be noted as such to the media and the general public."

"I'm sorry," she said. "I didn't mean that the way it came out," then she began to shake. "I heard the shots. I didn't know what happened. I saw an ambulance take someone away and then they carried two more out in body bags. You didn't come back."

Quiet tears suddenly slipped down her cheeks.

Mike reached down and pulled her up into his arms. Her hands snaked around his waist and when she hid her face against his shirt, he tightened his grip. He kept telling himself that he was simply offering her comfort, but the truth was he seriously liked it.

"I'm sorry you were scared," he said softly.

Poppy shuddered.

He rested his chin on the crown of her head. "I don't think anyone has cried for me since I was in the third grade."

Interested in hearing the rest of the story, she looked up, still wearing the tears she'd just shed.

"Who cried for you then?" she asked.

He got his handkerchief out of his pocket. It took a great deal of effort on his part not to kiss her as he began wiping her face.

"Oh, I was running all hell-bent for leather after a line-drive during recess and fell flat on my face on the playground. Busted my nose and drove my top teeth into my bottom lip. Bled all over my best blue shirt. I was too shocked to cry, so Marilee Whitson cried for me. At least I told myself she was crying for me, but it could have been because I also bled all over the front of her dress and the teacher's shoes, too."

Poppy blinked. "Are you telling me the truth or is this one of those stories cops make up to get people out of hysterics?"

Mike frowned. "You watch too many cop shows on TV. Yes, it's the truth and I have the scar to prove it."

He put the handkerchief back in his pocket then showed her the tiny, thin white scar on the inside of his lower lip.

She nodded. "I see it." When she suddenly realized how close they were and how blue his eyes were, she quickly stepped back. "Thank you," she added, swiping at her cheeks in sudden embarrassment, as if he might have missed some tears.

"You're welcome. I can't leave yet to take you home. Do you want to call your brother? I'll make sure they let him pass."

Her fingers curled into fists. "Yes. I want to go home."

Mike nodded. "Then call him."

"One more thing."

"What is it, Poppy?"

"I guess you called Justin... I mean, about what happened in there?"

"Yes."

"Is he... did he... I mean-"

"He didn't say much, but if I was guessing, I'd say today is probably one of the worst days of his life."

Poppy chose to ignore the tiny spurt of empathy. "I was just wondering," she said, and then looked around for her purse. "I need to call Johnny."

"And I'll let the officers know he's coming after you." He frowned at the expression on her face and then added. "You had nothing to do with what happened anymore than Justin did. Both of you were collateral damage to other people's choices, okay?"

Justin spent the night at Callie's bedside watching her sleep. He didn't know how to tell her what had happened, but he would have to before he left. It would be all over the news. People were going to talk. She was fourteen years old – too old to hide the truth about something as horrific as this.

He'd hired a private investigator to locate Wade Lee Tiller, and made a mental note to call Truman Epperson at the Edison Funeral home tomorrow.

There was an old saying running through his head that he couldn't shake. He couldn't remember exactly how it went, but he remembered part of the last line - '*... and miles to go before I sleep*'.

That's how he felt. Maybe there were too many miles between him and rest. The way his heart ached, he might never rest again.

It was midnight and Poppy had yet to go to bed. The television was on, but muted. The bowl of popcorn she and Johnny had shared was in the floor near her feet with a few un-popped kernels and two empty Pepsi cans stacked inside. The curtains were closed. The house was locked tight, and yet she couldn't shake the feeling she was standing naked in the world, and when the sun came up tomorrow, everyone would see.

Tomorrow, the news as to who killed Jessup Sadler would spread like wildfire, and it wouldn't take long for the reason why to follow.

Johnny kept telling her it didn't matter, that they would always be family – that she was his sister now and forever. But she knew there would be others from Coal Town who would disagree - who would suddenly see her as the bastard child of a rich man. They'd be expecting her to start flashing money and moving away from where she'd grown up, maybe even assume she would quit her job and move across the bridge to the north side of the city. She was so afraid to face tomorrow for fear what it might bring. She hadn't just lost her parents in this ordeal, she was losing her identity, as well.

And then there was Mike Amblin. This morning he'd been the cop still working her daddy's case, up until that moment in the van. The moment when they'd all heard Justin throw his mother's words back in her face - calling Sunny a cur who should have been tied up in a sack and thrown off the bridge into the river like an unwanted litter of pups. The moment when he'd reached for her hand and with a firm, but gentle grip, grounded her pain. That was the moment it hit her - remembering how many times he'd been there for her since this ordeal had begun. The moment when she'd looked past the badge and liked what she saw.

When the gunshots sounded at the Caulfield mansion, they were startling – even unexpected since it was supposed to be an arrest. But when he didn't come out – and the thought crossed her mind that he could be dead just like Daddy and she would never see him again - that's when she realized he'd gotten under her skin.

So here she was, unable to sleep, falling for a cop who was just being kind, waiting for sunrise and the next shoe to fall.

It was nearly midnight before Mike finished the last report and left the station. It was always a satisfying feeling when a case came together, but this one had blown up in their faces.

The only good thing was that it was over. Poppy Sadler would get her car back. She and her brother could bury their father and the world would go on.

At least that's how it should be, but Mike knew better. When word got around – and it would – that Justin Caulfield was Poppy's father, she would not know another moment of peace. She lived in Coal Town, but the truth about her birth father was automatically going to separate her from them, even if she didn't move. He wished he could protect her from that heartache, but he'd just run out of reasons to keep showing up in her life.

CHAPTER TWENTY

When Mike arrived for work the next morning, Prophet Jones was sitting on a bench outside the Caulfield police department, perched on the edge of the concrete bench with his hands folded in his lap and his head bowed in prayer.

There was a moment when he thought about going in through a side-entrance then chided himself for being afraid to face a helpless old man and got out of the car. He walked all the way to the entrance without seeing the old man move a muscle then just as he neared the door, Prophet raised his head and looked him square in the eyes.

A slight shudder ran up the back of Mike's neck. *That was weird.* It was like someone whispered in Prophet's ear that he was there, only the old man was alone.

Prophet stood. His state of grace disappeared as he came toward Mike in a crooked lope.

"Is it true?" he asked.

"Is what true, Prophet?"

"Is the Devil dead? Did you really kill the ones responsible for Mr. Sadler's death?"

Mike sighed. This would take a bit of explaining.

"Sit with me," he said, pointing to the bench Prophet had just abandoned.

Prophet settled back down then scooted closer. Once again, Mike tried not to imagine the transfer of fleas and lice and began to explain.

"Yesterday we were in the act of arresting Mrs. Caulfield and her bodyguard for the murder of Jessup Sadler, but we didn't kill them. The bodyguard shot Mrs. Caulfield then killed himself. It happened so fast we had no way to stop him."

Prophet was rocking back and forth as he listened. When Mike announced both their deaths, he leaped to his feet and raised his hands to the heavens.

"Praise the Lord, I have been delivered! The Devil and his minions are dead. My time of penance is at an end!" Tears began running down his face as he grabbed Mike's hand and shook it fiercely. "No more sackcloth and ashes. No more wandering in the wilderness. Thank you for hearing my words!"

"Yes, we heard you, Prophet. But now I want you to hear me."

The old man stilled, focusing on Mike's face as if he was listening for the voice of God.

Mike gripped Prophet by the shoulders to make his point. "There is no more Devil in Caulfield... at least not the one you've been preaching against. I know the Devil takes many forms, but so do God's angels."

"Yes, praise the Lord, yes, that is a fact!"

"Then hear me out, Prophet, because I don't want to find out you're still preaching against a family that no longer exists."

Prophet frowned. "Not a family. The Devil! The Devil, I say!"

Mike resisted the urge to shake him for fear he'd break the fragile bones beneath the rags.

"Prophet... you're not listening to me."

"I'm listening, yes, I am."

"Justin Caulfield helped us get the evidence we needed to make an arrest. He did it knowing his family might be incriminated and arrested. He did it with his heart breaking because he knew it was the right thing to do."

Now Prophet was hanging on Mike's every word.

"Justin Caulfield is a good man and not responsible for the actions of others, even if they were his parents. So, do we understand each other?"

Prophet put his hand over his heart as if he was about to take an oath.

"I hear. I understand. I will pray for him to be delivered from his sorrow."

"Okay then," Mike said. "And thank you again for your help. We might never have solved this without you. You are a hero, Prophet."

The old man blinked, then bowed his head and walked away, one leg dragging, his shoulders slightly stooped from the weight of the world.

It was just after daybreak when Justin got up from the chair near Callie's bed. She was still sleeping and he had calls to make before she woke.

He slipped out of the room and went down the hall to the waiting room to get a cup of coffee from the coffee machine. Thankful that the waiting room was empty, he took his first sip before he sat down to call Frances. He needed to catch her at home to prepare her for the day ahead.

He dialed her number then took another sip of coffee as he waited for her to answer. Just when he thought it was going to go to voicemail, he heard her voice.

"Hello?"

"Frances, it's me. I'm sorry to disturb you at home and so early, but I need to fill you in on what's coming up today."

"Yes sir, let me get a pen."

"No, it's okay. You won't need to write this down."

"Oh, okay. What's up?"

"I'm going to need you to cancel all my appointments for the next few days. I'm not sure when I'll be back in the office. Also, you'll probably be contacted right and left by newspapers and media. Tell them a statement will be issued later by the family."

Frances gasped. "You're scaring me, Mr. Caulfield. What's happening?"

"My mother and her driver, Oral Newton, were arrested yesterday for the murder of Jessup Sadler. Before the police could take them both into custody, Newton shot my mother and then himself."

"Oh dear God!"

Justin took a slow breath and closed his eyes, making

himself focus on her voice and not the pain in his gut.

"I won't go into the details. They'll be public soon enough. But I need you to hold down the fort for me. Can you do that?"

"Yes sir. You can count on me, and I'm sorry, so sorry."

"Yes, Frances, so am I."

Justin's hands were shaking when he hung up, but he made himself finish the coffee before he made the other call. It was more of a practical nature, but one that had to be faced. Last night while reading the local paper he'd noticed there were funerals being held today, which meant as long as there were bodies in the funeral home, they would have staff on duty night and day. He didn't know who would be there, but at least his call would be answered.

"Edison Funeral Home. Truman speaking."

Justin was relieved the person on duty was someone he knew.

"Truman, this is Justin Caulfield. I have a request."

"Of course, Mr. Caulfield, how can I help?"

Justin prepared himself to skim through the worst of it again. "This isn't a pretty story, but everyone will know soon enough."

Now Truman was anxious. "Please tell me this has nothing to do with your dear daughter?"

"No, it's not Callie. It's my mother and I don't need condolences. I just need your ear."

"I'm listening."

"Yesterday, as the police were in the act of arresting my Mother and her bodyguard, Oral Newton for the murder of Jessup Sadler, Newton killed her and then himself. And they were guilty. She confessed as much to me."

"Dear Lord, why?" Truman said, and then realized he'd spoken aloud. "I'm sorry. That's none of my business."

Justin still had to face Callie and refused to let himself weep.

"The reason will be common knowledge soon enough. Once the police release her body, I want Edison Funeral Home to pick her up. But there will be no service, graveside or otherwise, and there will be no viewing, is that understood?"

"Yes sir."

"She'll be buried beside my father. They deserve each other."

"Are you saying you don't want a pastor to bless the interment?"

"There's no need. She doesn't deserve any blessing here, and God will deal with her when she shows up there."

"I'm so sorry," Truman said.

"Just send me the bill when it's over."

"Yes sir, you can count on me."

"Thank you," Justin said, and headed back to Callie's room with his steps dragging.

Those calls had been a breeze compared to what came next. How was he going to explain Amelia's death and the scope of what she'd done, and not permanently traumatize the granddaughter who'd loved her?

"God help me," he said, then went inside.

It was six minutes after 7:00 a.m. when Gladys Ritter wheeled up into the Sadler's driveway. She'd just learned about the shootings during the police arrest and was a little put out that Poppy hadn't called her personally.

She'd gone to get milk for Mel's breakfast down at Millwood's Gas and Grocery, still wearing the black sweats she'd slept in, and heard Carmella Wyatt talking all about it. She was making snide remarks about Helen Sadler's past and Gladys had nearly gotten into a fight. During the scuffle, the banana clip holding up her hair had come loose and it was bouncing against the side of her head like the broke ear on a dog.

The house was quiet, which meant they were all probably still asleep, but Gladys wasn't shy. She'd known them too long to stand on ceremony. She doubled up her fist and began hammering on the door.

John woke with a start. He'd been dreaming about a thunderstorm. It took him a few moments to realize it wasn't thunder he was hearing but someone at the door. Anxious to get there before the noise frightened Poppy, he grabbed his jeans, pulling them on as he went. By the time he got to the door, he was running.

He opened the door with a jerk.

"Gladys? What the hell?"

She pushed past him, and let herself in.

John rolled his eyes as he shut the door.

"I just heard something down at Millwood's that I don't believe."

John sighed. Damn. Poppy had been right on target. This wasn't going to go away easy.

Then Poppy entered the living room with her hair in tangles, trying to tie her bathrobe with shaking hands.

"What's going on?"

John glared at Gladys. "She had the day from hell yesterday. I didn't think she'd ever get to sleep last night and now you went and woke her up at the crack of dawn. What's so damned important that you couldn't wait and call?"

Gladys put her hands on her hips in a gesture of defiance.

"I was at Millwood's getting milk for Mel's breakfast when Carmella Wyatt came in talking about an arrest in Jessup's murder and then people dying and talking all crazy about Helen and the Caulfields. I nearly got into a fight with her because I wouldn't believe all that would happen without Poppy letting me know."

Poppy shoved shaky hands through her hair, combing it away from her face and sat down in the nearest chair.

"Well it did happen. I don't intend to hurt your feelings, but after everything that's been going on the last two days, I haven't been in a mood to chat about it."

Gladys blinked. It was beginning to dawn that her indignation was minimal compared to everything else.

"I'm sorry. I didn't mean that the way it came out. I just don't like Carmella and I guess I was jealous she knew something about you that I didn't. I'm going home. You can call me whenever you want, or not. It's still okay."

"I'm going to get dressed," John said, and walked out.

"Sit down," Poppy said.

Gladys sat. "What happened?"

"You were Mama's best friend, weren't you?"

Gladys's eyes welled. "I like to think so."

Poppy sighed. It had to be said, and Gladys was the only one she could trust not to twist the facts. Ugly or not, Gladys would relate what she'd been told to anyone with a different story.

"Did you know Mama and Justin Caulfield had a thing her senior year of high school?"

Gladys gasped. "No she did not!"

"I found her diary in Daddy's things and yes, she did."

"Oh my word," Gladys said. "But what's that got to do with-"

"Mama was pregnant with me when she and Daddy got married, but I wasn't his. Justin Caulfield is my father. Daddy found the diary. He confronted Mama at the hospital and she told him the truth the night he died. He got mad. He'd been fired by the company. Mama was sick and dying and he'd lost his insurance. He went to Caulfield's home to ask for his job back, only Justin Caulfield wasn't there. So he told Amelia Caulfield that he wanted his job back or he was going to tell everyone Justin was my father."

Gladys clasped her hands over her mouth but didn't move.

Poppy continued. "It's even more complicated. Years earlier, my Grandpa Roberts had already gone to the family when they found out Mama was pregnant demanding money to keep it quiet. Mama was furious. She'd begged him not to, but he did anyway. Only Adam Caulfield wouldn't pay Grandpa off. He wrote a fifty-thousand dollar check out to Mama. Grandpa brought it home. Mama wouldn't cash it. She got back at Adam and she got back at Grandpa by not cashing the check. She wouldn't let herself be bought."

"My sweet lord," Gladys whispered. "Such a burden and she never told."

"That's not all. The Caulfields didn't tell Justin any of it. Apparently he was mad at his family and at himself for knuckling under to their demands to break up with her. He left for college without knowing she was pregnant, and because he was so pissed at his family, didn't come home for years. He didn't know about the payoff or the baby until two days ago, but by then it was too late to stop what had already happened. When Daddy showed up at their home to ask for his job back, Amelia Caulfield sent her bodyguard to get rid of Daddy. He's the one who killed him, but she gave the order."

"Poppy, sweetheart, I'm sorry. I had no idea-"

Poppy shuddered then took a deep breath. She wasn't ever going to tell this again. Might as well get it all said.

"The police talked to Justin. He wore a wire back to his house to confirm something I think he already feared and confronted his mother. She admitted the whole thing without a bit of regret. The police got it on tape and went to arrest her. The bodyguard shot her and then killed himself before they could stop him. So Mama is dead. Daddy is dead. Amelia Caulfield is dead, and so is her bodyguard. Justin Caulfield is my birth father, but he's a stranger I don't want anything to do with. He didn't want Mama enough to fight for her, so he doesn't get me, either. I have lost my family and my identity. Is there anything else you want to know?"

Gladys shook her head so fiercely the banana clip slid even farther down her head and bumped her on the nose. She was bawling when she fastened it back up and she was still bawling when she kissed Poppy goodbye and let herself out.

Poppy reeled. And now it began.

John walked up behind her. "It had to be said," he told her, then laid his hand on the top of her head. "Go back to bed if you want. I'll make breakfast for the both of us and call you later."

"No. I can't sleep, Johnny. Every time I close my eyes I hear that woman saying she wanted to put Mama in a sack and throw her off the bridge into the Little Man. She was evil and that blood runs in my veins."

"Mama's does, too. Love makes a family, not blood. Stop dwelling on things you can't change and focus on what's left to do."

"Like what?"

"We can bury Dad, now."

"Oh my God, how will I face all those people again? They'll know. They'll all know by then."

"It's not about what they think they know. It's about what you know. You're a good, strong woman. Mom and Dad made sure of that and it's up to you to prove it, which means keep your chin up, your mouth shut, and let them think what they want. Time will work everything else out."

Poppy closed her eyes and dropped her head.

He waited. Either she would get it, or she wouldn't. He couldn't make it happen for her.

"Poppy?"

She looked up. "Did you make coffee yet?"

"No, but-"

"If you make coffee while I get dressed, I'll make pancakes."

John grinned. "Deal."

"They have to release Daddy's body now, don't they? I mean, there's no reason not to anymore."

"That's right, and you should get the car back, too," John said. "I'll check on all that after breakfast. Do you want to go with me?"

"No. Do you mind?"

"Of, course not."

"I'm just not ready yet. You understand, don't you?"

"Yes, sister, I understand. Now stop worrying and go make those pancakes."

Poppy went to get dressed.

Justin was exhausted. He'd told Callie the whole ugly story, from the time he'd walked out on Sunny, to yesterday when he'd helped the police get his mother's confession of murder on tape. She'd been shocked, then horrified, and then she'd cried. In a way, her tears had been a blessing because it had finally given Justin an excuse to cry, too. He crawled up in bed with her, took her in his arms and let her cry herself to sleep. He still hadn't told her she had another father. He'd cross that bridge when he came to it.

Over the past two hours, the nurses had been very discreet, giving them time alone. When they had to come in to check Callie's monitors, they did so quickly, and without speaking. They didn't know everything, but they'd heard rumors. If even half of what they'd heard was the truth, it was enough to make anybody cry.

Justin was grateful for the solace. The headboard of the bed was his backrest, the top of Callie's head a pillow for his cheek. Every time she stirred, she whimpered. All he could do was pat her shoulder and rock her back to sleep.

It was close to noon when Callie woke up. She raised up, momentarily confused.

"Daddy?"

He kissed the top of her head. "I'm right here, honey," he said and then eased out of the bed and fluffed her pillows as she sat up on the side of the bed.

"Did I just dream that or was it true?"

"It's not a dream."

Her face crumpled. "Oh no."

"I wish I could make it go away, but I can't."

She was crying again, but without sound – just tears rolling down her cheeks, one after the other.

"Oh honey," Justin said. He grabbed a handful of tissues then wiped her cheeks.

"Are you sad, Daddy?"

"Yes."

She picked at a loose thread on the hem of her nightgown and then glanced up.

"What about your other daughter? Does she hate us because Nana killed her daddy? I mean, uh, I know you're her daddy, too, but I meant her other one."

Justin sighed. "I don't think she blames us for her father's death, but she's pretty mad at me. You can understand why, can't you?"

Callie nodded. "Do you think she's mad at me, too?"

"No. I'm sure she's not. She's actually a very nice person and would never blame you."

"Do you think I might meet her some day? I mean, she's my sister, right? I should know my sister."

"I think that's a good plan and something we will work toward. Right now I just need you to know you and I are good. We're as good as a Dad and his daughter can be. I think you're amazing and so brave. I don't want you second-guessing yourself about any of this mess, okay? These are all mistakes that grown-ups made. You just had the misfortune to be related to us."

She frowned. "Don't say that. You're not a mistake. You're very brave, too. You helped Poppy just like you're helping me. That's what good daddies do."

Justin wanted to cry all over again. Instead, he gave her a big hug.

"Thank you, baby. That kind of praise will take me a long way down the road."

"You're not going anywhere are you?"

He tilted her chin until he saw his reflection in the tears in her eyes and made himself smile.

"Nope. You're stuck with me forever and ever."

The door swung open. A nurse entered, carrying a tray.

"Looks like lunch is here," he said.

"Glad to see our favorite patient is awake," the nurse said. "You'll like what's on your tray today."

"Is it chicken something?" Callie asked, swiping at her tears.

The nurse nodded. "Yes, and I swear if you eat much more of the stuff you'll grow feathers."

Callie giggled and Justin smiled. Thank God for the resilience of youth. The sound was balm to an aching heart.

"So, now that you have food to eat, I'm going to go back to the apartment, shower and change into some clean clothes, okay? I won't be gone more than a couple of hours. You'll be all right until then, won't you, honey?"

"Yes, but when you come back, can we play Uno?"

"Yes, we will play Uno. See you soon."

He nodded at the nurse who was getting Callie settled and headed for the elevator. His phone beeped as he stepped inside. It was a text from the P.I.

Wade Lee Tiller located. Details sent via email.

He sent back a brief text. This wasn't bad news. In fact it

was good. It hadn't taken long to find him, which was what he wanted – what he needed for Callie. He wouldn't think about the new wave of sadness washing through him. He couldn't be concerned with how this could impact the future of their relationship. This was about saving her life. He'd worry later about having to share her with another man to make it happen.

CHAPTER TWENTY-ONE

As soon as John got the family car out of police impound, he took it to be detailed. It was cleaner now than it had been in years, even the black fender on the blue chassis was shining in lowly splendor. There wasn't a single remnant left inside to mark the thieves who'd stolen it, or the man who'd abandoned it as he was being murdered. A man from the detail shop followed John home in it, then handed over the keys and left with his ride back to the shop.

John entered the house with purpose, calling her name.

"Poppy! Hey Poppy!"

She came out of their parents' bedroom, her hair in a tangle with dust on her clothes.

"I'm here. What's up?"

He presented the keys to her with a flourish. "You are no longer afoot, little sister. It's clean, shiny, and full of gas."

Poppy smiled. "Thank you, Johnny."

"You're welcome." He swiped a finger down the bridge of her nose. "You're also dusty."

"I'm packing their clothes to take to Goodwill. Did you talk Mr. Epperson at the funeral home?"

"Yes. The police released Dad's body to the funeral home today. I guess they'll call and tell us what to do."

And just like that the mood in the room shifted. "I know what they'll want."

"I guess you do. You had all that to do by yourself before, didn't you?"

Poppy wasn't going to go there. John dwelled on his guilt

trip enough for both of them.

"Daddy didn't have a suit, but he had his khaki pants and that brown sports jacket."

"That will work," John said. "He needs to look like himself, not a banker."

"Pastor Harvard came by while you were gone."

John eyed the closed expression on her face. "And?"

"He offered to pray for me since it seems I have become the catalyst for the tragedy that brought about Daddy's death."

"You're kidding me. He did *not* say that."

"Not in so many words, but it felt like what he meant."

"Well damn it, sister. I'm sorry."

"It's what I expected, so it's not exactly a shock. Do you know if there's any more of that packing tape in the utility room? I needed to seal up the last two boxes and ran out."

"I'll check," John muttered, still pissed on Poppy's behalf.

A few minutes later he came back with a new roll.

"Last one," he said. "Which boxes are ready to go?"

She pointed.

He sealed them up and then shoved them against the wall with the others.

"How much do you have left to do?"

"About one more box to fill and then all the drawers and the closet will be empty."

John felt a little uneasy as he looked around the room. It felt like they were trespassing, and that his dad could come in at any minute demanding to know what the hell they were doing with his things. A wave of sadness washed through him, but he pushed it away.

"What are you going to do with the room?"

She dumped the last armload of clothing onto the bed and then stepped back, giving the room a sweeping glance.

"I've been thinking about taking this room for my own. It's a lot larger than mine. Maybe paint the walls and put some new curtains on the windows."

John frowned. "You wouldn't mind... being in here, I mean?"

Poppy looked surprised. "No. Why would I? Neither of them died in this room, although I think maybe Great-Grandpa

Roberts might have, but that kind of stuff doesn't bother me. I'm not afraid of the dead. It's the living who is dangerous."

John's frown deepened. "Are you going to be scared to live here alone?"

"No, of course not and that's not what I meant."

"I don't want to think about driving all over the country while you're here alone and scared out of your mind."

"I'll be fine. Give me a few minutes to box this up and then I'll fix lunch."

"You finish here. I'll make us something to eat."

"Okay," she said, and kept on working.

A short while later she went across the hall to clean up, then darted into her room long enough to put on a clean t-shirt. As she was coming up the hall, she heard a car pull up into their drive, then a knock at the door. She glanced out the window as she went to answer.

It was the police.

"Mike?"

"Hey, Poppy, sorry I didn't call first. Do you have a minute?"

"Sure. Come in. Johnny's making sandwiches. Are you hungry?"

Mike wouldn't have turned down the invitation to save his soul.

"You sure?"

"I'm sure. Hey, Johnny!"

John appeared in the doorway. "Mike! How's it going?"

Mike shrugged. "Okay. We're still dealing with the fall-out from yesterday. That arrest wasn't our finest hour."

"I had no problem with it," John said.

"I get where you're coming from. At any rate it's over, which is the most important thing. Oh! The invitation to eat almost made me forget why I came." He handed Poppy the large brown envelope he was carrying. "These are your father's effects. I need you to sign the sheet that's on it." He handed her a pen.

She signed the paper.

He took it off the envelope, folded it and put it in his pocket, then handed it to her.

It was somewhat shocking to be holding what they'd taken off his dead body, but she wouldn't let herself go there just yet. She dreaded what might be inside – that they would find something more that would rock their world. Whatever it was, she wasn't going to look at it now. She laid it on the end of the sofa and followed the men into the kitchen.

"Beer or Pepsi?" John asked, as he opened the fridge.

"I'm still on duty, so we better make it a Pepsi. Anything I can do to help?" Mike asked.

"Nah, I got it," John said. "You guys take a seat."

"I'll do the glasses," Poppy said.

"It's ham and cheese. Do you want mustard or mayo, Mike?"

"Mustard's good," he said.

"Remember, both for me," Poppy said.

Mike grinned. "You like mustard and mayo on your sandwiches?"

John poked a finger at Poppy in jest. "She sure does. When she was little she never could make up her mind. For a joke once Mom put both. The joke backfired. Poppy loved it and we've done them that way ever since."

Poppy shrugged. "So I'm a little bit weird, so what?"

"I'd say unique, and that's always good," Mike said.

John slid plates in front of Mike and Poppy and pointed to the bag of chips. "Help yourself."

"None for me," Poppy said.

They ate in easy silence for a few moments until John caught a look on Mike's face that made him smile. The cop had a crush on his sister. It would be great if Poppy returned the feelings. It would make going back to Atlanta a lot easier knowing there was someone he trusted who would be around when she needed help.

They were almost through when Mike's cell beeped. He glanced down at the text and then sighed.

"Duty calls. Thanks so much for the food," he said, and got up.

Poppy followed him to the door. "Thank you for bringing Daddy's things by."

"You're welcome."

She followed him out onto the porch, trying to think of something to say that wouldn't sound stupid. Then he stopped and looked back.

"I know John will go back to Atlanta soon. You know you can call me anytime if the need arises."

She smiled. "Thank you. That's a good thing to know."

Mike was all the way off the steps before he stopped again.

"Someday when you're feeling better, maybe we could drive over to Newport. They have a really good steakhouse. If you like steak, that is."

A wave of quiet joy slid through her. "I like steak."

"Great! That's just great. So I'll be seeing you."

"Yes."

And then he was gone.

Mike was still grinning when he crossed the bridge over the Little Man.

Poppy didn't mention the invitation to John when she went back inside. She knew he'd haze her about it non-stop until she went and she wasn't ready. Not yet, but soon. Definitely soon.

John had already dumped the contents of the envelope onto the card table and was sitting on the sofa going through them. He had tears in his eyes, but he was smiling when he saw her come in.

"Look at this. It's water-damaged, but you can still tell it's us."

Poppy sat down to look at the pictures he'd found in their dad's wallet. There was one of Helen leaning against the car with a big smile on her face, and another one of Poppy and Johnny eating watermelon on the front porch.

"Oh, my gosh! That one is so old. I couldn't have been more than nine or ten, and look at your hair," Poppy said.

"Hey, I was rockin' that mullet."

She looked up, and then out the window to the bird that just lit on the porch and wondered what it would be like to pick up and fly away from trouble. "Johnny?"

"Yeah?"

"I wish I knew how Daddy felt about me after he learned I wasn't his."

John slid an arm around her shoulder. "But Poppy, you were

his. You still are his. Just because he wasn't the sperm donor, does not nullify the years and love he gave to both of us. He was probably shocked, but he wouldn't have felt a bit different about you. If anything, he would have been afraid once you found out, you might want the rich man, instead of an out-of-work miner."

"Do you think?" Poppy whispered.

"I know," John said. "Now stop talking like that. Give the old man *some* credit."

"So okay, you're right."

"Of course I'm right because I'm older and smarter and I'm the man."

She punched him on the arm, but her mood had shifted.

"Is there anything else in the stuff that we can save?"

"The watch isn't waterproof. It stopped at 11:47, which is probably when he hit the water."

"Oh my God."

"Is it okay with you if I take this with me?"

She shivered. "Yes. I don't want the reminder. Why would you?"

"To remind me how precious life is and not to waste another day I'm still living it."

Poppy sat back, eyeing her brother thoughtfully. There was more to him than met the eye.

"That's good, Johnny. He would like that."

John nodded. He was trying hard not to break down and bawl. It wouldn't do either of them any good, and he was so damn weary of being sad.

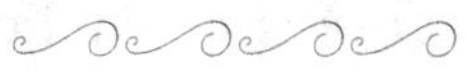

Justin wasted no time after locating Callie's birth father. Reading Tiller's background had been a relief. The man's record was clean - no arrests - no black marks of any kind against his name. According to the investigator's report, he owned a paint and body shop called Tiller and Sons, and had been divorced about ten years. Not so good for Tiller, but great news for Justin. There would be no wife in the wings to get pissed-off about an illegitimate child.

Justin was pulling out all the stops to make sure Tiller didn't say no when he confronted him. He was taking pictures of Callie and Deborah, as well as pictures of Callie at different ages - in her soccer uniform – at her thirteenth birthday party – and the latest ones of her in the hospital, including the one he'd taken with his cell phone last night, sitting in the hospital bed holding her favorite stuffed bear and surrounded by angel figurines. He would bare his soul to get her that transplant.

He'd contacted one of Callie's old babysitters, a retired teacher named Patricia Wayne, to spend time with Callie while he was on the road. Callie had no idea why he was leaving, only that he'd be back the next day, and she was excited to see Miss Patty again.

Now all he had to do was sleep – an impossible task. The bed in the apartment wasn't as comfortable as his bed back home, but the library was still being cleaned. Apparently it wasn't easy to get blood off of furniture and floors.

He fell asleep on the sofa watching the late-night news. When he woke up it was morning and the phone was ringing. He answered before his eyes were fully open just so he wouldn't have to hear it ring again.

"Justin Caulfield."

"Mr. Caulfield, this is Truman Epperson. I'm sorry to bother you, but we don't know what you want done about Mr. Newton."

Justin sat up, struggling to gather his thoughts. "You picked up his body, too?"

"Yes. Were we not supposed to?"

"No. Surely he has next of kin somewhere. I'll have Frances get that information to you, although I would have thought the police made those notifications."

"They told us he had no next of kin and there was no one to claim the body."

Justin's eyes suddenly narrowed. "Cremate him. Send me the bill and save his ashes."

"Yes sir. Thank you, sir. Sorry to bother you."

The call ended.

Justin glanced at the clock. It was already after 8:00 a.m. Time to get moving. Tiller lived in Clarksburg, which was a three-hour drive from Caulfield. With luck, he'd be there by noon.

It was just after twelve when Justin pulled up to the office of Tiller and Sons and parked. The building was neatly painted – white with red trim – and the area surrounding it had been enclosed by an eight foot privacy fence. Both garage doors were open with people working inside. On the surface, it appeared to be a thriving business.

He grabbed the envelope with Callie's pictures as he got out. The sun was warm on his face, even though the air verged on cold – a reminder that fall was here and winter not far behind.

As he started toward the office, two tall young men in their mid-to-late twenties walked out. From their matching strides to the white-blonde hair and blue eyes, it was obvious they were brothers. When they saw him, they stopped. One turned and politely stepped back and opened the door for him.

"Welcome to Tiller and Sons."

"Thanks," Justin said. "Are you one of the sons?"

The young man smiled. "Yes sir. I'm Hank, this is my brother, Ben. There are two more of us, but we're the cream of the crop."

Ben laughed, which made Justin smile. He'd always imagined what it would be like to be part of a big family. They were lucky.

Hank eyed Justin's car. "I'm not seeing a dent or a scratch on that fine Lexus you rolled up in, so how can we help you?"

"I'm looking for Wade Lee Tiller. Is he your father?"

The smile slid off Hank's face. "What are you, a process server?"

"No, no, nothing like that. It's personal business."

"What's your name?"

Justin pulled a card from his pocket. "Justin Caulfield, of Caulfield Industries."

The congeniality shifted to a protective formality. "Have a seat," Hank said, and left the office through a back door while

Ben stood guard.

Justin wondered how they would feel once they learned they had a sister. Would they still want to throw him to the curb, or even worse, try to claim custody? They wouldn't win, but the notoriety would destroy her.

Justin scanned his phone for text messages while he waited. There were none. God bless Frances for standing between him and the chaos he'd left behind.

A few moments later the door opened. Hank was back, followed by a man he assumed was Wade Tiller. He was burned brown by the sun, making his blonde hair appear whiter than it already was. His features had been passed to both of his sons – and as Justin looked closer, his heart twisted – on to Callie, as well. It was shocking to see his daughter's eyes looking at him from this man's face.

Demon Jealousy raised its ugly head, but Justin wouldn't acknowledge the presence. He stood up and extended his hand. "Mr. Tiller, I'm Justin Caulfield from-"

"I know who you are."

Justin froze.

Wade Tiller picked up the phone and dialed a number. "Penny. I need you back at the office. Yes, I know your lunch hour isn't over, but it's important. Tell Paul and Tommy to get to the house and tell Suzy to make extra. I'm bringing company."

Hank and Ben frowned. Their interest in Justin had suddenly increased.

"What the hell, Dad?" Hank said.

"You'll find out soon enough." Then he looked at Justin. "Mr. Caulfield, we're going to my house for this discussion. It won't put you out any because it's just across the street."

Justin felt a little like Alice must have felt when she fell down the rabbit hole. Nothing was as it seemed. As they crossed the street in tandem, he couldn't get past the feeling he was walking under guard. The fact that his presence might be received as a threat had never occurred to him and he was wishing he'd told someone where he was going. He couldn't afford to leave Callie an orphan – not when she was so young and so sick.

To his surprise, the two-story white house across the street was not only pleasing from the outside, but the inside was warm and inviting, as well. As they entered, he smelled something tasty.

"Yum, stew," Hank said.

"Show Mr. Caulfield to the bathroom so he can wash up. I'm going to the kitchen to talk to Suzy," Wade said, then left the room.

It was obvious Wade wasn't afraid or upset. More like fatalistic, as if he'd expected this might one day occur.

"This way," Hank said, and pointed to the last door on the right down a wide, airy hall. "When you've finished, follow your nose to the kitchen. Dinner's waiting."

"Okay, thank-"

But the words went unheeded. Like their father, he walked away, leaving Justin on his own. A couple of minutes later he walked into the kitchen and then stopped.

Wade saw him. "You can sit here," he said, pointing to a chair at his elbow.

Justin laid the envelope on the sideboard and sat.

"This really isn't necessary," he said. "I just need to-"

Wade shook his head. "This is how we do everything in this family. We share food. It's harder to pick a fight when your belly is full. And there are no secrets. Everyone knows what's going on at once. Secrets tear family apart."

Tears welled, shocking Justin into silence. The man was right about one thing, secrets were destructive.

Wade had not expected to see tears. His estimation of the man shifted somewhat slightly to the good, but he reserved the right to change his mind.

"Mr. Caulfield, you've already met my two oldest sons, Hank and Ben. That's Paul at the far end of the table and Tommy just to his right. Tommy is a senior in high school. Paul is a freshman in college. The two oldest have already graduated college and this fine woman on my left is my sweetheart, Suzy. She runs this house like we run the body shop. Neat, clean, and with no backtalk, right honey?"

Justin eyed them curiously. Wade Tiller had certainly put his mark on them. It was like looking at four different versions of the same man. The pretty, middle-aged woman sitting on Wade's right smiled. The smile never reached her eyes.

"Nice to meet all of you," Justin said.

Wade picked up his spoon. "The stew smells good, Suzy. Hey Paul, pass the cornbread," and so the meal began.

Conversation was awkward, but it eased as the meal progressed. The brothers chided each other about everything from girls and phone calls, grades and goofs on the job, to who ate the last piece of pecan pie last night. Justin could hardly eat for watching, wishing he'd grown up in a family like this instead of the sterile, polite environment of his youth.

Finally, the meal ended, the table cleared, and coffee and cookies were passed around. At that point, Wade gave the floor to Justin with a look.

Justin didn't mince words. "It's obvious you know who I am."

"Deborah's husband," Wade said.

Again, Justin felt side-swiped. Everyone had known about the affair except him.

"How is she?" Wade asked.

Ah, so he didn't know everything after all.

"Deborah died in a car wreck more than six years ago."

Wade paled. "I'm sorry to hear that."

"So were we. As I was saying, it's obvious you know who I am. I, however, did not know you existed until a few days ago."

Wade's surprise showed, but he said nothing as Justin continued.

"I found out during a fight with my mother. It was a shock, in more ways than one."

"I can imagine. Do your parents know that you're here?"

"My father's been dead for several years. My mother was shot and killed two days ago."

The collective gasp that went around the table shifted the energy again. Justin was gaining empathy, which was good considering what he'd come to ask.

"Really sorry to hear that," Wade said. "Was it a robbery?"

Justin reached for his coffee cup, unaware his hand was shaking. He took a sip, and then looked up.

"No secrets at this table, right?"

Wade nodded.

"Then to tell this right, I need to go back over twenty years. My senior year in high school I had a sweetheart from the wrong side of the tracks. Her name was Sunny. We sneaked around to see each other until my parents found out then it hit the fan. I was the only child, born with the expectation that I would follow in the footsteps of all the other Caulfield heirs who'd come before me and carry on the family business. It was no big deal to me until Sunny. My parents told me I'd be disinherited if I didn't drop her. I said I didn't care. Then they begged, threatened, and finally played their trump card. If I left them, there would be no one to carry on the family name – to take up the business that four generations before me kept flourishing. I was a kid. I caved in. I have regretted it ever since, but that was that. We broke up and I left for college bearing all kinds of guilt."

Wade nodded. "I see that, but I don't know what it has to do with me."

"You will. You wanted to know why my mother was shot, well it's because the past came back to haunt her. After I left town, Sunny found out she was pregnant. My parents paid her parents off to keep it quiet. Years pass. I marry Deborah and come home to take over the family business from my ailing father, completely unaware of what had happened. Last week, Sunny died of cancer. I didn't even know she was still in the city until I read the obituary. That's when I had the fight with my mother. That's when I found out about the daughter I never knew I had. At the same time, the man Sunny married found out about me. Ironically, he worked for my company and had just been fired. He went to my house to beg for his job back, but I wasn't there. My mother stepped in and told him to get out. He threatened to tell everyone about the illegitimate child if he didn't get rehired. She ran him off then sent her bodyguard to kill him."

This time the collective gasp that went around the table was one of retreat.

"The morning Sunny passed away, the police were pulling her husband's body out of the Little Man river."

"Sweet Jesus," Wade whispered.

"I've given you more details of my sordid family than I'm sure you care to hear, but it bears on why I'm here, so forgive me. Bottom line, I began to suspect what had happened and by then, Sunny's daughter found out about me. The police suspected me, but they didn't know all I knew. I wore a wire and went back for a second round with my mother, during which time she admitted to what she'd done. I'm still trying to come to terms with knowing she killed a man who only wanted his job back. When the police came to arrest her and the bodyguard, the man decided to spare them both the shame and embarrassment of public trial and prison, by killing her and then himself right in the middle of the arrest."

The room went silent, except for a faucet dripping into the sink and a cat fight in progress somewhere outside.

Ben cleared his throat then put a hand on Justin's shoulder.

"Really sorry, man."

Justin sighed. "And that leads me to why I am here. Deborah and I had a daughter. It's been tough raising her without her mother, but she's my life. I would do anything for her. But I have a problem my money can't fix. Last year she nearly died before the doctors were able to diagnose her disease. It took months for them to cure it. In the process, the disease and the treatment destroyed her kidneys. She's on the transplant list, but so far down it doesn't count."

"You can't donate?" Wade asked.

"I only have one kidney," Justin said. "But even if I had two, it wouldn't matter. I found out during that fight with my mother that she's not my child. She's yours, Wade, and I've come to beg for your mercy and your help."

The words were a sucker punch Wade didn't see coming. He stood abruptly, then sat down, then stood again and began pacing from one side end of the table to the other.

"Oh, my God. I didn't know. I swear I didn't know."

Justin gut knotted. The words were an echo of his only days earlier. "Believe me, I understand."

Wade moved down the table from one son to the next, touching a shoulder then a head - reading the varying expressions of shock on their faces. When he got to Suzy she reached for his hand and he grasped it like a drowning man reaching for a rope.

Justin got up, took the envelope from the sideboard and dumped all of the pictures he'd brought with him onto the table.

"Her name is Callie. She's fourteen years old and the light of my life. She's too weak from the disease to withstand the months of dialysis ahead of her as she waits to move up on the transplant list. She needs a kidney, and soon, or she will die."

Wade sat back down, staring in disbelief at the little blond girl who had his eyes. He went from photo to photo, lingering on the ones with Deborah and the child, but it was the photo Justin had on his phone, the one with Callie holding the bear, surrounded by her angels that signed the deal.

"I used to drink. I hope I'm still healthy enough to do this, but I'll gladly be tested," Wade said.

Justin shuddered. The relief was so great he couldn't speak.

Hank was staring at the picture of Callie in her soccer gear.

"I'm way healthier than Dad. I'll do it."

"I'll test, too," Ben said.

Paul and Tommy looked at each other, then at their dad. "We will, too," they echoed.

Tears were running down Suzy's face. "And I volunteer to hold down the fort until you all get back."

"There are no words to express what I'm feeling," Justin said. "Grateful doesn't cover it."

"Does she know about you?" Wade asked.

"Not yet. It was hard enough telling her that her beloved Nana was dead, let alone how it had happened. She cried for hours then woke up more concerned about her new sister, the daughter I didn't know I had. Her name is Poppy, and right now she pretty much hates my guts. In her eyes, I walked out on her mother, and got her father killed, even though she knows I helped the cops get to the truth. Callie is afraid her new sister hates both of us and she's probably right."

"Are you going to tell Callie about us?"

"Yes. Like you said, secrets destroy. There have been too many secrets in my life already. We need to start from a clean slate."

Hank punched Ben. "We're finally going to get that little sister we always wanted."

Paul and Tommy looked a little more anxious. "Is she going to live with us?"

"Of course, not," Wade said. "Mr. Caulfield is still her father. I missed that right by not being the one who raised her. That's what being a father is about. But maybe we can be extended family, if she likes us, and Mr. Caulfield doesn't mind."

Justin sighed. "I suspect she's going to adore all of you, and I will gladly share her with the world to save her life."

A look passed between Wade and Justin, and then the man extended his hand.

Justin took it.

"You don't know how much I have dreaded this meeting," he said. "I was afraid you'd resent a resurrection of the past. Afraid you'd be the kind of man who'd ultimately use her for the family money she will one day inherit. But I can honestly say, from one father to another, it's been a pleasure to meet you."

"Same here," Wade said. "Tell us where to go to get tested and we'll be there tomorrow."

"Thank you, thank you so much, and for the record, Deborah's parents were fools," Justin said.

Wade shrugged. "No. I was the one in the wrong. I was married. I had no right to do what I did, but sometimes the heart wants what the heart should not have."

Justin took a pen from his pocket and began writing info on the envelope. "I'll call Callie's doctor on the way home and tell him to expect you at Saint Anne's tomorrow. This is his name and the name and address of the hospital. I'm also going to give him your contact info. His office can tell you exactly where to go. As soon as you've finished, I'll find you and walk you to Callie's room."

Wade shook his head. "Oh my God."

Hank frowned. "What's wrong, Dad. Are you sorry? Are you changing your mind?"

Wade grinned. "Hell no, son. I'm just a little nervous. With you four, I had nine months to get used to the idea that you were coming. Less than twenty-four hours is pretty daunting."

"It'll be okay," Justin said. "I'll make sure this doesn't scare her. She'll need to understand that nothing will change between us, and that your family will be an addition, not a change in residence."

After another hour of trading information, Justin headed back to Caulfield, leaving not only pictures, but a piece of his heart behind. This was terrifying, bringing people into his world who Callie might come to love more than him. But it was a price gladly paid knowing she now had a chance to grow up and grow old.

CHAPTER TWENTY-TWO

Justin drove home on a high. He called Don Langley, Callie's doctor, and gave him the news about locating new family members. There was no need going into details. When Langley got the results back and saw the matching markers in the DNA, he'd figure it out on his own.

By the time he reached Caulfield, he was exhausted. More than six hours on the road, and the second most stressful day of his life had wiped him out. He wanted to go home, but didn't know if he could face being there.

He pulled in to a gas station on the outskirts of the city, refueled, then pulled away from the pump before he stopped to use the phone. His housekeeper answered on the second ring.

"Lillian, this is Justin."

"Oh, Mr. Caulfield, it's good to hear your voice. I don't know what to say except that I'm so sorry."

"I know, Lillian. I am, too. Has the library been cleaned?"

"Yes sir, the restoration company left just after three this afternoon. Are you coming home now?"

"Yes, Lillian. I believe I am."

"I'll make dinner."

"Something light. I'm just so very tired."

"Yes sir. I'm sorry."

He hung up, then folded his arms across the steering wheel and rested his head. The last few days had been about restitution and today was another step in that direction. He had guilt – so much guilt. There's been a time when he felt pride in being a Caulfield. Now it was a name he was going to have to learn to live down. The last thing still weighing on his mind was telling Callie.

"God help me," he prayed, then started the car and drove away.

Edison Funeral Home wasn't the only funeral home in the city, but for whatever reason, tonight it was a hotbed of business. It had never occurred to Poppy how many people might die in any given week in Caulfield, but in a city of more than 50,000 people and with the surrounding countryside in the same need, she supposed it could be a good number.

John was outside talking to his boss in Atlanta. She knew he was antsy about getting back before he lost his job. At least now that they were able to bury their dad, there would be nothing left to cause another delay.

She wasn't looking forward to living alone, but she had it better than most girls her age. Thanks to her family, she had a home free and clear and a job to go back to.

She looked up as the door opened, only to see another group of grieving family members enter. She quickly looked away. Even though she didn't know them, within these walls they were all part of a very sad club.

The door opened again. This time it was John. From the expression on his face, he seemed satisfied. He crossed the foyer and slid onto the sofa beside her.

"Do they have Dad ready yet?"

She shook her head.

He gave her knee a quick pat. "We picked out the casket at noon when we dropped off the clothes. Epperson told us to come back around five, but we've been here more than three hours. It can't be much longer."

She leaned over and whispered in his ear. "There are a lot of people here tonight. It's so sad. I never thought about how many people lose loved ones every day. Maybe we should come back tomorrow."

"We can if you want to. Oh, hey, here comes Truman now."

Normally Truman Epperson was calm and collected, but not

tonight, and it showed. His hair was a little messy and his tie was slightly askew. They'd kept bringing in bodies all afternoon and then another one just an hour ago. At the present, there were five bodies on the premises and he'd had a startling moment of his own back in the mortuary when he realized Jessup Sadler's body was under a sheet on one work table and Amelia Caulfield and Oral Newton were on tables nearby.

The irony that God had dealt his own brand of justice in this case was blatantly apparent, but he hadn't bothered to mention it to anyone else. When he entered the foyer, he approached John and Poppy with his usual grace.

"John. Poppy. I'm so sorry for the delay. As you can see it's been a difficult night for several families. Please follow me. Unfortunately, dear Poppy, you know the routine. If there's anything about your father that you want changed, you have only to ask."

John had already seen his dad, but this would be her first time.

"You okay, Poppy?"

She was tight-lipped and pale, but her gaze was steady.

"I'm not okay, but I'm ready."

They followed Truman into the viewing room. He shut the door behind them and led the way to the casket.

"This is a fine casket," Truman said. "I like the inlay of wood here, don't you? It's a nice, masculine touch." He brushed a non-existent speck from the lapel of Jessup's sport coat then straightened the collar on his shirt. "I'll give you a few minutes before I come back," he said, then quietly left the room.

Poppy stared down into the casket, afraid she would see the trauma her father had suffered, but to her relief, he appeared to be sleeping.

She felt empty. She wanted him to wake up and tell her he still loved her no matter what, but it wasn't going to happen. She would have to live the rest of her life without hearing him say it was okay that she wasn't his. She needed to cry, but the tears wouldn't come, which added another layer of sadness to what was left of her world. She gripped the edges of the casket then couldn't bring herself to touch him.

"Daddy, it's me, Poppy. We know what happened. We know everything. I'm so sorry. You'll always be my daddy, no matter what anybody says."

John eyes were burning and there was a pain in his chest the size of his fist. His dad had been such a vital part of his life that he couldn't imagine it without him. But it was Poppy that had him worried. He kept watching her, afraid that she would freak.

After a few moments of silence, John put his arm around her shoulder.

"I know this sound weird, but I'm actually relieved. This is a far better image to have in my head than the one from the morgue."

Poppy felt numb. "Are you okay with how he looks?"

He nodded. "He has his wedding band and I had Truman put the pictures from his wallet into his jacket pocket. I figured if he carried them all that time when he was alive, that he'd want to take them with him."

"Are they there?" Poppy asked.

John slid a finger inside the pocket and felt the edges of the photos.

"Yeah, they're there."

"I don't want anything changed."

"Neither do I," John said. "So do you want to stay or-"

"No. I'm just so tired. I want to go home."

"Then home it is." He paused to lay a hand on Jessup's chest. "Be seein' you, Dad."

When they walked out Truman was waiting. "Do you approve?"

"Yes, he looks good, and that's a relief," John said.

Truman was pleased. "I understand. Should any of your friends ask, he is ready for viewing. I'll see you day after tomorrow at the church."

They walked away, silently grateful to be leaving a place of such despair.

Poppy got the bathroom first and finished her bath, then went into her bedroom and dug some flannel pajamas out of storage. The wind had come up about an hour ago, making the house harder to hold heat. The days were already getting chilly and the nights were downright cold. The furnace was churning out heat to the rooms, giving the house a warm, cozy feel.

Pastor Harvard had asked her about her daddy's eulogy and what songs they wanted sung at the service, but she was drawing a blank. She couldn't quit thinking about the funeral home. Jessup had been alone in the morgue, and now he was alone in that viewing room. Maybe they should have stayed.

She was still struggling with her decision to come home when the phone suddenly rang. She glanced up at the clock. It was a little after 9:00 p.m. It rang again and she thought about letting it go to voice mail, but whoever it was, she'd eventually have to return the call so she picked up.

"Hello."

"Hello, Poppy, this is Justin. I apologize for calling so late, but I just got back into the city."

Her first instinct was to hang up. Instead, she froze.

"Poppy? Are you still there?"

"Yes, I'm here."

"Do you have a moment? I wanted to touch base with you before your father's funeral because I'm afraid the next few days are going to be a little hairy here. It appears we might have found a kidney donor for Callie."

Poppy frowned. Why was she getting this blow-by-blow review? She didn't care what he did as long as he left her alone. Still she couldn't be so unfeeling that she'd wish ill will on a sick child.

"That's good news."

"Yes, but not why I'm calling. Is there anything I can do for you?"

She flinched. "I think you've done enough. I hope your daughter's surgery goes well. Thank you for calling."

It hurt to hear the chill in her voice, but was no more than he'd expected.

"Wait, please!" When he didn't hear a dial tone, he kept talking. "I know you want nothing to do with me. I understand that. But I need for you to understand something. After I told Callie what her grandmother had done, she cried herself to sleep. When she woke up, you were the first person she asked about. She asked me if you were going to hate us, then in the same sentence, was happy you were her sister."

"I'm nothing to her. I'm nothing to any of you," Poppy snapped. "You don't need to call. You don't need to check on me."

"I'm not doing this because I think I need to. I'm doing it because I want to, Poppy. Just because you don't want me, doesn't mean I don't want you. I can't help how I feel. I want to make things good for you. I would give you the world if you would take it."

Anger surged through her so fast it left her breathless.

"The world? Wow! I knew the Caulfield family was wealthy, but I didn't know you owned it all. You keep your world, I'll keep mine. If you have issues with Coal Town, then that's your problem. We didn't create the divide, the city of Caulfield did. My family provided just fine for me. My home is free and clear. I have a job and a car. You're already paying to bury my father, but considering your mother was the one who killed him, I no longer have an issue with that."

She slammed down the phone just as John came out of the kitchen.

"Who was that on the phone?" he asked.

"Nobody," Poppy said. "What songs do you want sung at the funeral?"

John grabbed a handful of peanuts from a dish on the table and popped them in his mouth. "Dad liked Swing Low, Sweet Chariot a lot. He used to sing it in the car, remember?"

Poppy was still so pissed she couldn't remember anything but the sound of Justin's voice, but she wrote it down.

"One more," she said. "Pastor Harvard wants two."

"Old Rugged Cross."

"That's that," Poppy said, then shoved her notebook across the sofa. "This is as far as I got with the Eulogy. Can you fill in the blanks? You had Daddy eight years longer than I did."

"I remember," John said. "I also remember how happy I was when he and Mom got married. There were kids in my class who didn't have a father, but I was the only one who didn't have a mother. She filled a great big hole in my life."

Poppy got up. She needed to move or she was going to explode.

"I'm going to make some hot chocolate. Want some?"

John grinned. "Yeah, sure!"

She left him working on the Eulogy and banged a few pans until her mood began to shift. It had occurred to her that the longer she stayed angry, the more power she was giving to Justin. Little by little she let go until she was in a hot chocolate frame of mind.

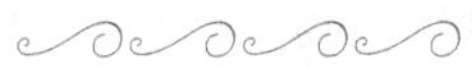

The click in Justin's ear was as distinct as Poppy's disapproval.

The woman had spoken.

He sighed, silently coming to terms with momentary defeat and sat for a moment, staring into space.

Outside, the wind was up, but the massive walls of the Caulfield mansion were a bulwark against any fit Mother Nature chose to pitch. As he sat, a log in the fireplace suddenly burned in two, sending a shower of sparks up the chimney as it fell against the firewall.

The phone call had been enlightening. There was no more wondering how she felt. Now he knew. Yes, she hated his guts. But he'd found out something else. She didn't mince words, which was a trait he admired. And there was something she had yet to learn about him. Justin Caulfield didn't quit on anything, most certainly not his own child. He'd already missed the first 20 years of her life and had no intention of missing the rest.

The sun rose on a cold day in Caulfield as Poppy stood at the windows watching the sky turn from blushing pink to a pale, blue-white. She was nursing her first cup of coffee and waiting for the rest of the house to heat up before she got in the shower.

From where she was standing, she could see the top three

floors of the Caulfield Building on the other side of the river. She was still fuming from last night's phone call, although she regretted showing any anger toward Justin's daughter. She and Callie were the true victims in all this chaos. They were the ones suffering, when in truth, all they'd done was be born.

John was still asleep and she was being as quiet as she could so as not to disturb him. She was beginning to think she might like the house to herself first thing in the morning. It was the calm before the storm. Outside, Coal Town was waking up as well.

Chimneys sent smoke signals into the sharp morning air as a warning of the day that lay ahead. School kids from Coal Town who were walking to the bus stops were wearing last year's winter coats, most of which were either too small because they'd outgrown them, or too big because they were wearing hand-me-downs. Dogs were curled up on the leeward side of the houses – the tips of their fur icy white from an early morning frost. They slept with their noses tucked beneath their legs. Poppy wondered if they dreamed of warmer days and fuller bellies.

Today was Jessup Sadler's day. His obituary and notice of funeral services were in the morning paper. She was beginning to think that Pastor Louis J. Harvard was enjoying the drama of the double funerals a little too much. He'd even asked her what she thought about slipping in a little 'come to God call' in the middle of her daddy's service. She'd told him since it was her daddy's funeral and not a revival, she didn't think it was the proper time to ask mourners to commit their lives to Jesus.

He'd looked a bit taken aback, and then quickly agreed. Personally, Poppy was just ready for all the drama in her life to be over so she could grieve in her own way, not with the world watching from the pews behind her.

When she heard the washing machine stop spinning, she abandoned her post at the windows to throw the clothes into the dryer. Since Johnny was leaving after Daddy's funeral, she wanted the clothes to be clean when he packed them back up.

Justin had been up since before sunrise. He felt like he was out of uniform as he went down to breakfast in slacks and a sweater rather than the two-piece suits he usually wore.

His footsteps actually echoed as he headed for the second-floor landing, and when he started down the stairs, the echoes followed. The original mansion had been built for the generations that would follow. It had been meant for large families and great parties, but for the past two generations, had seen neither.

Either the Caulfield seed had run its course, or the women the men had chosen were not the breeders they once had been. And for Justin, after the revelations of the past week, it no longer felt like a home. Maybe it was time to think about a new home - a place for starting over. It was something on his mind as he walked into the kitchen. The fact that he'd entered Lillian's domain without warning sent her into a fuss.

"Mr. Justin! I didn't know you were up. If you'll tell me what you'd like for your breakfast, I'll fix it and bring it right to you."

Justin shoved his hands in his pockets as he looked around the room – at the industrial-style appliances in shiny stainless steel – then at the worn down edges of the old wooden trestle table where the hired help ate.

"How about a couple of sausage links, two eggs over easy and some toast?"

"Yes sir. I'll bring it right out, and your coffee, too."

He thought about being alone in the formal dining room, and eyed that table again. It was warm and cozy in here and Lillian was a familiar face.

"Would you be offended if I sat at your table, instead?"

Her eyes widened. Never in the entire tenure of the twenty-something years she'd worked in this house had a member of the family sat down with the help, never mind shared a meal with them.

"No sir, it's your house. You can sit anywhere you please."

Justin smiled. "That's not what I asked. I asked if you would be offended. I promise I chew with my mouth closed."

Lillian blinked and then giggled, then blinked again, as if that shouldn't have happened. But he was still waiting for an answer, so she gave him one.

"I would be honored. Have a seat where you please. I'll start the sausage."

Justin hesitated a moment, then went to the counter and poured himself a cup of coffee.

Wade Tiller hadn't had a sleepless night in years – at least not since he and his wife had parted company. But he couldn't get his mind off the past. It had been a shock to learn Deborah was dead, but not nearly as big a shock as finding out they'd had a child together. His children were his life. Everything he did, he did in hopes of making a better future for them than the one that he'd had. To learn he had a daughter who was in a battle for her life had put him on his knees. He'd prayed more last night than he'd prayed in years. By the time the sun was up, he and his sons were on their way to Caulfield.

They'd started out in their usual boisterous manner, talking, teasing, and eating snacks non-stop, but the closer they got to their destination, the quieter the car became. The reality of the trip had begun to weigh upon them and Wade could see it in their faces.

"Boys, I want you to be honest with me. If any of you want to back out on getting tested, it's okay. No one will be mad at you and no one would blame you. It's a big thing to be asked to give away a part of your own body and it shouldn't be done lightly. You're all young. You might suffer an accident or illness as you grow older that causes damage to a kidney, but if you only have one to begin with, then it becomes a far bigger deal."

"Let it go, Dad," Hank said. "We all know the score. We talked about it last night after you went to bed."

"He's right," Ben said. "I kept thinking, what if it was me needing the kidney and I knew that any one of five people could save my life and they wouldn't do it. I can't imagine how scared the kid is, but when I was fourteen, the thought of dying never entered my head and she's been facing it for months."

Paul was the one who was most certain of his path in life.

He wanted to be a priest, and everything he'd done since he was twelve was aimed at the pursuit of that life.

"We don't know her yet, but God knows her and he sent Justin Caulfield to find us. So as far as I'm concerned, it's a done deal," Paul said.

Wade glanced in the rearview mirror. His youngest son was staring out the window and had yet to comment.

"So, Tommy, how do you feel about it?"

Tommy didn't answer.

Paul rolled his eyes and yanked the ear buds out of his brother's ears.

"Tommy! Dad's talking to you."

"Hunh? What? What did you say, Dad?"

Everyone laughed. When the teasing had settled down, Wade asked him again.

"I wanted to know if you were having second thoughts about getting tested. You don't have to, you know."

Tommy frowned, as if he'd just been insulted. "No, I'm not having second thoughts. She doesn't know it yet, but she's part of this family. Someone's gotta toss her a lifeline, right?"

Wade's heart was so full all he could do was nod.

"Yeah, Son, that's a good one. I like that. A lifeline. That's what we are, her lifeline."

Justin got off the elevator and started down the hall toward Callie's room. He was scared out of his mind to tell her yet another shocking truth, and the only thing that kept him putting one foot in front of the other was remembering the look on Wade Tiller's face when he'd announced there were no secrets in their family. When he reached the nurses' station, he paused.

"Good morning, Victoria."

The head nurse looked up and smiled. "Good morning, Mr. Caulfield."

"I have a favor to ask. I need to have a private conversation with Callie and wonder if there's anything pending regarding her care before I start."

"I don't think so." She picked up Callie's chart, scanning it quickly to see if there were any new doctor's orders. "Nothing is scheduled other than meds during the regular rounds, which won't be for another hour or so."

"Then could you see that we're not disturbed for a while? I hate to ask, but it's going to upset her and I need all the time with her I can get."

She frowned. "Of course I will. I'm sorry you're having issues. You two have had a pretty rough week."

"Not as rough as the Sadler family, but close," he said. "Thank you for being so considerate."

"You're welcome. I'll put a DO NOT DISTURB sign on the door."

Justin headed for Callie's room, paused to take a deep breath and then went inside.

CHAPTER TWENTY-THREE

Callie was lying on her side, curled up in a fetal position. She'd slept like that when she was a brand-new baby, and even now, when she was sick or sad, Justin knew it was the position that still gave her comfort. Seeing her with a hand tucked beneath her cheek and the covers pulled up beneath her chin, he almost turned around and walked out. She looked so comfortable, he hated to disturb her. But it was a case of tell her now, or surprise her later, and this wasn't the kind of surprise that lent itself to fun.

Quietly, he pushed the door shut and then moved to the side of her bed to watch her sleep. His heart hurt, remembering how enamored he'd been when she was first born, and how many countless hours he'd stood and watched her sleeping, just like he was doing now.

Only this time he wasn't just admiring her existence. This time he was looking for the differences in their faces, rather than the similarities. When Deborah was alive, she'd often pointed out a specific mannerism or facial quirk of Callie's that she swore mimicked his. Now, he wondered if she'd done it out of fear that one day he'd look at Callie and realize she didn't belong.

But there was something Deborah hadn't taken into account. The deal was that sperm had little to do with becoming a father. That came from the immediate fear the tiny little thing you brought home from the hospital would suddenly forget to take a second breath – from the hours of walking the floor to silence their fussy cries – from the panic of knowing that they hurt and you didn't know why.

Fatherhood was a fluttering heartbeat when they learned to say daddy – from bloody noses and trips to the doctor. It was the hug around the neck and the inevitability of pride in realizing they were growing up just fine in spite of everything you'd done wrong. But no one ever prepared a father for a moment like this. Justin still felt like he'd been blinded and tossed into a room full of land mines – one wrong step and everything could blow up in his face. Because of a mistake he made years ago, Jessup Sadler had gone through these very same feelings only a week earlier. He had no room to be indignant. All he could do was keep reminding himself that it wasn't about him, it was for Callie. Come what may, she was going to get her transplant and he'd gladly pay whatever the price to make it happen.

He glanced at his watch. In a couple of hours the Tillers would be in Doctor Langley's office being tested. Callie needed time to absorb the shock before being meeting the other side of her family.

God help me.

He leaned down and whispered her name. "Callie. Honey." As he brushed a finger down the side of her cheek, her eyelids begin to flutter. "Hey you," he said softly, as she opened her eyes.

"Daddy. You're back," she said sleepily, and wrapped her arms around his neck.

Justin closed his eyes as he returned the hug, savoring the moment. Once she knew, it would be the last of her innocence.

"Did you have a good day yesterday?" Justin asked.

She rolled over and scooted to a sitting position against the headboard.

"Yes. Seeing Miss Patty again was great. Did you have a good trip?"

Justin nodded, but there must have been something in his expression that alerted Callie to a different truth.

"What's wrong? Why do you have that sad look in your eyes?"

Her perception was surprising – again reminding him she was on the cusp of young womanhood – no longer a child.

"I'm not sad." *No more secrets in this family.* Justin dropped his head. "I'm sorry, Callie. That's not exactly true."

Callie reached for his hand. "Is it about Poppy? Did she refuse to talk to you?"

"No, it's not about Poppy. It's about you."

All the color faded from Callie's face. Her fingers curled around his wrist and then her voice faded with it.

"Is it bad? Is it my health? Did the disease come back, Daddy? Am I going to die?"

"No! No! I didn't mean to scare you like that. In fact, it's the exact opposite."

She rolled her eyes and then shoved shaky hands through her hair.

"Oh my God, Daddy, just spit it out. Nothing can be as bad as the fright you just gave me."

A peace washed through him as a slow smile spread across his face. "You know what, honey? You're right. The truth is I'm afraid because I have something to tell you about your mother and me, and I don't know how you're going to feel."

She frowned. "About you and Mother? What is it?"

He scooted onto the side of her bed. "Do you remember how I found out about Poppy?"

She nodded. "Yes. You had a fight with Nana and she let it slip."

"That's right. But she let something else slip that I haven't told you yet."

"And it has to do with you and Mother?"

"Yes."

"Why do I need to know?"

Justin kissed the palm of her hand then cradled it against his knee.

"Because Poppy's mother and your mother were in the same condition when they got married, and neither Mr. Sadler nor I knew about it until just this past week."

Callie took a deep sudden breath, like someone had punched her in the stomach.

"What are you saying?"

"That your mother was also in love with another man and was going to have his baby. But he was married. To make a long story short, she needed a husband and married me."

The shock on her face made him sick. When she started to weep, he wanted to cry with her.

"You're not my Daddy? You have to be my Daddy. Please, Daddy, please. I don't want to belong to anyone else but you."

Justin held out his arms. "Come here, honey. Of course I'm your Daddy. Being a daddy has nothing to do with who slept with who. That's why Poppy doesn't want anything to do with me just yet. She loved Mr. Sadler. He was her daddy. And you love me almost as much as I love you, which makes me your daddy, too. Legally and every way that matters, I'm all yours and you're all mine, okay?"

Callie crawled up into his lap, too stunned to move any further.

"And here's where the miracle comes in," Justin said. "I made your Nana tell me the name of your birth father so I could find him. That's where I went yesterday."

She shivered, and then covered her face with her hands. "Do I have to see him? I don't think I need to see him."

"I think you're going to want to. He's a very nice man. When he found out about you, he cried. He kept apologizing over and over, just as I tried to do to Poppy. He kept saying, I didn't know. I didn't know, just like I said. And do you know what else? You have four great big good-looking brothers who are very excited about meeting you."

She was motionless for a few moments then slowly looked up. "Four?"

"Yes."

"What does their mother think?"

"Their mother is not in the picture. I don't really know why, but I do know that all four of the young men still live at home. They work in their father's business with him."

"They do?"

"Yes."

"But that's still not the miracle. Do you know *why* I went looking for him?"

She shook her head.

"Because they are related to you by blood, that means any one of them should be able to donate a kidney to you."

He saw hope in her eyes, but there was fear in her voice.

"But they don't know me. They won't want to do that," she whispered.

"Oh honey, that's where you're wrong. Not only did your birth father immediately volunteer to be tested, but so did every one of his sons. In fact, they're all on their way here to Saint Anne's as we speak. Doctor Langley is going to test them all to see which one is the best match."

Callie's eyes suddenly widened, and then she kept staring at his face.

"Honey? What's wrong? I thought you'd be happy to get a chance for a normal life again."

"I am, Daddy. It's wonderful news."

"Then why are you looking at me like that?" He managed a smile, trying to tease her out of whatever was still upsetting her. "Do I have egg on my face?"

"I just realized something. You didn't have to do this."

Justin frowned. "I don't know what you mean? Of course I had to do this. I'd do anything... anything to make you well."

But Callie kept shaking her head. "No, when Nana died, you were the only one left who knew I wasn't really your baby. You didn't have to tell me because I'd probably get a kidney from the transplant list before it was too late. I could have lived my whole life and never known this. Oh Daddy, you don't even know what special thing you've done! This is just like the story in the bible about the two women who went to King Solomon, both claiming to be the mother of a little baby boy. The King didn't have any way of telling who the child really belonged to, remember? So he took out his sword and said he would cut the baby in half. He was going to give half to each mother and then they would be satisfied. But the real mother, the one who loved the baby enough to give him up, begged him to stop. She was willing to give him up to keep him safe. That's when King Solomon knew who the real mother was. She would rather lose the child than see him die." Callie threw her arms around Justin's neck. "Oh Daddy... you went to look for the other father especially for me! You were willing to chance losing me to keep me alive. You are the best, most wonderful daddy ever."

Justin knew he must be hugging her, but he couldn't feel his arms. Surely they had turned into wings because his heart was soaring.

Justin spent the morning with Callie, then stayed and had lunch with her just to reassure himself that there were no lingering questions she might have. The only thing she was worried about now was how she looked, which necessitated a quick call to a hair stylist who was, at the present, helping Callie wash and blow dry her hair. Justin had made a flying trip home to find a certain robe that she wanted, and stopped in a nearby pharmacy on the way back and picked up a tube of pale pink lip gloss. He had just parked and was on his way into the hospital when his cell phone rang. He paused outside beneath the breezeway and answered.

"Justin Caulfield."

"Hello, Justin. This is Wade."

Now Justin was the one getting nervous. "Hello, Wade. How's the day been going?"

There was a slight chuckle in his ear. "Hectic, interesting, nerve-wracking, take your pick or all of the above."

"I can imagine."

"Uh, we're wrapping up here now. Paul is finishing up some tests but the rest of us are through. I was wondering how it went with Callie?"

His heart sank, knowing that this was the first real step in separating her life from his, but it couldn't matter.

"Better than I could have ever imagined. I think she's torn between curiosity, fear, and an overwhelming gratitude that people who don't even know her would be willing to go through this for her."

"Bless her heart, and bless yours. I want you to know we will not betray the trust you've given us. We only want what makes her happy and for her to be able to live a long and healthy life."

"Then we're in agreement. So do I need to come find you to walk you back?"

"No. That's why I called. Doctor Langley said he'd personally walk all of us to her room. I just want to make sure you're there first."

"I'm at the hospital and on my way to her room right now. I'll be there waiting when you and your family arrive."

"Alright, then we'll see you soon."

Justin dropped his phone into his pocket and lengthened his stride. Callie would definitely freak if she wasn't properly dressed when they arrived.

A few minutes later he knocked on the door then peeked in. She was sitting on the side of the bed, her long blonde hair hanging loose and shining around her face.

"Hey, pretty girl. Your hair is beautiful. I'll be it feels better, too, doesn't it honey?"

Callie beamed. "Yes. It feels so good. Thank you for getting the stylist to come help me wash and dry it."

"Here's the robe you wanted. We need to get you in it and settled in fast. Mr. Tiller just called. It won't be long now before Dr. Langley brings them to your room."

All of a sudden she was in a panic again. "Hurry Daddy. Help me."

He slipped it on her, pretending not to notice how thin her arms were, and how fragile she really was beneath her hospital gown.

"Oh wow, sweetheart, how pretty you look. This blue robe is the same color blue as your eyes."

She beamed.

"I brought you something else that I thought you might want."

"Like what?"

He pulled the lip gloss out of his pocket. "It's gloss, not lipstick, but it has a little tinge of color."

"Daddy! Thank you! I need a mirror."

He lifted the lid of the tray table. "There's one underneath here, remember?"

"Oh, right," she said, and quickly applied a neat layer of gloss to her lips.

Justin watched with a lump in his throat. She was growing up. God willing she would also grow old.

Less than fifteen minutes later, there was a knock on the door and Callie's excitement shifted south. Suddenly, she was a frightened, little girl all over again.

"I'm right here, Callie. He's not your daddy, but he is the man who gave you to your mother. It's a good thing to know him."

And just like that, she lifted her chin. "I'm ready, Daddy. Please let them in."

Justin opened the door. He saw fear on Wade's face.

"Come in. Callie's been waiting for you."

An hour later, the mood in the room had done a complete one-eighty. Callie held court like the female she was, shy one minute and then flirtatiously giggling the next, but always with an eye on where Justin was in the room. He was her anchor.

It was obvious from the expression on Wade Tiller's face that he had fallen in love, but he was wise enough to keep his distance. Justin couldn't help wondering how many times today the man had thought of Deborah. Probably as many times as he'd thought of Sunny and wished he would have had the same chance with Poppy that Wade had here.

But there was that bit about a murder. What a difference a crime made.

After an hour, Callie began to fade and Justin saw it.

"I hate to bring a good thing to an end, but I see someone getting tired," he said.

Callie made a face, but it gave her permission to sink back against the pillows.

"Don't worry, kid," Hank said. "If I get to donate, not only will you get better, but you'll be strong. I'm the strongest one in the family."

Paul rolled his eyes. "You better hope it's me. It'll raise your IQ level to the max."

"You're offering to donate a kidney, not a brain," Tommy said, which made everyone laugh.

Wade had seen Callie fading, as well. He couldn't imagine the hell Justin Caulfield had lived through this year, thinking this child was going to die. He stood up, wanting to hold her, but it was all too new and too soon.

"As you can tell, there are no shy genes in the Tiller family, and your father is right. You need your rest, young lady. Thank you for receiving us with open arms. This day has been amazing in so many ways, but it's definitely one of the best days of my life."

Callie sighed. "It started off scary and ended good. Thank you for caring and for helping me."

Wade glanced at Justin, then back at his child. It had taken him all hour to get to this point – to giving himself permission to even think of her that way. He saw himself in her – the white-blonde hair and blue eyes - and he saw Deborah. He'd always thought of her as the biggest mistake of his life, but no more. Whatever they'd done wrong, this child made it right.

"No matter which one of us winds up being the lucky donor, you need to know we're proud to have a connection to you. One day we might share more than blood, but for now what you've given us is enough. Rest well. We'll be in touch."

"I'll walk you to the elevator," Justin said.

Callie waved from the bed, and then they were gone. The room had gone from high intensity to a silence so profound that it quickly sucked her under.

When Justin came back, she was asleep. He kissed her forehead, wrote her a note, and left to go home.

Bravest girl in the world. Love, Daddy.

Later, when she woke up and found it, she tucked it under her pillow for good luck.

It was the morning of Jessup Sadler's funeral. Coal Town was primed like a john with a hard-on. All they needed was a willing hooker and it would blow.

Plenty of people die. Not a lot of them get murdered and even less of them murdered by a member of the city's founding family. Everyone was curious. Did a murder victim look different than a regular dead man? According to the gossip on the streets, Coal Town was turning out to see for themselves.

John had the heads up straight from Aaron Coulter about what was happening, and to expect standing room only at the church. Poppy was already dreading the second funeral, but to realize it was about to become a spectacle only made things worse.

To add insult to injury, the cold front that had come through last night left some bad news behind. Right after the car from the funeral home came to pick them up, it started to snow.

"Look at that," John said, pointing out the window.

The flakes were so tiny they didn't have the weight to fall. Instead, they kept floating up and swirling down, caught in the air currents from passing cars.

Poppy shuddered. The cemetery was on a hill with no windbreak and she wished she'd worn pants and her boots instead of the same black dress and shoes she'd worn to her mama's funeral.

When they turned the corner leading up to the church, Poppy's heart skipped a beat. The streets were lined on both sides with cars as far as she could see.

"Oh my God!"

John reached for her hand. "It appears Aaron was right. How do you feel about being on show one more time?"

Poppy shivered. "Daddy would hate this."

He frowned. "Don't think of it that way. He's beyond all this crap. It's you I'm talking to. Can you do this?"

Her chin came up. "Yes, and don't play into this feeding frenzy, Johnny. Don't get indignant on my behalf. I can take care of myself, okay?"

He gave her hand a quick squeeze.

The church loomed. Moments later they were out of the car and being escorted in. The ones who'd been unable to get a seat inside were standing in the church yard and spilling out into the street.

Poppy tucked her hands into her coat sleeves, looking neither right nor left as she hurried inside. The blast of warmth that met them at the door was just as startling as the cold had been.

Pastor Louis J. Harvard got the signal that the family had arrived. He cued the organist, who ceased playing and instantly struck a chord.

"All rise," Harvard said, and lifted his hands toward the ceiling to indicate the congregation should stand. Considering everyone spoke English, it was a bit of overkill, but Louis J. always had been one to play to the crowd.

Poppy fixed her gaze on the casket at the foot of the altar as she and Johnny walked down the aisle. She already knew what a lot of the mourners were thinking. By virtue of blood alone, she'd lost her right to be one of them.

The service went by in a blur. By the time the last note of music had faded, she was as cried out as a woman could be and still be breathing. It wasn't until they raised the lid of the casket that she faltered.

John had his arm around her all the way through the service, but when she began to shake, he felt the tremors in her body all the way to his bones. He'd battled his own emotions, but seeing her like this hurt his heart.

"You can do this," he whispered.

She took a slow, deep breath then lifted her head. When the mourners began to move toward the altar, she bore silent witness to their passing.

Late that night when she'd finally gone to bed, she only remembered bits and pieces of the day.

Louis J. touching the crown of her head as if he'd been bestowing a blessing – or forgiving a sin.

Snow sticking to her eyelashes at the cemetery, leaving the world somewhat blurry to her view.

Hot coffee Gladys thrust in her hands as they came back to the church for the meal.

Aaron Coulter hugging Johnny and then walking away.

It was blatantly obvious that John was being held in higher esteem, and while she understood why, it didn't make it less devastating. The innuendoes abounded that she now thought herself above the other residents in Coal Town. The knowledge brought its own kind of pain.

This time next year Poppy would be old news, but right now

it hurt. Couldn't they see that she was grieving as much as Johnny? Why would they think the Caulfield blood in her veins would blunt the sadness of losing both her parents in one day?

The antagonism made no sense, and yet it was there. All she could do was pray for the strength to ignore it and the courage to endure it.

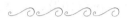

It was Mike's day off. Barring a homicide somewhere in Caulfield, he had the next twenty-four hours to himself. Today was the day of Jessup Sadler's funeral. More than anything, he wanted the freedom to go to that church in support of Poppy, but it wasn't his place to do so – at least not yet.

All day yesterday the police department kept getting tips that Jessup Sadler's funeral might become a detonation point for some kind of riot. It made no sense why it could happen, but it was enough to make him worry. He made it his mission to get to the Church of Angels early and park in a place where he had a clear view of the entrance. If he saw a situation beginning to develop, at least he was in a position to call it in before it got out of hand.

Within thirty minutes, people began arriving and soon after that, it began to snow. He was guessing a good number of the mourners were here only out of curiosity. It wasn't common, but not unusual for someone in Coal Town to die at someone else's hands. But Jessup Sadler's murder, and then the ensuing murder/suicide of his high society killers had turned this into a sensation.

By the time the funeral car arrived with the family, the church was full and the churchyard overflowing with mourners willing to stand in the snow for nothing more than a glimpse of Justin Caulfield's dirty little secret.

He got out, ready to make a run for Poppy should anything get out of hand, but John stood a head above most of the people there, and had her tucked tightly beneath his arm. They disappeared into the church without incident, which was a relief, but he wasn't going anywhere until he was certain the rumors were just that.

As he waited for the service to end, it felt more like a stake-out than monitoring security. When the pall-bearers finally emerged carrying the casket, he recognized some of them as men who'd worked Jessup's shift at the mine.

Then Poppy came out and paused. For few seconds she stood alone on the steps of the church with the snow swirling about her head, staring out into the crowd below. She was ghostly pale, and even from where he was sitting he could see she was shaking. Oblivious to the tears on her cheeks, she lifted her chin in a subconscious challenge. When John appeared behind her then helped her down the steps and into the car, she never wavered.

And that was the moment he fell the rest of the way in love.

CHAPTER TWENTY-FOUR

The snow quit before sunrise leaving a light dusting of flakes on the grass. John followed its exit, but not before eliciting a dozen promises from Poppy to call if she needed help, and that he'd stop in to check on her the next time he drove through West Virginia. Poppy hated to see him go, but in a way was also ready to get some order back in her life. The sooner she got used to living alone, the better off she would be.

She'd called Vic Payton to let him know she was ready to come back to work, and the joy in his voice had been obvious. She was back on the schedule, beginning tomorrow.

After spending all day yesterday at the church, she'd skipped Sunday services this morning. Today was about getting out her winter clothes and re-stocking groceries. Maybe she'd even treat herself to a burger and fries on the way home.

She was already dressed and in the kitchen making a grocery list when she heard a knock at the front door. It was Gladys.

And with her usual no-nonsense manner, went straight to the reason that she'd come.

"Hi sugar! I saw John's truck was gone so I guessed he was on his way back to Atlanta. I couldn't help thinking of you here by yourself and want you to know Mel and I are here for you any time you need us."

Poppy was relieved at least some of her friends weren't going to drop her.

"Thank you, Gladys. It's good to know you two are still speaking to me. After everything that's happened this past week, I wasn't expecting there'd be anyone left here who'd remember my name."

Gladys frowned. "I still don't see the reason for all this fuss. If anyone gives you lip, you tell them to kiss your ass."

Poppy grinned. "I suppose I could do that."

"Yes, you sure can. Oh, Mel wanted me to make sure you know to call him if anything goes wrong here in the house. He's a pretty good handyman. No need paying a service call for something he might be able to fix. Has the pilot light been lit on your furnace?"

"Yes. Johnny did it while he was here."

"All right then, I'll just be on my way. I have a load of stuff to do before work tomorrow." She gave Poppy a big hug and was out the door as fast as she'd entered.

Poppy was smiling as she headed back to the kitchen. Maybe this would all blow over sooner than she thought. She grabbed the grocery list then her coat and purse, and locked the door behind her as she left.

Justin was in his car, following the hearse bearing his mother's body out to the cemetery. A quartet of city employees was waiting by the open grave, ready to assist in moving the casket. He stood to one side as they lowered it into the void. In funeral ceremony vernacular, Amelia Caulfield was being laid to rest beside her husband, but Justin doubted her soul was at peace. Nowhere in the bible was it written that murderers got a straight shot to heaven.

As soon as the casket touched bottom, the men walked away to give Justin some privacy. Once they were out of sight, Justin walked to the edge. Without saying a word, he took the box bearing Oral Newton's ashes out of the sack he'd been carrying and tossed it into the grave. It hit the lid of the casket, bounced end over end, and tumbled into a corner of the pit where it slid out of sight.

Since they had colluded in life, they could spend eternity together as well. It would piss Amelia off to no end that she was being buried with the hired help, and he didn't give a damn what Newton would have thought.

He waved at the men, who then returned and began to cover it up. The first clods of dirt hit the casket with a thud. The shock of what his mother and her driver had done was passing, leaving him with nothing but shame. He stayed until the last shovelful of dirt was turned, then got in his car and drove away.

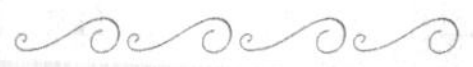

Despite the fact that Poppy had driven home with the window part-way down, the car still smelled like the burger and fries she'd had for lunch. Once she was home, other than unloading the groceries and washing one more load of clothes, she was nearly caught up. It felt good to be moving in a positive direction, although tonight would be the real test, sleeping in the house alone.

It wasn't like she'd never done that before, but she'd always known someone would be coming back, and this was no longer the case. She wasn't exactly afraid, just uneasy. But as Johnny had reminded her, all she could do was take it one step, one day, at a time.

When she turned the corner, she automatically glanced toward her house. Within seconds, her heart skipped a beat. The closer she drove, the more horrified she became. By the time she pulled up in the driveway she was crying.

The words, *rich bitch,* had been written across the front of her house in red spray paint. She got out with her legs shaking and stared at it in disbelief, then looked up and down the street, but it was empty.

Tears turned to rage as she headed for the neighbor's house. The old man who lived there was a widower with time on his hands and often sat by the window with his binoculars.

She saw a curtain fall back into place as she started up the sidewalk toward his house and realized that not only had he sat and watched them spray painting her house, but he'd done nothing to stop it.

She doubled up her fist and pounded on the door, but he didn't answer. She pounded again, this time shouting his name.

"Mr. Lewis, I need to talk to you. Please come to the door, I know you're in there."

Finally, she heard the sounds of shuffling feet and then the door opened just enough for him to peer out. It had been years since Poppy had seen him this close up. Not only had he aged drastically, he appeared to have shrunk a good foot in height.

"I'm busy. Go away," he muttered.

"You saw who vandalized my house."

"I didn't see nothin'," he muttered.

She started to cry. "Why won't you help me? Mama and Daddy were nothing but good to you. Is this the way you repay their kindness, by protecting the people who did this to my house?"

He frowned. "I don't know names."

"Did you see their car?"

"No, they was afoot."

"How many were there?" Poppy asked.

"Two boys, probably late teens, early twenties."

She swiped the tears off her cheeks with an angry swipe. "What did they look like? What were they wearing?"

"You don't tell no one I told you. I don't want no trouble."

"I don't want trouble either, yet I have it. What did they look like?"

"Both of them real tall, and skinny. Clothes hangin' on them like rags on a scarecrow. The clothes was all blue, like denim I guess. One of 'em had long brown hair pulled back in a ponytail. Other one had blonde curly hair hanging down around his face. Now go away. I got things to do."

Poppy stomped off the porch with single intent. The moment he'd said scarecrows, she knew exactly who'd done it and where to find them – two stoners named Freddie and JoJo who hung out at Millwood's Gas and Grocery begging for handouts.

She got back in her car and took off down the street, laying rubber as she went. By the time she got to Millwood's, she was furious. She wheeled into the station and stomped the brakes so hard the car slid sideways as it stopped.

Aaron Coulter was passing by in his Hummer and saw her pull in. He started to wave, then saw the look on her face and realized something was wrong. He hit the brakes and backed up, but by the time he got stopped, Poppy had already gone inside.

They were sitting in the corner near the heating stove with two empty long-necks at their feet and wrappers from candy bars wadded up beneath their chairs. Poppy headed toward them with her hands fisted.

"It figures you worthless bastards would be hiding out behind a shelf of toilet paper since you're both such assholes!"

Freddie fell backwards in his folding chair and JoJo tripped over him trying to run out the back.

Poppy kicked Freddie in the crotch and stomped on JoJo's fingers with the heel of her shoe. Both men were yelling and cursing, begging Old Man Millwood to call the police.

"Yes, call the police," she shouted. "It'll save me a trip downtown to file charges against the both of them for vandalizing my house."

"We didn't do no such thing!" JoJo yelled, cradling his fingers against his chest.

"Yes you did, you dumb ass, and the red paint is still on your fingers," Poppy shouted, and pulled his hair back so hard it popped his neck.

Freddie was doubled up on his side, moaning and holding his crotch. When she kicked him again, he screamed like a girl.

"Stop her! Somebody stop her! She's busted my nuts."

But Poppy wasn't through. She got down on her knees until she was only inches away from their faces.

"Both of you! Pay attention to what I'm saying! If this happens again, even if you didn't do it, I'll blame you. I won't go looking for anyone else, I'll go after you. It won't matter where you hide, I'll find you, and when I do, I'll be the one laughing when they bury the both of you without your dicks."

"Jesus Christ!" Freddie cried.

JoJo's eyes bugged out of his face. "You're crazy! Get away from me! Get the fuck away from me!"

"This isn't crazy. This is what fed up looks like!" Poppy

screamed, and started punching them.

All of a sudden someone was pulling her back and she began kicking and fighting all over again.

"Whoa, whoa, little sister! It's me, Aaron. Aaron Coulter. I'm not trying to hurt you, honey. Slow down, slow down."

Poppy threw one last punch that luckily missed him before she finally realized who it was.

"Let me go, Aaron! Let me go."

He stepped back and held up his hands, then eyed the pair of men on the floor.

"What did they do?"

"They spray painted my house. Wrote 'rich bitch' all across the front in red paint. There were witnesses and JoJo still has red paint on his fingers."

The smile on Aaron's face shifted. His eyes narrowed as a red flush spread across his cheeks.

"Is that true?"

Freddie was still cupping his privates and JoJo was bawling.

"We didn't mean nothin' by it," Freddie said. "It was just somethin' to do."

Aaron squatted down until he was on eye level with them.

"It never occurred to you that Poppy here has just had the week from hell? That she'd had to bury her mama and her daddy and have everything she knew turned upside down? Is that how we treat our own?"

"She ain't one of us. She's got rich blood. She needs to get out of Coal Town," JoJo muttered.

Poppy gasped, pushed Aaron aside and lit into him again, punching him in the nose before Aaron could stop her.

Blood spurted from JoJo's nose and he started screaming all over again.

At this point, Millwood yelled at all of them. "One more punch gets thrown and I'm callin' the cops!"

"Damn woman, I never knew you had this in you," Aaron muttered, as he pushed her back against the window. "Just hold it, okay? Let me finish this. I can make sure it won't happen again."

Poppy was so mad she was shaking, but the threat of police had finally gotten through her anger. The last thing she wanted was for Mike to find out she'd been brawling like the Coal Town trash she was.

"Get up!" Aaron said.

Freddie moaned. "I can't. My balls hurt."

He lowered his voice. "Get the fuck up. Both of you."

JoJo rolled over then staggered to his feet while holding the tail of his shirt against his nose.

Freddie finally got up, but was in so much pain he couldn't stand straight.

"Here's the deal," Aaron said. "None of us had a goddamned bit of choice as to who fucked who to get us here. Poppy Sadler was born and raised right here in Coal Town. She's no better off today than she was a week ago before her daddy was murdered. She's still driving the same piece of shit car, working at the same job, and living in the same house. What happened to her today better not ever happen again, and it's to your benefit if you spread the word. You tell them that anyone who messes with her answers to me." His voice got softer as he leaned in until there were mere inches separating them. "You do know what I'm saying, don't you?"

"Yes, hell yes, Aaron. We didn't mean nothin'. We won't do it again."

"Better not *anybody* so much as look at her wrong. John Sadler is my friend. She's John's little sister, therefore she's my friend, too. You know what happens to people who mess with *my* friends."

"Yes, yes, we know. We'll make sure no one messes with her."

"No. I'll make sure no one messes with her. Your job is to get on the other side of the street if you see her coming. Your job is to go out of your way to never look at her again. Do we understand each other?"

"Yes, hell yes."

"Then get the fuck out of my sight," Aaron whispered.

When they started to walk past him, he stopped them with a look.

"Go out the back you motherfuckers, so she doesn't have to look at you again."

They disappeared, leaving a trail of snot and blood behind

them.

Aaron turned around, but Poppy was nowhere in sight. He looked out the window. She was already backing out of the parking lot. As she took off in a flurry of flying gravel and dust, a slow smile spread across his face. That was one pissed off woman – one fine, pissed off woman. If he ever found one like that, he might actually settle down.

By the time Poppy got home she was in shock at what she'd done. She had never lost control like that, and was reeling from what Aaron had told them. She wasn't exactly afraid of him, but she would never want to be his enemy, either.

This time when she pulled up into the driveway she unloaded her groceries and carried them inside. After she'd put them away and changed into old clothes, she got a bucket of soapy water and began scrubbing at the paint. No way in hell was she going to bed until it, and the words, were gone.

Anger was a good cure for insomnia. When Poppy finally went to bed, she was exhausted. It had taken a little over four hours in the cold with her hands in water, scrubbing at the wood to get rid of the paint. Unfortunately, the white paint beneath it was also gone, too. Now the house needed a paint job, but that wasn't going to happen any time soon. She fell asleep without dreaming and didn't wake up until the alarm went off the next morning at 5:00 a.m.

"Oh my God," Poppy groaned.

She slapped at the alarm to turn it off, then threw back the covers and swung her feet off the side of the bed.

The house was cold and dark as she stumbled into the hall to turn up the thermostat then she staggered into the bathroom to shower. Fifteen minutes later she was out and running to find the clothes she'd forgotten to take in with her.

It was odd, getting ready for work without anyone to talk to.

She turned on the television just for the noise, and then went into the kitchen to make coffee. She ate a bowl of cereal standing up at the counter and poured herself a coffee to go. After a quick check of the house, she put on her coat, slung her purse over her shoulder, and locked the door on her way out.

She drove across the Little Man as light threatened the darkness across the eastern sky. No snow today, but it was cold. There was a man walking across the bridge's footpath. She glanced at him as she passed, checking to see if it was Prophet Jones. It was not. She wondered where the old man was now that winter had set in. Surely to God he wasn't still under the bridge.

As she stopped for a red light, a police car went flying through the intersection with lights flashing and the siren screaming. She muttered a prayer of safekeeping for whoever might be in trouble, and then drove on. It had been a little over a week since she'd been at work. It felt like a lifetime.

She parked in her usual place, and then hurried up the alley and in through the back door to the scent of freshly baked bread and fried bacon.

Sonny the chef looked up. His eyes widened with surprise, and then he nodded. It was more than he usually did, so she took it as a good sign.

She clocked in, ducked into the back room to stow her things in her locker then grabbed a clean apron on her way into the dining room.

One of the bus boys was filling salt and pepper shakers and another was folding napkins, but she was the first waitress here. Vic was at the till counting out money for the register and when he saw her, his face lit up.

Poppy sighed. Hopefully he and Michelle had made up. If they had not, she had a feeling it was going to be a long day.

She moved to the coffee urns and began making coffee, refilling sugar bowls with the little paper packets and falling back into her routine without hesitation. As soon as Vic had money in the till, he came to greet her.

"Good morning, Poppy. It's good to see you again."

"Thank you. It's good to be back and doing something normal."

"I can only imagine," he said. "I know you're going to need a lot of time to adjust to things, but if you ever need a break, or want to get away on your days off, just let me know. I'm a good companion."

"I know you are, Vic. You've been a good friend and I appreciate it. Friends are hard to find."

She could see the disappointment on his face, but it was better to get it said now than to let him think they could be anything but friends.

"Yes, right. So, I'll be in the office for a while. Got some orders to call in." He unlocked the front door, turned on the outside lights and then gave her a nod. "We're open for business."

"Where's Jewel?"

"She quit." He glanced at his watch and frowned. "There's a new girl. Her name is Mandy. She's been here two days and already late. We'll see how that works out."

Poppy didn't know about the new girl, but she was glad the old one was gone. Within a few minutes, regular customers began to trickle in.

About an hour later the new waitress showed up. Poppy had seen plenty of hung over people, but never one this bad who'd bothered to come to work. She walked in the back door as Poppy came through the kitchen for extra butter and syrup, and the uniform the girl was wearing looked like she'd slept in it.

"Who are you?" the girl asked.

"Poppy. You must be Mandy."

"Oh. You're the one who's old man got murdered. Tough."

Poppy stopped. The girl hadn't even bothered to mask her disdain. She started to respond, and then thought better of it, grabbed the butter and syrup and started to leave the kitchen when Mandy turned around, giving everyone a very good view of her ass and the pink thong underwear parting the crack.

"Hey, Mandy."

"What?"

"You might want to pull down your skirt unless that's your way of cruising for tips. Your ass is shining."

"Oh my God," Mandy groaned, and was reaching behind her as Poppy left the kitchen.

After her less than auspicious meeting with Poppy, Mandy toned down her attitude. By the end of the day she was almost friendly, but Poppy wasn't going to lose any sleep over her. The day went by faster than Poppy expected. A couple of her regulars expressed their condolences, and one looked a bit taken aback when she'd seen her, as if she had never expected to see her waiting tables again. But other than that, it was okay.

On the drive home, she became anxious again, fearing that she would see even more graffiti on her house when she drove up, but that wasn't the case. In fact, while she'd been gone, someone had brushed paint over the bare spots, trying to blend it in with the rest of the house. It was a bit whiter than the old paint, but it was better than the wood shining through. She didn't know who done the good deed and was too tired to try and find out.

She unlocked the door, kicking off her shoes as she stepped inside, and for a brief moment expected to hear her mama yell out, 'we're in here'. It was going to be a hard thing to remember that wouldn't happen again.

Instead of letting it pull her down, she went through the house, turning on lights. Since this was how it was going to be from now on, she wasn't hiding away in the dark.

Justin was still playing catch up at work, which meant he had less time than he would have liked to spend with Callie. After a brief consult with her, he decided to hire her old babysitter, Patricia Ryan, on a full-time basis. Miss Patty was tutoring Callie when she felt like studying, and entertaining her when she did not. Every evening Justin ate supper with Callie then went home. Once the Caulfield mansion had been his refuge, but it was beginning to feel more and more like a museum and less like home.

He was having a hard time finding solace in the place where he'd been raised. The air inside the place was heavy, like the way it felt when thunderheads began gathering before a storm. No matter how many lights he turned on, it still felt dark. It was as if the house had died along with Newton and Amelia.

When he finally got up the nerve to go into the library, the energy was so negative it stopped him in his tracks. He turned around and left without getting what he'd come for.

That's when he knew it was time to get out.

There were plenty of places on which one would expect a man in his position to choose to rebuild, but he kept coming back to the inevitable.

He had a daughter in Coal Town who wouldn't come to him. And in good conscience, he could hardly take his other daughter there. But he owned all the land surrounding the Caulfield Building, all the way to the river. Once he realized he could see the roof of her house from his office windows, he knew where he wanted to be. The closest he could get to her was to build a house on one of the hills above the river.

It didn't take long for word to get around that Poppy Sadler had given Freddy and JoJo a whipping for vandalizing her house, and that Aaron Coulter had not only backed her, but openly threatened anyone who bothered her again. All of a sudden she was 'one of them' again. In the vernacular of Coal Town, 'she'd whupped ass' and it was no more than the two stoners deserved.

It was somewhat pathetic that it took a brawl for her to gain the respect of her neighbors again, but she was grateful the pressure was off.

One day rolled into another. She painted the walls in her parent's old bedroom in a color called vanilla malt. With a throw rug on the floor by the bed and new curtains on the window, she was ready to make the move. The only thing holding her back was waiting for the new paint smell to fade.

Another weather front came through during the day on Friday and by quitting time it was snowing. Not the tiny flakes from before. These were serious, duck feather-sized flakes that stuck as soon as they fell, making the drive home a bit nerve-wracking.

Poppy slid sideways when she turned down her street and then slid again when she turned up into her drive. When she finally got the car stopped, she was so tense she'd given herself a headache.

"Thank God," she said, and headed into the house on the run.

She didn't realize until she'd locked the door behind her and kicked the snow off her shoes that the house felt different. It was snug and warm, but that's because Jessup always made sure to keep up repairs. It took her a few moments before she realized she felt welcome. The pervasive sadness that had permeated these walls was almost gone. The energy in the house was healing along with her.

Getting out of the uniform was always her first order of business, so she hurried down the hall to change. She put on sweats and a sweatshirt, brushed her hair and washed her face, and traded her work shoes for slippers.

A short while later she was in the kitchen peeling potatoes and chopping onions and celery to make potato soup. She had cornbread in the oven and the coffeemaker was churning out fresh brew. She couldn't help wishing she had someone to share it, but dwelling on shortcomings had never been her style. Within thirty minutes, the cornbread was done and the soup was simmering on a back burner when someone knocked on the door.

Poppy frowned, wondering who would come calling in weather like this, and then got a little anxious, wondering if Freddy and JoJo had gotten a fresh dose of nerve and were coming back for a face-to-face with her.

She turned off the stove, then turned on the porch light and looked out. There was a strange car in the drive and an elderly man on the porch. The dark overcoat he was wearing was peppered with snow and the blue sock cap on his head was pulled way down past his ears. He looked too old to be threatening, guessed he might be lost, and decided to open the door.

"Hello? Can I help you?"

"Good evening, Poppy. You told me if I ever wanted a free meal to knock on your door."

Poppy gasped. "Prophet Jones, is that you?"

"Indeed it is. Is this a bad time?"

"No, of course not. Please come in."

Prophet took off his overcoat, revealing even more clean clothes. When he took off his sock cap, she was shocked to see he was completely shorn of all but a couple of inches of snow white hair. With the wild hair and the rags he'd worn gone, it's no wonder she hadn't known him.

"You're just in time. I was about to sit down."

"Something smells very good," he said.

"Potato soup and cornbread. Follow me."

He beamed. "Manna from heaven."

Poppy dished up soup, cut a warm block of cornbread, and poured him some coffee, then remembered how he'd taken it before and added sugar and cream.

"We will eat and then we will talk. May I bless the food?"

"I would be honored," Poppy said.

It was all she could do not to stare as the old man gave the blessing. Right after the 'amen', he took his first bite, rolled his eyes in delight and then dunked a chunk of cornbread into the soup and ate it with his spoon.

"You are a fine cook. One day you will make someone a good wife," Prophet said.

Poppy grinned. "Thank you."

They ate in mutual silence. Once he was finished, as promised, he had things to say.

"I didn't just come to eat a meal. I came to say thank you, and goodbye."

"You're leaving Caulfield?"

He nodded. "It is time. Because you believed me, those who had trespassed against us have been brought to justice. I have shed my sackcloth and ashes. My years of wandering in the wilderness are over. I have no further need to stay."

"But how... I mean, your clothes, your car? You lived on the streets... under the bridge and God knows where else. How have you-"

Prophet shrugged. "I had means, I just chose not to use them."

"You aren't driving out tonight in this snowstorm are you?"

He smiled, which highlighted the bony angles of his face even more.

"I have been staying at a motel and won't leave until the roads are safe. I'm not as young as I used to be, you know."

"Where will you go?"

"Florida. It never snows there."

"I'm so thankful you came to tell me. I would have been sad if you'd left without saying goodbye."

"I have something else to say. You may think I'm interfering, but I was a pastor long before I became an advocate for justice. I am also a good judge of character."

Poppy frowned. She didn't know where this was going, but she felt a sermon coming on. Prophet stood up from the table, just as he might have risen to approach the pulpit.

"In all the years I've known him, Justin Caulfield has been a fair man. Considering what I thought about his parents, this is not an easy thing for me to say. I can't tell you how to feel, but it is my opinion that the sins of the father should *not* be visited upon the child. He and your mother were young and foolish, but he had nothing to do with the immoral crimes that were committed. The fact that he actually betrayed his mother to seek justice for you is remarkable and I hope when your grief is less fresh, you will realize it."

Poppy didn't want to hear this, but she sat in stoic silence. In her mind, letting Justin Caulfield into her life was a betrayal of both her mother and her father. Prophet Jones didn't know what the hell he was talking about, but she wasn't going to argue.

"Well now! I've said all I came to say," Prophet said. "It's time I got back before the snow gets too deep to drive in. I will keep you in my prayers, young lady. I hope you'll do the same for me."

Poppy stood. "You'll always be in my prayers, Mr. Jones. If it hadn't been for you, we might never have solved my daddy's murder."

"God works in mysterious ways, my child," Prophet said, then reached out and laid his hand on her head, as if he was blessing her. "Have a good life, Poppy Sadler. Don't live in the past or you'll miss what's happening to you now."

Poppy stood at the window, watching until his tail lights disappeared, then eyed the accumulating snow, thankful she had the next two days off.

CHAPTER TWENTY-FIVE

Justin woke abruptly then rolled over and looked at the clock. It was already after 8:00 a.m. He threw back the covers and climbed out of bed before he remembered it was Saturday. It had been slick driving home from the hospital last night and still snowing when he'd gone to bed. A glance out the window confirmed his decision had been a wise one - white as far as the eye could see and still coming down. He was going to have to break out the four-wheel drive Range Rover to get anywhere today.

Then he thought of Poppy. Granted she'd managed twenty years without his help, but only because he hadn't known she existed. Now that he did, and knowing she was either out in this weather, or in that little house all alone, he was going to worry whether she liked it or not, so he reached for the phone.

There was no need planning what to say to her because he knew she'd be pissed no matter what, and her number was now a fixture in his memory so he didn't have to look it up.

It was a sad commentary that the only sure thing he knew about her was a damn phone number.

After he made the call, he sat down on the side of the bed and counted the rings. If she didn't answer, then she was already at work. He'd have to drive by to make sure she was there and not stuck in a snowdrift somewhere between her house and The Depot. Just when he thought it was going to go to voicemail, she answered, and he could tell by the confusion in her voice that she'd been asleep.

"Poppy, sorry to wake you. It's Justin. When I saw how

much it had snowed, I wanted to make sure you weren't going to have to drive in this."

Poppy raised up on one elbow. "I don't know what you think I did for the past twenty years without your interference, but I don't need your help."

"What I think is that your father looked after your welfare during that time, and I didn't know you existed. What I know is that he's no longer here and I still am, which means you're stuck with my interfering phone calls now and then whether you like it or not."

She blinked. If he'd been coaxing, or apologetic, she would have felt like he was trying to get on her good side, but he'd challenged her. That was unexpected. And then she remembered he was still on the line and hung up.

Justin heard the click and sighed. That wasn't the smartest thing he'd ever done, but she wasn't the only hard-headed person on the planet. He dialed her number again.

She answered on the second ring.

"What?"

"Do you have to go to work today?"

"No."

"Do you have food in the house and is it warm?"

"Yes, what do you think I am, a moron?"

"I'm fairly certain you aren't a moron. If you need help, feel free to call."

This time, he was the one who hung up.

The click in Poppy's ear was startling, and then she sighed. Yes, she'd been rude when he'd only been trying to help, but if he thought she could be won over like this, he had another think coming.

Justin smiled. If they ever managed to have a relationship, he was guessing she'd be hell on wheels if crossed. Satisfied that one daughter was taken care of, he headed for the bathroom to shower and shave. As soon as he ate some breakfast and checked his email, he was going to Saint Anne's to check on the other.

However, Justin's phone call had put Poppy in just enough of a mood that she couldn't go back to sleep. Still irked by the call, she got out of bed, turned up the heat on the thermostat, and raced to the bathroom across the cold floor. Dressing in her warmest and most comfortable clothes, she turned on the television to catch the early morning news and went to the kitchen to make coffee. As she was putting bread in the toaster, the phone rang again.

"Hello?"

"Hey, honey, it's me."

"Johnny! Hi! Where are you?"

"I'm in L.A., but heading back toward the East coast this morning with a load. I saw on the news that it was snowing there and wanted to check in."

"Yes, it's snowing a lot, but luckily I'm off the next two days so I'm safe inside."

"That's why I was calling, to make sure you were okay."

"You're not the first one who's called to check on me this morning."

"Who else called, Adam?"

She wished. "No, Justin."

"Caulfield?"

"Yes, and it's not the first time. I don't know what he's trying to prove, but I don't want anything to do with him."

John didn't immediately answer, which told her he wasn't in total agreement.

"What?" she asked.

"I don't know. Just don't write him off without giving him a chance."

"That's easy for you to say," she snapped.

"Actually, it's not," John said. "His mother is responsible for Dad's death, but he's the one responsible for bringing her down. I have a lot of admiration for a man with that kind of moral strength."

Now she was the one without a comment.

John sighed. "Change of subject, okay?"

"Okay."

"Are you getting any flack from the community?"

"I was, but I think it's behind me."

"Oh hell, honey. I'm sorry you're dealing with that on your own. You know if it gets to be too much you can pack up and move to Atlanta with me. My apartment is small, but we can always get a bigger one."

"No. This is home, and it's over."

"What happened?"

She hesitated to say anything, but knew if he ever talked to Aaron again, he was bound to find out, and then he would be mad she hadn't told him.

"I came home from work earlier in the week and found the house had been vandalized. Someone had painted the words rich bitch on the front of the house in red paint."

"Damn it! Did you call the police?"

"No. I went across the street to Mr. Lewis and made him tell me what he saw. The descriptions he gave me fit those two stoners, Frankie and JoJo, perfectly. I got in the car and drove straight up to Millwood's, which is where they hang out. They were there, sitting in the back of the store by the beer case and JoJo still had red paint on the ends of his fingers."

"What did you do?"

"I kicked Frankie in the balls, stomped JoJos hands and popped him in the nose. After that, I proceeded to act like the Coal Town trash that I am and lit into both of them. I could tell by all the yelling they were doing that I was winning, too, until Aaron Coulter pulled me off."

John knew he shouldn't laugh, but he couldn't help it.

"Oh my God, are you serious? Did you really do that?"

"Yes. You know what they say about the last straw. That was it."

"What about the graffiti on the house?"

"I scrubbed it off right down to the bare wood and when I came home from work the next day, someone had painted over it with white paint to try and help. Part of the paint is whiter than the rest, but it's better than it was."

John sighed. "And this is supposed to relieve my mind."

"I'm a grown woman, Johnny. You drive your trucks. I will take care of myself and I'll see you when I see you, okay?"

He laughed. "Yeah, okay. Love you, little sister."

Poppy smiled. "Love you, too, Johnny."

Justin had a new DVD, a box of microwave popcorn and two cans of Dr. Pepper with him as he got on the hospital elevator. It was a good day to take his best girl to the movies. As he exited the car, he met Dr. Langley, Callie's doctor, making rounds.

"Hey, just the man I needed to see," Langley said. "Got a minute?"

"Always," Justin said.

Langley pointed toward the waiting room. "Let's sit a bit while we talk. I haven't been home since yesterday and my feet are killing me."

Justin followed him into the waiting room and sat down. Langley chose a chair beside him.

"Good news," he said. "Both Wade Tiller and his son Paul are the best candidates for a donor transplant for Callie. I've spoken to them, and it's going to be Paul. Paul is twenty-one. He's old enough to make his own decisions and Wade is forty-eight. Paul claims he's going to be a priest and that God will make sure he doesn't need but the one kidney, however I have to say that's a remarkable family."

Justin beamed. "That's wonderful news! When are you going to schedule it?"

"It'll take a few days to set up. I want to send her to Charleston for the transplant."

"Whatever, whenever, we're at your disposal. Can I tell Callie?"

"Of course, and before you go, there was one other thing I need to ask. It's about the Tiller family."

Justin held up a hand. "I'll save you from trying to find a kind way to word it. I am well aware that Wade Tiller is Callie's birth father and that his sons are her half-brothers. It's why I went looking for them. Oh, and she knows it, too."

Langley nodded. "Well then, that's all that needs to be said. I'll call you as soon as the transplant team can schedule her in."

"Do you think it will be long?"

"No, but I'll let you know for sure later today."

"Thank you, Dr. Langley, for everything. Now I'm going to go give Callie the news."

Justin couldn't quit smiling. Who knew it would take a

blizzard to put their lives back on track?

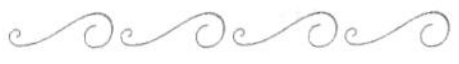

Poppy had skipped Sunday services again. She was trying not to let it become a habit, but the trust she'd once had for the members was still a little shaky. The streets in front of her house had not been plowed and she wasn't in the mood to slide off in a ditch, or deal with any lingering attitudes. By noon, the weather front had shifted and snow was beginning to melt. Every so often a big chunk slid off the house with a plop, startling Poppy into thinking someone was stomping around outside.

Disgusted with her jumpy attitude, she decided to put her energy into good use. By mid-afternoon she was in the middle of baking cookies when the phone began to ring.

She set the timer so the pan in the oven wouldn't burn then ran to answer, thinking it would be Mike. They'd been playing phone tag since yesterday.

"Hello?"

"Hello. Is this Poppy Sadler?"

Poppy frowned. It wasn't Mike. It sounded like a young girl.

"Yes, this is Poppy."

"Hi, Poppy, this is your sister, Callie Caulfield."

Poppy gasped then realized Callie must have heard it because she began to talk very fast.

"Please, please, don't hang up. I really need to talk to you, okay?"

"Does Justin know you're calling me?"

"No, and please don't tell him. I just wanted to say how sorry I am that you hate us. I've always wanted a sister, and now that I have one, it's sad she doesn't want me."

This was weird. Poppy didn't know how to talk her way out of this without hurting the girl's feelings, but the truth was that she wished they didn't exist.

"Does your brother hate you?" Callie asked.

The question was so ridiculous Poppy answered before she thought. "No, of course not. Why would he?"

"Because your grandmother had his father killed."

The skin crawled on the back of Poppy's neck. She'd never thought of what happened like that, and Callie was still talking.

"The truth is that we're the innocents who got caught in the middle of adult lies and crimes. When Daddy and your mother were young and in love, they didn't mean to hurt each other. I don't think they knew how to stand up to all those grownups, do you?"

"I suppose not," Poppy said.

"My daddy is no more to blame for your father's death than I am to blame for my Nana's death. I keep thinking how much Daddy must have loved your mother to be willing to turn in his own mother for you."

"I know what he did," Poppy said. "I was there. I heard everything that was said."

"Really?"

Poppy sighed. "Yes, really."

"And your heart is still angry?"

"I guess it is," Poppy said. There was a moment of silence before she heard a long, drawn-out sigh.

"Okay, I understand that you have to feel what you feel. People should never pretend to love someone they don't. Just look what happened to us because of that."

Once again, Poppy was struck by her wisdom. "How old are you?"

The bubble of enthusiasm came out in Callie's answer. "I'm fourteen, almost fifteen but I'm small for my age. Oh, there's one more thing I wanted to tell you."

"What?"

"They're flying me to Charleston tomorrow. I'm going to have a kidney transplant in a couple of days."

"Isn't that a good thing?"

"Yes, but I have to face facts. A lot of things could go wrong. I might not make it through surgery, and I just wanted you to know what a special man our daddy is. I hope you find it in your heart to give him a chance, because if I die, not only will he be very sad, he'll be alone."

Tears welled, but Poppy blinked them away. "I'm sure you're going to be fine."

"I hope so," Callie said, and then giggled. "Bye Poppy. Thank you for talking to me."

"Yeah, sure," Poppy mumbled.

The line clicked.

The girl was gone.

The timer went off.

Cookies needed to come out of the oven.

She hung up the phone and then got a potholder out of the drawer by the stove.

It was strange how life worked. One minute you're hating with every cell in your body and the next thing you know, WHAM! sideswiped by logic.

She cried the rest of the way through the cookie baking and was trying to get herself together when the phone rang again.

She started to let it go to voicemail then realized if it was Mike, they'd be doing that phone tag dance all over again. She swiped the tears off her face and then took a deep breath.

"Hello."

Mike frowned. "Have you been crying?"

Poppy sighed. "How do you know this stuff?"

"I hear it in your voice. Is something wrong? If you need me I can be there in about fifteen minutes."

"It's just been a long day," she said. "I baked cookies."

"Please say you need me so I'll have a good excuse to come sample them."

A slow smile spread across her face. "You can always come anyway."

"I called because I want to see you. I know I said I wanted to take you to Newport to eat steak, but I'd rather wait for better weather to make that drive."

"That's okay. We can do it another time. I'm off work by 5:00 p.m. every day this coming week, and I'm off again next weekend."

"But in the meantime, who's going to help you eat all those cookies?"

Poppy laughed, and it felt good to be laughing, like sparklers were going off in her belly – making her all tingly and hot.

"I guess that would be you," Poppy said.

"What if I bring take-out to your house and we eat the cookies for dessert?"

"That would be great."

"Would you rather have barbeque, pizza, or Chinese?" he asked.

"Chinese."

"My kind of woman! See you in about an hour?"

"Okay."

This time when the line went dead, Poppy did a little dance, then stopped suddenly, feeling guilty that she'd felt joy when she was supposed to still be grieving. It took a few moments to remember Mama and Daddy would have been happy for her if they'd still been here, so she was going to be happy for herself.

Two orders of Spring rolls, Sesame Chicken and fried rice later, Mike and Poppy had run out of polite conversation. He'd dreamed of this moment, being alone with her in this house. He wanted to kiss her. But there was propriety - and those damn cookies yet to be eaten.

Poppy had removed the take-out boxes from the table and was pouring fresh coffee in their cups.

"Cream or sugar?"

"I'll take you."

She sloshed coffee onto the table then quickly wiped it up. For a second she was certain she'd heard him wrong.

"I'm sorry. What?"

Mike stood up. "It's like this, Poppy. You are driving me somewhat crazy." He circled the table, slid one hand around her waist and the other behind her head. "Do you mind?"

She blinked.

"I'll take that as a no," he said softly, and kissed her.

It lasted only a few seconds, but it was long enough to make him try it again. The second time when he came up for air, he tilted her head a bit to the right, and then went in for the kill.

That kiss put him somewhere in the red zone, which meant back off now before they both got burned.

"Lord have mercy," Mike said, and ran a thumb across her

lower lip. "Do you know what I'm thinking?"

Poppy felt like she was floating. "Probably, but I think for tonight, you need to satisfy your hunger with cookies."

Mike threw back his head and laughed, and once again, the sparklers went off in Poppy's belly. This was going to be a good thing. She could feel it.

And she'd been right.

For Poppy, the ensuing month passed in a series of emotional mood swings. Even though phone calls from Justin had trickled down to what she referred to as a duty call once a week, she heard through the grapevine that Callie Caulfield's kidney transplant had been a success. And there was Mike, patiently worming his way into her heart.

It had been quite a while since Wade Tiller had an occasion to go to Charleston, but never for a reason as momentous as the one that brought him and his family here today.

Somewhere beyond these walls, two of his children were having surgery and the thought of how many things that could go wrong was driving him quietly insane.

He was still uncertain that giving in to the family's insistence and letting Paul be the donor for Callie's kidney had been the right move. Wade was the oldest and she was his daughter. It should have been his right. But that reason was also why he'd finally given in. Because she was his daughter, he wanted only the best for her, and a forty-eight year old kidney that he'd put through years of hard living and drinking was certainly not the best.

He kept watching Justin Caulfield's face, looking for anger, waiting for him to assess blame for all those years of deception, but it just wasn't there. Deborah might not have loved Justin when she married him, but between the two of them, she had damn sure married the best man.

His gaze shifted to his sons. In all the years since their birth, he had never seen them this quiet. They'd bunched up together on the single sofa, sitting with their elbows on their knees, their heads down, staring at the floor. If he had to guess, he would say they were praying. God knows he done nothing but pray ever since he'd found out he and Deborah had a daughter. Callie had the Caulfield name, but Wade had definitely marked her just as he'd marked his other children. There was no mistaking where the white-blonde hair and blue eyes had come from.

All of a sudden there was a flurry of activity out in the hall then one of the surgeons walked in.

"Paul Tiller family?"

"We're here," Wade said, as he stood up.

"Paul did great. He's in recovery. As soon as he's taken to his room, they'll let you know."

"What about the patient receiving the kidney? What about Callie?" Justin asked.

"Are you her parent?"

"Yes."

"All I know for sure is the transplant procedure is in progress. Her surgeon will be out when he's finished to give you the details."

Justin nodded, then turned and thumped Wade on the back. "Good news, right? One down. One to go."

"Yes, good news." But Wade knew Justin was right. They were only halfway through this ordeal.

The waiting room was littered with empty paper cups, candy wrappers, paper plates and an empty pizza box. Eating had been a way to pass the time and keep emotions as low-key as possible. It has been more than four hours since the last surgeon had been in and Justin was literally sick at his stomach with fear. If he'd been waiting by himself, he would have already lost it. Wade's sons kept a running commentary of what was happening in the NFL, what they'd done last week, and even a quick update on Paul, who'd finally been taken to his room. Wade had gone up to see him and had yet to come back.

Justin kept pacing from one end of the waiting room to the other, pausing every now and then to stare out the window. He felt so damn helpless.

"Hey, Mr. Caulfield, there's a surgeon out in the hall," Ben said.

Justin recognized him as Callie's surgeon and met him as he came into the waiting room.

"Callie did great," the surgeon said. "The transplant was a huge success. Her skin color already looks better. It's amazing how the human body does work."

"Thank you! Thank you!" Justin said. "When can I see her?"

"Soon. You know we're going to have to isolate her for a while. We need to make sure she isn't exposed to anything her body can't handle. However, we'll put a mask on you and you can walk beside her bed when we take her from recovery to ICU."

Justin didn't care if they made him wear Haz-Mat gear if that's what it took to get her well.

"So, I'll have a nurse come get you when she's ready. In the meantime, feel free to let all your family know that the surgery was a success."

Justin nodded in agreement, but the truth was, there wasn't anyone to call but Poppy and he was pretty sure she didn't give a damn. He'd call his housekeeper later and let her know everything was okay, but the only other people who cared were in the waiting room with him.

The Tillers were grinning from ear to ear as they began to clean up the mess that they'd made.

"Man, that is such good news, isn't it, Mr. Caulfield?" Ben said.

Justin sat down. "Yes, Ben, it is amazing news. God is good."

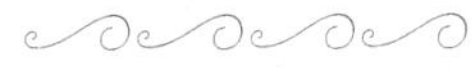

Back in Caulfield, Poppy's relationship with Mike was heating up. Two weeks and a half-dozen dates later, she ended what Mike referred to as training camp by taking their relationship to bed. It was, for Poppy, the inevitability of her growing love for this big, crazy man. He'd saved her, he'd fed her, he'd loved her, and now he'd branded her. She would never be the same.

Oddly enough, it was also a turning point in how she felt about Justin. She kept remembering what her mother, Sunny, had written in her diary after she and Justin had first made love. *I felt my body take flight.*

After making love with Mike, she now knew what her mother had meant, and was beginning to understand how love could blind the truest heart.

Poppy was eating breakfast one morning when she happened to glance at the calendar. The moment she saw the date, she jumped up in a panic and dumped the rest of her food into the trash. Within moments she started to cry. It was her mother's birthday and she'd forgotten. She cried all the way to work, managed to pull herself together enough that no one noticed, then skipped her lunch break to go to a florist to get flowers. Her anxiety was at an all-time high, fearing something would delay her at quitting time.

It didn't happen.

The moment she clocked out, she made a flying trip to the cemetery, knowing they locked the gates at dusk.

The ground was still soggy from the last rain and the trees, having long since lost the glorious colors of autumn, were not only bare sentries to the passing of lives, but to the passing of seasons, as well.

She got out of her car and began to run, eyeing the sun as it continued to slide ever farther into the west. The weather they'd been having had barely begun to settle the bare mounds marking her parents' graves. They were still as raw as the pain left behind from their passing.

Poppy laid the bouquet of lavender and yellow chrysanthemums onto the muddy mound, and then touched the headstone.

"Happy birthday, Mama. You know I miss you. You know I love you. And you also know that I'm going to be okay because you raised me to be strong." Her gaze slid to the other mound. "Hey, Daddy. I don't know what all goes on in heaven, but I hope they allow dancing because you know how Mama loves to dance. I miss you so much and I'm trying to do what's right. It breaks my heart that you died with the burden of my birth on your heart. I know about the other man who is my father, but you know I love you best."

Then she glanced up at the sky. The sun was hovering just above the horizon.

"I have to go. Love you both."

She raced back to her car and drove out as fast as she'd come in. Just as she passed through the gates, the sun gave way and slipped below the horizon, as if it had finally become too heavy to sustain the height. She waved at the policeman who was getting out of his car to lock up, and headed for home.

CHAPTER TWENTY-SIX

Nearly three weeks had passed before Callie Caulfield was released to come home, and for Justin it was a day for celebration. His daughter had been given such a gift – the gift of life, and through it, was forging a tenuous bond with the people who'd made it happen.

After she'd been moved out of ICU and into a private room, the Tiller family was at her side almost as much as Justin. Callie was no longer uncomfortable with Wade or her new brothers, but the extent of their future relationship was still a work in progress.

She and Justin left the hospital in Charleston in the middle of the afternoon and after a two-hour helicopter flight back to Caulfield, met up with an ambulance at the airport that was taking them the rest of the way home.

The last time Callie had been out of the hospital, the grass was green and flowers had been in bloom. Now, except for some small evergreen shrubs around the old mansion, everything was bare and brown.

The time between had been long and scary and there were many, many days when she believed she would not see it again, yet now she was here. It was nothing short of her miracle.

"Daddy, I can't wait to see my room. Did you move all my angels back from the hospital?"

"I sure did," Justin said. "Everything's there, although I think for sure you're going to need some new clothes. You've grown at least an inch through the summer, which is amazing considering how sick you've been."

She giggled. It was almost more than she could stand, waiting to get out of the ambulance.

"We're almost there," Justin said.

Her smile shifted suddenly. "Is Lillian still here? She didn't leave after... uh, I mean when Nana..."

"She's there, and anxious to get both of us home," Justin said.

Callie reached for Justin's hand. "I hope she makes me rice pudding. I love her rice pudding."

Justin brushed a lock of her hair from her eyes. He still thought of her as his little girl, but she was turning into a young lady in spite of him.

"I believe she mentioned something about it when I spoke to her this morning."

Callie sighed. "Perfect."

"I know you're going to want to look at everything, but your doctor cautioned you against doing too much at once, so let's take it easy this evening, okay? I mean, you've had such a huge day with all this travel."

"Okay, Daddy. I'm not going to argue. I am tired, but in a good way for a change."

Moments later, the ambulance took a turn and then began slowing down.

"We're here," Justin said.

The back doors opened. The driver and the paramedic who'd accompanied them got her into the wheelchair then wheeled her up to the front door.

"Welcome home, little lady," the paramedic said.

Callie beamed. "Thank you. Thank all of you so much."

Justin opened the front door then held out his hand. Callie grabbed it as she stood and they walked back into the house, a family again. The ambulance was driving away as Lillian came scurrying toward them, talking and crying at the same time.

"Welcome home, Callie, welcome home!"

Callie hugged her. "Thank you, Lillian."

"I made rice pudding," Lillian added.

Callie beamed. "Yay!"

"You have some mail. I put it all in your room. Mr. Justin,

is there anything I can do for you? Do you want dinner at the same time?"

"I don't need a thing now that Callie is home and yes, let's have dinner at 6:00. She's going to need some early nights for a while until she gets a little stronger."

"This is wonderful, just wonderful," Lillian said, and then grabbed the suitcase and hurried up the stairs, leaving them to come at a slower pace.

By the time they reached her room, Callie was shaky and after a quick trip to the bathroom, she stretched out on the bed.

"Daddy, would you help open my mail?"

"I sure will," Justin said. "Hey, you even have a package. How about that? What do you want to see first, the cards or the package?"

"The package!"

Justin turned it end over end looking for a return address, but there was none. He tore into the outer wrap to the box beneath.

"Hurry Daddy," Callie said.

He grinned, but when he opened the box, they realized there was more packing around an even smaller box inside.

"What on earth?" he said, and pulled it out.

They finally got it open to find a red crepe paper flower on top of a small silver angel. Callie reached for the angel, but when she picked it up, quickly realized it was a bell.

"Daddy! It's a bell! It's an angel bell. And look what the engraving says on the inside. 'Every time a bell rings, and angel gets her wings.' What does that mean?"

"It's a line from an old Christmas movie called 'It's a Wonderful Life' starring Jimmy Stewart."

She frowned. "I don't know who that is."

Justin grinned. "Yeah, he's probably too old to be on your radar."

She giggled. "Who's it from?"

Justin looked all through the packing but to no avail.

"I don't know. There's no card."

"What's this?" Callie asked, as she twirled the little flower in her fingers.

"It's a flower that military veterans give out to

commemorate Veterans Day. Disabled veterans make them and take donations from people they give them to."

"The rose is a pretty red color, but it got mashed in the box. See how flat it is."

"No, that's not flat honey, and it's not a rose, it's a-"

All of a sudden the hair rose on the back of his neck.

"It's a what, Daddy?"

Justin swallowed past the lump in his throat. "It's a poppy. The flower is called a poppy."

A wide, happy grin spread on Callie's face. "I know who it's from! It's from my sister, Poppy. I wonder how she knew I liked angels? I've been praying she would quit hating us, maybe this is a sign."

"Oh you have, have you?"

Callie nodded, hesitated a moment, then added. "I talked to her."

He didn't bother to hide his surprise. "When? What about? Why didn't you tell me?"

Callie gave him a quick glance then had to look away for fear she'd start crying.

"It was before my transplant. I called her just in case I died. I wanted her to know what a really good dad you were, and that I hoped she would change her mind about us. I told her that you would be very sad if I died and that she needed to let you love her."

Justin heard what she was saying, but he'd had no idea her fears about the transplant had included both her healing and his welfare.

"Oh honey, I don't know what I did to deserve you, but I'm very glad you're mine."

"Me, too," Callie said. The tears in his eyes made her sad so she handed him the flower. "Here Daddy, the angel is for me, but I think this should be yours."

He put it in his pocket without comment and began opening the rest of her mail, but the weightless little flower was as heavy on his heart as the burden of his guilt. He'd done so many things wrong in his life. If he could just make peace with his first child, he would die a happy man.

It was later that night before he finally went to bed. He took the small red flower out of his pocket and fastened it to the lapel of his suit.

He was going to wear that paper flower every day until Poppy Sadler found a way to forgive him, or until it fell apart - whichever came first - and moving out of this house was going to be the first step in making that happen.

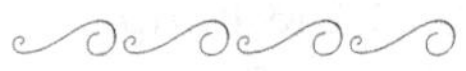

While Justin and Callie had been in Charleston, a logging crew had begun cutting a road up through the trees leading to the hill overlooking the Little Man, and when that was done, another crew had gone on to clearing the actual building site. People in Caulfield noticed the fresh cut on the hillside, but had no idea what was happening. All they knew was trees were down and concrete had been poured for some kind of foundation. Progress was slow-going during winter weather, and when inclement weather swept through, progress came to a halt.

Like most everyone else in Coal Town, Poppy had seen what was happening in increments - from the first trees going down to make way for the road, to the larger site cleared away on the hill.

She had no idea Justin Caulfield was building a new home and would have felt somewhat cornered if she had, because once they took up residence, he would be able to see the entire front of her house from any river-facing window in his house.

John came through Caulfield the week before Thanksgiving to celebrate the holiday with her, albeit a week early. They spent the time he was there playing catch-up.

It didn’t take him long to realize the relationship between his sister and Mike Amblin had undergone quite a change. There were little signs, like razors and men’s aftershave in the bathroom, even a couple of extra shirts in the closet that were far too big for her.

"Hey little sister, is there something you want to tell me?" John said, holding up the razor.

"Not really."

He grinned. "Is it Mike?"

"Yes."

"I'm cool with that."

She smiled. "So am I."

"Is he coming to eat turkey with us?"

"If nothing happens to change the plan, yes."

John frowned. Something about the way she answered told him that issue was of some concern.

"Does the plan change often?"

Poppy shrugged. "He's a cop. It happens."

"Are you okay with that?"

"I'm okay with him and all that comes with him."

"How's it going with Justin?"

She frowned. "It isn't."

"Did he quit?"

"No. He calls regularly."

"And...?"

"I listen. I hang up."

John nodded. "Okay, it's your business. Did you make a grocery list?"

"Yes."

"You made sure we've got everything we need to make Mom's cornbread dressing for the turkey?"

Thankful he'd shifted from the personal inquisition to worrying about what went in his belly, she handed him the list and then he was gone.

Mike showed up an hour later with a pecan pie he'd picked up at the bakery and a bouquet of yellow roses.

"Those are beautiful," Poppy said.

"So are you," Mike said, and kissed her soundly. "Oh my God, you even taste good."

She laughed. "It's the cranberry jelly. I tasted it to see if it was sweet enough."

He kissed her again for good measure and then cupped her backside and pulled her close.

"So I'm guessing John's not going to be gone long enough

for any fooling around?"

"You'd be right."

"Damn," he said, and then grinned. "You know me. I had to ask."

"I adore you," Poppy said.

"I love you," Mike said, and then took pleasure in the shocked expression on her face. He'd never said it before although he'd been thinking it for weeks. "You know how I am, always gotta one-up somebody."

Poppy didn't know whether to laugh or cry. "I adore and love you back," she said softly.

Mike hugged her. "Such a teaser," he said softly. "You finally tell me this with your brother on the doorstep. So what am I going to do about this overwhelming desire to make mad crazy love to you?"

"Put it on the back burner for another day?"

He grinned. "I can do that."

"I knew I could count on you."

"Just don't forget the cop motto. We always get our man, or woman as the case may be."

Poppy laughed. "That's not your motto. It belongs to the Royal Canadian Mounted Police."

"But think how good it sounded," Mike said, and then laughed, which made his eyes crinkle at the corners.

After John returned with the groceries, he and Mike spent a total of two minutes sizing each other up.

Mike sensed John's concerns and decided to allay them before it became an issue.

"So, John, I think it's only fair to tell you that I have the best of intentions of bugging your sister until she breaks down and marries me, no matter how long it takes."

Poppy gasped, her face turned red, and then she saw the devils dancing in Mike's eyes and laughed. He took such joy in causing friendly chaos.

It wasn't until John saw Poppy laugh that he knew what was happening was not only right, but good for her. What had begun as the Sadlers' first holiday alone was turning into a celebration.

"Mom and Dad would be real happy for you, Poppy," he

said.

"I'm gonna be real happy, too, especially when we finish this dinner," Mike said. "I'm starved. How about we continue to discuss all the lovey stuff after we have a tiny piece of that pie?"

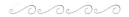

It was because of her early celebration that Poppy wound up working at The Depot on Thanksgiving Day, giving another waitress the time off to spend with her family. No one really wanted to work on holidays, but it was an understood hazard in the food industry that, at one time or another, everyone pulled a holiday shift.

The day had started out slow. Very few diners were opting for breakfasts, choosing to save up their appetites for the feast ahead. By noon, the place was packed.

Poppy was juggling food and orders with her usual calm demeanor when she looked up and saw Justin Caulfield walk in with a pretty young teen on his arm. At that moment, her calm took a walk. The girl was as blonde and fragile as Poppy was dark and tall. It had to be Callie.

The urge to bolt was strong, but it was foolish. This meeting would have eventually happened anyway. Then to her horror, they were seated in her section and she could tell by the apologetic expression on Vic's face that Justin had asked to be seated there.

Poppy sighed. The sooner she got this over with, the sooner they'd be gone. So she lifted her chin, grabbed menus and two glasses of water, and headed for the table.

"Happy Thanksgiving," she said, as she set the water on the table and handed them their menus.

She was about to recite the daily special when she saw the little red poppy fastened to the lapel of his suit and the words got tangled on her tongue. She took a deep breath and tried to focus again, then caught the girl looking at her with unconcealed interest.

Callie smiled. "Surprise?"

It was the understatement of the day. "Yes, it is a surprise."

"I hope it's a good one," Justin said. "I already asked your boss if you could take a break and eat with us, but he said you were too busy. I'm sorry. I didn't want you waiting on us. I would have rather been able to treat you, instead."

"I had an early Thanksgiving with my brother and my... with a friend last week, but thank you for asking. The special of course is turkey with all the trimmings, but if you'd rather see a menu I can get one."

Justin shook his head. "No, we'll have the special, right, Callie?"

Callie nodded, but had other things on her mind. "Did you get my thank you note? I loved the angel bell. Did you know I collect angels?"

Poppy was a little surprised. "No, I didn't know that. Yes, I got your note and I'm glad you liked it. I'd better turn in your order. What would you like to drink?"

"I'll have coffee and Callie will have water with some lemon."

Poppy turned on her heel and headed for the kitchen, desperate to put space between them until she could get it together. It was obvious they could have had a far nicer meal in their home and that they were here because of her. She didn't know what to make of the poppy he was wearing and wasn't going to ask.

A short while later she returned with their food. "Is there anything else I can get you?"

"This looks great," Justin said.

"You're really pretty," Callie said.

Poppy sighed. God love the kid, but she wasn't going to let up.

"Thank you. So are you." Then she eyed the white-blonde hair and almost smiled. "I always wanted to be a blonde."

"And I always wanted to be a tall brunette so I would be like Daddy."

Poppy flinched. She'd never thought about physically looking like him, and couldn't bring herself to search for the resemblance. It had been bad enough sharing blood. God in heaven, how was this ever going to end?

"Enjoy your food," she said, and made another quick exit.

Callie sighed. "I think I ran her off."

Justin grinned. "You just keep hammering away at her, honey. One of these days she's bound to buckle."

Callie nodded as she eyed his plate. "Are you going to eat that cranberry sauce?"

Justin laughed out loud. "I planned on it. If you run out, we'll get you some more."

Poppy heard the joy in his voice but refused to look. She didn't want to like him. Not even the sound of his laughter. But she did her job and did it well, keeping their drinks topped off and hot bread on the table. When it came time for the complimentary pumpkin pie, she even added an extra dollop of whipped cream on Callie's piece.

Justin saw it and smiled. He glanced up just as Poppy looked down. For a split second their gazes locked, and then she lifted her chin and looked away. But in that brief moment, he'd seen something that gave him hope and at the same time, made him sad. There was a very frightened child beneath that tough exterior.

He left a twenty-dollar tip and his phone number with a "call me sometime" written on the credit card receipt.

They were gone by the time she found it, which left her she with nothing but dirty dishes on which to vent her frustration, instead of the dirty look he would have gotten.

It was the morning of December 9th when Poppy woke up and found Mike sitting cross-legged in the bed. He'd been watching her sleep. She rolled over with a frown.

"Was my mouth open?"

"Yes, and you were drooling. It was absolutely disgusting."

She laughed and then hit him with a pillow, which prompted a tussle that ended in a deep, lingering kiss. When Mike finally pulled back and raised up on one elbow, Poppy was breathless.

"Happy birthday, my sweet baby," he said softly.

She beamed. "Oh my gosh, it is! I'd completely let it slip my mind."

"I guess it's a good thing it didn't slip my mind, too," Mike said. "I can't bake, so we'll have to buy your cake at the bakery, but I did buy you a present."

"What is it?"

He thrust his hand under his pillow and pulled out a small black box.

Poppy gasped, and sat up.

He opened the box, revealing a perfect one-carat emerald-cut diamond. His voice began to shake, but his hands were steady as he took it out.

"Even though we met under the worst of circumstances, you have become the best thing in my life. I love you, Poppy Sadler, so very much that I can't imagine my life without you in it. Will you marry me? Will you be my wife?"

"Yes, yes, yes," Poppy said, and was crying and laughing at the same time when he slipped the ring on her finger.

"It fits," she cried.

"Just like us," he said, and then he kissed her, just to seal the deal.

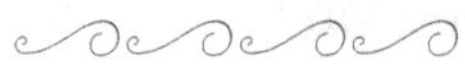

By the time Christmas had come and gone, Poppy's engagement was common knowledge and Mike was in permanent residence. After everything she'd lost, he'd instinctively known she would want the grounding of familiar surroundings. Rather than coaxing her into his north-side apartment on the other side of the river, he moved his things into her simple house down in Coal Town.

Little by little, they began doing small repairs, adding shelves, painting walls, and even putting down new carpet in the living room so the floors would be warmer. Their next project on the list was a fresh paint job on the outside of the house, but they were waiting for better weather.

Across the river, the bare bones of a new house were slowly rising above the treetops. By now everyone knew it belonged to Justin Caulfield.

At first Poppy had been irked, then finally let it slide, accepting the fact that he would be part of her view for the rest of her life. She hadn't thought about it working both ways.

By the time May rolled around, Mike and Poppy's house had a fresh coat of white paint, and they'd added neat black shutters to the front windows. She'd found two old wicker chairs at a used furniture shop and painted them both red. The little house stood out from all the rest on the street like a new penny, prompting one neighbor to clean up their yard while another painted the fence around their house. Gladys even got into the swing and planted flowers up both sides of her walk.

John popped in and out of their lives with regularity and Poppy was beginning to feel like life was worth living again.

If it hadn't been for Justin Caulfield's persistent presence, life would have been just about perfect.

It was the weekend of Memorial Day.

Mike got a call before daylight that a body had been found in an abandoned warehouse on the north side of Caulfield and the M.E. was calling it a homicide. Reluctant to leave without telling her where he was going, he finally kissed her awake.

Poppy rolled over and kissed him back. She was beginning to get the hang of the abruptness of his job.

"What's wrong?" she asked, rubbing sleep out of her eyes.

"Hey sweetheart, I've got a case. Don't know when I'll be home but I'll call you later, okay?"

Poppy threw her arms around his neck. "Be careful. I love you," and tasted coffee on his lips.

It was all Mike could do to tear himself away from her sleepy-eyed look and that long, love-tangled hair.

"I'm always careful and I love you, too. Stay in bed. It's still dark. Remember you're off for the next two days."

Thankful for the reminder, she snuggled back down beneath the covers, heard his car start up and drive away, then soon fell back asleep. It was two hours later before the phone began to ring.

Her voice was still husky from sleep as she grabbed for the receiver.

"Hello?"

"Poppy, it's me, Kenny Duroy."

Her heart skipped a beat as she sat straight up in bed. "What's wrong?"

"Mike's been shot. They just took him into surgery, but I promised him I would call you so you could be here when he gets out."

Panic splintered into a thousand different directions as she threw back the covers, stripping off her pajamas and grabbing clothes as she talked.

"What happened?"

"The shooter was hiding in the warehouse all the time we were working the crime scene. Mike heard something and went to investigate and that's when we heard the shots."

She yanked a pair of jeans up over her long legs and grabbed her t-shirt off the doorknob. "Did you get him? The shooter, I mean?"

"Yeah. The bastard is dead."

"I'm on my way."

Poppy had gone into survivor mode. She was dry-eyed all the way to the hospital, focusing on stopping for lights and obeying the laws of traffic because she had to. But when she got to the surgery floor, everything inside her began to come unwound. There was a large crowd near the entrance to the surgery unit, more than half of whom were wearing uniforms of the Caulfield P.D.

It felt like she was moving in slow motion as she walked toward them. Her thoughts had gone into freefall while her body was going numb. She couldn't believe God was actually putting her through this again. Then she saw Kenny coming toward her and clutched his arm to steady her shaking legs.

He saw the shock in her eyes and quickly led her toward a sofa.

"Where was he shot?" Poppy asked.

"One in the chest. One in the leg."

She was unable to hear this without remembering Jessup.

"How close to his heart?"

"Nicked a lung for sure, but it missed his heart. Not sure about anything else. Is there someone I can call? Do you have some family or friends you want to be here with you, too?"

Justin's face flashed through her mind, and then she shook

her head.

"There's no one."

"Well, you have us," Kenny said, and gestured toward the crowd of uniformed officers. "We're here for Mike and for you. If you need anything to drink or a place to lie down, just let me know. I'll make it happen."

"What about his parents? Did anyone call his parents?"

Poppy had spoken to them a time or two on the phone, but they had yet to meet. They weren't in good health and for the past five years had been living in Michigan to be closer to his sister, who had the only grandchildren in the family.

Kenny nodded. "Yes, they were notified. I was told they're not well enough to fly."

She could imagine their fear, living so far away and unable to be here with him. Her grip tightened on his arm.

"Is there anything you're not telling me?"

"No, honey, no! I swear. You know as much as the rest of us. But Mike's tough, as tough as they come. I have to believe he's going to pull through this just fine."

"From your lips to God's ears," she whispered, then leaned back and closed her eyes.

Another hour passed. A nurse came out long enough to tell them that he was holding his own, and that the doctor would be with them after surgery was over.

Poppy had moved from shock to panic. Her heart was hammering so hard against her ribcage that it hurt to breathe. She kept wanting to scream, but was afraid God wouldn't listen.

Then all of a sudden she looked up and saw Justin coming toward her. There was a moment of disbelief that he was even here and tried to work up some anger, but it didn't happen.

Without a word of greeting, he sat down beside her and pulled her close against his side, and just like that her head rolled against his shoulder as if he'd cradled her countless times before.

"I'm here," he said.

She couldn't find the focus to reject him for wallowing in the strength of his embrace. And, it was finally his empathy that broke her.

The first tears came softly and then once they'd begun, turned into harsh, ragged sobs until the sound of her despair tore at the hearts of every man there.

It cut Justin to the core. He felt every tremor of her body as if it was his own. The depth of her despair was understandable considering the seed from which it had grown. She'd already lost so much. She had no strength to lose anything more. So she cried and he held her until there was nothing left of her grief but a silent, trembling fear

When the surgeon finally appeared, asking for Mike Amblin's family, Justin stood, pulling Poppy up with him.

"This is his fiance'."

"And he's my partner," Kenny added, as everyone gathered to hear the verdict.

The surgeon saw the panic on Poppy's face and purposely focused on her.

"The good news first. He came through the surgery just fine."

Poppy went weak with relief. "Oh, thank God."

The surgeon kept talking. "One bullet nicked a lung. We fixed that, but it also tore though muscle on its way out. That will take time and therapy to fully heal. The wound in his leg was a through and through, but he lost a lot of blood. He's weak. He's got a fairly long road ahead of him, but barring any complications, he should expect a full recovery."

"And that's it?" Poppy said.

The surgeon smiled. "That's it."

"When can I see him?"

"He'll be in intensive care for a couple of days. The nurses will give you visiting hours."

"Well then," Poppy said, as her eyes rolled back in her head.

Justin caught her before she hit the floor and laid her back down on the sofa. Kenny ran to get some water. By the time he got back, she was already coming to.

"Did I faint?"

Justin smoothed her hair away from her forehead. "Yes."

Kenny set the water down on the table. "Just like you did when we first met you, remember?"

Poppy's eyes welled with tears. "Yes, I remember."

Justin frowned. "When was that?"

"The day they came to tell me they pulled Daddy's body out of the Little Man."

Justin felt the accusation as sharply as if she'd screamed it at him.

Kenny sighed. "We didn't know she'd just gotten the call from the hospital about her mother. It was a bad time."

"But that's in the past and I don't live in the past. Not anymore," she said.

She felt Justin looking at her. The words were hanging on the tip of her tongue. They had to be said now, when it mattered, and to him.

"Thank you for coming."

It was a shock. It was a relief. It was more than he'd expected.

"You should have called me."

"I didn't think."

They both knew that was a lie, but they let it lay.

That's when she noticed he was still wearing that crazy paper flower.

He caught her looking at it and waited for her to ask, but she didn't, instead she shoved her hands through her hair.

"I must be a mess. I just got out of bed and drove here. I don't remember even washing my face."

Justin wanted to hug her, but all he said was, "you're fine, but you need to put something in your stomach or you'll fade out on yourself again."

"I can't eat."

"Yes, you can. Mike's alive. I'm thinking it would be to your advantage to stay strong for him."

She stifled a frown. Why did he have to be right, too?

Kenny overheard the conversation. "I'll get you something," he said, and headed for the vending machine on the other side of the room.

Justin didn't say a word until she had eaten an entire sweet roll and finished a cup of coffee. Once it was obvious that Mike had come through the surgery, the police presence on the floor thinned considerably. Kenny returned to the precinct to write up the reports, leaving Justin and Poppy in the waiting room alone.

"I'm going to say something now that you're not going to like, but I can't fall any farther in your eyes than I already am, so what the hell. You are such a strong, beautiful woman. You remind me so much of your mother that it makes my heart ache. I'm very proud of you and whether you like it or not, I'm growing to love you."

Poppy felt cornered.

"And having said that, I think it's time for me to leave. You weathered your crisis like the survivor that you are, and would have done just fine without me. I needed to be here for you, more than you needed me and that's okay. Call if you need me."

He kissed the top of her head then walked away without looking back.

Poppy didn't say goodbye. She'd already thanked him. It was all she could manage for one day. Her panic did not fully subside until she was allowed to see Mike. Between the steady blip of his heartbeat on the monitor and the warmth of his skin beneath her touch – she finally allowed herself to believe he would survive.

CHAPTER TWENTY-SEVEN

It was close to sunrise when the nurses came to tell her Mike was waking up. The moment ICU was open to visitors she made a beeline for his bed, but he hadn't moved since her arrival. Now, she was standing at his bedside willing him to regain consciousness while she was there. The frustration of limited visiting hours was driving her insane. He had to wake up soon. This was her last day off from work, and come hell or high water, to keep her job, she had to be at The Depot tomorrow.

All of a sudden, he moaned. It was the first sound she'd heard him make since they'd moved him from recovery. She took his hand, threading her fingers through his and gave them a squeeze.

"Mike, it's me, Poppy. I'm here, sweetheart."

His fingers suddenly tightened around her hand.

Her heart skipped a beat. "Yes, honey! I'm here. You're okay. You're going to be okay."

His eyelids began to flutter. She glanced at the clock. Only seven minutes more and then they'd make everyone leave. She waited, willing them to open as she cupped the side of his face. The whiskers were like sandpaper against her palm - tough like the man who wore them.

He blinked.

"Hi honey."

He blinked again and then suddenly his eyes were open. Momentary confusion began to escalate until he saw her. His grip tightened as Poppy whispered in his ear.

"Welcome back, Michael Amblin."

"Love...."

Her smile ended on a sob. "I love you, too."

"Sorry," he said, and then his eyelids fluttered again as he slid back under.

This time when the nurses ended visitation, she was leaving on a high. He was coming back to her. It no longer mattered how long it took. All that mattered was the journey had begun.

When she went home, she called Johnny and told him what had happened.

"Oh my God, sister, are you okay?"

Poppy sighed. "Yes. I've come to understand something I'd never understood before."

"What's that?" Johnny asked.

"The human body can only take so much damage before it dies, but the human spirit is different. No matter how many times it's wounded, it rejuvenates itself by nothing more than the passing of time. Remember that old saying, 'time heals all wounds?' I finally get it."

John was silent.

"Are you still there?" Poppy asked.

"Yes, I'm just trying to come to terms with the fact that, although I'm older, my baby sister is wiser now than I ever will be."

"Don't feel bad, Johnny. I thought you already knew women are smarter than men."

By the end of the day Mike was remembering everything, including the fact that right after he'd been shot, he feared he was going to become the next person in Poppy's life to let her down. Eternally grateful he'd been wrong, he lived for the moments when she was with him, and gave her all the confidence she needed when she had to leave.

Their relationship had just been tested in the most difficult of ways, and Poppy Sadler had come through with flying colors. During the ensuing days, every time one of the guys from the precinct came by to visit, he heard it over and over again. It was everyone's opinion she had the makings of a damn good cop's wife.

Justin's new house was rising like a phoenix from the ashes of his past. It was now apparent it would be majestic, but what surprised most of the residents was how scaled down in size it was compared to the massive mansion in which he'd been raised.

There was also something else going on down on the north side of the riverbank that they had yet to figure out. A few weeks earlier ground had been cleared of brush and trees and the earth had been turned and worked. First guesses from the community were that the head offices were going to expand. But when a small tractor suddenly appeared one morning pulling a seeder, they realized something was being planted – most obviously some kind of ground cover. After that, it ceased to draw interest.

They had no idea that it was the single thing on which Justin was most focused. It was his last ditch effort to show Poppy how much she meant to him, and that he was not above shouting it to the world.

Callie called Poppy every Saturday - sometimes to issue an invitation that was never accepted - sometimes just to remind Poppy that she and Justin were in her life, whether she wanted them or not.

Justin saw her on a regular basis at The Depot, and continued to wear the red poppy, although its bedraggled state was pitifully obvious. When it was a business lunch, he greeted her warmly and introduced her to his dining companions as his daughter, leaving Poppy with no option but to bear it silently or lose her job for causing a ruckus.

He knew it irked her, but what he didn't know was that, for Poppy, his dogged determination not to quit was also beginning to wear away her disdain. The fact that John held him in high esteem and Mike liked him as well left her riding that fence alone. And the truth was that Mike filled her with so much love, it was impossible to maintain hate.

July 4th:

It was the end of Mike's first week back at work. They'd put him on desk duty, which rankled, but at the same time he was so grateful to be back at work he wasn't about to complain.

An invitation to Justin Caulfield's housewarming was on the kitchen counter where Poppy left it the day it arrived. It promised food, wine, and fireworks over the river and begged an RSVP which she had ignored.

The new house in question was sugar-frosting white - straight out of the old South and sporting four massive pillars that ran the entire length of the front façade. They supported a two-story roof over a deep wrap-around porch. It wasn't hard to imagine that some southern belle in a long hoop-skirted dress might come strolling out onto the veranda at any moment.

The black-top road leading up to the property was like an arrow pointing the way to the new diamond shining in a bright green rough.

Poppy resented it for the constant reminder it was, that she was in any way attached to the owner, and at the same time felt small for being so petty. It had been nearly a year since her life had unraveled, and to date, she had yet to find a single critical fault with the man her mother had so desperately loved.

The crop he had planted months earlier had turned out to be nothing more than a huge long field of tall, uncut grass. She supposed it was to prevent erosion and run-off, which was a positive difference from the muddy, brushy riverbank where Jessup had been murdered.

She hadn't been able to discard the housewarming invitation, but at the same time couldn't bring herself to go. While her feelings for Justin and Callie were slowly changing, they were still too fragile to air them in such a public fashion.

Tonight she and Mike were going to grill burgers and hot dogs in the front yard and feed anyone who happened to swing by, and after it got dark, enjoy the promise of Caulfield's fireworks from their side of the river.

As she drove over the bridge on her way back home, she glanced toward the river. The thick greenery on the riverbank looked different. There were subtle color changes here and there and some flashes of scarlet. Clover was a common cover crop. If he'd planted the crimson clover variety it was probably putting on blooms.

Her thoughts shifted to preparations for their cookout and reminded herself to ask Gladys and Mel to bring folding chairs when they came. Kenny had already warned them he was going to drop by and liked his burgers rare. It was going to be their first official party as a couple and she couldn't wait.

When she pulled into the drive, she gave the new exterior of their house a critical examination. Mike still didn't know about the vandalism she'd endured, or about her fight in Millwood's store, and she wasn't going to tell him. If it came out, then fine. If not, so much the better. The longer he thought he was marrying a lady, the happier he would be.

She quickly unloaded the groceries and then began prepping for the grill.

Mike was in his element over an open fire. It was all Poppy could do not to laugh. He handled the spatula and tongs like he handled his gun - with skill and speed – and the running commentary that went with it kept everyone laughing.

As it neared sundown, people began walking up on foot while more cars began driving by the house. Word was getting around that Poppy and her cop were entertaining. She was on her way out of the house with a new bag of ice when she saw a big white Hummer turn the corner and come slowly down the street.

Oh my God, it was Aaron!

Everyone, including the police, knew the Coulter family

was up to their ass in illegal activities, but they had yet to prove it or put one of them behind bars. She paused, wondering if he would acknowledge her as he passed the house. Having Mike on this side of the river had probably made them antsy. But to her surprise, not only did Aaron pull up and park, he got out, carrying a six-pack and a big bag of chips.

She grinned. No one had ever accused Aaron of being shy.

She dumped the ice into the chest and then wound her way through the crowd toward him.

He looked a little uneasy when he saw her. "Am I going to put a kink in the festivities?"

"No. Have you met my fiancé?"

He smiled. "I can happily say I haven't had the pleasure."

Poppy laughed.

Mike's radar where Poppy was concerned was always on high alert. When he heard her laugh, he turned toward the sound. The man she was talking to looked familiar, and when they started toward him, he realized who it was, but his inner cop was off duty tonight.

He also remembered it was a tip from Aaron Coulter that had been part of what turned the tide in solving Sadler's murder, so he couldn't be all bad.

"Hi honey." Poppy slipped a hand under Mike's elbow. "You haven't met Aaron yet. Aaron, this is my fiancé, Mike Amblin. Mike, this is Aaron Coulter. He and Johnny have been friends since high school."

"Nice to meet you," Mike said, as he shook Aaron's hand. "I'm glad to finally get the chance to thank you for the tip you gave us that helped catch Sadler's killer."

Aaron was surprised by the cop's genuine friendliness, but hid it behind a big smile.

"It never hurts to keep an ear to the ground, you know?"

Mike smiled back. "Yeah, it's the same in my profession. Grab yourself a burger and good luck in finding an empty chair."

What could have been an uneasy moment passed without a hitch as Aaron headed for the table where the food was spread out buffet-style.

"That deserves a pat on the back," Poppy said.

"I'll settle for a kiss," Mike said, and got what he asked for.

The sun finally gave up and disappeared, but the porch lights were coming on all along the block, keeping lights on the party still in progress.

All of a sudden there was a loud, thunderous boom that shocked everyone into sudden silence. They turned toward the river just in time to see the falling sparks in the sky and realized it was coming from Caulfield's new residence.

"Looks like the fireworks are about to begin," Mike said, and when Poppy frowned, he pulled her back against his chest and whispered in her ear. "Keep an open mind, my love. They are innocent fireworks and have no part in your personal war."

She snorted beneath her breath but didn't comment.

The fireworks began and as expected, were a spectacular show that added another layer of fun to her party. She watched for a few minutes, but couldn't stop thinking about a perky little blonde who wanted an older sister and a boy who'd been her mother's first love. Finally, she begged off the show, using a trip to the bathroom as an excuse.

Once inside the house, she skipped the bathroom and went into their bedroom and closed the door. She needed to get a grip on her emotions, but didn't know how. It was just a house. The people who lived there meant nothing in her life, so why did she feel guilty that she wasn't there?

She sat down on the bed, wishing she could just curl up and sleep when the phone suddenly rang. She answered it without thought.

"Hello?"

"We missed you," Justin said.

Poppy sighed. How had he known to call the moment she'd crawled off into the quiet to hide?

"Mike and I are having a block party."

"It's probably more fun than my housewarming."

She didn't answer.

"Callie says hello. She was hoping you would come because she's going to spend a couple of days with the Tillers and wanted to see you before she left."

The news was actually surprising. Not only was Justin generous enough to share his child, he was giving her birth father a big foot in the door.

"Really?"

"Really." Her silence was painful. No matter what he did, she didn't seem inclined to accept the olive branch he kept offering. "Do you still hate me, Poppy?"

She sighed. "No, but it's not for lack of trying," she muttered.

He chuckled, and the sound washed through her. Then his mood shifted again to a more serious note.

"Are you ever going to forgive me for abandoning your mother?"

"It's not my job to forgive you for that."

"Then I don't understand. What's left? What's keeping you from just meeting me halfway?"

"I live here. Being connected to you makes it hard for me to stay."

"You didn't have to."

"I don't want to leave here. This is home. Mike and I are going to live here even after we're married."

"You're getting married?"

"Yes."

"When?"

"December 1$^{St.}$"

There was a moment of silence before he spoke. "Do you think I might be invited?"

"I suppose the possibility exists. Tell Callie if I decide to have a bridesmaid, the job is hers if she wants it."

He smiled. That was more than he expected.

"Oh she'll want it, trust me. Are you watching the fireworks?"

"I was, but I came inside."

"You might want to go back out, because the last one's for you. I'm not ashamed of you, Poppy Sadler and want everyone to know it. I live for the day when you're no longer ashamed of me."

The dial tone was sudden and unexpected. Poppy stared at the receiver. He'd hung up. All of a sudden she remembered what he'd said and hurried outside.

"There you are," Mike said, as she slipped under his arm

and then wrapped it around her. "Are you okay?"

She nodded.

"Oh wow! Would you look at that!" someone yelled.

All eyes turned toward the sky and the exploding rocket, then down to the grounds in front of the house where a fireworks display had begun to light up.

"It's spelling a word! Look! Look!" The crowd began to spell in unison as one by one, the letters lit up on the hillside.

"P" "O" "P" "P" "Y".

All of a sudden, the yard went quiet.

Poppy could feel their shock and waited for the judgment that would follow. Mike's arm tightened around her, reminding her she wasn't bearing this alone. But nothing happened.

There were a few whispers and then someone giggled.

She took a deep breath and closed her eyes. *What was he thinking?*

Then someone in the crowd started clapping. She dared a peek, but it was too late to see who had started it. The sound was spreading as more and more people began to join in, then Aaron came through the crowd, clapping and grinning. She should have known.

"Way to go, girl," Aaron said. "Maybe he heard about Frankie and JoJo."

Poppy glared at him, and then quickly looked at Mike.

That made the crowd erupt as the clapping and jeering got louder.

Mike frowned. "Who's Frankie and JoJo?"

"Uh..."

But Aaron was still riding the spotlight. "Yeah, I'll bet that's why he wrote her name in fireworks. She's one woman you won't want to cross, and if you don't believe me, Frankie and JoJo will tell you. In fact, I heard they've not only given up huffing, but they quit their graffiti tagging altogether. Frankie's still walking bowlegged and JoJo's nose healed leaning toward his right ear."

That set off a roar of delight that made everyone laugh. Even Poppy started to grin.

"Jesus Christ, Poppy. What did you do?" Mike asked.

She shrugged, as if it was no big deal.

"Oh, two worthless stoners decided to entertain themselves by writing rich bitch across the front of my house in red paint. I made them sorry."

Mike's eyes widened. "You went after two men by yourself? Why didn't you call me?"

"Honestly? It never occurred to me. I grew up here, Mike. I'm as tough as they are."

"I can vouch for that," Aaron said. "She had both of them on the floor begging for mercy and Millwood threatening to call the cops. It took all I had to pull her off."

Poppy waited. Either Mike was going to be horrified, or it would be okay.

All of a sudden he grabbed her hand and held it high. "The winner and new Coal Town champion in a double TKO is Poppy 'the ball-breaker' Sadler."

Poppy grinned. This time when they laughed, it no longer mattered. The only secret she'd kept from him was finally out in the open and he was laughing.

She took the teasing in good fun, but when no one else was watching, looked across the river to the house on the hill. The walls between them kept coming down. Even if she could, she was no longer certain that she would stop them.

Two days later:

The sun wasn't yet a full hour old, but already hot and promising to get hotter. Mike had already left for work. She'd traded days with another waitress, so having a day off in the middle of the week was unusual. She had a dozen things planned and was up early and already busy cleaning house. Johnny was coming by in a couple of days and she also wanted to do some baking before the day got too hot.

She'd dressed in an old pair of jeans and a tank top, pulled her hair up off her neck in a ponytail, and was looking all over the house for her other tennis shoe when the phone rang.

"Hello?"

"Hey honey. It's me."

"Hi Mike, what's up?"

"Go down to the river."

She frowned. "Why?"

"You'll see when you get there."

"You know I don't like surprises. What is it?"

"He keeps telling you in every way he knows how that you matter. Pay attention, woman. This is why your mother loved him."

"Mike, what-"

The line went dead.

"Oh for God's sake," she muttered. "Whatever. I still have to find my other tennis shoe."

She finally found it under the edge of the sofa, then locked the house and headed toward the river on foot. There were only three blocks between her street and the riverbank so it wouldn't take all that long to get there, but her steps were dragging. She knew exactly who Mike had been talking about but wasn't in the mood for more fireworks.

A dog barked at her from inside a fence as she walked past an empty lot, then continued to bark and was still barking when she finally reached Front Street, which ran the length of the Little Man. The closer she got to the river, the more anxious she became, wondering what embarrassing stunt he was about to pull now.

There was that cheap little paper flower he'd worn all winter on his expensive designer suits until it had fallen apart. He'd turned the hill overlooking the Little Man into a marquee with her name lights. All she could think was, what next?

Then she turned the last corner and the sight was so startling that she stumbled. The entire north bank of the river had exploded into a waving cascade of red. Whatever he'd planted had burst into bloom, but she couldn't think what it meant. It was beautiful – so beautiful it made her eyes burn, but why did this prove he loved her?

An old woman coming from the other direction saw Poppy's expression and took the opportunity to strike up a conversation.

"Ain't that somethin?"

Tears were welling, but she managed to nod.

"Them's poppies, you know. My mammy used to grow

them, but nothing like that. I never seen a whole field of poppies before. Someone went to a mess of trouble to grow it up that purty."

Poppy grunted as if she'd been punched in the gut. When she could breathe without thinking she was going to pass out, her gaze went from the riverbank to the top floor of the Caulfield Building rising above it. When she realized there was a man standing at the windows, the hair rose on the back of her neck.

It was him!

He might have been waiting to see her reaction, but she was too stunned to think beyond what this meant - a field of poppies stretching all the way from the bridge over the Little Man to the east bend in the river. A field of poppies too beautiful too ignore, announcing her place in his life in a way only she could understand.

The sun was in her eyes and then so were tears as the poppies blurred and melted into the river. Her chest was burning, like she'd been holding her breath forever, and when she finally exhaled, the last of her anger went with it.

He had never denied her. Not from the moment he'd learned of their connection. He'd worn his heart on his sleeve for the world to see while she continued to deny him. She'd turned her back on the truth out of anger and pain, but no more.

She started walking toward the bridge, and the closer she got, the faster she moved, until she was running.

Justin had been standing at the window overlooking the riverbank ever since his arrival in the office. He'd shed his suit coat and tie the moment he walked in, and although the air conditioning was churning out a continuous blast of cold air, he still felt hot and anxious.

He'd known the day was imminent, but even he had not been prepared for the magnificence of the sight. The field of poppies far surpassed his expectations. If she didn't respond to this, then the cold war between them had to be over. He would accept his defeat like a man and allow her to live her life without him in it. The urge to call her a half dozen times had come and gone without following through. This was his last hurrah and he was scared out of his mind it wouldn't work.

He'd been pacing at the window for almost an hour when he suddenly realized Poppy was standing on the street across the river. Shock was evident in the posture of her body, but she was too far away for him to read the expression on her face.

When he saw her look up, he froze. Was this where she turned her back on him in anger?

Tension grew as he waited for her reaction.

He held his breath when she started to move, then it took a few moments longer for him to realize she was going toward the bridge, not back to her house. His heart skipped a beat. The farther she went, the faster she moved, and that's when it hit him. She wasn't running away. She was running to him!

He bolted toward the elevator, then out of the building and across the parking lot toward the river in an all-out sprint. The closer he got to the bridge, the faster he went.

Poppy reached the bridge and quickly jumped onto the footpath, still running north across the Little Man while the cars flew past her, leaving hot air and exhaust fumes in their wake. Sweat was trickling down the middle of her back. The thunder of her heartbeat was a roar within her ears, but she had to keep moving to outrun her past.

Out of nowhere, a man suddenly appeared at the far end of the bridge. At first it was just his height and the stark white of a shirt against darker skin that caught her eye. But then she saw who it was and that he was coming toward her. After that, everything shifted into slow motion.

The assault of heat against her skin.

The jar of foot to pavement all the way to her bones.

The man running toward her.

Coming closer.

Running faster.

Close enough that she finally saw his tears.

Then he opened his arms and her feet left the ground.

She leaped forward, safe in the knowledge that he would not let her fall.

THE END

ABOUT THE AUTHOR

As a farmer's daughter and then for many years a farmer's wife, Sharon escaped the drudgeries of life through the pages of books, and now as a writer, she finds herself often living out her dreams. Through traveling and speaking and the countless thousands of fan letters she has received, Sharon has touched many lives. One faithful reader has crowned her the "Reba of Romance" while others claim she's a magician with words.

Her stories are often dark, dealing with the realities of this world, and yet she's able to weave hope and love within the words for the readers who clamor for her latest works.

Always an optimist in the face of bad times, many of the stories she writes come to her in dreams, but there's nothing fanciful about her work. She puts her faith in God, still trusts in love and the belief that, no matter what, everything comes full circle.

Her books, written under her name and under her pen name, Dinah McCall, repeatedly make the big lists, including The New York Times, USA Today, Publisher's Weekly and Waldenbooks Mass market fiction. Sharon Sala. www.sharonsala.net

CPSIA information can be obtained
at www.ICGtesting.com
Printed in the USA
LVHW080952280222
712209LV00017B/167

9 781469 937175